I0724339

Cover Design and Interior Format

DEMON'S BANE

INDIA POWERS

for my loved ones

CHAPTER ONE

———

Northern England
1450

THE PUNISHMENT FOR TREASON RANG
in Julian Rutherford's mind like a church bell
calling sinners to repent.

Hanged. Drawn. Quartered.

Swearing at his morbid thoughts, Julian reined
up his stallion at the top of the limestone ridge.
Behind him his army pounded to a stop, the
thud of hoofbeats fading until only the clank of
chainmail remained. Hundreds of the Mage High
Council's soldiers flooded the valley below, a red-
cloaked sea flowing past muddy white tents and
dark smoldering fires.

Today he would end the war his brother started.

A grey palfrey rode up to his left, as Evelyn joined
him. The hood of her brown cloak was thrown
back, exposing thick honey-gold hair that gleamed
in the few rays of sunlight that broke through the
heavy clouds. But her hollow cheeks and weary

green eyes told a different story about lean days and the ravages of war.

Julian's gut twisted into knots. He and his men—a ragtag band of mageborn rebels, humans, and half-bloods—outnumbered the opposing army, but every single one of the council's soldiers had magic. Only Julian's mages and some of the half-bloods had power. "You shouldn't be here," he said.

"I'm your wife. Of course I had to come." She glared at the soldiers below, and then her shoulders dropped. Her left hand pressed protectively against her belly where their unborn child lay. Tears welled in her eyes. "You have to win. We need you." Her husky voice broke over him, molten and sweet.

Love and determination surged hot through his body. "Don't worry. I will."

"You'd better. I'm a healer, not a miracle worker. I can fix a lot of things, but I can't cure death."

He squeezed her hand reassuringly. Her answering smile was a shadow of her usual one, but it warmed him regardless. "Come on. It's time to go."

He nudged his bay stallion down the slope towards the enemy camp. The council's soldiers parted at his approach, forming thick barricades on either side of the packed earthen road.

Ashes drifted on the air, glinting darkly in the cold morning light before falling to stain the white-frosted field. All nine members of the Mage High Council waited within a fifty-foot ring seared into the dried winter grass. Their luxurious purple robes were cinched with gold braid. How many villages could have been fed with the cost of their clothing alone?

The Chancellor of the Mage High Council, a stately man with grey hair and steel blue eyes, stood at the forefront of the group. His fingers caressed a hammered gold disc dangling from a chain around his neck. A reminder of who was in charge here.

The scent of scorched heather stung Julian's nostrils as he swung down off his horse.

The Chancellor unfurled a scroll. "Due to the high number of casualties sustained over the last seven years to the mageborn population, the Mageborn War will be settled by single combat per the accords signed last week. The Marquis of Harbrook will represent the Mage High Council, while Julian Rutherford, the second son of the Earl of Lindsay, will fight on behalf of the rebels. If Lord Harbrook wins, Lord Lindsay's followers agree to quit this insurrection and return to their homes. All leaders of the rebellion will then suffer a punishment deemed reasonable by the council."

Once again, a church bell tolled in Julian's mind. If he lost, he and his men would not receive an honorable death by magic. They'd be hanged, drawn, and quartered, a punishment reserved for human offenders—and mageborn traitors.

"*When* I win, the Mage High Council will accept our terms—all edicts against mageborn and human concourse will be abolished."

"Agreed." The Chancellor's lips pursed as if the word were bitter upon his tongue.

"In addition, all laws banning the rights of human–mageborn offspring to inherit will be struck down." Eric had begun the rebellion to ensure his son Alex would inherit his title and property, and by all that was holy, Julian would finish it. He would see the laws against half-bloods changed. His nephew would receive his rightful inheritance.

The Chancellor searched the Accords. His narrowed gaze fell on Julian, more frigid than winter's deepest frost. "As stated in the Accords, so it shall be done."

"Very well," Julian said. "Let's begin."

"Lord Harbrook." For the first time the Chancellor acknowledged Harbrook's presence.

"Chancellor." Harbrook approached the councilors. His worn brown cloak, extraordinary height, and burly chest made him seem like a bear in the midst of children. He pushed his hood back, revealing wavy blonde hair and rugged features women had swooned over in their youth.

Harbrook. Foster brother, best friend, comrade-in-arms.

Enemy.

The ache of betrayal flared in Julian's chest. Harbrook used to believe in rights for humans and half-bloods. Why would he join the council's forces?

"Gentlemen, the rules of combat are as follows: the first to step outside this ring loses. If you cry mercy or are unable to fight, you cede the contest. You will stand back to back, then walk ten paces. When the horn sounds, you may turn and engage."

Julian studied the rigid features of the man

who'd once been like a brother to him. The muscle ticking in Harbrook's jaw showed anger churned just below the surface. By His Blood, what had Julian done to raise the man's ire against him? *Harbrook* had betrayed *him*.

"My lords, take your places." The Chancellor gestured to the middle of the circle. Then he led the other councilors to the perimeter, where the soldiers dispersed to give them room.

"Lindsay." Harbrook's familiar voice rumbled.

"Harbrook." Julian moved until they stood back to back on the rocky field. Bloody hell, fighting Harbrook would be like battling his own brother.

"If you stand down now, the Chancellor said your life would be spared."

The first words in two years Harbrook spoke to him, and he wanted Julian to quit? Did his best friend even know him anymore? So much churned inside Julian, but he couldn't speak the words. "That's not what the Accords say."

"The Chancellor gets to choose the punishment. He would grant you clemency and spare your life."

"And in exchange I lose the war and watch the men who followed me hanged as traitors? Never."

"*One...*" The Chancellor's voice boomed across the open meadow.

Julian moved forward as Harbrook stepped away.

"You would keep your title and estate," Harbrook said.

"You know me better than that."

"*Two...*"

"I'm a demon hunter. You can't win against me."

Thanks to his demon-hunter lineage, in addition to his ability to track demons, Harbrook was bigger, faster, and more powerful than ordinary mageborn. He definitely had the advantage.

Julian clenched his teeth. "I trained and hunted demons with you. I can hold my own."

"*Three…*"

"Don't say I didn't offer you a chance."

"You offer me dishonor."

"It's an opportunity to spare your life."

"No." An icy wind blew across the stone-riddled field, sweeping a lock of black hair across Julian's eyes.

"*Four…*"

"What about Evelyn?"

Julian's gaze flicked across the field to Evelyn, who clutched a rosary in her hands. The beads slipped slowly through her fingers, prayer by prayer. She carried their child. What would happen to them if he failed?

He sucked in a deep breath. The frigid morning air seared his lungs, and he was grateful for the icy burn that forced him back to the situation at hand. "You know I can't."

"*Five…*"

"You've always been too stubborn for your own good!"

Julian almost laughed. How many times had the old earl, his father, yelled that at him? It'd become a badge of honor for him to resist.

"*Six…*"

Julian took another step and assessed the rocky

terrain. Boulders as tiny as finches and large as wolves littered the uneven field. The exposed limestone fell sharply to a rocky ledge on his left. If he got trapped between the limestone terrace and the edge of the ring, he would be at Harbrook's mercy.

"*Seven…*"

Julian surveyed the field before him and considered his choices.

"*Eight…*"

His sister-in-law and nephew were in hiding after two attempts on their lives. Julian wouldn't let them down. He had to win. *For Eric, Cecilia and Alex.*

"*Nine…*"

He called forth the magic in his blood, feeling it surge through his veins, raw, powerful, dangerous. Thick currents flowed hot beneath his skin. Scanning the rough terrain before him, Julian planned his first strike.

"*Ten…*"

He took the last step, his muscles taut. His blood pounded through his veins in anticipation.

The horn's deep wail reverberated across the valley.

Julian dove to his right, flattening himself behind a large boulder. A sharp sizzle hissed near his left ear. He leaned forward and darted a quick glance around the pitted stone that shielded him. A blackened patch marked the spot where he'd been standing moments ago.

Harbrook didn't bother to take cover. He stood in the middle of the field, lips moving, hands cupped before him.

Julian rose. Magic burst from his fingertips, streaking blue across the field, sucking moisture from the air as it went. Harbrook's hands separated and he held them up, palms out in a defensive position. Julian whispered and the water froze, shattering into a million shards of ice as it hit Harbrook's hastily constructed shield. Blood welled bright red on Harbrook's cheek where a stray sliver found its mark.

Julian's pulse raced as he harnessed his mage energy once again.

Harbrook cupped his hands and flung them outward. Stones littering the field jolted into the air, then arced towards Julian like a barrage of arrows.

He dove off the edge of the terrace. The sharp-edged rocks pummeled his back and arms. He clenched his teeth and rolled to his feet on the terrace below, too close to the ring's blackened outline for comfort. His chest constricted. He was trapped. His father had called him a failure, a wicked imp he should have drowned at birth. But not Eric. His brother had been the sun of both their lives and shielded his younger brother from their father's unholy rages. Julian had failed to save Eric, but he wouldn't fail Eric's cause.

Harbrook reached the edge of the terrace, his expression hard and angry. His upraised hands glowed.

A blast of wind threw Julian backwards. He wrenched his body and landed just inside the marked edge of the arena. Desperation squeezed around his lungs like iron bands. He hurled his magic with a flick of his wrist. A fiery whip slashed the earth. Harbrook eased back from the cliff.

Crack! Harbrook dove and rolled to his knees. The lash smacked the ground in a shower of sparks. Julian scrambled up the slope.

Crack! The rope of fire wrapped around Harbrook's ankles and flung his feet out from under him. Julian's blood thundered in his ears as he drew the whip back.

Harbrook rose onto one knee, and his lips and hands motioned feverishly. Sweat beaded on his forehead.

Crack! A ghostly hand grabbed the lash mid-strike. Harbrook yanked and Julian fell to his knees. Something large and heavy hit his back, knocking Julian flat to the ground. The musty odor of earth and dried grass filled his nostrils. He gathered his thinning magic and thrust upward. The boulder flew off him and exploded.

When he looked up, orange flames were dancing on Harbrook's left hand. Fireballs struck the ground around Julian. The dead grass and heather burst into flames.

He pressed his hands into the winter-hardened turf, tremors rippling through his body. The constant use of magic was taking its toll. The ring of fire edged closer, whipped higher by the stiffening wind. Julian's muscles shook with exertion, but he wasn't about to die in a cloud of ash like a suckling pig roasting in a pit. He heaved himself to his feet.

Julian harnessed the breeze, sending it spinning

around the field. Frost and ashes rose into the air, hovering as he dug deep for more mage energy. He hauled the breeze towards him and closed his mouth and eyes. A shower of frost and ashes dampened the flames.

The air shimmered from the heat. He wiped the moisture and ashes from his eyes.

Harbrook braced his form and lifted his hand, palm up. "Rise."

Julian's body rose upright into the air, spinning in accord with the stirring motion of the marquis's hand. His limbs trembled, his blood and muscles nearly drained of all magic. He searched his body for some remnant of power.

He rotated faster, forming the center of a large vortex. His stomach heaved. He squeezed his eyes shut, tucked his head into his shoulder. Dirt and grass swirled around him, whipping his face and clothing. His mind clouded.

A rope of magic connected the whirlwind to Harbrook. The whirlwind lurched.

Evelyn's face flashed in Julian's mind, followed by images of Eric, Cecilia, Alex, and all his soldiers who depended on him—mageborn, human, and half-blood. Bile burned the back of his throat. Death by hanging. Cecilia and Alex alone. Evelyn devastated. His child fatherless. He couldn't let them down.

His mind cleared.

He focused on his bloodstream. A single spark of power remained. He coaxed it. Fed it energy from his sinews.

Then the heavy pressure of Harbrook's magic flickered. Once. Twice. An old signal. Disbelieving, but determined to be ready, Julian poured his remaining power into his hands and waited. Flicker. He flung his magic down the line connecting the whirlwind to the marquis.

A boom like rolling thunder shook the ground. The whirlwind died.

Julian fell to the ground. He spat a tuft of grass out of his mouth, then wiped his damp face with the back of his hand. He was still inside the ring. He searched the area for Harbrook.

Harbrook lay prone on the ground outside their arena. The backlash had thrown him across the field.

Julian had won.

The Chancellor's voice echoed across the field. "Abiding by the rules set within the Accords of Wizardry, Julian Rutherford, second son of the Earl of Lindsay, has won the challenge. The Mageborn War is ended. All edicts regarding mageborn and human concourse will be modified, per the terms agreed upon by all parties."

A huge cheer rose from Julian's men as they approached. He staggered to his feet. Griswald, his second-in-command, threw a heavy woolen cloak across his shoulders. Evelyn raced towards him, and Julian opened his arms to pull her close. He stared across the battleground at Harbrook, whose men were helping him stand up.

Harbrook. Demon hunter. Foster brother. Best friend. Chosen of the Mage High Council.

Robert Westcott, the Marquis of Harbrook, had intentionally won the war for the rebels.

CHAPTER TWO

———◆———

THE REBEL CAMP RANG WITH joy and celebration after Julian and his men returned. Food and drink flowed abundantly after months of rationing, and the campsite echoed with song and laughter. A large bonfire burned bright in the center of the camp, its orange-red flames streaking high into the black sky.

"A toast! A toast to Lord Lindsay, who has won justice for us all!" the half-blood Griswald, his second-in-command, shouted.

Julian raised his cup. "To the end of the war." He took a deep swallow of mead, and then beckoned to one of his soldiers. "Make sure the men stay on alert. The war is over, but we'll keep our guard up until we return home." The man nodded and headed for the nearest sentry post.

The ride back to camp had passed in a blur. Exhaustion still bit deep into Julian's bones, but after food, drink, and Evelyn's healing magic, he no longer craved a week's worth of sleep. She sat curled against him, her head resting on his shoulder, her fur-lined cloak wrapped tight against the chilly night air. Julian kissed her hair. The scent of lilacs, her favorite flower, surrounded him.

Her chin lifted, and she looked at him questioningly. "You seem terribly gloomy for a man who just won a war."

He stared down at his goblet, wondering how best to explain. Flames reflected off the engraved sides, dark shadows next to shimmering gold. He gathered his thoughts. "Did I ever tell you about my father's visits when I was fostering with Harbrook?"

"A little."

"He'd make me duel with Harbrook." Julian could still picture the courtyard, the audience circling him and Harbrook, the sweat trickling down his spine under the hot afternoon sun as his father watched from the shadows. "Whenever I lost, my father beat me. He called me a coward and disgrace to the family."

Evelyn rubbed his shoulder, her green eyes moist, but said nothing.

"Harbrook was more than a foster brother. He was my best friend. Everyone knows that demon hunters have the advantage, but that didn't matter to my father. One day Harbrook came up with a plan. He'd ease back on his power. Just the faintest flicker. Twice, so I'd know it was my signal. On the third withdrawal I was to attack with all my strength."

"Did it work?"

"Yes. Harbrook pulled back his magic just enough for me to beat him. Nobody ever knew. It was our secret." While everyone else congratulated Julian on his win, not one word had passed his father's lips. Instead, the earl had turned and left. Harbrook, his eyes full of sympathy, had clapped Julian on the back. *Come on*, he'd said. *Let's go celebrate.*

"Harbrook loved you like a brother."

"When we fought today, his magic faltered, the same as when we were kids."

Her hand flew to her throat. "Do you think he did it on purpose?" she whispered.

"Yes." He stared into the flames, seeing nothing but memories of his old friend. The boy who had lost to save his best friend from a beating had never stopped guarding his back. Julian had been wrong about Harbrook. His foster brother hadn't betrayed him. Instead, he'd betrayed the council. Julian prayed they never found out.

"Well, the next time I see him I'll be sure to thank him."

Julian laughed. He gently pushed a lock of hair behind her ear. Contentment flowed over him as he gazed at his beloved wife. "Now that the war is over, we can return to our estate and raise a family."

"Yes, we can." She smiled, and her eyes twinkled. "Don't you think it's time we joined the celebration?" She nuzzled the column of his throat. Heat rushed to the surface of his skin as her warm breath caressed his neck. His body tightened in response. She brushed a kiss on his stubbled chin.

"Evelyn," he groaned, as his blood pounded through his body. He wrapped his arms around her. His love for her stole the breath from his lungs, overwhelming him with its intensity. She'd chosen him, even though he was only the second son of an earl, and had chosen the hardships of the battlefield in order to be near him. He would sacrifice body and soul to keep her safe.

He kissed her, loving the way her generous mouth opened beneath his. She slipped her arms around his neck. Her soft breasts pressed against him and he slid his hands up, stopping short of cupping their fullness.

He broke away, breathing hard. "Let's return to our tent," he whispered, pressing his forehead against hers. "They can celebrate without us."

Her husky laugh filled him with warmth. Long lashes framed mischievous green eyes that never failed to captivate him. "I like that plan."

Images of the many different ways they could celebrate filled his mind. Julian grinned, feeling the weight of the war slipping from his shoulders.

Suddenly Evelyn's breath hitched. Her sun-kissed cheeks paled in the ruddy firelight and her pupils enlarged until her eyes were black. "Not now," she whispered hoarsely. Her fingers stilled on his neck.

A low moan broke from her mouth and fear twisted Julian's gut. Tears welled in her dark eyes. Evelyn had had visions before, but he'd never seen her react like this.

"Evelyn, tell me what you see." He kept the urgency pulling at him out of his voice as he gently held her.

"No." Her voice was ragged but firm.

His jaw clenched and a vein throbbed in his temple. What was she hiding? How could he protect her if she kept her vision secret? "Tell me."

Evelyn caught her breath. She stared past him, her eyes wide and unfocused. She shook her head vigorously, as if rejecting what her vision showed her. Her hair loosened from its coil, the strands falling down her back in a honey-gold curtain.

Tension arced through Julian's muscles as the urge to battle filled him. His hands flexed on her waist. The logs in the bonfire cracked and popped as they burned, loud compared to her silence. Her skin grew cold to his touch.

Her fingernails dug into his shoulders.

"Tell me what I can do."

An uneven laugh broke from her lips, jarring his nerves. "Nothing. There's nothing anyone can do." She flung her head back and inhaled deeply, eyes squeezed tight as tears streaked down her cheeks. When she opened them, they were green once more.

Julian gathered her close. She wearily laid her head against his shoulder. "The camp will be attacked tonight."

"You saw this in your vision?"

"Yes."

He beckoned to one of his soldiers. "My lady has had a vision. There will be an attack tonight. Spread the word." The man ran to alert the others.

"Who will attack? The council's army?" Did the Mage High Council discover Harbrook's betrayal? Would they risk restarting the war, knowing more mageborn lives would be lost?

"I don't know. All I saw were you and your men with your swords drawn, staring towards the field in front of the camp." Her arms slid around his waist and held him tight.

"What else did you see?" Visions of battle had never affected her to this extent. He sensed there was more that she hadn't told him.

"I saw a portal the size of a castle gate. It was wreathed in red and black magics, and another color I couldn't distinguish. The sight filled me with great pain and loss."

"Why?" *Red for blood. Black for evil.* Both magics were banned. Plus one more. What could it be?

She hesitated, then said, "Someone close to me will die tonight."

His heart thudded against his chest. No wonder her vision had disturbed her so much. "Will it be me?" he asked gently.

She looked up at him, her eyes wide and scared. Her body trembled against him. "I don't know."

Julian grabbed his goblet of mead. "Drink. You need to restore yourself."

She raised it to her lips and had barely taken a sip before she spat it out. Red liquid gleamed darkly on the ground.

Men all over the campsite were either retching or spitting.

"It's blood." Shock filled her voice. She wiped a dot of blood from her bottom lip with shaky fingers. "The attack has begun."

Horns blared across the night as sentries sounded the alarm.

Julian pulled her to her feet. He grabbed a flask and opened the top. The warm scent of mead drifted up. He handed it to her. "Here. This one is untainted."

She took a small sip, rinsed her mouth, leaned over to spit it out. Then she drank.

Julian shouted to Kikson, head of his personal guard. "Take my wife to safety and make sure no harm comes to her." He drew her into his arms and kissed her. The heady warmth of her mouth mixed with the lingering sweetness of mead. She clung to him, the press of her lips desperate against his own.

Her arms wrapped tight around him. "Let me stay here with you. I can help."

The clang of metal swords and shields rang in the background. There was no time to pursue the matter further. "No. It's too dangerous."

"Hurry, my lady," Kikson urged.

Julian held her tight, then loosened his grasp. He glanced across the campsite where his soldiers stood ready for battle, then addressed Kikson. "Take care of her."

"Don't worry, milord." He clasped Julian's hand. "I will."

Evelyn released Julian and stepped back. His guard closed ranks around her, heading for the secret entrance to a cave network they'd stumbled across years ago. She'd be safe there.

Julian's gaze clung to her as she followed his soldiers. He hoped her vision about someone dying was wrong. They didn't always come true. She glanced at him over her shoulder.

"I will come for you as soon as I can." His promise rose above the din.

"Godspeed." She raised gloved fingers to her lips and kissed the tips in a gesture of farewell.

CHAPTER THREE

EVELYN TRAILED KIKSON AND THE other two guards as they slid into the dense woodland shadow. They headed for the limestone cliff that backed the forest. Julian had men stationed at the top, so no attack was possible from behind the camp.

A lump rose in her throat. Her husband might die tonight. Her vision had shown her a black portal on the moors, but nothing else. All she knew was that someone close to her would die. That is, assuming the vision came true. They didn't always. Often, they were simply warnings. Regardless, it felt wrong leaving Julian so she could save herself. But he was right. The campsite wasn't safe, and she had to protect their unborn baby.

Evelyn and her guards moved single file through the forest. She pulled her cloak tight to better navigate the shrubs and undergrowth. Kikson led. He held his right hand outstretched before him. A faint green glow hovered above the ground, lighting their way.

Soft swishing noises reached their ears followed

by the distinct snap of branches.

"Wait here," Kikson said. He moved silently in the direction of the sounds.

Loud shouts rang out from the camp, and the clang of metal joined the din. Her fingers clenched on her kirtle and she held her breath. Every fiber of her being trembled with the need to return to Julian. *Dear Lord, please keep my husband safe.*

It seemed an eternity before Kikson rejoined them. "It was only a boar."

"What about the camp?" Woodrow asked. "They're under attack."

"We escort Lady Lindsay to the caverns first. Afterward you may return to the camp."

Evelyn's vision from earlier taunted her. Someone close to her would die tonight. "Maybe Woodrow and Clark could return and you could take me?"

"No. Our orders were to take you to safety. If we are attacked in the woods, we'll all be needed."

After an hour, the darkness eased as they reached the edge of the forest. The limestone cliff towered ominously above them, black against the deep night sky. Evelyn stepped onto a pebbly slope riddled with boulders.

"Not much farther, milady," Woodrow said. He was the youngest of her guards, his features hardened into maturity by years of war.

"Thank you," she spoke quietly to keep her voice from carrying in the still night air.

She followed Kikson down the slope until they reached a jumble of large boulders interspersed with trees and shrubs. Kikson moved to the right of a slab of rock that stood higher than his head. He pushed some low-growing shrubs aside, exposing a hole that reached no higher than her knees at the base of the cliff wall.

"In here, milady. Woodrow will go first."

Woodrow dropped flat to the ground and pushed his sheathed sword before him. A few moments passed, and then the yellow glow of a lit torch illuminated the entrance.

"Milady, you're next."

Evelyn dropped to her knees. She overlapped the edges of her cloak to form a pad in front of her stomach, and then stretched out flat on the sandy soil. Propping her upper body on her elbows, she rounded her back to raise her belly above the cold earth. Thank heavens the baby was still small. She ducked her head and inched her way forward.

She hated tight spaces. Especially when the weight of an entire cliff pressed down above her. Although she kept her head bent, her hair brushed against the dense stone above. Her breaths came faster and faster. Grit dug under her nails. *Don't panic.* Torchlight flickered faintly before her, and she focused all her energy on reaching that light, inch by painful inch.

A hand reached down and Evelyn choked back the sob of relief that rose in her chest. Woodrow hauled her to her feet.

She inhaled sharply and released her breath. The damp air was stale and cool. She dusted the sand and dirt from her clothes then wrapped her cloak tight. Her head still spun from the panic induced by crawling through the rock. She took long breaths to calm her racing heart.

A torch flickered in an iron holder. She yearned for the welcoming dark of a night sky, not the impenetrable black that spread high above her head. She stepped away from the entrance as Clark, and then Kikson, crawled through.

The cavern air was dank and tinged with a fetid animal stink. Bats? She listened intently but heard nothing except Woodrow rooting through his pack. For now, they were the only living creatures in this vast underground hole.

Clark lit two torches. Kikson took one, and Woodrow grabbed the torch from the wall.

"We need to move away from the entrance," Kikson said. "There's a spot we can set up camp further inside."

He and Clark stepped around her onto a natural stone ledge surrounding a viscous-looking black pool. The torches cast flickering circles on the massive ochre-colored icicles that stabbed down from above. The shifting shadows resembled giant claws scraping the walls. Evelyn shivered. Her imagination was running away with her. These caverns meant safety. She needed to settle herself.

She slid carefully onto the narrow ledge and pressed her back against the wall. A pebble tumbled into the water. The soft plop reverberated in the suffocating quiet, and the stagnant water quickly absorbed the ripples. How deep was the pool? It was impossible to tell, but the rock had sunk quickly.

Kikson and Clark stopped, waiting patiently for her to move closer. Their orange-red torchlight flickered across the pool's inky surface, reminding her of the portal in her vision.

Julian.

Her stomach lurched, and she slammed back against the damp wall, panting.

"Milady, do you need assistance?" Kikson asked. The flickering torchlight distorted his features, making his hooked nose resemble the beak of a bird of prey.

She pulled her hands away from the wall's rough surface, feeling the indentations on her palms. "Thank you, but no. I needed but a moment."

Kikson eyed her as she continued her slow progress along the ledge. "It's only a little further. We're almost there," he said.

Another cave opened to the right of the pool. The limestone rose to a large platform a few feet from the water. Kikson reached back to haul Evelyn up. He looked past her to Clark. "Drop the pack."

Clark placed the pack of supplies on the floor of the cave.

"Everything seems to be in order, but let's be sure before you return to the camp." Kikson gestured with the torch to the black reaches beyond the platform. Evelyn strove to pierce the darkness, but couldn't. Her skin crawled. Anything could be lurking in those shadows. She moved closer to the light.

"This cavern branches into two separate cave

systems. Woodrow, follow the one leading to the back exit. Clark, check the branch that follows the water and make sure no one else has been here."

The men jumped down to the walkway that skirted the water to their left. Woodrow headed for the cavern that opened beyond. Clark moved to the right, following a tunnel that sloped downward.

Kikson lit two torches in holders on the wall. He knelt and pulled a thick wool blanket out of the pack and laid it on the ground.

"Milady, would you care to sit?"

"Yes, thank you." Despite the many layers of cloth in between, the cold from the stone seeped into her bones.

Kikson paced the broad shelf, every now and then jumping down to the path below.

"Do you think the council's soldiers attacked the camp?" she asked after he'd surveyed all the exits.

"That would be my guess."

Lights bobbed in the far caverns. Woodrow and Clark soon reached them.

"All is well," Clark said.

"I went to the back exit and patrolled briefly outside. Nothing was out of place." Woodrow hesitated. "I heard no more shouts from the campsite. Everything was quiet."

Did that mean the attack was over? Was everyone dead?

"Nothing is amiss here. You two may return to the camp." Kikson's face was somber. "Good luck."

"Milady, we hope to return with good news

for you." Woodrow bowed before he and Clark ran along the water's edge back towards the forest entrance.

Evelyn's skin itched with the need to know what happened. She was the rebellion's only mageborn healer. She had to know if it was safe for her to return. "I'm going to summon a vision. I need to see what is going on at the camp."

Kikson's brows furrowed above his beaked nose, but he nodded. "I'd like to know what is happening as well."

Evelyn closed her eyes and focused on the mageborn magic flowing through her blood. "*Show me the campsite.*"

Nothing happened.

"Did you see anything, milady?"

"No, but I'll try again. Maybe the water can help me focus my sight."

Kikson helped her climb off the platform. She drew her remaining magic into a tight knot. Her hand hovered above the stagnant pool.

"*Show me the campsite.*"

Mage energy flowed down her arm. Blue specks dripped from her fingertips to puddle atop the water as she moved her hand in slow circles. Her vision darkened, and then she saw the moors in the grey light before dawn. A misty portal hung in the air, made up of black motes of magic intermingled with purple and red, then a streak of white joined the colors in the black mist. A sense of death permeated her vision. The intense grief accompanying her sight meant the person who died was very close to her.

Her visions weren't infallible. Sometimes people made choices that changed the outcome. She hoped that would hold true tonight.

Her vision dissolved, and the cave's pool came into her sight. Power left her body in a rush, and she placed a hand on the wall to steady herself. The drain on her energy had grown greater since she'd become pregnant.

"Did you see anything, milady?" Kikson asked.

"No." Instead, her vision had shown her the portal again and the types of magic involved. Black—evil. Red—blood. White—death. Purple—demon. But it hadn't shown her the camp, the battle, or Julian, which is what she had wanted to see.

With careful precision, she climbed back up the ledge on shaky legs until she collapsed onto the folded wool blanket. Maybe a demon had attacked the camp. That would explain the purple magic in her vision.

Kikson pulled a flask from the pack and held it out to her. "Drink. This will help restore you."

She grabbed the flask and gulped the mead. Warmth flooded her body. "Thank you."

As she passed the flask back, her vision blurred and her hand wobbled. The magic in her blood subsided, slipping from her grasp.

"Milady, are you well?"

She lifted a hand to her forehead and blinked repeatedly, but the cavern continued to spin. "No. I feel quite dizzy. This mead seems to be quite strong."

"It's not the mead, milady, but a little herb I added to it." Kikson's form shimmered, elongating and widening until he towered above her. She scrambled away from him, even as her limbs weakened. A long snout with sharp teeth grew from his face. Yellow eyes flickered like flames as his skin thickened into a rough hide. Large claws gripped the flask she had just handed to him.

Once again the image of a giant black mist wreathed in demon and blood magic flashed before her. Evelyn's stomach roiled as the meaning of her vision became clear. Now she knew why her magic had shown her the portal instead of the camp.

Not Julian's death.

Hers.

CHAPTER FOUR

JULIAN TURNED HIS GAZE BACK to the camp and snapped, "Men! To your posts!"

His soldiers fell into position around the perimeter of the campsite. They placed torches in holders at regular intervals and added wood to the bonfire burning at the center of the camp.

Heavy darkness reigned beyond the campsite. Clouds scurried across the sky, alternately obscuring and revealing the stars. The frost covering the field only dimly reflected the torchlight. Here and there rocks jutted, resembling hunched trolls. A muscle ticked in Julian's jaw as he searched for some hint of the attack to come.

It was the perfect night for dark magic.

At least Julian knew who his adversary would be. The mead had changed to blood. Only demons had the power of transmutation. Thank goodness he'd sent Evelyn away from the camp. She'd seen the attack occur here, not in the caverns. She'd be safe.

It had been years since Julian hunted demons with Harbrook. He tried to remember what he knew about demons. They could perform the same magic as the mageborn but didn't weary. Harbrook said it was because they had the power of the mageborn souls they consumed. A demon that had never eaten souls was easily defeated.

Demons also healed quickly from wounds—unless the weapons were coated with demonsbane oil. Since he quit hunting them, Julian no longer carried a jar with him.

Demons had one other ability. The worst, in his opinion. They were shapeshifters, able to transform into the likeness of any soul they had taken. Since they also retained the victim's memories, they were nearly impossible to detect. A demon could be in the camp, and Julian would never know it.

He needed a demon hunter. He needed Harbrook.

Since Julian didn't have his old demon-hunting friend, at least he had cold iron. Iron repelled dark magic, and it didn't get any darker than a soul stealer.

Griswald, his second-in-command, came up on his left. He was stocky with the burly arms of a blacksmith. "Have you figured out who's going to attack us?"

"A demon."

"Damned soul eaters." Griswald crossed himself.

"I wonder who summoned the demon and what its task is."

Griswald leaned forward on his sword, the sharp point digging into the hard earth. He chewed on the edges of his mustache for a minute.

"Could be the council. Could be some other mage. A lot of mageborn hate us for starting this war."

"Pretty extreme reaction to commit a crime you would hang for."

"Anger turns some people into fools." Griswald shifted his grip on his sword, raising it up before him.

Julian looked over at him. "Your blade is useless against magic."

"Mebbe. But not against other things." The plume of his breath gleamed briefly in the chilly air before evaporating.

A ground fog began to swell around the camp. The moor mist often arose on cold nights. Julian shifted his feet and watched as tendrils eddied about his legs. Something was wrong. "There's no mist in the field."

"What?" Griswald shifted his gaze from the camp to the field.

Thin vapor trails flecked with purple seeped past the torchlight. *Demon magic.*

"Beware the mist. It's an attack!" Julian shouted.

Ghostly human forms crawled out of the miasma. The scent of decay and rotting flesh permeated the air. Disgust and pity churned in Julian's stomach. They were fighting the souls of the demon's kills.

Shadowy arms snaked out of the gloom to wrap tightly around his legs. Julian sliced down with his sword. The arms dropped to the ground. The misty forms inched forward and the arms reconnected with their bodies. "Back away from the fog!"

Griswald determinedly hacked away at the heads and limbs coming out of the vapor.

Although the beings were dead, their staring eyes shot chills down Julian's spine. He thought he recognized one of them, but his sword cleaved its face and it dissolved. His men chopped away, but they were slowly being backed into the middle of the camp.

"Iron repels dark magic. Channel your magic through your swords to amplify its power." Julian didn't know if these eerie creatures could capture souls for the demon, but he didn't plan on finding out. Death would be better than eternal servitude.

His sword gleamed a brilliant blue as mage energy ran down the blade. The ghostly figures shrank from the light. He stabbed the mist. "Disperse!"

Blue flames shot from the tip and spread like lightning through the fog, sparking on the iron weapons of his men. The mist fragmented and evaporated like smoke. The putrid odors faded from the camp.

Julian inhaled deeply of the fresh night air. "I pity those poor souls, trapped forever and enslaved to the demon's whims."

"Not joining them tonight is enough for me," Griswald said.

"A rider approaches from the north," called a sentry.

Julian squinted into the darkness. A chill swept over him. The rider approached from the base of the cliffs where the hidden trail came out.

As the horse drew closer, Julian could distinguish the shadowy forms of two riders. The first he noticed was the demon. Larger than a giant, its dark leathery hide stretched taut over sinew and bones. Its skull reminded him of a predator, jutting forward into a snout filled with deadly, sharp teeth. Its yellow eyes flickered like flames fanned by a stiff wind.

The demon clasped a woman with honey-blonde hair before it on its mount. Her head and arms bounced loosely with the horse's gait. Julian's muscles froze.

Evelyn.

"Steady, man, steady," Griswald said.

The demon stopped just outside the range of the torchlight. Evelyn sat limply, her features curiously lax. What was wrong with her?

"Give me my wife," Julian demanded. He tried to focus on the demon, rather than Evelyn's frightened face. Kikson was dead…or Kikson was the demon. By God's Bones, had he sent his wife away with this creature? Guilt burned inside his chest. He strode towards them until he stood within sword range.

"Lord Lindsay, how nice to see you again."

Julian recognized the voice. "Kikson."

"Yes. I've been Kikson for months." The demon laughed.

"Who summoned you?"

"Tsk tsk. You know I can't tell you."

"What is your task?"

"Ah. Much better question. It seems you have angered quite a few people, milord. I was tasked with, shall we say, eliminating the problem. In other words, *you*."

"I'll go with you, but release my wife."

The demon chuckled, a harsh sound that rasped over Julian's skin. Evelyn shuddered. "Unfortunately, my task included your progeny as well, and your wife is carrying a newborn soul inside her." It shook its head in mock sorrow.

Julian would die before he let the demon kill his wife.

"No!" He leaped forward, swinging his sword at the demon's left arm. The cold iron struck solidly against bone then bounced back. Purplish-black blood poured from the wound, then slowed as the blood congealed. The sides of the wound drew together. Within seconds, the cut had completely healed.

His men's shouts clamored behind him. Julian saw them pounding on a purple-flecked mist that surrounded the camp.

His enemy opened his jaw in a half-laugh. "Your men cannot help you."

Julian swung his sword again, slicing into the ropy muscles of the demon's thigh.

The demon howled in pain. It raised its newly-healed arm and slashed at Julian. He dove beneath its horse, but not quickly enough. Sharp claws tore across his shoulder.

A second shout rang out. "A rider comes from the southeast!"

Hooves thundered on the turf. A sword flashed blue in the dark night. Harbrook. "What in the name of all that's holy are you doing here?"

"I'm a demon hunter, remember?" Harbrook's bright sword slid into the beast's hulking shoulder, and one claw dropped away from Evelyn.

Julian attacked from the opposite direction, trying to break the demon's grip on her.

She struggled weakly, but it was apparent she didn't have the strength to break free. Julian struck the demon on its right side, trying to sever its grip on Evelyn. Harbrook slashed down and severed a claw. Dark purple blood sprayed the air. Julian winced as several droplets landed on his glove and burned through the thick leather to his skin.

Julian and Harbrook raised their swords and struck in unison. The demon bellowed. Its arm flashed in a blur of movement and swatted the marquis out of his saddle. The injuries inflicted by Harbrook's demonsbane-oil-coated blade still bled, unlike the wounds caused by Julian's weapon.

The fiend's horse advanced on Harbrook, legs raised high to trample the fallen man. Julian ducked under the horse's snapping jaws and stabbed its chest. It reared and the demon leaped from its back, still holding Evelyn. The horse shuddered and collapsed to the ground, jaws snapping. Julian pulled his sword free.

Julian raced towards her, but the demon was faster. It hoisted Evelyn over its shoulder and fled with preternatural speed. He heard it growling words in an unfamiliar language. He sheathed his sword and sprinted after them.

Hoofbeats pounded behind him. "Take my

hand!"

Julian turned and grabbed Harbrook's hand, leaping up behind him on his horse.

The demon raced across the moor as the sky began to lighten in the east. It headed for the limestone cliffs, whose extended shadow remained black in the coming light of dawn. The beast ran faster than any two-legged creature Julian had ever seen.

The marquis urged his horse to greater speed. They gained on the demon.

Suddenly the demon stopped at the base of the towering cliffs. It ripped its claws across Evelyn's chest and shoulder. Blood seeped through the slashes, soaking into her woolen dress. The demon's dark spell still poured from its throat.

Julian sucked in a giant lungful of frigid air to quell the pain that wrenched his heart. Only a rocky field separated him from his wife.

Please don't let her die, he prayed. *Let me save her.*

CHAPTER FIVE

———

EVELYN DANGLED ACROSS THE DEMON'S back as he bounded over the limestone field. Blood rushed down to her head, and the smell of his smooth hide reminded her of saddle leather. The hard angle of his massive shoulder dug into her gut. Even in her dazed stupor she knew she had to protect her child. She shifted, but his strides slammed her back into place.

She'd been at his mercy for the past hour, drugged by the mead and drifting in and out of consciousness. She forced her brain to focus, to climb out of that drowning fog in her mind. Her baby. She had to protect her baby and get away. If she didn't, the demon would take their souls.

She struggled to get free, but he only clamped down harder on her back. She collapsed against him, turning her face away from his ribcage to draw in a deep breath of air. Her exposed face tingled from the rush of the biting wind, and her body ached from the demon's jarring race across the moorland. Threads of magic stirred in her veins.

Behind the cliffs the sky lightened from inky

black to a soft grey-orange as dawn approached. An involuntary shiver shook her. The time of her vision neared.

The demon swung her to the ground. Her legs wobbled like a newborn fawn, then buckled. He caught her against his torso. "It's an effect of the drug. It'll wear off. Eventually."

"I hate you." She tried to push him away, but she was too weak. Tears burned her eyes. How was she going to save her baby's life when she couldn't even stand without her enemy's help?

The demon growled, a deep angry rumble that raised the hairs on the back of her neck. "The demon hunter is on my trail now. If my summoners sent him, I'll be able to return home without completing my task."

"And if they didn't, your gate won't open, and Harbrook will kill you."

The evil fiend glanced back towards the camp they'd fled. "Even on horseback, they can't reach us in time. If my spell fails, I'll still be able to escape."

Evelyn grasped her magic, but its response remained sluggish. She needed more time. "If you leave now, you could get away. I'm sure you know there are ways to mask your trail, even from a demon hunter."

The demon hissed and snarled. It sounded strangely like laughter. "I always liked you, milady. I think I will enjoy having your souls with me for eternity."

Souls. That's right. He would take both of their souls. The thought of being trapped forever inside a demon, never free to move on, caused a chill to run down her spine. She dug her nails into her palms. She would kill herself and her child before letting that happen. "Never."

"Never is a long time, as I well know." He lifted her chin. The tips of his claws lightly pricked her chin and her eyes watered. "Don't let your stubbornness blind you to reality. I am going to open the gate to my world—you've been around demon hunters enough to know what that means."

Her life's blood would be the sacrifice that opened the portal. "Use me to return home, but don't take our souls. Please."

His snout curled in what looked like a smile. "Ah, but I like you. Even your child burns with mageborn magic. Your souls will help me heal." He glared at his forearm, where blue sparks hovered over a vicious slice oozing purple blood. "It's time to get started. I see your would-be heroes approaching, and I would like to be finished before they arrive."

Evelyn's choices quickly narrowed. Julian and Harbrook wouldn't reach the meadow in time to save them. If she didn't act soon, she and her baby would die. She could feel her magic begin to flow again. The drugged mead he'd given her was wearing off. "How do you know the bargain was broken?"

"If the gate opens, I'll know. If it doesn't, I'll still have completed part of my task."

"Your task? What were you summoned to do?"

"Kill your husband and his offspring. He'll be

here soon. I might return to my world before mid-morning regardless." He hissed and snarled again.

"Julian or Harbrook will kill you before then."

The moment had come. She needed more time but the sands in the hourglass had run out. Her power blasted the demon, packed with the punch of a lightning bolt. He dropped her and fell back a couple of steps, shaking his snout from side to side.

"You bitch!" He dragged her up from the ground. His sharp jagged teeth snapped shut inches from her face, and she flinched. "The power of thousands of souls resides within me. You think one puny mageborn witch can thwart me?"

He raised his hand, the curved ivory claws like daggers. Evelyn braced herself. *I'm sorry, little one. I failed.*

The demon's sharp claws pierced her shoulder. She gasped and doubled over. The wicked instruments pierced deeper into her flesh, then ripped her chest and abdomen. The edges of her vision dulled. She sagged in the demon's grasp.

He chanted. Harsh, guttural words bombarded her ears. Purple, red, and black motes swirled, clustering together to form a portal to the demon's hell.

Evelyn's lifeblood drained from the gashes, and her child's heartbeat slowed. Warm tears leaked from the corners of her eyes, sliding down her jaw. She used the threads of her magic to examine her body. She started to shake. She'd lost too much blood. The damage to her body was too great for her to heal. She and her baby were dying. White motes of death magic clustered on her skin, sliding up her limbs. The demon's spell droned on.

Her daughter's heartbeat faltered. Evelyn held her breath. Waited.

One beat…

Two…

Silence.

She swallowed hard. Tears streamed down her face, but she bit back the moans that rose in her throat. She didn't want the demon to kill her or take her soul. Not yet. Anger burned inside her. How she hated him. He'd killed her daughter. He had to pay for what he'd done to her and her family.

The most powerful magics in the world lay within her reach. Death magic. Demon magic. Blood magic. Black magic. So what if their use was banned? She'd be dead before the council could send anyone to arrest her.

Her body was weakening by the second, although her magic still flowed in her blood. She decided to curse the demon. It would tie her to him, but that meant she'd be the one who could exact her revenge.

First, she needed her blood. She struggled to touch one of her wounds. Her hand fell heavily to her chest. Holding her breath against the pain, she forced leaden fingers deep into a gash. Knife-sharp pain flared throughout her body and her vision darkened. Her breathing quickened and she fought to remain conscious. She coated her fingers with her blood.

Next, she needed his blood.

With slow jerky movements, she placed that same hand on the demon's arm where purple-black blood oozed slowly down his slick hide. She slid her fingers into the cut. Her heartbeat stuttered, then throbbed hard against her ribs as power unlike any she'd experienced before coursed through her body. She felt light, and her hair fluttered in the air around her.

She remembered her vision in the cavern. At the end, a flash of white had joined the other colors wreathing the portal.

The white motes of death magic gleamed on her skin, mingling with the purple-black haze of the demon's blood and the red of her own. She grabbed onto death, and held tight to its power as it traveled closer to her heart. She wove the magics together as though spinning wool into thread.

"By my blood and thine, our lives intertwined." She whispered the traditional opening words. "I curse you, demon, to be trapped in this world and barred from your own, until the day my heart is reborn."

"What are you doing?" The demon shook her hard.

Black magic had a price, but Evelyn didn't care. Whatever the price was, she would willingly pay it. This demon had killed her child and their futures. He had to suffer.

"One day we will meet again. And when that happens, you will die, not I." Her voice was the merest thread.

Her power infused the combined magics with the words of her curse. A mist shot with black, purple, red, and white magics surrounded Evelyn and the demon, the magics binding them together in her curse even as the last of her life drained from her body.

Evelyn's soul floated into the air. Her limp form lay on the ground in front of a misty portal of black motes mixed with purple and red, and streaked with white. The demon jumped through the gateway and disappeared.

The world brightened around her as the sun rose over the cliffs. Her view encompassed the moor, the dales, and beyond.

A new vision—of life, love, and family—appeared. Visions didn't always come true. She knew that. But now she had more than revenge. She had hope.

Julian.

Until we meet again, my love.

CHAPTER SIX

JULIAN SHOUTED AS THE DEMON flung Evelyn to the ground next to the misty portal. She landed on her side with a thud and laid unmoving, her body curled away from him on the winter grass, head resting on an outstretched arm. The red gown tangled around her legs, exposing her calves and ankles. She resembled a child's doll, cast carelessly aside.

He lunged for the demon.

Yellow eyes flickered and a low snarl reverberated in the air. The fiend dove into the thick black mist and disappeared.

Evelyn's head slid off her arm. Julian's heart paused in its frantic beat, then thumped roughly back to life. He leaped across the remaining distance. His knees buckled beneath him and he collapsed beside her.

Let her survive this. Please.

"Evelyn." Julian touched her shoulder. No response. He slowly rolled her onto her back. Her head fell to the side, and the metallic tang of blood saturated the air. He'd seen terrible wounds during the war, but none like this. Even Evelyn, with all her skills, couldn't have healed these injuries.

Though he had little hope, he checked for breath, a heartbeat, anything to prove he hadn't lost her.

Nothing.

She was dead.

His body throbbed with the need for vengeance. He wanted to kill the demon as brutally as that monster had killed his wife.

He wrapped his wool cloak around her, hiding her ravaged torso. He laid the palm of his hand over the gentle slope of her belly. Throat tight, he said goodbye to the baby who never had a chance to see the world. Then he moved Evelyn away from the portal, where her blood stained the earth.

He gathered her into his arms and cradled her against his chest. He'd failed to protect her, and now his family was gone. He'd been unable to save them, the same way he'd been unable to save Eric.

A quiet footfall sounded behind him. Harbrook laid a hand on Julian's shoulder, not saying anything, his strong grip conveying more than words.

"It was my fault. I sent her away with the demon, and I didn't even know it."

"Demons are expert impersonators. Were it not for my heritage, even I would be fooled."

"I've never envied your demon-sensing ability more." Julian bowed his head over Evelyn. More than anything, he wanted to bring her back to life. "She carried our first child. Did it take their souls?"

"I'll need to touch her." Harbrook knelt and placed his hand on her head. A frown grew between his eyes. He sat back on his heels. "I can't tell."

"What do you mean, you can't tell?"

"When a demon takes a soul, there's an emptiness, like a vessel that's never been filled. When death takes a soul, there's still a hint of the person left behind. The shadow of memories from that person's life. This feels…different. She isn't an empty husk, but there's no trace of her life that death would leave. I'm not sure what happened."

"So the demon might have gotten their souls?"

"I don't know. Maybe…maybe not."

Julian stared down at his beloved wife's face. Maybe wasn't good enough. If the demon had taken his wife and child's souls, they would be trapped forever—unless someone killed the demon and freed them. He raised his head to look at the portal still flickering in the air. "I have to go after it."

"That gate leads to the demon hell. You'll sacrifice your own soul."

Julian smoothed Evelyn's golden hair away from her face. The scent of lilacs, her favorite flower, wafted up. His chance of success was small. But if he could free their souls, any sacrifice—even losing his own soul—was worth the cost. "I have to try."

Harbrook paced in front of the black mist. "You aren't a demon hunter. I'll go."

Gratitude flooded Julian. Here, once again, was his best friend, who would willingly risk his life for him. "I appreciate your offer, but this is my failure. My responsibility. It's up to me to make this right."

"I understand. Evelyn was my friend too." Harbrook untied a black leather sheath holding an ornately scrolled cross-hilt dagger, then reached into his jerkin and pulled out a brown earthenware jar. "The blood of a demon was used to forge this dagger. It takes time for demons to heal from the wounds this causes. You're already familiar with demonsbane oil. Make sure you coat your weapons with it."

Julian took the dagger, hefting its solid weight with one hand. He slipped the jar and sheathed dagger inside his pocket.

"One more thing. If the demon took her soul, you need to be prepared."

"What do you mean?"

"If it transforms into Evelyn, could you do what needs to be done?"

Julian's mind reeled with the implications. In order to save his wife and unborn child's souls, he might have to kill somebody who looked like her, sounded like her, and had access to her memories.

"Remember that it won't be Evelyn, but the demon."

Julian rubbed his eyes with his left hand. He might see Evelyn again, but it wouldn't be Evelyn. It would be the demon. And there was a part of him, deep inside, that didn't care, as long as he got to see her alive. "I won't forget."

The edges of the portal were fraying. He needed to leave before the magic failed.

He pressed a kiss against her forehead and carefully laid her out on the grass. "I won't fail you, Evelyn. You and our child will be avenged."

Julian stood up and faced his old friend. "Give her a proper burial and let our families know what happened. They might not believe you, but make them. Especially my father. Alex is his only heir now. My father needs to find Cecilia and her son."

"I will." Harbrook stared across the limestone field towards the rebel camp. He turned to Julian. "Somebody summoned that demon to destroy you. I'll find the summoner and make sure he's brought to justice. You have my word."

Julian clasped his hand, and Harbrook folded him in a hug. A lump choked Julian's throat. This would be the last time they saw each other. He was glad they'd had the chance to mend their friendship. "Thank you…for everything."

Harbrook's old smile flashed, and the years of separation fell away. "Godspeed and good luck. I won't let you down."

"I know you won't. Farewell." Julian strode into the black mist.

CHAPTER SEVEN

———◆———

Northern England
1804

GRULIK SQUINTED AND TURNED HIS snout away from the scorching midday sun. Yet again he cursed that witch bitch and her unborn child. He'd planned on returning to his demon world, but Evelyn's curse had been more powerful than he'd realized. Instead of the hot dry heat of his world, he'd found himself exiting the jump in the early dawn next to cultured fields on the outskirts of a sleepy village. He'd traveled *centuries* into the human world's future.

Little whore. Should have taken their souls while I had the chance.

He'd had plenty of opportunities to fulfill his task. But he hadn't been able to resist temptation. The war allowed him to steal souls undetected, and his magic had grown stronger with each one.

He stumbled over a rock, jostling the wounded arm clutched tight to his chest. Pain from his severed claws and myriad gouges stabbed at him. *My summoners betrayed me. As soon as the war ended, they sent a demon hunter after me.*

He could no longer make his summoners pay. They were long dead by now.

He traveled for hours, heading for the deep caves under the limestone cliffs some miles distant. His wounds had quit bleeding, but even so his trail would be obvious to any with the eyes to see it. He needed to go underground, give his body time to regenerate. He briefly considered venturing into the town to secure some souls to speed his healing, but decided it wasn't worth the risk. Injured with nowhere to hide in a small town, the odds weren't in his favor.

His clawed feet slipped on the shale, and white-hot pain seared along the edges of the lacerations inflicted by the demon hunter's blade. He fought the urge to howl his bitterness and pain.

Quiet. Quiet.

He looked to the north where the cliffs he'd been seeking jutted out sharply from the land. The ground grew rockier and climbed steadily as he reached the foothills. A thick grove of trees filled the valley below. He needed to find a cave where he could hibernate until his wounds healed.

"Sssssss," Grulik hissed softly.

He went still as the scent of saddle leather, horse, stale ale, and humans carried to him on the breeze. The rhythmic clipping of hooves on turf and stone was followed by the soft jingle of leather harnesses from the trail he'd been paralleling.

Grulik closed his eyes and sniffed. *Four souls, all*

reeking of magic. Perhaps the healing process would begin sooner than he'd anticipated.

"My body's aching with every hoof beat. Couldn't we have slept in a little longer, Warren?" A young man whined.

A hearty laugh rang out. "Perhaps you shouldn't have celebrated with the wine and ladies as much as you did."

Grulik crept higher above the trail to see the mageborn travelers. One man cradled his forehead, while another lightly held the reins as his body slumped in the saddle. With the exception of the man dressed in hunter's garb, the rest of the party was young.

The man Grulik guessed was Warren spoke somberly. "If we'd waited till later, it'd be well after nightfall when we reached the hunting lodge. Although things have quieted since the times of my grandfather, this is still no land to be caught wandering after dusk."

Grulik surveyed the steep terrain. The trail bent around a large rockfall. For a few minutes, as each passed around the tumbled boulders, the riders would be strung out single file. It was the perfect site for an ambush.

He'd take the hunter first. The rest should fall easily, as they were young and dulled by a night of excess.

With their souls, the worst of the pain would go away and his regeneration would start immediately. It was risky, but he had surprise and the power of his demon form to aid him.

The first rider passed within range.

He leaped onto the hunter. He punched him unconscious and tossed him to the ground, then broke the horse's neck. The second rider's horse reared back. Grulik sliced its throat. He hooked his claws in the young man's jerkin and tore him off the horse. He stomped on him, crushing his chest but not killing him. The horse collapsed, blocking the trail.

The other riders tried to back away, but the path was too narrow. Grulik sent his magic to calm the horses. The last mage threw a fireball at him, which he easily deflected. Pathetic. The man was so weak from his carousing he could barely control his magic.

Grulik jumped on the horse of the third rider. He tore the man's arms off before kicking him off his steed, and threw the arms at the last rider, who flinched and almost fell off. Then Grulik dove over the last horse's head and knocked the mage to the ground. He cracked the man's head against a rock. When the man went limp, Grulik stood up to survey the damage.

All of the mageborn were unconscious, except the one whose arms he'd ripped off. That one was nearly dead. The man's eyes fixed on his face. "Never fear. Your soul will be safe with me." Grulik laughed.

Purple mist flowed over the mage, down his throat and into his body. Grulik leaned in. He could feel the soul separating from the body as his demon magic took hold. Then the mist poured out of the mageborn's mouth, the purple now tinged with the colors of his soul. Grulik inhaled.

The man died when the last of his soul left his body.

Raw power surged through Grulik's limbs, and he flexed his muscles, revitalized. The minor cuts had healed, but he was still missing three of his clawed fingers. He looked at the two other men whose souls he'd planned to take. One down, two to go.

When he was done, Grulik stretched his clawed fingers. He had five on each hand once more, the missing ones regenerated from the power of the souls he'd consumed. It was too bad taking their souls killed them. Once the life was gone, the blood was useless.

The horses waited on the path, still under his control. He cleared the trail until all signs of his attack were gone. He didn't plan on staying long, but it never hurt to be careful. Then he brought the bodies and horses to a small forest clearing. The last rider lay next to a thick oak. Blood pooled on the leaves below the man's head.

A gurgling sound came from his victim. The man's eyelids flickered. Grulik's long legs ate up the distance between them in three steps. His claws scored deep into the vulnerable chest. The man's features creased with pain.

Good.

It was time to return home.

He hissed the words of the spell. The spilled blood infused his demon magic with the power needed to open a gate to his world. Black specks swirled in the clearing before him, purple flecks around the edges. The motes shivered but did not solidify.

Grulik repeated the spell. Nothing.

He couldn't return home. If the spell didn't work now, it never would. He was trapped in this human hell because of that witch's curse. He growled and kicked the mage in the ribs. The man gurgled and coughed.

Evelyn had died. Her curse should have been broken. But it wasn't. That meant she was alive, somewhere in this time.

The curse bound him, but it also tied him to the witch. Since she had used their comingled blood for the spell, he could use his blood to find her.

He sliced the palm of his hand and let the blood drip to the earth, the wound already closing. Hissing softly, he performed a tracking spell. The blood changed color from purple to red, slid southward, then stopped.

Tracking her was going to be tedious.

Grulik headed back to the remaining man and took his soul. He dragged the man to the pile of bodies. Since he was stuck in this time, he had to hide his tracks. It took a lot of time and energy to dissolve bodies, but news of an attack like this would quickly spread across England. Better to take the time now than have demon hunters on his trail later. Purple motes landed on the bodies, multiplying until only a darkly pulsating mist remained. The mass shivered and slowly shrank. A faint hum vibrated at the edge of his hearing.

Several hours later small dust heaps occupied the clearing where the bodies had been. A flick of his talon and the breeze carried the dust away.

An elegant house in London floated to the surface of his mind. It belonged to the owner of the one horse he'd kept. According to the young man's memories, a very large mageborn population resided in that city. London was far to the south. He might as well head in that direction, until his tracking spell told him otherwise.

An image of the red-headed mage formed in his mind. Glowing purple flecks surrounded Grulik, and his demon shape shimmered and shrank. Smooth white skin replaced green hide, and long claws transformed into short stubby fingers. He ran his hand through the curls covering his head and yanked out a strand. The color was reddish-blonde. He was now Lord Higginbotham.

Wherever Evelyn was, he would find her. Because there was only one way to break a witch's curse.

Kill the witch.

CHAPTER EIGHT

London
1804

REGINA FLIPPED THROUGH *A DIS-COURSE on Magic*, searching the heavy tome—futilely, so far—for some actual instruction in magic. Her brother Gabe slouched in the leather chair in front of their father's massive desk, pounding his fist against his thigh. Thump-thump-thump, the rhythm conveyed his anxiety. She needed to find a lesson fast, anything to distract him while they waited for Aunt Agatha's return.

"I've found the origins of mage magic and the differences between mageborn and humans, but nothing yet on how to use magic." She closed the book and offered him an encouraging smile. "Why don't you show me one of your latest tricks?"

Gabe stopped and frowned at the worn Persian carpet. "Do you think Uncle Matthew will agree to train me?"

Her heart broke at his expression—hopeful and despairing at the same time. Uncle Matthew was the only one of the brothers who acknowledged their existence, but he suffered from the same prejudices as the rest of the mageborn. Humans and half-bloods, no matter how magically gifted, should not be trained as mages. Holding back that truth from Gabe, even to preserve that bit of hope in his face, was wrong. "We're half-bloods. I would be very surprised if Aunt Agatha managed to change his mind."

"But I have power. Aunt Agatha says so. Look!" A fierce expression crossed his face. A miniscule flame flickered in the palm of his hand, before disappearing with a sharp hiss. He slumped back, drained. "I'm only fifteen, but I can create fire. She says even Father couldn't make fire before he was sixteen. And he was pure mageblood."

Things would be so different had their father lived. He could have trained Gabriel himself. Instead, they had to rely on Aunt Agatha and her uncooperative brothers.

"Aunt Agatha has taught you everything she knows. Perhaps we can learn more from these old texts." Regina glanced back down at the book and placed her finger on the spot she'd read last.

"It's not fair. Why did Father have to die? Why didn't you get any magic?" He stopped. "I'm sorry. I didn't mean to say that."

Why didn't you get any magic?

How many times had she asked herself that same question? She wished she could shut away the world of mages and half-bloods, but this was Gabe, her younger brother. After their father died, she vowed that she would watch over Gabe and see him trained. That she'd never let him down. "I know you didn't. And I don't know why I didn't get any magic. It's just the way it is."

"Are you sure? You never tried my lessons with me. If you did, maybe you'd be able to work magic too!"

His eyes were wide with excitement, as if this had never occurred to her. It was true, some people developed their magic late. But try as she might, she could not forget their grandmother's words to her when she was twelve.

You're a half-blood, child. Some half-bloods, like your brother, are born with powerful magic. Others, like you, take after their human parent. I'm sorry, my dear, but you have to accept the fact that you are magicless.

She remembered protesting. *But isn't it possible I could get magic when I'm older? I have these dreams sometimes, where I'm a witch and a healer. Doesn't that mean I might have magic?*

Her grandmother had looked at her sadly and shaken her head. *Those dreams are your hopes, dear. They're not reality.*

Regina was twenty-three now and no longer a child. And her grandmother had been right. She remained a magicless half-blood.

"I've tried, Gabe, many times. I can't do your lessons. There's no point when I don't have any magic."

"When was the last time you tried?" His jaw jutted out.

"Two years ago." On her twenty-first birthday.

She didn't say that every year on her birthday she had tried to work magic, hoping by some miracle she'd succeed. Two years ago, she'd finally accepted her fate. "We still have some time before Aunt Agatha's return. Since this book doesn't have any exercises that I can find, why don't you practice one of yours?"

"Why don't you try again? You don't have to do my lesson. You could try to make a light. That isn't too hard."

For you, maybe, she thought wryly. "There's no point."

"It's been two years. At least try."

She hated to disappoint him, but her trying to work magic was useless. "Gabe, I'm a magicless half-blood."

"Don't say that! You sound like a mageborn."

"But it's true. I've accepted it." Because she had to. Wishing didn't create magic.

"Please. Just once and I won't bother you again."

She closed the book, since she was about to prove her own lack of magic. "If it fails, I don't want to discuss this anymore."

"Agreed." He leaned forward and rapped his knuckles on the desk, the same way she did to get his attention. "Now close your eyes and pay attention to your body."

Regina closed her eyes, but her mind wandered. Did Aunt Agatha manage to convince at least one of her brothers to train Gabe? She frowned.

"You have to focus on your body, Gina! Stop worrying about other things!"

She jumped. He must have seen her frown. "I'll try."

"When I do it, I think about my breathing."

She focused on her breaths, each slow inhale and exhale.

"Then I try to hear my blood. Put your hands over your ears—"

"Then I won't be able to hear you."

"Just do it!"

She placed her hands over her ears. The world narrowed to the rhythmic sound of her breathing, the roar of her blood coursing through her body.

"Now search deeper. Look at your blood and find the threads of magic there. They're. . . *sparkly*. Find them and grab them. Pull the magic up in your blood."

A chill gripped her at the thought of blood magic, and her concentration broke. No, that wasn't right. *Magic in the blood*. Not blood magic. What had made her think of blood magic? Blood magic was forbidden.

She fought to bring her focus back. Would she find anything? Was it possible she did have magic?

She breathed deeply to slow her racing heart and tried again. A feeling of calm dissipated the chill. Suddenly she felt aware of every hair on her head, of her weight positioned on their father's chair, of her forearms resting on the ancient oak desk.

"Deeper. Search deeper."

She dove down, imagining herself swimming in her blood, searching, searching for threads of mage energy and finding. . .

Sparks of gold. Only a few. Scattered widely.

Impossible. Was that what magic looked like? She'd never seen them in her previous attempts.

She gathered those tiny bits of gold. They expanded in her blood, overtaking her vision until it was like trying to hold back a wave—

Total darkness washed over her. Her breath caught, and then an image of a young, redheaded gentleman riding an exhausted steed blossomed in her mind. He was on a country road with fields to either side. His chin suddenly lifted, and he sniffed, scenting the air. He turned his head, and she saw his eyes—light blue with pupils of yellow flame. Her breath stilled in her throat. He met her gaze, as if he could see her too—

He smiled, and she began to shake.

"Gina? Gina!" Her brother's frantic voice rang in her ears.

Regina blinked, and she was back in the library. She slumped in her seat, drained, as if she'd just raced across the fields at home. Gabe squeezed her hands so tightly her fingers ached. Her gaze lifted to his pale face.

"What happened?" Gabe's eyes were wide. "Why were your eyes black?"

A vision. Grandma was wrong.

Regina wasn't ready to talk about it though. "Nothing happened. It must have been a trick of the light."

"Did you find any magic?"

"I'm not sure. I thought I saw something, but I don't know." A vision meant she had magic. But could she do it again? Should she? That man with strange eyes—she didn't want to see him again. Could he find her through her visions?

The sound of hooves outside the townhouse made them both jump. Gabe crossed the study to look out the window.

"Aunt Agatha is home." He continued to stare outside, his worries about Regina apparently forgotten.

"Would you ask cook to prepare a tea in the morning room? I'm sure she would appreciate it."

"I will." Gabe dashed out of the study as if grateful for a distraction.

Regina rested her head in her hands and closed her eyes. All those times she had tried to perform magic, she had never found anything in her blood. And then today, not only had she found magic, she'd had a vision. Why? After all these years of thinking herself without magic, it was so easy to doubt. But she knew it was real. That gentleman in her vision wasn't a dream. She hadn't imagined his yellow-flame eyes.

Something deep down told her he wasn't human or mageborn. That he was dangerous. But that wasn't what worried her the most. Although it had been her vision, he had seen her too…and been pleased.

CHAPTER NINE

Northern England
1450

THE DEMON'S OTHERWORLDLY POR-
TAL GLEAMED black and ominous in the
early dawn light, a dark blight on the pale, frosted
meadow that stretched from towering limestone
cliffs to rocky hills. Stepping through that obsidian
gateway would separate Julian from the world of
humankind.

For Evelyn, he would enter the demon's hell.

The people he'd leave behind wouldn't understand. He'd never see his sister-in-law or his nephew
again, nor see the fruits of the Mageborn War. He
wouldn't find out who summoned the demon and
bring him to justice. None of that mattered now.
When the demon mauled his pregnant wife and
left her bleeding into the dirt, Julian's entire world
had vanished. He only had one goal now—find
the monster and kill it. If he failed, the souls of his
loved ones would be enslaved for all eternity. He'd
rescue them or die trying. That was the only future

that mattered.

Julian sucked in a breath and plunged into the heart of the demon's portal. Bone-aching cold pierced his body, reminding him of the time he'd fallen through the ice into the lake behind the blacksmith's shop. The water had closed above his head, the grey winter light growing more and more distant as he struggled to reach the surface. That same feeling of slipping away from the world filled him.

One step later all sensation fled. He tried to blink but no longer had a body to do so.

The mageborn called the demon realm a hell. Because it had flames and burning pits of fire—or because any place full of demons had to be a hell—who knew?

An image of the monster running across the moors with Evelyn slung over its shoulder, and Julian's own desperation to reach her, filled him with rage and anguish. He felt a tug on his mind that strung across this black space. He had the impression he was traveling now, following a thread that connected him to the evil fiend.

A pinprick of light appeared in the inky dark. The light rapidly expanded, and his body plummeted through the glare to solid earth below.

Julian groaned, every bone complaining from the hard landing. The earthy scent of moist soil filled his nostrils. He shielded his eyes from the bright morning sun, noting the soft blue sky and fluffy white clouds floating lazily in the warm spring breeze. This was the demon's hell?

He rose to his feet, his body clumsy and heavy after the formlessness of the void.

Julian stood in a cultivated field on the outskirts of a sleepy village. At least he was in a world that looked like England and not some godforsaken demon hell. Maybe he would have a chance of surviving after all. Unless it was an illusion. Was this truly the demon's world?

He wouldn't find any answers standing like a dolt in the middle of a field. The demon had been injured. There had to be a sign of its presence somewhere.

Several rows over, thick purplish-black liquid coated the recently-plowed earth. The back of his left hand burned where the demon's blood had fallen upon it. He compared the liquid on the ground to the purple splotches on his hand.

He had found the demon's trail.

From here its path was easy to see. Its huge prints resembled human footprints, except each foot was topped by five claws. The creature had headed for the woods.

I've got you now.

He followed the tracks northward. Based on the prints, the demon remained in its natural form. It made an effort to avoid open areas, even when a direct path would be faster. More and more, Julian suspected this actually was England. The countryside had a familiarity that nagged at him. He had seen humans in the distance, but no demons or other strange creatures. Why would the fiend hide if it were in its own world?

The terrain grew steeper as Julian entered some foothills. Four horses had followed a well-worn trail to this spot, but none continued on past the curve of the road. Signs indicated a fight had taken place, and he suspected the demon had ambushed the riders. He followed the drag marks and hoofprints to a forest clearing, where blood pooled on the ground next to the demon's claw prints. He found nothing else—no bodies, no horses, no equipment.

The marks indicated only one horse had left the woods. He followed its trail to a large crossroads near a river where an abbey lay in ruins. Wagon and horse tracks traveled in all directions. Julian ground his teeth in frustration. He couldn't tell which way his quarry had gone.

He stumbled to the drystone wall that ran beside the road and slumped to a seat. Julian recognized this dale and the river that coursed along its bottom, but any hope of seeing people he knew vanished. Where missing walls and solitary arches rose from the grass, he remembered a functioning monastery. It was England, but not his England. He'd thought demons could only travel between earth and their own realm. Why had the demon traveled forward in time instead of returning to its own world? It didn't make sense.

He flexed his swollen left hand. Red streaks radiated from the splotches where the demon's blood had spattered him. He removed Eric's gold signet ring and transferred it to his right hand. He'd forgotten to give it to Harbrook. He'd always meant for his nephew Alex to have it.

He pulled out the jar of demonsbane oil. He hated to waste it, but his wound was getting more inflamed. He smoothed the cool liquid over the lesions.

Julian bent over, his forearms resting on his thighs, the energy seeping from his bones. If this was truly England in a future time, his family's estate lay about a half-day walk to the east. Perhaps there he could find some assistance. He lifted his weary body and forced himself back to the road that hopefully still led home.

The sun hung low in the sky as Julian approached the Lindsay estate. He trudged beneath stately elms, fading sunlight angling through the leaves. Did Lindsays still live there? Would they aid him? He turned a corner of the road and stumbled to a stop. The world wavered before him. He shook his head but the vision didn't change.

The greystone castle of his childhood was gone, replaced by a defenseless rectangular-shaped building with an enormous number of windows arranged evenly across the front. A large expanse of lawn spread in every direction. His home—the one thing he'd been sure would not have changed—was gone. He sagged against an elm for support.

The old manor no longer existed. He'd hated the place because of the memories it evoked, but it had been his home.

Instead of heading for the front entrance, he turned towards the area where the gardens used to be, on the off chance they were still there. That had been Evelyn's favorite place. She said being in them gave her a feeling of peace, no matter how upset she was. Julian could use a dose of peace right now. Seven years of war hadn't destroyed him as much as the losses of the past day. He'd lost everything he'd cared most about in the world. He should have listened when Evelyn begged him to let her stay at the camp. Instead he'd sent her away to her doom. He was a failure, just like his father always said.

No one seemed to be about the estate, although he heard a horse's neigh in the distance.

The garden appeared to be unchanged from his youth. Even the placement of the walls looked familiar. He wandered past the delicately scrolled iron gate. Shrubs with beautiful purple and white flowers edged the paths, perfuming the air with their warm fragrance. A measure of peace fell over him. Walking the old paths, he could almost pretend Evelyn was by his side, breathing in the sweet scent of roses and lilacs.

A faint metallic snip disturbed the background of buzzing insects. Julian snapped out of his reverie and searched the garden. Across the lawn, an elderly man bent down, deadheading roses on an arbor.

A surge of energy propelled him towards the gardener. Hopefully he'd be able to find refuge before evening fell. "Good man."

The weathered groundskeeper straightened and turned. His blue eyes widened in his sunburned face, and he hastily executed a bow. "Milord." He kept his eyes downcast.

"I need rest and food. Do you think I could stay here this night?"

"I…I don't know, milord. If you will excuse me, I will find someone who can answer your question." The gardener turned and shuffled away, as quickly as his aged legs could carry him, heading for the servant's entrance.

Angry red streaks covered the entire back of Julian's hand, spreading towards his wrist. The oil hadn't helped much. Demonsbane used to grow at the back of the garden. Perhaps it still did. The fresh herb might be more effective. He might as well check while he waited for the gardener's return.

With luck—not that he'd had any—the master of the estate would give him a place to sleep tonight, and tomorrow he could be on his way. They must have demon hunters in this time. He'd find one and enlist his aid.

A massive, ancient oak rose majestically near the back wall. Julian searched around it, looking for demonsbane in the fading afternoon light. He spotted the low-growing plant behind a stone bench.

He picked a handful of the succulent leaves and chewed them to make a paste. The sound of boots on gravel had him rising to his feet. He hoped the owner of the estate would let him stay the night, even if he had to sleep in the stable.

"I thought I told you never to come back," the man stalking up the path said. Julian froze. The gentleman was tall, a little over six feet. His hair was a dark raven black, except for two white streaks on the sides, which made him look distinguished rather than old. His narrowed eyes were a steely blue-grey. The hair was cropped short, and the clothes expertly tailored.

The man could have been Julian advanced thirty years. Julian resembled this lord more than he did his own father. There was no doubt Lindsays still controlled the estate.

Julian spit the demonsbane paste into his palm, his gaze steady on the disturbingly familiar features of the gentleman before him. The man seemed to recognize him. Who did he think Julian was? Probably a relative. Their resemblance to each other was too strong for anything else. "I've fallen on hard times recently. I stopped here in hopes of a meal and some rest." The truth, such as it was.

He glanced down to rub the paste onto the back of his hand. He couldn't feel his fingers on his skin.

The man frowned and glanced at his injury. "What happened to you?"

"A poisonous plant I encountered in the woods," he lied. He doubted the man would believe he'd fought a demon.

"You were in the woods? Last I heard, you were in London with that mageborn rabble you call friends. You're a disgrace. Did you come here thinking I'd release your funds?"

"I came only for a meal and a night's stay. And some demonsbane to treat my injury. I'll leave now if that is your wish." He stared at the gentleman. When the man didn't answer, Julian headed for the path to exit the gardens.

"Wait," the man called. His eyes were fixed on

Julian's right hand.

Julian looked down, but all he saw was his ruby signet ring. He glanced at the older gentleman.

The mageborn lord's features hardened. "You're not my son. Who are you?" He raised his hand.

The house's lack of defenses and the garden's quiet tranquility had fooled Julian. He'd let his guard down. A blast of wind threw him backwards against the oak.

The world went black.

CHAPTER TEN

REGINA WENT DOWN THE STAIRS and into the hall, where she watched Aunt Agatha remove her gloves and pelisse and thrust them at the butler. She could tell from the angry precision of her aunt's movements that the meeting had not gone well.

"Was Lord Burlington at home?" Regina asked.

"Yes, he was," Aunt Agatha snapped. Her lips pursed together, and she glowered at the butler, who quickly moved out of her way. "Let's discuss this in the morning room. Where is that boy?"

"Gabe went to ask cook to prepare a tea. We heard your carriage arrive."

The tightness around her aunt's eyes and mouth eased slightly. "He's a good child." She addressed the butler, "Please ask my nephew to join us in the morning room."

He bowed. "As you wish, madam."

"Thank you, Deeds."

Aunt Agatha led the way into the morning room. Yellow floral wallpaper provided a cheerful glow in the afternoon sunlight, lifting Regina's spirits after her disturbing vision of the man with the yellow-flame eyes. The world seemed normal again with her aunt back home. She settled onto the damask-covered sofa and squeezed her hands together, while her aunt took the Chippendale chair across from her. A moment later, Gabe's footsteps raced down the hall.

A frown crossed Aunt Agatha's face, but Regina inwardly heaved a sigh of relief. Gabe running indoors meant he'd put aside this morning's events. Her brother was growing up fast, but he was still a boy. She'd often wished to be a girl again, to ride her horse wildly across the fields of their Yorkshire estate, or slide down the banister of their oak staircase with no worries about what people would think. But now they were in London, and Aunt Agatha was staying with them to chaperone Regina in her fourth season. It was bad enough being a half-blood, without adding the dreaded term *hoyden* on top of it.

Gabe slid to a stop outside. A moment of silence ensued, and then the door to the morning room opened. "Good afternoon, Auntie," he said with a little bow.

"Harrumph." Her eyes—the same dark green Regina and Gabe had inherited from their father— narrowed dangerously. "I have ears, I'll have you know. And it hurts them to hear your feet pounding on those old oak floors like that. You're not a little child anymore."

Gabe hung his head. "I'm sorry, Auntie."

She still frowned at him.

"I asked cook to include lemon cakes with the tea." A mischievous grin crossed his lips. Cook's lemon cakes were his aunt's favorites, as Gabe well knew.

No one—not even Aunt Agatha—could resist that look. She maintained her frown for a few moments longer then gave up. "Oh, get on with you. But I want you to apologize to Deeds for scuffing up his floors."

"Yes, ma'am."

Aunt Agatha's features were very similar to her brother but with a more feminine cast—straight nose, high cheekbones, soft rounded jaw. She'd been the toast of the *ton* in her youth, and Lord Carlisle had proposed a week after meeting her. Regina liked her aunt's husband, but didn't see him often, since he preferred his country house and rarely came to London. Regina had often envied her aunt's delicate beauty. Although she, too, had inherited the Westcott nose and cheekbones, Regina and Gabe had both inherited their mother's jaw—square and stubborn. The only softening of the effect was Regina's full lips, also a gift from her mother.

"I presume you would like to know the results of my meeting with Lord Burlington this afternoon?" Aunt Agatha looked directly at Gabe, and her eyes softened. "I'm sorry, Gabriel, but Lord Burlington refused to train you."

Gabe went still. "Did you tell him I could make fire?"

"I did, my boy. But there's no arguing with him.

You could have the power of the greatest mage-born ever to live, yet he still would not train you. Like all the mageborn, he thinks it an abomination to see a human trained in magic."

"But I'm half-mageborn!"

"That doesn't matter to him or those of his ilk. All they see is your human blood." She turned to Regina. "I mean no offense, my dear, but you exemplify their arguments against intermingling."

No mage would marry Regina, because her human blood could result in a magicless child just like her. Even her generous dowry was not enough to compensate. But was it true she was magic-less? Hadn't she had a vision earlier? She debated whether to tell Aunt Agatha what happened, then decided against it. She'd tell her once she was sure the magic was still there. "Is there anything else we can do? What about our other uncles?"

"I already tried them. For shame, they won't even acknowledge you."

The memory of the Hartley ball last year came to mind. She'd run into Uncle Miles at the entrance to the ballroom, and he'd given her the cut direct, nodding only to Aunt Agatha before moving past. It had hurt, knowing that like most of the mage-born, he saw only her half-blood. She would never be good enough to join their ranks.

Gabe suddenly sat up. "Could we pay someone to train me? People hire tutors—why couldn't we find one to teach me magic?"

Regina and her aunt had discussed this, but not with Gabe.

"No, no, no. That would never work," Aunt Agatha stated firmly.

"Why not?" Gabe persisted.

"No tutor would ever agree to train a half-blood, because no mageborn would hire him afterward. He'd lose his livelihood."

"But there are other half-bloods like us. Couldn't they hire an instructor too?"

"There aren't enough of you to make it worthwhile. The wages among the mageborn are higher than any paid by humans, and the jobs more plentiful. A tutor would truly have to be desperate to accept a position with us."

Regina twisted her ring. There was another option. But could she do it? How likely was it that she would get married? *Realistically*, as her grandmother would have said. She'd spent three seasons standing against the wall, with no one approaching her aunt to ask for an introduction, nor her to ask for a dance. With every year, her hopes of marriage and a family of her own faded. But if she did this, her small chance would drop to none. She let out a breath. "We can offer a tutor my dowry. Then he'd never have to work again."

Gabe's head jerked back. Aunt Agatha gasped and touched her throat.

"I'm a half-blood. In three seasons, not a single mage expressed interest in me, and humans want nothing to do with me because of my powerful relatives." The irony grated at her. "I have no need for a dowry. We might as well put it to some use."

Aunt Agatha looked thoughtfully at Gabe. "That's

an interesting idea. It's possible—"

"No," Gabe interrupted angrily. "You will not give up your dowry."

"Gabriel! Your sister has proposed an excellent plan. I'm almost positive we could—"

"No. I refuse."

"Gabriel," Regina pleaded. "You could learn to control your magic."

The determined cast of his features showed the man he would become in a few years. "I will not let you use your dowry. I could use my own funds, if it came to that."

Aunt Agatha shook her head. "Your guardian would have to approve that outlay. Lord Richter is mageborn. I doubt he'll agree."

Gabe crossed his arms. "We'll find another way. I refuse to use your dowry."

At that moment, the door swung open and the maid brought in the service. Aunt Agatha prepared the tea, complete with lemon cakes, cucumber sandwiches, and crumpets.

"But Gabe, it's *my* dowry," Regina asserted.

"Exactly. It's *your* dowry. Who'll marry you without a dowry? Even if you were full mageblood, you wouldn't have a chance at marriage without one."

"I haven't much chance now."

"Gabriel's right, my dear. Once your dowry is gone, you wouldn't have a mage's chance in Hades of finding a man." A steely glint entered Aunt Agatha's eyes as she scanned Regina from her head to her toes. "There's only one option left."

She was almost afraid to ask. "And that is?"

"Marriage."

Regina fell back against the settee as the tension left her. "In case you don't recall, I've attended three seasons, and no one expressed even the slightest interest in me."

"There are other ways of garnering a proposal. Gabriel, take your tea and leave the room. Regina and I have some things to discuss that are not appropriate for young ears."

No one could miss the interest that lit up Gabe's eyes.

"And do not attempt to listen at the doors. I may not be as powerful as my brothers, but I can certainly blanket a room with silence."

Gabe looked crestfallen. "Very well." He grabbed a few sandwiches, a couple of crumpets, and with a baleful sideways glare, swiped a handful of lemon cakes, leaving but one upon the plate.

After he left the room, Aunt Agatha sat very still in her chair. "Quiet." The air seemed to spark to life for a moment in a bright bubble around Regina and her aunt. Aunt Agatha relaxed in her seat. "There. We can talk freely now without fear of being overheard."

That feeling of dread was back. "What do you have to say that required Gabe to leave the room?"

"My dear, there's only one solution to your situation. You need to marry, and Gabriel needs a mentor, preferably a powerful mage capable of training him." She paused to take a sip of tea. "No mage would willingly marry you. So you must take matters into your own hands."

"What do you mean?"

"You are a beautiful young woman. If you high-lighted your assets a bit—" she looked pointedly at Regina's full bosom—"and developed a more flirtatious manner, you might be able to entice a mage into—*ahem*—acting inappropriately." Her aunt blushed.

"You want me to encourage a mage to seduce me?" Regina was shocked.

"It doesn't have to go quite that far. If the two of you are alone in a room, or in a secluded part of a garden, a kiss would be sufficient. People always think the worst."

Mageborn society was very strict. Kiss a woman—or heaven forbid, do more—and the mage was obligated to marry her or be ostracized. That part would probably succeed, if she could find a mage interested enough. But this was for Gabe, not to satisfy her own desires for marriage and a family, and her aunt's plan had a huge flaw. "If I succeed in this, wouldn't the mage hate me for forcing him into marriage? I doubt he'd agree to train my brother."

"The powers of the marriage bed can work won-ders, my dear. Some women choose to keep their men happy, others to deny them. Either method works." She paused, and a faint line of red rose up her chest. "I, myself, *ahem*, prefer the former. It is a much more satisfactory option for both parties, in my opinion." She pinched her lips and said no more, but her fiery blush spoke volumes.

Regina disliked her aunt's plan intensely, but

after three failed seasons, what choice did she have? She had promised herself she would do whatever it took to see Gabriel trained in magic. If this was the only option, so be it.

"Very well. I'll do it."

CHAPTER ELEVEN

———◆———

WATER DRIPPED ON STONE, MAKING a soft plopping sound in the oppressive silence. Julian opened his eyes. He lay on a thin pallet in a small chamber cut from rock. Orange and yellow torchlight flickered through a small barred rectangle set high on an iron door. He struggled to rise and fell back. Thick iron bands attached to chains encircled his wrists, throat and ankles.

The edges of the room were hidden in darkness, but a sense of familiarity nagged at him. If he guessed correctly, he'd been imprisoned in the dungeon beneath his family's estate. He sat up, pulling the clanking chains with him. His muscles were stiff and cold. He stretched. Would anyone come at the noise? Where were his jailors?

He listened, but only the steady drip of liquid on stone broke the silence. If he was alone, this was his chance to escape. He gathered his magic. Power surged through his veins, burning away the cold. Strangely, the iron fetters also warmed up. A reaction to his magic?

He focused on the bands shackling his wrists.

"Open."

The metal cuffs glowed red. A stifling pressure surrounded him. He fought to open his chains. The force opposing him increased and tightened around his chest. He couldn't breathe.

He released his magic, and the pressure dissipated. He sucked in a breath.

"Effective, isn't it?" A voice came from outside the door. Julian glimpsed a shadowy figure through the barred window. A clink of keys and the iron-bound door swung open.

"What is?"

"The dampener. When you try to use magic, the dampener turns your magic back on you. It's a good thing you stopped when you did. You would have suffocated otherwise." The man's voice was cultured, his tone matter-of-fact. As if it didn't matter to him one way or the other if Julian had died. The voice didn't sound like the lord from the garden.

His jailor placed a torch in a holder. Approximately Julian's own age and height, he had brown wavy hair, swarthy skin, a broad muscular build. The light was too dim to determine his eye color. Brown? Hazel? The man's expression was hard to read. He had a feeling this man held many secrets.

"I'm not a threat to you."

"That remains to be seen." The man grabbed a stool from the corner. "How's your hand?"

Julian flexed his fingers. The swelling and numbness were gone. Tiny scars were all that remained of the demon's blood burns. "Fine. While I appreciate you treating my wounds, the rest of your hospitality is sadly lacking." He shook his chains. "Why am I here?"

The man leaned back and smiled, crossing his arms across his chest. "Funny you should ask that. I was about to ask the same of you."

"As I told the gentleman before—how many days ago was that?"

"Five."

Five! The demon's trail would be cold by now. "What did you do to me?" He couldn't keep the snarl from his voice. He yanked his arm forward, but the chain prevented him from reaching more than half a foot from the edge of the pallet.

"Treated you, healed you, gave you a little something to drink. To be honest, we didn't expect you to sleep this long. We've been waiting for you to wake up these past three days."

"You have to let me go."

"Not until you answer some questions. Who are you?"

"Julian Rutherford."

His jailer shook his head. "See, this is why we can't let you go. You're a liar."

"I'm not lying," Julian gritted. "My name is Julian Rutherford."

"You're saying you are the son of the Marquis of Thornwood?"

Julian remembered the older gentleman in the garden, who had exclaimed "You're not my son" before blasting Julian with magic. "No."

"Then why are you trying to pass yourself off as

his son?" The man uncrossed his arms and leaned forward. "You have to admit this looks suspicious."

"I'm not trying to pass myself off as his son. That's my name. It's a common name in my family."

"And coincidentally identical to that of the marquis's son."

Julian yanked on his restraints as anger and frustration rocked through him. They were wasting time. "Listen to me. It's obvious to all of us that there is some familial connection between me and the marquis. He looks more like me than my own father did. I assume I'm a distant relative of his—" Ha! That was putting it mildly. "—based on my name and the resemblance between us. But I am not his son. I was in the area and needed some demonsbane to treat the wound on my hand. I'm guilty of trespassing, but nothing else. I was leaving when I ran into him."

He couldn't tell if the brown-haired man believed him or not. The man reached into his pocket and pulled out a signet ring with deep red rubies embedded around the seal.

Julian glanced at his own bare fingers and fought to keep his body still. He wanted to tackle the man to the ground and snatch the ring from his hand. "That's my ring."

The man held it up in the faint torchlight, making the rubies glow a deep red. "It's beautiful. How did you acquire it?"

Julian ground his back teeth as he debated answering. "I inherited it."

The man turned the ring around in his fingers.

"Who did you inherit it from?"

"My brother, after he died." The words stuck like sand on his tongue. Even now, the thought of Eric's death affected him.

"What was his title?"

"The title was lost long ago. It doesn't exist now. The ring is a family heirloom. It's all I have left of him." Surely that was plausible enough.

The man's gaze narrowed on him. "What are you doing here?"

Should Julian tell the truth or not? "I was looking for someone, but I lost his trail. This was the only place I knew of that might have demonsbane, and I needed to treat my wound."

"Your clothes look like those from the fifteenth century. Are you an actor?" The man snapped the words out.

Julian choked on a laugh. The thought was absurd. "No."

"Then why are you wearing those clothes?"

He shrugged.

"What is your occupation?"

"I don't have one. I'm merely passing through."

"Who are you searching for?"

Julian met the gaze of his questioner straight on. "A monster."

The door opened, and the man Julian had met in the garden entered.

The brown-haired man stood up and offered his seat to the Marquis of Thornwood. The marquis sat on the stool and gestured for Julian and the other man to continue.

Julian looked up at his inquisitor. "What's your name?"

"Nothing you need to know at the moment." He leaned back against the wall. "You said you were chasing a monster. What kind?"

"A demon." Since they'd had his wound treated, they already knew it was caused by demon's blood, not a poisonous plant. "It killed my pregnant wife. If it got their souls, they'll be enslaved for all eternity. I have to find it."

The marquis frowned. He seemed lost in thought.

"Are you a demon hunter?" the brown-haired man asked.

"No."

"Then how do you expect to find it?"

"I was hoping to find a demon hunter to help me track it."

The man exchanged a look with the marquis, then he said, "The demon hunters are all but extinct."

"What? Their family lines died out?"

"No, but one family only has daughters. Another has a half-blood son, who is too young and has no one to train him. Another disappeared, and the last is somewhere in Scotland."

"What do you do when there's a demon on the loose?"

"It's not a problem. Nobody summons demons anymore. It's against mageborn law." There was the faintest edge of mockery in the brown-haired man's voice, as if he were repeating something someone had said to him many times.

Summoning demons was against the law in Julian's time too, but that hadn't stopped mages from doing it. "The demon has already killed four people. It needs to be stopped."

His inquisitor didn't seem surprised.

"You know about this? Who were the men? If you know their names, I can find the demon."

The marquis shook his head and joined the conversation for the first time. "We didn't hear about any deaths, only the disappearance of four noblemen from London who'd gone on a hunting trip."

"Three. One returned to London," Julian's original inquisitor commented.

"They're all dead. Including the fourth one." Julian's voice was flat.

"You can't be sure of that," the man by the wall scoffed.

"I found an empty meadow in the forest, scored with drag marks and the demon's claw prints. Blood spattered the grass and soaked into the earth. They're dead. The demon is the man who rode to London." Julian yanked on the metal links that chained him to the wall. "You have to release me. Now there are more souls that need to be freed. I have to kill it!"

"We'll release you," the marquis spoke quietly, "as soon as we know who you are. Tell me again how you got this ring?"

"It was my brother's ring. When he died, it came to me."

The marquis gazed at Julian and then held out his hand to the man next to him. The brown-haired man leaned forward and dropped Julian's signet ring into the marquis's palm. The older lord examined the ring for a long minute, then looked up and spoke. "Did you know my ancestors fought in the Mageborn War?"

Julian jerked at the odd turn of the conversation. He didn't remember any Thornwoods from his time. He shook his head.

"Perhaps you've heard of my other title, the Earl of Lindsay," the marquis said. "My name is Edward Rutherford. My great-great-etcetera grandfather is infamous for starting the Mageborn War."

The man's name confirmed their connection. The marquis descended from Eric's son Alex. Julian bowed his head to hide the welter of emotions that filled him. Gratitude that the Mage High Council had fulfilled their part of the Accords, and Alex had received his birthright. Despair that he had failed to save Evelyn and hadn't stayed to raise his nephew. He'd won a war, but lost everything that mattered most to him.

"What's wrong?" the marquis asked.

Julian struggled to regain control. After a moment he released his breath and addressed the marquis. "Nothing. I was surprised by what you said."

The man by the wall commented. "The fact that you are surprised is surprising. How could you not know this? Every child in England is practically born with this knowledge."

"He said he was the Marquis of Thornwood. I didn't realize he was also the Earl of Lindsay," Julian retorted.

The marquis directed his sharp blue gaze at Julian. He seemed to come to a decision. "After the Mage High Council conceded to the terms of the Accords, Lord Lindsay's wife was murdered, and he disappeared. Are you familiar with that story?"

His throat tightened. He'd lived that story, but he wasn't about to say that to these men. They'd think he was mad. "No."

The marquis continued. "The facts have never been clear. Some claim that the baby Lindsay's wife was carrying—did I mention she was pregnant at the time? —was not his, and he killed her in a fit of jealous rage. The other tale says that a demon killed her and used her blood to open a gate back to its demon hell. That story says the magelord followed the demon to its world, hoping to kill it and save his wife and unborn child's souls."

Although he knew the answer, Julian forced the words past the thickness in his throat. "What does that story say happened next to Lord Lindsay?"

"That he died. What else?"

That was exactly what Julian had expected to happen to him. He'd only hoped he would have a chance to kill the demon and save Evelyn and his child's souls first. "Why are you telling me this?"

"Our family has always believed there was a demon involved. We'd assumed Lindsay had died in the demon world. And yet..." He raised the signet ring up until the torchlight made the rubies glow a clear claret. "You have his missing signet ring, you're wearing clothes from that time period, and you have the same story and name."

The man by the wall jerked upright, and his head snapped towards the marquis. "You aren't suggesting—" He shook his head hard. "That's impossible."

The marquis reached inside his jacket and pulled out another ring. He held them out to Julian's gaze. The rings were nearly identical. Julian's ring bore rubies, the other tiny sapphires. Both rings were wrought of heavy gold, but the engravings were slightly different. The sapphire signet ring had the addition of a tiny sun.

"Look at the rings, Langley," the marquis told the man by the wall. "The gold of his ring shines bright yellow, there are few scratches. Mine is aged and worn. When the original ring was lost, this one was made to replace it."

"His could be a copy. If it was made recently, of course it would be new," the brown-haired man stated.

"It's a poor copy then. His is missing the sun that was added to the crest."

"When was the sun added?" Langley pursued.

"When this replacement was made. Around 350 years ago."

"I still say it's a trick," he repeated stubbornly.

"The healer said it looked like he had demon's blood poisoning."

"So the monster he's chasing really is a demon. It doesn't mean he's a man from the past." Langley bit the words out.

Julian glanced between the two of them, his mind racing. The marquis had figured out who he was, and, oddly enough, believed. The other, naturally, was skeptical. Should he admit the truth? Would that convince the marquis to release him? Or would they keep him here indefinitely, convinced he wasn't in his right mind? "Does it matter who I am? I'm chasing a demon, who is five days ahead of me now. All I want is to find it."

Langley took a step forward and loomed over Julian. "And what will you do when you find it?"

"Kill it."

"Release him, Langley," the marquis said.

"First, he needs to answer this question. How did he get here from his time period? Demons can only travel between our world and theirs. They do not travel through time. *Mages* do not travel through time either."

Julian would never forget charging across the meadow, the limestone cliffs black against the rising sun, the pain of watching Evelyn struggling to get out of the demon's grasp and the knowledge he couldn't reach her in time. "The demon had sliced my wife's body with his claws. He used her blood to open a portal."

"Yes, we know a sacrifice is needed to open the gate between our worlds." Langley waved him on, seemingly indifferent to the action that had destroyed Julian's life.

Julian clenched his hands and fought the anger that burned inside his chest. He needed to convince them of the truth. Otherwise they might never release him from this dungeon. "I saw a burst of magic around them both before she died. She was a powerful witch. All I can guess is she somehow changed the direction of the gate. The demon jumped through it, and I followed soon after. I expected to land in the demon's world, but instead I ended up here. What year is this?"

"1804," the marquis answered.

The word hit him like a punch in his gut. More than three hundred years separated him from the world he'd lived in. Everything he'd known was lost. He rubbed his forehead, the chains heavy on his wrists. There was no going back. Mages couldn't travel between worlds, only demons. And until now, nobody had ever been able to travel through time. "I guess Evelyn was more powerful than I'd thought."

"Release him, Langley." The marquis gave the younger man a hard stare.

"Yes, sir." Langley placed his hands on the iron bands around Julian's wrists. He uttered a spell and the clamps fell open. He did the same for the ring around Julian's neck and the bands around his ankle.

Julian rubbed his wrists as Langley stepped back. He considered trying to overpower them and make his escape, but he needed their aid. "You believe me?"

Langley crossed his arms and leaned back against the wall. "Only a fool would believe that tale. But I believe a demon killed someone you love, and that you're determined to hunt it down. A demon roaming free in England is an abomination. I'll help you."

"Why?"

"To keep an eye on you. And if we kill a demon in the meantime, so much the better."

CHAPTER TWELVE

THE LONDON AIR WAS SOOTY and rank. Grulik nudged his horse down the busy cobblestone street lined with shops. Elegantly-dressed women and men leisurely strolled the pavement, followed by their servants carrying a number of packages in their arms. The odor of meat pies floated through the air from a vendor hawking his wares from the corner, and Grulik stiffened at the pang of hunger that ripped at his middle.

He was hungry. Starving. But not for food.

Grulik closed his eyes and inhaled deeply. The rich aroma of magic-laden souls greeted his nostrils. He swallowed the low growl that rose in his throat in response. It'd been three days since he'd last taken a soul. Now he was surrounded by them. He'd never been to this time, and London was teeming with people. Their souls burned bright. He wanted to snatch them and feast until that emptiness inside went away. But it'd be foolhardy to do so. Who knew how many demon hunters existed in this time? No point in making his presence known. Not when he couldn't escape back to his world.

Still, he yearned to fill that emptiness and craving inside him with the mageborn souls' bright beauty.

He'd already circled London and performed his blood tracking spell. He knew the witch was somewhere in this city. He didn't know where. Not yet. London was too large for him to find her quickly with his spell. He'd give mageborn society a try first.

Saliva pooled in his mouth. Tonight. He'd quench his thirst tonight.

CHAPTER THIRTEEN

———◆———

The Lindsay Estate
Northern England

JULIAN AWOKE IN A SOFT bed. Sunlight slipped through velvet curtains onto a polished oak floor. For a moment he struggled to remember where he was, then he sat up as the memories flooded back. After he'd sworn an oath not to leave, he'd been escorted to this room.

They'd all agreed Julian would pretend to be the marquis's son, the Earl of Lindsay. He looked like him, and it was easier than trying to explain the fantastic truth. Strange events were commonplace among the mageborn, but no one would believe he'd traveled through time.

The Marquis of Thornwood told the servants that his son had joined an acting troupe, then come home when it hadn't worked out. Julian hadn't seen the slightest flicker of surprise on the butler or footmen's faces when he and Thornwood ascended from the dungeon into the manor above. Either the servants were extremely well-trained, or this wasn't the first time the marquis's son had been tossed into the dungeon.

A soft knock sounded on the door. A valet entered with clothing neatly folded over his arm and a small leather satchel. Footmen followed with a tub and buckets of water.

"I've come to help you dress, milord." The valet's tenor voice was polite. He laid the clothing on a bench in the dressing room.

"Very well." If Julian was going to find the demon, he needed to blend into this time period. Then he would find out what the marquis stood to gain by helping him. There had to be more to it than merely catching the demon or helping a supposed ancestor. Did the marquis truly believe his tale, or was he playing a game of his own?

After a bath, haircut, shave, and new clothing, Julian joined Thornwood and Langley in the library. They sat in wingback chairs before the marble fireplace, where a fire burned in the grate, chasing the damp morning chill from the vaulted room.

Julian couldn't help glancing at the family portrait hanging above the mantle. The marquis, his wife, and son were depicted in an outdoor landscape. The young man had wavy black hair, piercing blue eyes, and his father's height. Julian did indeed resemble the carefree young man in the painting. They could have been twins. But that air of insolence—betrayed by the faint curl of the young man's upper lip—belonged to the marquis's son alone.

"The resemblance is uncanny," Thornwood finally commented. "Even I mistook you for my son at first. With Langley at your side, I don't think you'll have any problems posing as the earl."

"Do I need to pretend I'm your son? Why don't we just search for the demon?"

"If people see you, they will assume you are the Earl of Lindsay," Langley said. "Lord Higginbotham was part of the hunting party you said was attacked. He rode back to London. Whether he is the demon or not, we need to speak with him."

Julian nodded. "I agree, since this is our only lead."

"You will need a title and money in order to move around London society with me. So if you want a chance to question Higginbotham, you'll have to play the role of the marquis's son."

"Won't that be a problem if the earl is in London?" Julian asked.

"I already sent a missive telling him that I will reconsider his latest request for funds, but only if he comes to see me in person. That will get him here. In the meantime, you'll stay with Langley until we know my son has left London. Then you can take up residence in my London townhome."

"There's only one problem. Your son does not associate with polite society," Langley said.

"That's true." Thornwood drummed his fingers on the armrest of his chair. "We can pretend that my son and I have reconciled. That would even explain your presence, Langley. People will believe you are there to make sure my son no longer gambles, associates with the Mageborn Purity League, or overindulges with alcohol."

"I think that would work," he agreed.

There was no doubting the strong bond that existed between the marquis and Langley. From their conversations, Julian knew the marquis had immediately sent for Langley after imprisoning him, and Langley had come right away to handle the interrogation. Was there another connection Julian wasn't aware of? "You said this would explain Langley's presence. Why?"

"Because I'm the earl's cousin on his mother's side. But mainly because I have spent many years hauling his son out of gambling dens. People are used to me trying to keep him out of trouble."

"Impersonating my son might pose some difficulties for you," Thornwood said to Julian.

"What do you mean?"

"My son is infamous throughout mageborn society for his prejudices against humans and half-bloods. When you enter society, many people will give you the cut direct or avoid you."

"That one fell very far from the tree," Langley commented.

Julian tried to understand this, but it didn't make sense. Eric had died, and Julian had traveled to the future, so there was only one person who could be the marquis's ancestor. "Aren't you descended from Alexander Rutherford? The half-blood son of Eric Rutherford?"

Thornwood gave a bitter laugh. "Yes, we are. Alexander was the strongest mage in our family history. But despite the Mageborn War, half-bloods and humans still aren't accepted as equals in mageborn society. My son has tried to minimize his background—even going so far as to join the Mageborn Purity League—in order to gain greater acceptance from his unsavory associates."

Anger burned in Julian's chest. A war had been fought generations ago so that the entitled young lord in the portrait could deny his heritage? Julian had lost Evelyn for this? For a society that still turned its back on half-bloods? He glared at the marquis. "Why are you helping me? It's more than hunting the demon, isn't it?"

The marquis met his gaze. "Yes. There's nobody left in our family line besides me and my son. If he doesn't marry, the estate will revert to the crown. He needs to find a wife, but no woman of decent stock will marry him. With your help, we might be able to reform his image enough for him to find a wife."

"No." Julian had just lost the woman he'd loved most, the mother of his child. And the marquis wanted him to participate in society so his son could find a wife?

"Then we won't help you find the demon, and you'll be thrown back in the dungeon," Langley said. His brows rose over his cynical brown eyes. "I thought nothing mattered more to you than killing that demon?"

Julian ground his teeth in frustration. "Fine. I will do my best to reform your son's image. However, I refuse to court any women on his behalf." God willing, he'd find the demon and accomplish his mission quickly.

"Agreed."

"What happens to me after we kill the demon? What if I don't have time to reform your son's reputation?"

"You'll be free to go," the marquis answered, "but if you stay and help improve his standing in society, I will set you up in a place of your choosing."

New clothing, new era, new life. Those alone were bad enough. But now Julian had to redeem the reputation of a mageborn bigot so the disreputable earl could find a wife? He swallowed his disgust. "If that's what I have to do to find the demon, so be it."

CHAPTER FOURTEEN

A Gaming Hell in London

GRULIK SHUFFLED THE DECK WITH trembling hands, then slowly dealt the cards around the green baize-covered table. Orange candlelight flickered from the sconces dotting the dingy aquamarine walls, but most of the smoky room was shrouded in darkness. He rather enjoyed the gloom. Tonight he wore the shape of a feeble elderly gentleman, Lord Bernson.

Three young men sat across from him, all of them already far in their cups. He looked at the cards in his age-spotted hands and bit back a smile.

Sometimes, it was almost too easy.

The young men looked at their hands. Their expressions told him whose cards were good, and who would soon drop out. Grulik eyed the hulking young lord across from him. Drunk and slumped in his seat, the man had raven hair and blue eyes, just like a certain warrior Grulik had once known. But this one had a brutish attitude Julian Rutherford had never had. This man wasn't his nemesis from the past, but the resemblance was too much to be coincidence. A plan blossomed in Grulik's mind, and this time, he did smile at his cards.

Raven Hair shoved his bid to the center of the table. "I raise you ten quid."

The man to his right, whose eyes were half closed from the copious amounts of whiskey he'd already imbibed, studied his cards and slurred, "I'm out."

Grulik spent some time examining his hand, as if he didn't know whether to stay or drop. He pushed his bid to the center. "I'll match."

The man to his left pushed his money to the center. "Match."

They went around a couple more times. The gentleman on his left dropped out. Grulik squinted at his cards as the bids went higher. Raven Hair clenched his teeth as he shoved the last of his money onto the table.

"Match," Grulik said.

The angry young lord turned to the somnolent companion on his right, the one Grulik privately called Whiskey. "Lend me some money."

"I beg your pardon?" Whiskey's eyelids lifted and for a moment he looked wide awake.

"I need to borrow some money to finish this hand. You'll have it back as soon as I've won."

"You still owe me from last time." He shook his head.

"I'm going to see my father next week. I'll pay you everything I owe you when I return."

Whiskey studied him then slouched further in his chair. "Very well. Take what you need."

Raven Hair took half and moved it to the center. "Your bid."

"Match. Your cards?" Grulik said.

The young lord turned over his cards, triumph in his gaze. He held one of the highest hands.

Grulik revealed his cards. "Sorry, you lose." He reached out to claim the money.

The angry youngster leaned forward and grabbed Grulik's wrinkled hand in a numbing grip. "You cheated."

"I did not." He looked at the other gamblers at the table. "Ask them."

The other players looked back and forth between the two men. Lefty shrugged, while Whiskey frowned. "I didn't see anything." His mouth pulled down at the corner. He looked at Raven Hair. "You still owe me half my stake."

The player's face flushed a dark red. He released Grulik's hand and threw the money towards him, eyes narrowed.

Grulik pocketed his winnings. "Thank you for an enjoyable evening. Perhaps we can play together again sometime soon." His gaze lingered on the angry young man. "Good night."

He turned and left the gaming establishment.

He shuffled slowly down the street, pausing frequently as if overcome by the alcohol. It didn't take long to sense Raven Hair's presence behind him. He turned into a dark alley between two brick buildings. Good, it was empty.

A hand grabbed his shoulder and slammed him against the wall. Pain shafted in the back of his head.

"Give me your money," the young man growled. "Cheaters don't deserve to keep their winnings."

"I agree completely," Grulik said. He had cheated, but so had the young lord before him. The only difference was that he had done a better job. He looked into the florid face of the brute before him and recognized the cruelty in his eyes. He was going to enjoy taking this one's soul.

His body shimmered as he changed into his demon form. The angry young man let go and staggered back, shaking his head as if the alcohol had bested his senses.

Grulik hissed and snarled his laugh.

"My dear Earl of Lindsay, it is time you learned some manners."

CHAPTER FIFTEEN

REGINA HID BEHIND A LARGE palm in the corner of the Sherrington ballroom and tried futilely to pull up the low bodice of her costume. Aunt Agatha had insisted she wear the costume of Marie Antoinette. Regina's honey-colored hair was obscured by white powder, and her green eyes looked a startling sapphire blue thanks to a demi-mask that Aunt Agatha had bespelled.

The mask didn't stop there. Her square jaw now looked fashionably soft and rounded. Regina had always wished for her aunt's delicate jawline, but she felt uncomfortable with the change. She missed the determination of her own chin.

"No one can possibly guess who you are in this disguise," Aunt Agatha had marveled when Regina was fully dressed.

"People will recognize you, though, and know you are accompanying your niece."

A sly look slid over Aunt Agatha's face. "Lady Marleigh is going to ride with us, and everyone knows that her daughter is attending the ball as Marie Antoinette tonight."

"Oh, no, Auntie, what did you do?" Panic flared in Regina's chest. Lady Marleigh was Aunt Agatha's dearest friend. Lady Marleigh's daughter, Felicity, was one of the most sought-after debutantes of the mageborn *ton*, and rumored to have turned down four offers of marriage in her first season alone. Regina had always been ignored by the mageborn at these events, but in this disguise she'd be the center of attention. *Remember, you're doing this for Gabe. You'll have a better chance of trapping a mage in marriage tonight.*

"I promised I would get her an invitation to the Dellingham soiree."

Regina gasped. The Dellingham soiree was *very* exclusive. Invitations were highly sought after and almost impossible to get. "How can you possibly fulfill that pledge?"

"Lady Dellingham owes me a favor for a spell I worked on her behalf years ago."

"And you're sure she'll remember this?"

"She'll honor it. In fact, she'll be delighted to be let off so easily."

Regina wondered what spell Aunt Agatha could possibly have cast that would require payment years later, but knew better than to ask. Surveying the glittering crowd, Regina once again questioned the wisdom of her aunt's plan. She needed to find a mage who would be powerful enough to train Gabe, but not resent her actions so much as to refuse her request.

Regina gave up wrangling with her bodice. It was a futile endeavor, anyway.

Lady Marleigh had stood next to Regina when they entered, announcing Regina simply as "Marie Antoinette" with a wicked smile. Lady Marleigh was dressed as the famous courtesan of Louis XV, Madame de Pompadour. It had been an odd experience, entering the ballroom with Lady Marleigh. Everywhere she looked, the mageborn lords and ladies smiled back, and young gentlemen had surged forward to beg her for a dance. No one seemed to realize she wasn't Felicity.

Aunt Agatha had whispered, "Regina, do not disappear to the library or behind the palms or wherever it is you usually abscond to. Take note of any mage who looks at you. A glance can often signify further interest." Then she and Lady Marleigh joined the dowagers seated in a corner of the ballroom.

Regina danced with many mageborn lords for the first hour. Men who'd never deigned to acknowledge her presence at a ball fought for the privilege of leading her to the dance floor. How did Felicity stand the constant attention? After ten minutes of non-stop chatter, Regina had longed for her old quiet anonymity. Eventually she fobbed off the rest of the dance requests by saying she had a slight headache. She saw an opportunity and ducked into a corner behind the palms. When no one followed her, she leaned against the wall with a sigh of relief.

She mentally reviewed the list of mages she and her aunt had drawn up. She'd been so busy dancing and talking that she hadn't had time to search for them yet, and the lords she'd danced with so far weren't powerful enough to train her brother. She leaned forward from her position behind the palms to view the mass of people crowding the elegantly decorated ballroom. Lady Sherrington was one of the few leaders of the mageborn *ton* who invited half-bloods to her balls. Although none dared say so outright, it was rumored she had a human ancestor somewhere in her family tree.

Shepherdesses, Roman emperors, a king or—Regina stifled a laugh—ten, fairy princesses, pirates, what looked to be the entire English court, and even a mermaid, complete with two oversized shells, packed the ballroom. Most of the men, fortunately, wore demi-masks that hid their eyes only. It made recognizing them easier. Which was the point, of course.

Lord Falsworth had been Aunt Agatha's first choice for Regina. He was a powerful mage looking for a second wife. He was older than Regina would have liked. However, he'd already secured his heirs, so he might be more open to a half-blood. Plus, he didn't associate with the Mageborn Purity League. She didn't see anyone who matched his stocky form.

Next on their list had been Regina's top choice—Baron Ilwich. He too was a powerful mage. Not quite at the level of Lord Falsworth, but in his favor, he had always been polite to her. She spotted him dressed as King Neptune, dancing with the woman in mermaid costume. Their choices seemed unusually fortuitous. After observing their mutually besotted expressions for a minute, Regina scratched the baron off her list. She would not come between a man and his mermaid.

Her aunt's third choice had been the Earl of Lindsay. Regina's cheeks had burned at the suggestion, and she had vehemently refused. She'd encountered the handsome lord at the Prinsworth soiree the season prior. Rumor had it that the only reason he attended the ball was because he'd lost a wager to the Mageborn Purity League.

Regina still bristled at the memory. She had taken a wrong turn on her way back from the ladies' retiring room and encountered the earl in the hallway. He'd been in his cups, and he crushed her against the wall. She tried to push him away, but he placed his wet mouth over hers, squeezing her tight against his body. Shuddering with horror and tasting the alcohol on his breath, she kicked him as hard as she could in the shins. His grip loosened. She backed away and wiped her mouth with the back of her hand as he leaned down to rub his shin. His narrowed eyes promised retribution.

"You!" He spat. His spittle landed at her feet.

Regina backed away further, trembling now.

"You're that half-blood spawn of the Marquis of Harbrook." He straightened up and his lip curled. "I must be cup-shot not to have recognized you. What is Lord Prinsworth thinking, inviting half-bloods to his ball? It's like inviting livestock, except animals at least are useful. I'm going to talk with Lord Prinsworth and let him know his choice of associations leaves much to be desired."

He turned and left.

Regina had stood there for several minutes, shaking. The man was little more than the beast he'd accused her of being. She didn't care that he was the most powerful mages of her generation. Aunt Agatha—who knew of this encounter—said the earl was obviously attracted to her and that she could use this to her advantage. In this disguise, Regina probably would be able to trap him. But she couldn't stand the thought of marriage to such a brute, and doubted he would train her brother, no matter what her aunt said about the powers of the marriage bed.

A commotion to her left caught her attention, as people scurried away from the entrance. A tall, dark-haired man strode into the crowded ball-room. He was elegantly dressed in a black tailcoat, snowy white shirt, cream waistcoat, black breeches and shiny Hessian boots. A domino masked the top portion of his face. The gentleman's looks were so striking that she couldn't stop staring. His midnight-black hair gleamed from the chandelier above, and she caught a glimpse of dark blue eyes. His profile was strong—straight nose, cleft chin, the slightest hint of a dimple bracketing his lips. Her heart thumped wildly in her chest. She was sure she knew him. They must have met before, but where?

When her memory placed him, she shook her head. No, it couldn't be. That man's shoulders had never been so broad, nor his build so muscular. Plus, this lord surveyed the ballroom like a general would a battlefield. He wasn't cupshot and stumbling through the crowd. Her breath caught in her throat. He must be someone else.

He examined the balcony, and Regina finally got a good look at his face. Chagrin swamped her. She was wrong. Her mystery man was that horrible, handsome, despicable Earl of Lindsay.

———◆———

Julian scanned Lady Sherrington's ballroom for the man he believed to be the demon—Lord Higginbotham. He and Langley had stopped at the lord's house several times since arriving in London, but the man was never there. The butler told them Higginbotham accepted an invitation to tonight's masquerade ball, so Julian and Langley attended as well.

The young lord had reddish-blond hair. It should make finding him easier, assuming he was here.

Julian had never seen so many people together outside of the battlefield. The room reeked of stale perfume and warm bodies. He envied Langley, who had taken one whiff of the stuffy air and said he'd check the gardens.

Lord Langley had accompanied him everywhere, like a leech. The marquis's son—the real Earl of Lindsay—had disappeared several days ago. Langley learned that the earl had gone to a notorious gaming establishment the night he disappeared. The mage owed large sums of money to quite a few people, and rumor had it that he'd fled London to escape his creditors.

Like any good impostor, Julian had immediately moved into the earl's townhouse and taken possession of his home, clothing, and title. The earl's clothing and personal effects were still there, which indicated he'd left town in haste. The servants had been glad to see Julian. It was evident they didn't like the earl, but they didn't want him gone either.

Julian dragged his thoughts back to the ball. So far he'd spotted five redheaded men. Two were too old to be Lord Higginbotham. The other three might be his quarry. That is, of course, if the demon still wore that man's form.

A woman with white-powdered hair and a jeweled mask hovered behind a group of palms to his left. Her spine snapped straight when she caught him staring. Their gazes locked, then she flipped her fan open and turned away. A knot formed in his throat. Evelyn had possessed that same height and statuesque figure. One evening, Evelyn had waited for him at home in the library, hiding behind the door. When he found her, she laughed and wrapped her arms around his neck, and gave him a lingering kiss.

Odd that this woman would trigger a memory he'd almost forgotten. His eyes clung to that familiar form, as the ache in his chest built. He would do anything to have his wife back.

A hand clapped him hard on the back. "That doesn't look like a redheaded man to me," Langley said. "Did the definitions of redhead and man change over the centuries?"

Julian tore his gaze from the lady behind the

palms. He squashed the pain of his memories and focused on why he was here. He wasn't about to tell Langley that this woman reminded him of his dead wife. "Any luck outdoors?"

"No. Here?"

"Five, but only three are the right ages."

"Let's go. We have a lot of people to meet."

Over the next few hours, Langley introduced Julian to every redheaded and bewigged man at the ball, as well as other acquaintances, using the pretext that the Earl of Lindsay was newly reformed and back in the good graces of his father, the Marquis of Thornwood. Julian bowed and smiled politely. He lost track of the names and costumes, and frustration ate at him as every encounter failed to turn up Higginbotham.

"The demon must have switched to another form." Julian glanced at the top of the stairs. A liveried footman still waited to announce guests, even though there hadn't been any new arrivals for at least half an hour.

"What now?"

"I don't know. Is there any matron, maiden, shepherd or lord left in London that you haven't introduced me to?"

Langley laughed and leaned back against the white fluted column behind him. "Other than Higginbotham, I think you've met them all."

Julian smacked his gloves on the balcony railing as he surveyed the crowded dance floor below. "I'm not ready to leave yet. There has to be a way to find the demon or some trace of him if he's here."

"Perhaps there is." Langley joined him at the railing. "Do you see the woman in the light blue dress with the wide skirts? The one dancing with Julius Caesar."

There was only one woman on the dance floor who matched that description—the mysterious woman who had snapped her fan at Julian earlier. The gentleman she danced with wore a toga and laurel crown. Even discounting the towering pile of curls on her head, she was taller than her barrel-chested partner. "The one with white-powdered hair?"

"Yes. Let me introduce you to Marie Antoinette."

"The lady is French?" Julian didn't know why, but he felt oddly disappointed.

"I meant the woman *dressed* as Marie Antoinette. Your education is sadly lacking, cousin."

Julian made a mental note to find out who Marie Antoinette was. "You know my story. It'll take time for me to catch up." He jerked his head toward the woman below. "Who is she?"

"I believe that is Lady Marleigh's daughter, Felicity. Her father was a demon hunter. He passed on several years ago, but maybe she knows something that could help us."

He watched as she gracefully stepped through the forms of the dance. Once again that jab of remembrance stabbed him. He didn't really want to approach her, not when she reminded him so strongly of Evelyn. It was absurd, since she looked nothing like his wife. But there was something about the way she moved that brought all his memories and longing for his lost love to life.

"Is something wrong?" Langley asked.

Julian shook off the weight of the past. He was a warrior, not a weepy-eyed poet. If he was going to save Evelyn's soul, they had to find the demon. "No. Let's go talk to the lady in the blue dress."

CHAPTER SIXTEEN

GRULIK WANDERED AROUND THE SHER-RINGTON masquerade dressed in a black domino. Tonight he was Lord Falsworth, a middle-aged widower. He'd been searching all week for the witch without any luck. London was too large to pinpoint her location. So he attended yet another ball. Maybe he'd find her in mageborn society. Or if not, his next victim. He grinned to himself.

He headed towards the French doors leading to the balcony. As he passed a group of dancers, he caught the witch's scent. Euphoria swirled through him.

She wore a light blue dress and a half mask. He couldn't tell what she really looked like beneath her costume. It didn't matter though. Her soul was bright with magic. He inhaled deeply, unable to resist. Her soul was tinged with different memories now, although the core was the same. Did she realize she'd been reincarnated? Did she remember who she was?

He caught a whiff of another person from his

past. Julian Rutherford. Surprise filled him and he searched the ballroom. It didn't take him long to spot his old nemesis on the balcony above him, sporting the clothing of this new time period. Same old soul, same old memories. Grulik had never imagined Julian would follow him through the portal and leave poor dead Evelyn behind, but souls never lied.

He was sure the lord wanted revenge. But without his foster brother Harbrook to help him, Julian had no idea who Grulik was or where to find him. According to Lord Falsworth's memories, there weren't any demon hunters left in London. Poor Julian wouldn't recognize him now any more than he had when Grulik had impersonated Kikson back in the rebel camp. If Grulik had been in his demon form, he would have hissed with laughter.

Fortune had smiled doubly on him tonight. Time for some fun.

Kill the witch. Break the curse. And then... *home*.

CHAPTER SEVENTEEN

REGINA THANKED HER DANCE PART-
NER, a robust fellow dressed as Julius Caesar,
for their dance as he escorted her off the oak dance
floor. Now that the Scottish Reel was over, she
wanted nothing more than to find a spot to rest
and hide from any more suitors. This was the first
time she had ever been the center of attention, and
she longed for her previous anonymity. Being popular was greatly overrated.

"Lady Antoinette!" A gangly young lord dressed
as a highwayman came towards her.

Regina stifled a sigh. She'd missed her chance to
escape. It took her a moment to recall the man's
name. "Lord Pratchett. What are you doing here?"

"I came to find you. Lady Marleigh suggested we
take a walk in the garden, since it is such a pleasant
night."

Of course Lady Marleigh had sent him her way.
She'd been sending mages in Regina's direction
the entire night. Was this what it was like for Felicity? Suitors constantly searching for her, asking her
to dance or stroll in the garden? How did she han-

dle the constant barrage? If Regina had Felicity's popularity, she would fake a cold in a witch's snap to avoid attending these balls.

Regardless, no matter how much Regina wanted to refuse, she had to make the most of every opportunity. *For Gabe*. She pasted a warm smile on her face. "That would be very nice."

They passed through the French doors and down the stairs to the garden. The cool air was refreshing after the stuffy heat of the ballroom. Lanterns hung from the trees along the path, swaying lightly in the warm evening breeze.

"I'm so glad you agreed to take a walk with me. You've been so busy dancing that I wasn't sure I'd get a chance to approach you, much less speak with you."

"It's actually very pleasant out here. Thank you for asking me."

"At the end of this path there's a pretty little arbor. Would you care to see it?"

Regina wasn't familiar with this garden, and already the number of people were thinning on this path. She hesitated. Did she want to be alone with him? *Remember your goal. You need to trap a mage into marriage.* Lord Pratchett wasn't the most powerful of mages, but his magic was strong enough. "I'd love to."

As they strolled through the garden, Regina's hand on his arm, Lord Pratchett babbled about her beauty. He prattled on about the wonder of her blue eyes—she started a bit at that, until she remembered her bespelled mask—her lips like ripe plums, and many other extravagant references. His gaze delved frequently to her bosom.

Regina wished she had dressed as a nun.

"Here we are." He stopped at the entrance to a secluded alcove. Trees and flowering shrubs hid the little nook. Stepping stones on the grass led to a wrought-iron bench. Lantern light drifted from the path, but the rear of the refuge lay in darkness. It was lovely, but a strange buzzing filled her head.

"Won't you have a seat?" Lord Pratchett placed his hand on her back and nudged her forward.

Regina didn't budge. Pressure built around her, as if the very air hung on the edge of violence. Her muscles tensed. "I think we should go back."

"I beg your pardon?"

"I'm not feeling well. I'd like to go back." Her blood thrummed in her ears, and the urge to flee grew stronger.

"You can sit and rest. There's a bench right there." His hand tightened on her waist. His gaze dropped to her breasts once more.

Lord Pratchett was on the list Regina and her aunt had compiled. He seemed more than willing to attempt a little seduction. That sensation of lurking danger increased. She looked up at Lord Pratchett, but despite his obvious interest in her, he wasn't the source. Her skin prickled. "I need to go back. Come with me."

"Won't you stay a little longer?" He loomed over her as he pulled her close. The excitement in his eyes scared her. She'd been so focused on that other threat that she hadn't realized the risk he posed.

"I'm sorry, but I must go." She twisted out of his grasp and fled back toward the manor.

"Milady, wait," he called, running his hand frustratedly through his hair.

She glanced back, half afraid he would chase her, but he didn't follow. He remained near the alcove.

The path was empty. She'd been more isolated than she'd realized out in the garden with Lord Pratchett. She raced down the tree-lined aisle until the path curved and people came into view as they strolled across the lawn. She slowed to a walk. Her heart hammered within her chest, but that strange pressure and unreasoning fear was gone. She'd been so close to obtaining her objective with Lord Pratchett, but that sense of danger had overwhelmed her.

What had triggered those reactions? She'd never felt them before, so they must be related to her newfound talent. Was her magic trying to warn her? What had triggered it? The cause had to be supernatural, because there'd been nothing—besides Lord Pratchett's little attempt at seduction—to threaten her. Unless her power perceived Lord Pratchett as a threat. Did her magic care that she had been *planning* to be seduced?

She climbed the flagstone steps leading up to the patio. Aunt Agatha might know, but Regina couldn't ask without divulging she had magic. Until she could prove to herself that her power was here to stay, she would keep her discovery to herself. After all, her aunt wouldn't believe she had magic without proof. So far, the only evidence Regina had was a vision—which Aunt Agatha would probably say was a figment of her imagination, like her dreams of being a witch and healer—and tonight's eerie sense of lurking danger. None of which, when it came down to it, was solid proof of anything other than wishful thinking.

No, she wouldn't tell anyone yet. Not until she could prove her magic was real.

———◆———

Grulik watched the witch wrench herself out of the arms of her young suitor and flee back to the ball. Frustration ate at him from his hiding place at the back of the alcove. Only a few more steps and she and Lord Pratchett would have been completely hidden from sight of the path. Grulik could have taken her soul and killed them both. The curse would have been broken, and he could have returned to his home world.

But instead she'd fled.

The young lord she'd left at the alcove cursed. Grulik sympathized. The young man had had plans. Different from his, of course, but just as thwarted.

At least the night didn't have to be a total waste. Grulik shifted into his natural form.

CHAPTER EIGHTEEN

———————

JULIAN LEANED AGAINST THE BALUS-TRADE overlooking the gardens, waiting for the return of Marie Antoinette. A young lord dressed as a highwayman had approached her after her dance, and she left the ballroom on his arm. He and Langley had followed them onto the flag-stone terrace, but not the gardens that stretched away from the manor. Langley chatted nearby with a young lady dressed as a shepherdess and her mother. Thankfully he hadn't suggested Julian join them.

Julian had always assumed when the war was over, he and Evelyn would settle on their estate to raise a family. He never imagined that he'd be alone, staring at the clear night sky, wondering how to find the demon that killed her. He should have let her stay at the camp like she'd asked. He would have been able to protect her then. Instead, he'd sent her to her death.

A breeze carried the scents of evergreens and flowers, wiping away the cloying scents of cologne and sweaty bodies, but not his guilt. Could he ever cleanse himself of the blood that was on his hands?

Langley strode up beside him, and Julian thrust the past aside. "She's coming."

The wide skirts of Marie Antoinette's costume were unmistakable as she rushed along the gravel path. She frequently glanced behind her, but nobody followed her. The other guests enjoying the warm evening paid no attention to her. Her companion was noticeably absent. What had happened out in the garden that she returned without him?

She climbed the flagstone steps to the terrace.

"Let's go." Langley crossed the patio and met her as she reached the final step. "My dear lady, I have someone here who begs to make your acquaintance."

Her eyes closed for the briefest moment, and she sighed. "And have I made your acquaintance, sir?" She examined Langley's red wig and false beard with the slightest twitch of her lips. "I don't believe I know a Pirate Red Beard."

At the sound of her voice, a little crease appeared between Langley's brows. Then his features smoothed, and he bowed deeply. "Red Beard the Pirate, also known as Lord Langley, at your service, milady."

"Ah yes, I seem to recall you now."

"I'd like to introduce you to my cousin, Lord Lindsay."

"We've met before, but never been properly introduced." Her chin lifted, and she gave Julian a sideways glance. "I must admit I'm surprised to see him here."

Julian had the impression that encounter hadn't gone well. He met her gaze and his breath caught in his throat. He had the unmistakable sense that he knew this woman. Knew her well.

"Forgive my mistake. I should have said, I'd like to introduce you to my *recently reformed* cousin." Langley emphasized the words he'd left out in his last introduction.

"I see." She measured Julian with an icy stare. For some reason he expected her eyes to be green, but instead the eyes behind the mask were a deep sapphire blue. Was it simply because her height and form reminded him of Evelyn?

Julian bowed deeply, just as Langley had earlier. After all, they needed her help. "If I have given offense, milady, I beg your pardon and hope we can start anew. As my cousin says, I am a changed man."

"Let's hope so." Her mask sparkled for a moment in the light, and her features shimmered. Was her mask hexed?

What he was about to do was considered the worst breach of etiquette, but he released his magic and stretched it towards her. The mask vibrated. He pulled his senses back, now seeing the distortion the mask cast over her face and throat. A disguise to mask her real features, in order to better resemble the person she masqueraded as? Or something more sinister?

Could she be the demon? He discarded the thought right away. The demon was a shapeshifter. It wouldn't need an enchanted mask to hide its features. Still, it seemed odd. Julian didn't recall seeing any other hexed costumes, but then again, he'd been looking for a redheaded man, not trying to see what magical enhancements guests might have made to their outfits.

A mage in a Harlequin costume spotted Marie Antoinette and changed course, a huge grin on his face. If this kept up, Julian would never have a chance to ask her his questions. He placed himself so he blocked the young buck's path. "May I have the pleasure of your company for the next dance?"

She glanced behind Julian at the lord heading towards them and rapidly moved forward to take Julian's arm. "I would be much obliged, my lord."

The sound of violins tuning signaled the next set would begin soon. He led her inside. When they reached the dance floor, the first notes of a waltz filled the air. "I forgot to ask—do you have permission to waltz?"

"Would I still be on the floor with you if I didn't? This is a masquerade. Everyone has permission to waltz this night."

"Of course." Julian pulled Marie Antoinette into his arms. He did his best to ignore the way his hand fit snugly into the curve of her waist, the way her fingers curled around his hand. Memories of dancing with Evelyn in the great hall on their wedding day bombarded him. She had fit into his arms just like this. But thankfully Marie Antoinette smelled like roses, not lilacs.

She released a breath and relaxed as the bars of the dance began. He thrust his grief away as best he could, using the scent of roses to help him focus on the present. This young lady was a Marleigh, one of the remaining lines of demon hunters. He needed her help.

◆

Regina looked up at the sinfully handsome Lord Lindsay. She couldn't fathom her reaction to him. His cousin, Lord Langley, was almost as good looking and was one of the few mageborn who had always been courteous to her. But it was Lindsay—with his dark blue eyes and intense gaze—who drew her.

Had the earl truly changed? So far, he had been unfailingly polite. Exaggeratedly so, such as when he'd bowed and begged her forgiveness, claiming to be reformed. But then again, he probably thought she was Felicity Marleigh, who was full mageborn. Perhaps he'd always treated magebloods this courteously.

She couldn't hide the smile that rose to her lips as he spun her into a curve of the waltz. The earl was the worst of cads as she well knew, yet he danced divinely, guiding her expertly through the crowd. His physical form had changed since her encounter with him last year. His body was harder, his skin darkened by the sun. She'd heard he'd done nothing but drink and frequent the worst establishments London had to offer, yet powerful muscles rippled beneath her hand. She fought the urge to stroke those rugged shoulders and corded arms.

Regina stared at his bronze skin rising above the

folds of a perfectly-tied cravat and swallowed the urge to touch her tongue to the strong column of his throat. What was wrong with her tonight? The earl was the worst of beasts. A member of the Mageborn Purity League. A blackguard of the worst order.

Or was he? Unlike last year, he didn't reek of alcohol. Instead he smelled of the outdoors, scents that reminded her of her family's country estate in Yorkshire and filled her with a longing for home. She decided to test him. "My lord?"

"Yes?" His voice was so deep, she imagined she could feel the vibration beneath her fingers. His dark blue eyes focused on her, instead of scanning the crowd around them. Her breath caught at the connection that surged between them when she met his gaze.

She knew next to nothing about him, but had the strange sense she had known him all her life. What did he see when he looked at her? Did he feel the same way? She couldn't ask. He'd think her a lunatic. "Your cousin said you are reformed. Does that mean you are no longer a member of the Mageborn Purity League?"

"Absolutely not. I refuse to be part of that organization." His voice was hard.

"But weren't you a member?"

"Not anymore."

So far, so good. He'd quit the league, which was definitely a step in the right direction. She stared at his firm lips and wondered how they'd feel upon her own. If he'd been kind to her that night a year ago, would she have been able to resist him? Maybe Aunt Agatha was right, and the earl would be a good choice for her.

"I'm glad you accepted my invitation to dance. I wanted to speak with you earlier, but a highwayman beat me to it." Unlike all the other men she'd danced with tonight, whose voices were so warm that she'd often found herself blushing at their compliments, Lindsay's tone was crisp and businesslike. She'd completely misread his look of determination. He had no interest in courting her.

She writhed inside with embarrassment. He had only approached her because he thought she was Felicity Marleigh. More than ever, she regretted participating in this deception. "What did you want to discuss?"

"I understand your father was a demon hunter."

"Yes, he was." At least she could answer that honestly. Regina's father had been a demon hunter as well.

"Do you—"

Screams from the garden rent the air of the ballroom. Lindsay abruptly stopped dancing. Regina stumbled against him, but he didn't seem to notice. Instead, he stared across the bewildered crowd, then ran for the French doors leading to the terrace. Her hand was still in his, and he pulled her along. She was glad she had worn her normal slippers instead of the French heels of her costume or she wouldn't have been able to keep up.

Lindsay threaded his way through the crowd down to the gravel path she had strolled earlier that evening. They followed the cries deep into the garden. A group of costumed partygoers stood outside the alcove that Lord Pratchett had shown her. Regina's stomach twisted in fear.

A man dressed as a highwayman lay prostrate on the grass in front of a wrought-iron bench.

She gasped. "It's Lord Pratchett. I was just with him." Lindsay glanced at her and released his grip. She surreptitiously massaged her hand. He entered the alcove.

"What happened?" the earl asked. The people surrounding Lord Pratchett's body responded to the calm note of authority in his voice and straightened up. He looked at the young lady who had been screaming when they arrived. A dowager had her arms around the distraught girl, who hiccuped and sobbed into the older woman's fulsome bosom.

"Lady Iris here said she was coming back from a walk in the gardens with Lord Humphrey," the dowager gestured with her chin towards a skinny young man who stood hovering nervously near them both, "when they stumbled upon Lord Pratchett in this alcove."

Lady Iris looked up long enough to nod, then she caught a glimpse of the body and wailed again.

"There, there, my dear," the older lady soothed.

"Is he alive?" Lindsay asked.

The young man, Lord Humphrey, blushed with embarrassment. "We didn't check, sir."

The earl approached and knelt beside the body. He placed gentle fingers on the man's neck then lowered himself to place an ear next to the man's mouth. He sat back on his heels. "He's dead."

Regina wondered how Lord Lindsay could possibly have the experience to know this for certain, when a chill swept over her. She had a whiff of something *other*—the same sense of wrongness she'd touched that day she and Gabe had tried to use their magic. She looked back towards the darkened garden, with its pathways faintly lit by lanterns swaying in the trees. Was something out there?

"Could someone have attacked Lord Pratchett?" Lord Humphrey asked.

"I don't see any injuries or indications of a fight, but he seems too young to have died of natural causes," Lindsay said.

Regina remembered that sense of unease that had caused her to flee earlier. She too had her doubts.

"Are you sure he's dead?" She moved forward to kneel beside Lord Lindsay, strangely feeling as if she had done this many times before. She touched Lord Pratchett's arm, and froze at the sense of evil that swept over her.

When Regina's father had died, she had been clasping his hand between hers. One moment his soul had been there. The next his soul had hovered above her before disappearing. She'd still been gripping her father's hand, could feel the echoes of his memories and life. But there was nothing left of Lord Pratchett. She had no sense of him at all. His body was an empty shell. She couldn't help the words that issued from her mouth. "His death isn't natural. His soul is gone."

The dowager made a patronizing tsking sound. "My dear, *of course* his soul is gone. That's what occurs when a person dies."

Old biddy. That wasn't what Regina had meant. His soul had been *taken.* She swallowed the retort that jumped to her lips. No one here would take her word over that of a dowager.

There was a commotion outside the alcove, and a short barrel-chested man in the dress of King Henry VIII pushed his way inside. "What's going on?" He ignored Regina and Lord Lindsay, looking instead at Lord Humphrey, who nervously shifted his weight from foot to foot.

"We found Lord Pratchett lying dead here on the grass, my lord," the youth answered.

"You're sure he's dead?"

"Yes," Lord Lindsay said.

King Henry snapped his fingers and four servants squeezed past him. Regina and Lord Lindsay moved out of the way. "Have the body removed to Lord Pratchett's home."

"This young lady says the soul is gone," Lindsay said.

The servants holding the body paused to look at King Henry's reaction. The man turned beady black eyes on her. "Are you a demon hunter?"

"No, I'm not." Since she was a woman, they both knew she wasn't, but that didn't mean she was wrong.

King Henry shook his head in exasperation.

"Then how can you possibly know that? Proceed."

The servants exited the alcove with the body. The remaining crowd milled around uncertainly. The young woman who'd originally stumbled across the body had stopped sobbing, instead staring wide-eyed at King Henry.

"What are you all waiting for?" he snapped. "Go rejoin the ball. I hear the music starting back up."

The little group dispersed. Regina stepped onto the path, followed by Lord Lindsay.

"You, young lady, hold on a minute," King Henry snapped.

Regina stopped. What did he want with her?

King Henry approached her and his face twisted in anger. "We don't need a troublemaker fear-mongering among the guests. I don't know what advantage you think to gain by attributing Lord Pratchett's death to unnatural causes, but I do not want to hear that rumor bandied about again. If so, I will see you banned for the season. Do I make myself clear?"

"Yes, my lord."

King Henry brushed past her.

She glared at the brutish little man. "It's times like these that I wish I weren't mageborn at all."

"Ignore him. He's just a small man seeking to make himself important."

"Didn't you recognize him? Lord Ponseby is the Chancellor of the Mage High Council." She hastened down the now familiar path. Why had she ever considered gardens to be romantic? "I'm not surprised he dressed as King Henry VIII. Aside from his vanity of dressing as the most infamous mageborn king, he's already on his third wife. Through *natural* circumstances, I'm sure."

"How could you tell Lord Pratchett's soul was gone?"

"You believed me?" She turned to face him. In the lantern light beneath the trees, his eyes seemed to glitter behind his mask. He stared at her as if nobody else mattered, and she found she wanted to share her secret.

"Yes. How did you know?"

"My father passed away some years ago." Her throat thickened at the memory of him lying in his bed, suffering from the demon blood that poisoned his body. She struggled to keep her voice steady. "I was holding his hand when it happened. One moment he was alive, the next he was gone. But I could feel the imprint of who he had been. There was still a trace of his memories, even though he was no longer here."

"And Lord Pratchett was different?"

"Yes. When I touched him, I couldn't find any hint of his memories or who he'd been. His body was completely empty, as if he'd never existed." She couldn't imagine anything more horrible, and it had happened to a man who'd been with her right before his death. Was that the danger she had sensed? Would she be soulless now too if her magic hadn't warned her?

"What's wrong?"

"Nothing." She wished she had told Lord Pratchett of her fears and made him leave with her. But her magic was still a mystery to her. She hadn't understood what it tried to tell her.

"You strolled the gardens with Lord Pratchett earlier."

"Yes."

"Did you go near the spot he was found?"

She wasn't sure where these questions were leading. "Yes. He actually led me there and wanted me to go in. But I felt uneasy and left."

"Did you see anyone else?"

"No. That was one of the reasons I returned. We were too isolated." She'd ruined any chance of getting herself compromised, but maybe that had saved her from Lord Pratchett's fate.

He studied her for a moment, then continued leading her down the path back to the ballroom. "You have a remarkable gift. In fact, that leads me to why I wanted to speak with you tonight."

Finally, she would learn what he wanted. They'd reached the edge of the manicured lawns, and she paused.

"I've been told the Marleigh line has had many demon hunters. I was hoping you could assist me."

She lifted her chin and held her head high like her mother taught her. Her impersonation had been too successful. She'd only had a chance of trapping a mage tonight because everyone had thought she was Felicity. Now, when she'd found a mage she was interested in, he only spoke to her because he thought she was a Marleigh.

The time had come to end this charade. Like Felicity, Regina came from a line of demon hunters. However, she couldn't help him, and Gabe was untrained and too young. "I'm sorry, but I can't be of assistance."

She didn't wait for the earl's response. Instead, even though it was cowardly, Regina fled.

CHAPTER NINETEEN

GRULIK STARED AT THE ELEGANT row of houses in Grosvenor Square. He'd followed the witch home after the Sherrington masquerade, then hidden in the mews until the house quieted and all the lights turned out. From here he could feel the tug of her soul, that connection that kept him trapped in this bloody human world.

He slunk over the refuse and manure that littered the alley, then slid through the deep shadows until he reached the back gate. He grabbed the latch.

The iron turned bright blue. Flames licked his hand and he jerked back.

What was going on? He touched the top of the gate. Once again the metal turned as blue as the flames that had danced along Harbrook's blade. His palm burned as if a hot poker had stabbed it. His breath hissed through his teeth. The blue fire engulfed his hand and traveled up his arm. He released the gate. The flames died to random sparks, but the burns refused to heal.

There had to be a way inside. Glancing both ways down the dark alley and seeing no movement other than scurrying rats, he shifted into his demon form. The rats fled down the alley, and he bared his teeth. *Run away, little rodents. You're not my prey tonight.*

He leapt toward the top of the brick wall. The air glowed blue. He bounced off an invisible shield and fell to the ground. His thick hide smoked where it had made contact with the barrier.

Pain seared his hide, but he shifted back into human form. He walked up the pavement in front of the house and reached out a hand. Once again blue flames engulfed him, burning his skin.

He circled the townhouse, then the house next door, and the one after. Iridescent blue fire flared at every attempt to gain entrance. The entire block had been warded against demons.

He looked up at the witch's window and snarled. She was sleeping now. Defenseless. But he couldn't get to her.

He needed a new plan. If he couldn't attack her at her home, he'd have to find a way to get her in public. His flesh smoked, and the pain couldn't be ignored any longer. He needed to heal.

Time to hunt.

CHAPTER TWENTY

JULIAN PACED HIS STUDY WHILE he waited for Lord Langley to arrive at the Lindsay town-house. He and Langley had discreetly questioned the guests at the Sherrington masquerade after Lord Pratchett's body had been found. It had been easy enough to do—the mysterious death was on everyone's lips. The last person seen with the young highwayman was Marie Antoinette, when the two of them had gone for a stroll in the garden. No one had seen Lord Higginbotham.

Julian and Langley had searched the entire garden—for clues or any more bodies—but come up empty. Afterward they spent the night scouring London for Lord Higginbotham. The man never returned to his residence, and no one had seen him at his usual haunts. The demon had changed forms again.

They needed help.

As soon as Langley arrived, they would visit the Marleighs. Lady Felicity had refused her assistance last night, but Julian hoped to convince her other-wise. If he were lucky, the Marleighs would have a male relative who could help them find the fiend. He would not endanger another woman's life.

A carriage rolled up, and the butler announced Langley's arrival. Today Langley was dressed as the perfect gentleman—fawn-colored breeches, black jacket, blue waistcoat, and a cravat. There was no hint that he knew the seedier sections of London as well as the better ones, as Julian had learned last night. "I think the pirate costume suited you better."

Langley grinned. "The wig and beard itched too much."

After their long night traipsing London, he and Langley had reached a truce of sorts. Langley still doubted Julian had traveled from the past, but as long as Langley helped him find the demon, Julian didn't care. "Shall we go?"

"We'd better. If we don't leave now there will be such a crush at the Marleighs we won't have any chance of getting close enough to speak with them."

"I noticed last night that Lady Felicity is very popular."

"That's an understatement. Believe it or not, she usually has many more admirers."

Julian climbed in opposite Langley, and the footman closed the door. The carriage, pulled by four horses, jolted forward. Although the overstuffed seat cushions made traveling over the rough cobblestones of London streets comfortable, Julian would have preferred riding horseback.

Could Felicity Marleigh be the demon's new

disguise? It didn't seem likely, especially given the fact she'd mentioned Pratchett was missing his soul. His nemesis was too smart to give himself away so easily. But the monster had fooled him once and cost Julian everyone who mattered most. He had to consider the possibility. "What can you tell me about the Marleighs?"

Langley looked up from staring at his fingernails. "What do you mean?"

"Does Lady Felicity have any relatives who are demon hunters?"

"None that I'm aware of. Her father was the last one. He died about two years ago."

"Then there's no one here in London who can help us?"

"There's only one I can think of—the Marquis of Harbrook."

Julian started at the name *Harbrook*. He remembered the last time he saw his best friend—the dawn light breaking over the field, Harbrook's solemn expression as he shook hands with Julian and promised to find the person who had summoned Evelyn's killer. Julian's chest tightened, as if a blacksmith had fastened iron bands around him.

"However, the marquis died in a battle with a demon some years ago. His heir is a half-blood. It's quite the pity. I've heard the boy has some ability."

Demon hunters only appeared in certain mage-born bloodlines. Harbrook's was one of them. "Is there a chance he could hunt demons?"

Langley shook his head. "Assuming he's old enough, he'll never receive the training he needs to do so. No mageborn who values his position in society would teach him to use magic."

"Why not? I thought humans and mageborn had equal rights?"

"They do, but he's a half-blood." Langley looked at him quizzically. "There's still a social hierarchy, even if there isn't a legal one."

"But if he could be a demon hunter, wouldn't that justify training him?" Could this society be so blinded by their prejudices?

Langley laughed for a long time. "Nobody thinks demons are a threat anymore. It's against the law to summon demons. So naturally nobody will do it."

"You really believe that?"

"Of course not. Demons appear periodically, but the Mage High Council keeps this quiet. I haven't heard of any for a few years though. Not since Lord Marleigh's death."

"I thought the Mageborn War would change things." Julian looked out the window at the hawkers and wagons teeming the streets. He yearned for the simpler luxuries of his previous life—the camaraderie of the camp, a tent shared with his wife, the glorious blue sky above the moor on crisp fall mornings. There'd been hardships—it'd been war, with everything that entailed—but he'd always known he fought for a just cause. It was disheartening that winning the war had made so little difference.

"It did. It gave half-bloods and humans the right to inherit property and titles. But there's prejudice on both sides. Humans don't feel comfortable intermingling with the mageborn either."

The carriage slowed to a stop before a massive Georgian home on the outskirts of London.

"Don't forget who you're playing. The Earl of Lindsay was a brute who despised humans. If the conversation should turn to humans or half-bloods, remember to emphasize you've had a change of heart and no longer hold to those views."

The Marleigh drawing room was a model of elegance and comfort. A thick green and gold carpet warmed the room, and chairs and sofas with thick cushions were cozily arranged in front of a massive marble hearth. Lady Marleigh and her daughter sat together on a green damask settee with a tea service already prepared on the table before them. A pleasantly smoky aroma drifted from the pot.

Lady Marleigh was one of the women Julian had seen leaving with Marie Antoinette the night before. Both she and her daughter had red hair, although Lady Felicity's was a deeper, more vibrant shade. Lady Felicity, while as tall as he remembered, did not match his memory of Marie Antoinette. Her eyes were still the deepest blue he'd ever seen, but her chin was more pointed than rounded. Her figure wasn't as curvy as he remembered either. She looked leaner and stronger, her shoulders straighter. The differences seemed to go beyond costuming.

Last night she had reminded Julian so strongly of Evelyn that he had partially dreaded coming here. Today that mysterious connection he'd felt was missing. He had the strange sensation that he'd never met this woman.

"Lady Marleigh, Lady Felicity." Langley paid his respects to the women.

As Langley's dark head bowed before her, a look of unutterable sadness filled Lady Felicity's eyes. She banished it with a brilliant smile before Langley straightened, and Julian wondered if he had truly seen that fleeting expression.

"Lord Langley." Lady Marleigh greeted him warmly. Then she looked at Julian and her expression hardened. "My dear Lord Langley, who have you brought with you?"

"This, my lady, is my recently reformed cousin, Lord Lindsay. Lady Felicity, I believe you had the pleasure of meeting my cousin last night."

"Ladies." Julian bowed.

Lady Felicity glanced at her mother. Lady Marleigh answered Langley's question. "I believe there's been a mistake. My daughter did not feel well last night, so she did not attend Lady Sherrington's ball."

"But I thought Lady Felicity was attending the ball as Marie Antoinette. Was I mistaken?" Langley asked.

"I had planned on going as that famous member of the French court," Lady Felicity said, "but since I could no longer attend, I let the niece of my mother's bosom friend borrow my costume. We're nearly of the same height, and I so hated to see my lovely costume wasted." Her vowels were rounded, cultured and elegant. Melodious. But there was no doubt. Her voice was not the same as that of Marie Antoinette.

If she hadn't attended the ball, then who had Julian danced with that had the ability to sense souls? Had his partner been the demon after all? Had the creature been toying with him?

"We had hoped to ask you about last night's events," Langley said, "but since you weren't there, we'll have to ask you some other questions instead."

"Such as?" Felicity lifted the lid off the teapot and glanced inside. "The tea is ready now."

"Is there anyone in your family who hunts demons?" Langley asked.

Her hand froze mid-air, then she carefully replaced the lid. "No. Why do you ask?" She poured a cup of tea and handed it to her mother.

"Did you know Lord Pratchett was found dead in the garden at the Sherrington masquerade?" he continued.

"Yes, I did."

"Lord Pratchett's soul was taken," Julian interjected. "That means a demon was there last night."

Lady Marleigh gasped and looked at Felicity. "I hadn't heard that."

Felicity's gaze turned intense. "How do you know the soul was taken? Only a demon hunter can tell."

"The woman wearing your costume told me," Julian said.

"Lady Regina?" she exclaimed. "Mother, is that possible?"

"I don't know." Lady Marleigh shook her head. "I thought she didn't have magic."

Langley gazed at the two of them. "You mean

Lady Regina Westcott? The daughter of the Marquis of Harbrook?"

"Can you tell us where she lives?" Julian asked. "I'd like to speak with her."

"I'm surprised you would have any interest in Lady Regina," Lady Marleigh said. "After all, her mother was a human."

There it was. His cue. Julian bit back his disdain for his namesake. How a man descended from a half-blood wizard could spit on his heritage was incomprehensible to him. "As Lord Langley said, I am a changed man. I bear no ill will towards humans or half-bloods."

"So you no longer associate with your Mage-born Purity friends?" Lady Marleigh's voice was frigid.

"No, madam, I do not. In fact, I can't remember the last time I associated with any of them." All of which was true. Julian had no idea who the earl's friends were. He'd never met them.

"I see. We have chairs, you two may be seated. Felicity, please pour the gentlemen a cup of tea." Lady Marleigh settled back against the settee.

Julian had passed his test. "What do you mean Lady Regina does not have magic?"

"She's a half-blood. Her brother has magic, but it is well known that she does not." Felicity frowned. "Their father was a demon hunter, but without magic, it doesn't make sense that she could sense souls. That's part of the gift. You're sure she said the soul was taken?"

"Yes." If what Lady Felicity said was true, it looked

more and more like Lady Regina was the demon's latest victim. "We are trying to find the demon. I was wondering if you know of any demon hunters, or perhaps have a relative who could assist us?"

"Or maybe you could help us," Langley said.

"I'm sorry, but I don't know of any demon hunters since my father passed away. Nor can I help you. I did not receive any of my family's demon-hunting talents."

Julian stood up. "At least you told us who wore your costume at the Sherrington ball. We'll speak to Lady Regina, in case she has more information. Ready, cousin?"

"I see we're done for today." Langley rose. "A pleasure, as always, ladies. Thank you for your hospitality."

Lady Marleigh nodded at the footman, who opened the drawing room door. "Langley, you never visit as often as you should. Please come again soon." She glanced at Julian. "I hope you are mistaken about Lord Pratchett's death. A demon in London would be disastrous."

"I agree." Julian itched to leave this house. If Lady Regina was the demon, they needed to find her as soon as possible.

"That wasn't good *ton*, cousin," drawled Langley from behind Julian as they descended the town-house steps.

Julian ignored his "cousin" and stepped onto the pavement as they waited for the coach to be brought around. "We need to speak to Lady Regina. We don't have time to waste drinking tea in Lady Marleigh's drawing room."

"Are you sure you're not the marquis's son?"

"Who is Lady Marleigh's bosom friend?"

"Lady Carlisle. She's the sister of the old Marquis of Harbrook. She and Lady Marleigh attended Miss Emmett's School for Ladies together."

"If the niece is a half-blood, why is she attending mageborn balls?"

Langley slapped his hat against his leg. He squinted at Julian in the mid-afternoon sun. "She's looking for a husband. I believe this is her third or fourth season. With her looks and dowry, she'd be considered a diamond of the first water in other circumstances."

"What do you mean?"

"No mageborn worthy of the title would marry her."

In this era half-bloods seemed to be despised almost as much as in Julian's time. "Then why does she come to mageborn balls? Couldn't she find a human to marry?"

"The Marquis of Harbrook was an extremely powerful mage. No human would want to marry into such an intimidating mageborn family." Langley considered him. "Sometimes you act as if you really were from the past."

"Is it true Lady Regina does not have magic?"

"That's what I've always heard. Even her aunt, Lady Carlisle, has said so on occasion."

"Lady Regina was the last person seen with Lord Pratchett." Langley was an intelligent man. Julian didn't have to spell out what he was thinking. "Do you know where Lady Regina lives?"

"Yes."

"Good. I think that should be our next stop." Julian had to determine if she was the demon in disguise.

CHAPTER TWENTY-ONE

REGINA SAT IN HER FAVORITE chair by the fireplace, her feet curled beneath her. An elaborate tea had been laid in the morning room, because her brother had a bottomless pit for a stomach. The sun streamed pleasantly through the curtains, but Regina's mood was dark. A demon was loose in London. What should she do? What *could* she do?

"Tell me about the ball last night." Gabe happily munched on a crumpet. He reclined on the settee, long legs slung over the armrest, with a plate of sweets and savories balanced on his stomach. "Did anyone guess you weren't Lady Felicity?"

"Surprisingly, no. I think I received more requests for dances last night than I had in my previous seasons combined." The masquerade had been the closest she'd ever been to being the belle of the ball, and yet she hadn't enjoyed it. People who had never once acknowledged her presence had fawned over her. The entire evening left a sour taste in her mouth.

Hold your head high, child. Your blood is nothing to

be ashamed of.

How many times had her mother told her that?

Too many. But her mind had never quite grasped the lesson. It was easy enough to be proud, when you had powerful magic, like Gabriel. But Regina had exhibited no magical gifts until now, and she had told no one about her discovery. The mageborn only permitted her presence at London events because of her father's powerful lineage.

Her mother's side of the family had welcomed and loved her. However, that same powerful legacy that granted her access to mageborn society barred her from the human community. Despite her lack of magic, humans—even her beloved relatives— had always eyed her warily, as though one day she'd spout spells and turn them all into toads. Had she not seen her parents' love for herself, she would have thought it impossible for a mageborn-human marriage to succeed.

Her mother had been beautiful, strong, coura- geous. Human. No matter how poorly mageborn society treated her, she never bowed down. She raised her chin higher and insisted that whether the mageborn aristocracy acknowledged it or not, she was their equal. Human and *sans* magic. *She* was their equal.

Her father had been smitten by their mother's confidence and beauty. She had intrigued him, and their match had been for love. Her mother had weathered even more disdain from the mageborn after she became Lady Harbrook, but she'd always laughed. They were bitter, she said, because she—a human—had managed to do something none of the mageborn ladies could—capture the love of Lord Harbrook.

Regina had wanted to emulate their mother in all respects. But she had failed miserably in one aspect—she could not ignore the barbs the mageborn threw at her. Each had lodged under her skin, tearing at her, making her feel less than she was. Although she wanted to be accepted by them, she wasn't sure she wanted to *be* like them. Why would she want to be like the people she despised, who were so superficial as to judge everyone by their bloodlines? Her own brother, who bode well to be one of the most powerful mages of his generation, was ignored by his own kin, all because of his human heritage.

Gabriel was too young to be exposed to mageborn society, but he needed to know about last night.

"Not a single person noticed you weren't Lady Felicity?" A look of disgust crossed Gabe's face, as if he couldn't believe the stupidity of London gentlemen.

She shook her head. "I didn't talk much. I held my tongue and let them prattle on about the wonders of my costume, my perfect form on the dance floor, and their delight in being in my company."

"You're bamming me! Gentlemen don't speak like that!"

Regina delicately shrugged her shoulders. "I must admit I was quite disillusioned."

Gabe scowled, and she laughed.

"Well, it wasn't quite as bad as that, but I'm not exaggerating by much." She plucked a lemon cake from her plate and held it in the air, as if for a toast. "My respect for Lady Felicity—already high—has increased ten-fold since last night. I have no idea how she maintains her composure in the face of such admiration." She popped the treat into her mouth. Gabe wasn't the only one who liked lemon cakes.

"What happened next?"

This was the crux of it. Even though he was younger than her, Gabriel took his responsibilities as the man of the house seriously. Should she tell him about the demon or not? He wanted to be a demon hunter. That was his heritage. But would he be foolish enough to try to hunt the demon without any training in magic or weaponry? She'd have to tread carefully.

"I toured the gardens with Lord Pratchett." Gabe didn't need to know about her plot to trap a mage into marriage. "We were at the far end of the garden when I suddenly felt uneasy. I returned to the ballroom, but Lord Pratchett stayed behind. He was alone when I left him."

"I bet he was mad you left him there." He ate another crumpet.

She laughed. "Probably. Yes." She took a deep breath, and despite the warmth of the room, she suddenly felt cold. "It wasn't long after that Lord Pratchett was found lying in the garden alcove. He was dead, Gabe."

"Dead! At the ball? Was he old or something?"

"No. He was a young man. There weren't any signs of injury or a fight."

"Are you sure he was dead?"

"I checked, and so did another lord." Her brother looked so young and innocent. She had to warn him. He needed to be on guard. "There's something else you should know. His soul was missing."

"How did you know it was missing?"

"I could tell when I touched him." Demon hunter gifts needed more than blood lineage. They also required magic. Would Gabe realize that? She frowned as the implications hit her—she'd also sensed their father's soul when he passed away. If she'd always had power, why couldn't she use it until recently?

"You touched the body?" He perked up and pushed himself up until he was sitting upright on the sofa.

"I did. His body felt empty. There wasn't any hint of who he'd been at all."

"What do you think happened to him?"

"It must have been a demon. They're the only creatures I know of that can take souls."

"A demon in London? It can't be!"

"When I was walking in the gardens with Lord Pratchett, I had this odd feeling of danger. What if I was sensing the demon?"

"If Father were still alive, he would be able to answer our questions. Why did he have to die?" He slammed his fist on the armrest. "We are twice cursed he didn't have time to train me!"

They were twice cursed, but not for the reason Gabe thought. After their mother died, their father's will to live had died too. He could have survived the demon's blood poisoning if he had sought a healer right away. But he hadn't. Instead he had abandoned them.

"We know some things. We have to remember as much as we can. Demons eat souls. Once taken, the soul is trapped for eternity."

"Unless the demon is killed."

"That's right."

Gabe went still. When he raised his head, he looked pale but determined. "Gina, if it's a demon, I have to find it and kill it."

"Gabe, no! You can't. You aren't even trained in magic or fighting. How could you possibly defeat one? You saw what it did to Father!"

"I'll learn."

"How? Father was the last hunter, and he's gone."

They fell silent. Regina recognized that flicker of light in Gabe's eyes. He was scared, but he yearned to follow in their father's footsteps. Demon hunting was in his blood.

Hers too, a voice whispered. Hadn't she sensed the demon's presence?

Lord Lindsay had wanted to talk with Felicity about demon hunting. Maybe he'd be willing to talk with Regina, assuming he could get past her human heritage. There was a demon on the prowl in London. She had to take action, before Gabe did something foolish.

CHAPTER TWENTY-TWO

JULIAN SAT ON A PLUSH velvet chair at the back of Countess Allensworth's musicale. From this vantage point he could see all of the guests as they arrived. A string quartet tuned their instruments at the front of the room.

He was tired of running all over London without any tangible results in their hunt for the demon. He and Langley had been rebuffed at Lady Regina's townhouse. They'd been told she was not at home. Julian couldn't help but be reminded of their attempts to locate Lord Higginbotham. He, too, was never at home. The butler said if they wanted to see her, they had to attend the countess's event. So here they were. Waiting.

The real Julian's unsavory reputation served him well, as few people—other than a couple of determined matchmaking mothers—dared approach him, despite his supposedly reformed character. Langley stood at the adjacent wall, chatting with some young lords. Langley also watched the entrance, as they waited for the arrival of Lady Regina and her aunt.

The musicians finished tuning their instruments and ran through some warm up exercises. The guests migrated towards the chairs arranged in rows down the center of the ballroom. Langley settled next to Julian.

"I believe the acoustics are better towards the front." Julian gestured at the many vacant seats still available, as matrons and their daughters continued to chat around the edges of the room.

"But no matrons nor their unmarried daughters will join us here," Langley said with satisfaction.

For the moment, he and his cousin were in perfect accord. After losing Evelyn, the last thing Julian wanted was to be involved with another woman. He'd prefer not to be here at all, except he needed to find out—was Lady Regina the demon? The line of new arrivals shortened, but he didn't see anyone tall enough to be Marie Antoinette. "The performance is about to start. I don't see her."

"There's plenty of time. People often arrive late." Langley leaned comfortably back in his seat.

The servant announced Lady Carlisle and Lady Regina. Finally. Julian turned to see what Marie Antoinette looked like without the mask.

A diminutive woman with an enormous ostrich feather in her cap entered, followed by a woman who made his heart stutter. A tall honey-blonde glided into the ballroom, with graceful movements that triggered his memory. Marie Antoinette. That pull he'd felt at the masquerade was back, but stronger. She adjusted the green shawl covering her shoulders and leaned down to listen to something her aunt said. She laughed, and then she pivoted in his direction.

A smile Julian could have drawn in his sleep curved across her face. A smile that he had longed to see again, with an ache that tinged his every thought. A smile that even now squeezed his chest and stung his eyes.

He couldn't breathe. Couldn't move. Could it be…?

Evelyn.

The crowded ballroom faded into the background. All he could see were those familiar beloved features, the gentle curve of her cheekbones, the determined chin. He wanted to rush forward, hold her tight in his arms, and kiss her with all the longing in his soul. His heart began to race, the urge to go to her overwhelming, but his mind resisted. He remained frozen to his seat.

At his shoulder, Langley whispered in Julian's ear. "That's Lady Regina, the Marquis of Harbrook's daughter."

No, Julian wanted to argue, that was Evelyn. The wife he had loved and lost, the woman whose bloody body he had cradled in his arms on the wintry moorland, the woman who had left a hole so deep in his chest he swore he'd never let another fill that space.

"Lady Regina?" Julian asked. "Are you…are you sure?" It wasn't possible. How could a woman centuries from the future look exactly like his dead wife? Unless…unless she was the demon.

"Of course I'm sure." Langley's voice was grim.

"There's our quarry."

Unlike Marie from the night before, Lady Regina's eyes were not a deep indigo blue, but an unusual shade of green that reminded Julian of cool forest glens. Her lips were a deep luscious pink, and her jaw was square and determined, not delicately rounded as the mask's spell had conveyed. Honey blond hair fell in golden ringlets around her face, the rest gathered back into a loose knot. "Has Lady Regina always—" he cursed himself for the stupidity of the words he would utter next—"looked like this?"

"A tall, blond, green-eyed beauty?"

No, Evelyn. Instead, Julian nodded. He drank in the sight he'd never expected to see again. He could pretend, just for a moment, that his wife was back and alive.

"Yes."

Julian jerked to his feet. "Introduce me."

Langley looked up at him from his chair. "The earl despises humans and half-bloods. People are going to talk if you approach her."

"I'm reformed, remember? I need to question her about last night. Introduce me." *I need to get closer. I need to see. I need to know.*

"As you wish." Langley rose and weaved through the crowd towards the ladies.

Lady Regina's green eyes widened when she saw him approaching. Her skin flushed, and her steps faltered. *She's not Evelyn,* Julian reminded himself. *She's Lady Regina, or the demon in disguise.* Plus, her curves were much more pronounced.

A memory niggled at him. Evelyn's figure had once been as generous, before she left the comfort of her father's home to join him on the battlefront. He shoved the memory to the back of his mind before grief and guilt overwhelmed him.

He needed to discover if Lady Regina was the demon in disguise. But how? Kikson had been the demon, and Julian had never once suspected the head of his personal guard.

"Ladies, may I present to you my cousin, Lord Lindsay?" Langley bowed to the women. "My lord, Lady Carlisle and her niece, Lady Regina, daughter of the Marquis of Harbrook."

"It's a pleasure to make your acquaintances." Julian raised Lady Regina's hand slowly to his lips. He could feel the heat of her skin through the thin calfskin glove she wore. It was a shame demons were warm-blooded. There was no way to tell a human from a shapeshifted demon unless you stabbed the creature's heart. Then it bled purple.

He bowed over her aunt's hand. "Lady Carlisle," he murmured.

Lady Carlisle's eyebrows rose in a high arch. A mischievous glint sparkled in her eyes as she looked at her discombobulated niece's expression. "Lord Lindsay, would you care to join us?"

Lady Regina glanced at the few remaining seats in the center of the ballroom. "I'm afraid that isn't possible, Auntie. Lady Quimby has kept seats for us as she promised, and only two remain." Her voice was low and husky, with the rich warmth of honey. Her voice had a different timbre from the night before. Julian hadn't realized her voice had been masked as well. A lump closed his throat. By His Blood, even her voice reminded him of Evelyn.

"I'm sure Lady Quimby won't mind if we add a couple of chairs to the row," Langley said, as he waved over a footman.

"Excellent," Lady Carlisle said. "It's all settled then. Come along, dear. We mustn't keep Lady Quimby waiting."

Julian took the seat next to Lady Regina as the orchestra began to play. The delicate odor of lilacs—Evelyn's favorite—wafted from her hair, and another pang struck him. Her perfume had been roses the night before, but she had been wearing Felicity Marleigh's costume. Perhaps she had worn a different perfume to keep people from guessing who she really was.

But if the demon had taken Lady Regina's soul, it wouldn't surprise Julian if the fiend was taunting him with a reminder of his dead wife.

Regina held her head high, but her nerves jangled. Beneath her floor-length skirt, she locked her ankles to keep her heels from knocking. Lord Lindsay was too close for her comfort. His shoulder pressed against her own, and she swore she could feel his breath warm upon her skin whenever he glanced at her or spoke to her aunt. It disconcerted her having a handsome magelord willingly sit beside her.

She didn't understand why he had asked Lord

Langley to formally introduce him to her. Aunt Agatha would say it was because Regina was a beautiful young woman, and the fact Lord Lindsay kissed her at the Prinsworth ball last year meant he'd noticed. Of course, he'd also insulted her as soon as he'd realized she was a half-blood.

Lord Lindsay had been very polite and courteous so far, which seemed to indicate his claims of reform were genuine. Part of her wanted to talk with him about Lord Pratchett's death. Why had he believed the lord's soul was missing, when no one else had? How did he think she could help him? But to do that she'd have to admit that she—not Felicity Marleigh—had been dressed as Marie Antoinette.

She gave him a sideways glance and chewed the inside of her lip. Had he somehow realized that was her? Did he want to finish their conversation? She hadn't been prepared to sit beside him in the first place, and now she worried he'd somehow figured out she was Marie Antoinette. What if he asked her again to help him? She didn't think he'd let her escape so easily this time.

His eyebrows rose as he caught her glance. "Yes, milady?"

Drat. She turned to face him. In for a penny, in for a pound. "I was wondering if you realize we've met before."

"Yes, I did. Marie Antoinette, I presume?"

"How did you know?"

"I saw Lady Felicity and her mother earlier today. They mentioned that you attended the ball as Marie Antoinette." He didn't sound bothered by her deception. Most mageborn would have been livid over the trick she had played. She added a point in his favor.

"Did you visit them because you were looking for me?" Was he interested in Lady Felicity, or had he wanted to finish the conversation Regina fled from last night?

"Yes. I wanted to ask you a couple of questions, but you left before I could. Forgive me for calling you Lady Felicity. I had assumed incorrectly who you were."

Strange that he was apologizing, when she was the one who had deceived everyone. "That's understandable. Everyone knew she was attending the ball as Marie Antoinette."

"Does the fact you are talking with me mean you are open to answering my questions?" His smile took the edge off his words.

"Yes, but later." She nodded at the crowd around them. She didn't want people overhearing their conversation. "We can talk during intermission."

"I look forward to it." This time his smile was so warm it could have melted snow, but the ice in his eyes made a nervous shiver run down her spine.

What had she agreed to? Had he truly changed?

He turned away and settled into the concert. Their conversation was over.

The music swept over her and her mind drifted. The Earl of Lindsay had been named after Julian Rutherford, the hero—to humans and half-bloods, that is—of the Mageborn War. Did he hate his name? She closed her eyes in an effort to focus on the intricate notes of Bach, but instead she found herself wondering about the rebel warrior who had ended the Mageborn War.

An image of Lord Lindsay filled her mind. He stood on the tor near her family's estate. The wind tousled his raven hair, and the sky behind him was a cobalt blue that matched his intense gaze. Her ears sang with soaring birdcalls and the moor wind whistling among the rocks. A brisk breeze blew against her face as she clambered up the hill towards him. He smiled—a look filled with love and joy—and she knew it was meant for her alone.

Magic surged in her bloodstream. She opened her eyes, but black filled her vision, obscuring the ballroom. Panic rose in her chest.

Julian's broad-shouldered form filled the doorway. His lean features were hard and still, and his eyes glittered with an emotion she couldn't read. He wrapped his arms around her in a brief hug then let her go.

"Why did your father want to see you?" She'd been wondering this ever since Julian received the summons from his father.

"He wanted to tell me he was pleased with me."

Her head jerked in shock. His father despised him. "What?"

"He was glad I had more sense than my brother, who, in his words, was 'throwing his inheritance away' by starting this foolish war."

"What did you say?"

"I told him Eric wanted his son to inherit the title. And he said—'If Eric had wanted his son to inherit, he

should have married a mageborn lady, not that human wench.' Suddenly, I'm my father's favorite son." His lips twisted.

"I'm so sorry." How many times had Julian striven and failed to please his father? And to receive the man's approval this way? He must hate it.

"It doesn't matter. I told him I agreed with Eric. That I didn't want a title that rightfully belonged to my nephew."

"What did he say?"

"He laughed. He said I'd change my tune as soon as that title was in my hands and everyone was calling me Lord Lindsay."

"And then?"

"I said that would never happen and I left." Julian's blue eyes bore into her, then he stepped forward and clasped her tight against his chest, burying his face in the crook of her neck. "I hope you can forgive me."

"What do you mean?"

"I joined Eric and his rebels."

Loud clapping jolted Regina. She blinked and the vision was gone. She inhaled sharply. The darkness faded from her eyesight, and rows of seated ladies and lords appeared before her. The orchestra played on a dais at the front of the ballroom. Unlike the vision she'd had of the redheaded lord with the eyes of a monster, this one had seemed to be of the past. The scene reminded her of the world of her dreams. The ones where she was a witch and healer. But she had never had a husband in them until now. Why had he looked like the Earl of Lindsay?

Was this a true vision of the past, or had her imagination, fueled by her uncontrolled magic, used Lord Lindsay to create a romantic story about a mageborn hero she adored?

No matter how real her vision had seemed, it was only a dream. A fantasy. She needed to focus on her situation. Lindsay was a magelord, powerful enough to meet Gabe's needs. The earl wanted to ask her questions, but she wanted answers too. She would ascertain if he had truly changed. If so, her brother would get his mentor, and she would use Lindsay's interest in demons to do it.

CHAPTER TWENTY-THREE

WHEN THE MUSIC STOPPED FOR intermission, the clapping rang loudly for several minutes. Members of the audience rose from their seats and dispersed to the edges of the ballroom to chat or for refreshments. Julian had been waiting impatiently for this moment. The orchestra could have sounded like squawking chickens or a heavenly choir for all the attention he'd paid.

Lady Carlisle stood up and said, "Lady Quimby and I are going to mingle with the other matrons for a while. You should tour the gardens. The countess had the trees lit with authentic lanterns from the Orient."

"That's an excellent suggestion," Julian said.

"While the lanterns sound fascinating, I'll pass. I see someone I need to speak with." Langley slapped Julian on the shoulder. "Have fun."

Julian looked at Lady Regina. "That leaves the two of us then. Would you like to see the lights?"

"It would be my pleasure." Her smile transformed her face, and his breath caught in his throat at her beauty. Every time he looked at her, it was like seeing Evelyn. His mind told him he was wrong, but his heart didn't listen. She laid her fingers on his arm. His muscles tensed at her light touch, even as his pulse raced. He searched her face, but he couldn't see any clues that would indicate she was a demon. She looked human. Just like Kikson had.

He led her through the French doors to the patio outside. She gave him a questioning glance. "I'm surprised you want to be seen with me, considering my heritage."

Crickets and the loud croaking of frogs from the lake filled the balmy night. He guided her past other couples to a less trafficked part of the garden. "What man wouldn't be interested in a stroll with a lovely young lady?"

"That wasn't your attitude at the Prinsworth Ball last year. Nor is it the attitude of most of the mage-born."

The marquis's son had despised humans and half-bloods. Langley had warned him people would talk if he approached her. Julian had thought he referred to the earl's attitude. Now he realized Langley had meant the mageborn. He needed to determine if she was the demon, but couldn't if she refused to spend any more time with him. "I've changed."

"Are you saying you no longer despise humans and half-bloods?"

What had happened in her previous encounter with the Earl of Lindsay? Whether she was the demon or not, he needed to allay her suspicions. "I do not dislike humans or half-bloods. And I'm sorry, but I have no recollection of the Prinsworth Ball."

"I'm not surprised you don't remember. I have never seen a man so deep in his cups shamelessly appear at a ball," she snapped. Her anger seemed to translate to her legs, because he had to walk faster to keep up.

"What did I do?"

"You accosted me."

Should Julian ever encounter the marquis's son, the man would suffer a beating he'd never forget. No man deserving of the name would ever force himself on a woman.

"Did I hurt you?"

She looked confused by his question. "I fought you and escaped your grasp."

"What else?" He could see there was more she wasn't telling him.

"You truly do not remember?"

"No. I beg you, please enlighten me." He couldn't help the rage in his voice, but he was infuriated that a man who looked like him and carried his name could be such a blackguard. His anger seemed to frighten her, for she took a step back.

"It was nothing. I should return."

He grabbed her hand. "Wait. Please." He softened his tone. "Tell me—what else did I do to you?"

She pulled back against his grasp, but he didn't let her go. This was the stumbling block he needed to get past if he was going to earn her trust.

"You spit on the floor when you recognized me. You had mistakenly kissed a half-blood and your disgust knew no bounds."

The paper lanterns swung in the breeze, casting a warm glow over the path. Lady Regina seemed somehow vulnerable in the flickering light, and Julian felt a pang of doubt. Could a demon feign such deep emotions? *Remember Kikson. He was your personal guard. Demons are expert impersonators.* "You are right to despise me and my actions. But I promise you, I am no longer the same person I was then."

She looked away from him for a few moments. When she met his gaze this time, she looked resolved. "I believe you."

Her mood changed so quickly, he was taken aback. "Langley said there is a maze in the back worth seeing. Would you care to see it?"

"I'd love to." She seemed as eager to be alone as he was. If she was the demon, was this a trap? Or did she want to be alone for some other reason?

Watching her carefully, he placed her hand on his arm and led the way towards the maze.

"Forgive my curiosity, my lord, but considering how much you disliked humans—until recently, that is—" she hastily corrected, "did it bother you that your father named you after the hero of the Mageborn War?"

He was positive her question wasn't as innocent as it seemed. Was this her way of testing to see if he had really changed? "I'm my own man. It doesn't matter to me what someone else with my name has done." Especially not some half-baked brute who resented his own mixed heritage.

"As a half-blood, I have always wondered about Julian Rutherford. He was pure mageblood. Why would he join the war? Why would he give up the title for his nephew? Was he truly that noble?" She examined the lanterns as they walked down the gravel path. "But maybe I understand."

"What do you mean?" He stiffened as he remembered the arguments he and Eric had had with their father. The Mageborn War had torn their family apart.

"If I'd had a father like his, I would have joined the rebellion out of spite too."

Julian caught his breath. How did she know? Of course he'd wanted his nephew to inherit. But if his father hadn't summoned him and said he was pleased Julian hadn't joined the war, would he have gone to Eric and the rebels so quickly?

He stared at the woman who was Evelyn's twin. A few more questions and he would know whether or not she was the demon. Could he kill her if she was? Dread filled his soul as he soaked in those familiar uptilted eyes and sweet features. "How did you know about Julian Rutherford's relationship with his father? Is that in the history books?"

She laughed and shook her head. "I don't know why I said that. I don't know anything about the father except that he'd been against the war. It was just my imagination running away with me, like my aunt always says."

Julian had never told anyone about the conversation with his father that had pushed him to join the war. Only Evelyn. And while he didn't like Lady Regina's characterization of him, he had joined the war out of anger to show his father just how wrong the magelord was about him.

There was only one way a magicless half-blood could know about this. Lady Regina was the demon, and the demon had taken Evelyn's soul.

———◆———

Regina had never seen this section of the Allensworth garden. Constructed of eight-foot tall hornbeam hedges, the maze loomed at the end of the gravel pathway. Faint strains of music drifted from the ballroom. The wind rustled through the branches of the trees. No one was in sight. She wasn't sure she wanted to enter, even though it presented the perfect opportunity for her to further her plan.

Lord Lindsay no longer seemed to despise half-bloods, but every time he looked at her, his eyes held a wariness she didn't trust. She should turn back, but this was her best chance of securing a mentor for Gabe.

She stepped forward, her hand still on his arm. Darkness swallowed them, except for the soft glow of the lanterns lining the pathways. The path split to the left and the right.

"Which way?" he asked.

She thought back. What had her aunt said about the Allensworth maze? "Left. The trick to reaching the center is to always touch the hedge with your left hand."

He followed her instructions, each choice leading

them deeper inside the labyrinth. Regina couldn't hear the music anymore. No sounds disturbed the night other than their own footfalls on the crushed gravel path. She felt foolish. Why had she told him her vision about the Julian Rutherford from the Mageborn War and his father as if it were fact? Imagine how he would have laughed if she'd said he looked exactly like that earl from the past. He'd know just how drawn she was to him, despite their wretched encounter the previous year.

The soft scrabble of claws on gravel reached her ears. "Did you hear that?"

Lord Lindsay paused, but there were no further noises. "Probably a rodent of some kind."

The night suddenly seemed very quiet to Regina. The crickets had quit chirping, and even the distant croaking of the frogs had faded. Dark leafy hedges, small lanterns, and thick shadows stretched along the natural corridor. Goosebumps rose on her arms.

"I feel like something is watching us." An image of eyes like yellow flames popped into her brain. "Can you see anything?"

He searched the gravel path, looking ahead and behind them, as well as the trees edging the grass. "I don't see anything or anyone."

She moved a little closer to him, seeking comfort from his strength.

"I've heard your brother has magic, but you do not. Is that true?"

She hadn't told anyone, not even her family, about her secret. "It's common knowledge that I do not have magic. Why do you ask?" Other than the soft scrape of their shoes on the gravel path, the night was extraordinarily quiet. Why did she feel like something was stalking them?

They reached the center of the maze, where a stone bench lay in the middle of a circle surrounded by statuary of Classical figures. Compared to the light of the full moon, the lanterns seemed dim.

"If you don't have magic, then can you explain how you knew Lord Pratchett's soul was missing?"

She released his arm and faced him. Was this one of the questions he'd wanted to ask about Pratchett's death? Tension weighed heavy between them. "I just knew."

"Ordinary mageborn cannot tell if a soul is missing," he drawled. "Neither can humans nor magicless half-bloods. Only someone of demon hunter lineage can tell, and only if that person has magic. Do you have magic or not? Or were you lying when you said Pratchett's soul was missing?"

She didn't want to answer him, but he was correct. To deny her magic was absurd in light of the evidence. "I recently started having visions. So yes, I think I have magic, although I haven't told anyone yet. And I wasn't lying. I'm sure Lord Pratchett's soul was missing."

"Very convenient. The entire mageborn community, including your own family, believes you don't have any magic. Yet you say you recently discovered it and have told no one?"

"It's the truth."

"What happened to Lord Pratchett when you walked in the garden with him?" He stalked closer to her, moving until he blocked the only exit from the heart of the maze.

She backed away from him. "He was fine when I left him. You think I had something to do with his death?"

"I'm sure of it." His stance shifted. She had the impression that he was readying for an attack.

Pride be damned, she listened to her instincts and scurried away from him. "You're mad."

"Am I?" He moved closer, a beast stalking its prey.

"Whatever it is you think I've done, you're wrong. I had nothing to do with Lord Pratchett's death."

"I think you're the demon that took his soul."

The man was clearly insane. "You saw me at the ball. I left him in the garden."

"Exactly. I saw you with him at the ball and walking in the garden. And after that, Lord Pratchett's body was found and his soul taken—by your own words."

"That doesn't mean I'm the demon." Her pulse roared in her ears. His expression struck a fear unlike any she'd ever known into her heart. If she couldn't convince him of her innocence, the look in his eyes told her he would kill her.

Regina backed away and stumbled. She flung a hand to the stone bench behind her and caught herself before she hit the ground.

Lord Lindsay surged forward and hauled her

against his chest. His arm came up and something thin and metallic touched her throat.

"I have been searching for you for weeks," he growled.

She pulled back from the blade so she could speak. "Well, you found me." She cursed the faint edge of sarcasm that tinged her voice. *Stupid chit. Don't bait him.*

His arm tightened around her shoulders, and once again the knife's cold edge lay against her skin. She fought the urge to swallow. "*Why did you kill my wife?* Who summoned you?"

She spoke with as little movement of her throat as she could. "I didn't even know you had a wife. How could I be the demon?"

"You think to play games?" He whispered hoarsely. "I lost everything because of you."

"We met for the first time at the Prinsworth Ball last year. I've only seen you twice since then. I know nothing of your family."

"You lie."

He pulled her tighter against his body and the blade shifted closer. The edge nicked her skin, and she inhaled sharply. Who would help Gabe if she died? "Please don't hurt me. I'm not a demon."

"You knew why Lord Lindsay joined the Mage-born War. The only way you could know that is if you are the fiend who killed my wife."

"That's your reasoning? It was a dream, a vision I had earlier this evening during the musicale. I told you, I probably imagined the whole thing!"

"You have a very accurate imagination then. This

is your last chance. *Who summoned you to kill me?*"

"Nobody. How many times must I tell you, I am not a demon!"

"I have to free my wife's soul." His voice was harsh. The blade dug into her throat.

Hot pain sliced her, and warm blood trickled down her skin. Regina closed her eyes and braced for her death.

CHAPTER TWENTY-FOUR

JULIAN GRIPPED HIS DAGGER FIRMLY. The sharp edge of the blade dug into Lady Regina's throat. Their bodies touched from shoulder to thigh. Her curves fit perfectly against him, soft and familiar. The scent of lilacs rose from her honey-gold hair. He could be holding his wife in his arms.

This isn't Evelyn. It's just the fiend in disguise.

Harbrook had warned him. Could he do what needed to be done if the demon looked like his wife?

Julian had thought he could, but the feel of her against him, the scent of her hair—it would be like killing Evelyn, the mother of his unborn child.

He shifted his grip, and Lady Regina stiffened in his arms. She hadn't said anything since her last denial. It didn't matter what the evidence against her was. Julian couldn't bring himself to draw the blade across her throat.

I can't do it. I can't kill Evelyn, not even to save her soul.

He removed his dagger from her throat and

pushed her toward the stone bench. "Take a seat."

She collapsed onto the bench. "Why didn't you kill me?" Her eyes shone with unshed tears.

"I still might, so don't try anything foolish." He waved the blade at her and paced. He needed to figure out what he was going to do with her. He couldn't let her leave and go home.

If she was the demon, why hadn't she transformed? She'd had many opportunities once they'd entered the maze. Maybe Lady Regina was telling the truth about her magic. Or maybe the Marquis of Thornwood could toss her into his dungeon until they could find a demon hunter who could tell them for certain if she was the creature who killed his wife. Until Julian had zero doubts—or she shifted forms—there was no way he could slice her throat.

She pulled a handkerchief out of her pocket and pressed it to her neck. The cut he'd made had been so shallow that only a few drops had fallen. She looked at the white cloth, folded it, and patted it against her neck. When she checked it again, the cloth remained clean. She put it away.

Whenever Julian looked at her, he saw no recognition, no love. Instead, hate raged behind those eyes. He was almost certain she was the demon, but he still couldn't kill her.

Lady Regina's head jerked up, and she inhaled sharply. She stared at the path they'd come from earlier. "Something's out there."

"What do you mean?"

"At the masquerade, I had felt uneasy, as if danger

lurked nearby. That's why I left Lord Pratchett in the garden, and he ended up dead. I feel it again now." She glared at him. "Obviously I'm not talking about you. Could it be the demon?"

"It's possible." Whenever a demon was near, Harbrook said it felt like an arrow aimed at his back. Julian tried to sense something—anything—but all he could feel was the quiet of the night. He wondered if this was a trick of some kind.

"I've never had these feelings of danger until recently." She looked around the heart of the maze.

Julian searched the area around them too, but only Greek statues stood out. A faint scratching reached his ears from the path. It reminded him of bone scraping over rock. Lady Regina shrank back on the bench.

More scrabbling noises of claws turning over gravel, then two squirrels chased each other out of the maze. Bloody hell. Rodents.

Lady Regina huffed out a breath. She gave a croak of relief. "Squirrels."

He stared at her, unsure if she was the demon playing games with him, or if the real demon was out there. "Is your feeling of danger gone?"

"No. Whatever it is, it's closer." She rubbed her temples. "The pressure in my head is building."

He strode to a position where he could watch her and the entrance to the maze's heart. His blood was pounding. He wanted to fight. "If you aren't the demon, I will protect you."

"Of course I'm not the demon, you imbecile! And you cannot possibly protect me. My own father—an experienced demon hunter—succumbed to one. Who are you to think you can do better?"

Julian couldn't track demons, but he'd killed plenty of them with Harbrook. If she was right, his nemesis was near. "Shush."

"I will not—" she angrily hissed back, then abruptly stopped.

A portly lord walked out of the dark corridor. "Ah, Lord Lindsay and Lady Regina, what a surprise finding you two together."

Julian looked between the middle-aged lord and the young miss. He'd expected a demon to walk out of the maze, not a mage. "The surprise is all mine. You're not what I was expecting."

Lady Regina moved behind the bench. She pointed at the gentleman. "It's him, Lord Falsworth. He's the source of the danger."

"Tut tut," scolded Falsworth. "It's not polite to cast aspersions."

The demon could be either one of them, although Julian was leaning towards Falsworth. If he was right, nothing would hold him back from his revenge. "I've been looking for you."

"How fortunate for all of us then, since I've been hunting you too."

"You took Lord Pratchett's life," Lady Regina said.

Falsworth waved his hand, and a blast of wind threw Julian off his feet. "Correction, my dear. I took his soul." His form shimmered and grew, until he towered over the life-size marble statues in the center of the maze. Pale skin transformed into thick leathery hide, and the reek of animal musk saturated the air. Long dagger-like claws curled from each fingertip, menacing and too close for comfort.

Julian scrabbled backward out of the creature's reach. His heart thudded, but he held his ground, keeping one eye fixed on his enemy's shimmering form while he searched for Lady Regina. He jerked his head toward the hedge opening, prayed she saw his signal, and rose to his feet. He extended his dagger, the metal glinting in the light of the moon. He'd been waiting centuries for his revenge. Tonight, the demon would die.

Julian gathered his magic. This fiend had destroyed his family and future. Death would have to be good enough. "Why did you kill my wife? Who summoned you?"

"It doesn't matter who summoned me. They're all long dead."

Lady Regina backed away from the bench, stopping near a large statue of Adonis. It was as far from the demon as she could get and still have protection.

"Your summoners betrayed you. You were no longer obligated to fulfill your task. *Why did you kill my wife?*"

"I needed a sacrifice to open a gate to my world. She was convenient." It hissed and snarled in laughter.

"You spawn of hell." Julian stalked toward the demon. "I'm going to make you regret killing my family. But before I do, tell me why you're here."

"Let's just say I have unfinished business."

"And that is?"

"My concern, not yours." The yellow flames in the demon's eyes blazed.

Julian didn't need to hear more. He couldn't get revenge on the demon's summoners—that was up to Harbrook now—but he could avenge Evelyn and free the souls the demon had taken. He charged. Sharp claws swiped at his head. He sliced the fiend's arm and darted out of range.

He circled the creature. Lady Regina watched them as she scrambled for the aisle leading from the maze's center.

"Run!" Julian shouted at her, as he kept his eyes on the demon.

The beast snarled. "She can't leave. Her soul is mine."

It raised a leathery arm and clicked its claws. A purple-black mist filled the gap between the hedges. The mist glowed briefly in the flickering lantern light and then winked out.

Demon magic. They were trapped.

"I won't let you get our souls." Julian flicked his fingers and an opening spell flew towards the path. A sullen orange flare hit the center of the aisle, which glowed purple-black once again. The flame disappeared. The dark haze lingered then faded.

Lady Regina skidded to a stop at the entrance. She reached out and touched the doorway. Violet flames surrounded her hand and she snatched it back, cradling it against her chest with her other hand. She shook her head. His spell had failed.

She sprinted along the hedge until she was behind Julian once again.

He slowly stepped around the circle, careful not to get trapped between the monster and the statuary. There was no need to tell Lady Regina to stay behind him. He could hear her soft footsteps on the grass, keeping pace with him. Smart woman, to keep Julian between her and the soul sucker.

He'd failed Evelyn, but he vowed to kill the demon and keep Lady Regina safe. Guilt pricked his conscious about his earlier actions but he shoved it aside. There'd be time for remorse later.

The full moon illuminated the heart of the maze, so bright the Greek statues cast shadows. Julian felt as if he were in one of the famed arenas of old.

He hurled a binding spell. Bright orange specks enveloped the beast. The hulking figure froze in place as Julian's magic took effect, its arms falling to its sides. He had mere moments before the monster shook off his power. Purple-black motes ate away at the orange mist as Julian tackled the demon to the ground. He stabbed its unshielded neck.

The demon broke free and knocked the dagger out of Julian's hand. Julian slammed his fist against the creature's skull and leapt off. He grabbed another blade from his boot and sliced the monster's gut.

The fiend kicked out with a clawed foot and Julian jumped out of range. The creature rose, clutching its abdomen. Dusky purple blood oozed from its wound. Julian's nostrils pinched at the putrid smell.

"Did you take my wife and unborn child's souls? Tell me and your death will be merciful. If not—" Julian struck and sliced its forearm—"you will beg me to kill you. I coated all my weapons with demonsbane oil. Your injuries won't heal."

"You don't know?" Moonlight glinted on its canines as it hissed and snarled. Its yellow eyes sparkled with amusement.

The need for revenge charged cold as winter ice down Julian's spine. "It doesn't matter. If you took their souls, they will be freed tonight."

The flames in the demon's eyes glimmered wildly in the moonlight.

The world narrowed to the two of them. Julian's body tensed as he planned his next attack. This monstrous fiend had shredded Evelyn's body, killing her and their baby. It had to die.

Julian leapt and ground the dagger's sharp tip into the juncture of the creature's collarbone and neck. The demon knocked him off, flinging him across the gravel where he hit one of the stone benches. His dagger flew from his fingertips, and the demon kicked it out of reach as it approached.

"A few more souls, and I'll heal soon enough." It raised a clawed foot and aimed a kick at Julian's head.

CHAPTER TWENTY-FIVE

S TATUES OF GREEK GODS GLEAMED white in the moonlight and cast shadows on the maze's heart where Lord Lindsay and the demon fought. Regina's heart leaped every time the creature landed a blow. She edged along the hedges, praying she could reach the exit and get help.

The demon kicked Lord Lindsay in the head. The magelord slumped to the ground. Her pulse and mind raced. Was he dead? What could she do? She wasn't a demon hunter and couldn't control her magic yet. She didn't have any fighting skills.

The demon loomed over the unconscious lord. He crouched down and grabbed Lindsay's shoulder with a clawed hand.

Regina's entire being recoiled. She came from a line of demon hunters. She wouldn't be worthy of her ancestors if she didn't stop the fiend from taking the earl's soul.

"Leave him alone!" she shouted.

The monster's head snapped around on his thick neck. Yellow-red eyes gleamed in the dark.

Her breath caught in her throat at the soul hunger in those flame-filled eyes. *Move, Regina. Get to the exit.* She reached the gap between the hedges. She braced herself for the pain and pressed her fingertips against it. No purple flames appeared. The blocking spell was gone.

She stood in the doorway between the hedgerows and faced him. On her family's country estate, she'd been able to outrun every boy and young man she'd ever known, a gift of her demon hunter heritage. "If you want a soul, take mine. If you can catch me."

The demon hissed and snarled, a strange noise that somehow resembled laughter. "Ah yes," he said. "I suppose it wouldn't be very sporting to steal a soul from an unconscious man. And you remind me of my priorities."

He rose from his crouch and leaped toward her. Pulse pounding in her throat, sure now that the demon would follow her, Regina lifted her skirts and dashed down the leafy corridor.

The beast chased her. His clawed feet scraped over the gravel, striking fear in her heart. She fought to remember the turns she and Lindsay had taken to get to the maze's center.

Follow the hedge to the right.

Run, Regina, run.

Her blood pounded the refrain in her ears.

Male and female voices chattered ahead.

"Help!" she yelled. She had to reach the group. The scrabble of claws on gravel grew closer. The demon was gaining on her. The urge to look behind her was strong. She resisted. If she looked, she'd slow down. That might be all the fiend needed to catch her.

Daggerlike claws scraped her shoulder and slid off. The demon was breathing down her back. *Run!* She fled, running faster than the time a boar had chased her through the forest.

She caught her breath and yelled. "Help!"

Sharp talons scored her back, snagging her dress. Hot pain ripped down her spine. The demon's fetid breath lifted her hair. He held the muslin fabric in his grip, but not her. She could still get away. She plunged ahead against the resistance of her clothing. The thin material of her evening dress ripped. She stumbled forward, clad only in her chemise and stays, and flew down the hedgerows.

She gasped, dragging humid air into her burning lungs. Another burst of speed—another right turn—and the maze exit came into view. She sprinted for the opening where she heard voices calling her name.

"Help!" Regina burst into the crowd of people outside the entrance. "There's a demon in the maze. Lord Lindsay is trapped inside."

She looked behind her, but the path was empty. Shadows filled the gap between the hedgerows. Was the demon lurking beyond the torchlight at the entrance? Or had he gone back to take Lord Lindsay's soul?

The group of mageborn lords and ladies murmured all at once, deep male tones and higher-pitched female voices mingling together in a rising cacophony. No one moved toward the entrance of the maze, but Lord Langley began pushing forward from the back of the crowd.

"A demon?"

"She's mad."

"Summoning demons is against the law. No one has heard of any demons in England in years."

"Lindsay must have given her some of those alcoholic beverages he used to be so fond of."

"Where is Lord Lindsay? Wasn't he with her earlier?"

"What happened to her dress? She's in her underclothes!"

Regina shivered and shoved her way past them into the cluster of lords and ladies milling beneath the trees. She'd be safe from the demon here. An old lord leered at her. She shrank into herself and turned away from him, crossing her arms over her bosom. Where was her aunt? Every direction she turned, the mageborn closed in, like wolves around their prey.

Never show them any weakness, her mother's voice admonished. Regina choked back the sobs rising in her chest and searched for her aunt's familiar face.

"Regina!" Her aunt bustled forward, sharply rapping men on the arm with her fan. "What happened?"

She stumbled into her aunt's arms, swallowing back her tears. She tried to say—*a demon tried to kill me*—but the words wouldn't come out. The faces around her held disapproval, scorn. A few wore sardonic smiles.

"There, there, child, you're safe now." Aunt Agatha rubbed her back. "You—" she pointed at a tall lord who stood there ogling Regina in her chemise, "hand me your greatcoat." He reluctantly removed his outerwear and handed it to Aunt Agatha, who immediately wrapped it around Regina.

"My dear, are you all right?" Lady Quimby asked. She and the Countess Allensworth accompanied her aunt.

Regina nodded and pulled the greatcoat tight around her. "Yes, thank you. But there's—" *A demon* trailed off her tongue.

The chatter ended and a few women gasped. A shadow formed in the depths of the wooded passage. Regina gripped the edges of her sleeves and her heart raced. Was the demon coming after her? Was she wrong to think she'd be safe in the crowd?

Lord Lindsay staggered from the hedgerow maze, weaving on his feet. Regina's tattered dress dangled like a washrag from his large grasp.

CHAPTER TWENTY-SIX

———

G RULIK HID IN THE DARK depths of the maze, waiting for the furor to die down. The wound in his shoulder ached and resisted healing. Demonsbane oil. He wished that plant would die out. A few mageborn souls would help him recover, but the lords and ladies had flocked as a group back towards the ballroom.

Croaks and chitterings of frogs and insects filled the night once again. Carriages leaving the countess' estate rumbled over the rough cobblestone drive. Grulik waited. He needed to regenerate before getting into another battle, and killing another lord or lady so recently after Lord Pratchett's death would not be wise. Lord Lindsay knew about him, and another suspicious death might cause someone to send for a demon hunter. Just because no one knew of any demon hunters in London, didn't mean none existed in England. Best to lie low for a while, until he got another opportunity to go after Lady Regina.

He hissed and snarled softly in laughter. The earl thought Grulik had taken the souls of his wife and unborn child. He'd heard Lindsay threaten to kill Lady Regina before he confronted them in the heart of the maze. The mageborn lord had no idea that she was actually Evelyn reincarnated. Grulik laughed harder. That oaf had almost killed his own wife and broken the curse for him. The snarls poured from Grulik's throat.

He should have taken Rutherford's soul, but the insolent young witch had reminded him that breaking the curse was more important. Plus, Grulik couldn't resist a challenge. Demons were predators. They enjoyed the chase and watching their prey run.

She was faster than he'd expected. The mageborn said she didn't have magic, but her demon-hunting lineage ran true. He could sense her raw power. She'd also inherited the agility, size, and quickness of her forebears. Lindsay's wife had been one of the strongest witches of her time, but Regina melded her demon-hunting lineage with Evelyn's abilities. Grulik was lucky she didn't realize her strength. She would be a formidable foe if she ever learned to harness her magic.

He hissed and snarled once more. The magebloods of this era despised half-bloods and humans as much as their ancestors had. Fortunately for him, he didn't have to worry about anyone training the half-blood witch.

The night quieted a few hours before dawn. Grulik slunk out of the maze, still in his demon form. The dark green of his hide made it easier to blend into the shadows of the trees along the river. If he could have shifted into an animal shape, it would have been easy to disappear. But demons could only shift into the form of a soul they'd taken.

He reached central London, still in his demon form. A mageborn thief hid in an alley behind a row of brownstone buildings. Grulik smiled. The road to recovery was about to begin.

An hour later, he stretched in satisfaction. After stealing the thief's soul, he'd gone to the docks. Five souls more and all his wounds were healed, even the deep puncture in his neck. He weighted down the last body and tossed it into the Thames.

Whose house did he want to sleep in tonight? He scanned through the souls he'd culled over the past few days. Definitely a lord. Preferably wealthy. He could use a good meal.

The soft thud of leather on stone alerted him. He turned and a bright blue sword swung down as a figure clad in black from head to boots jumped off the wall behind him.

He scrambled back as the sword sliced his shoulder. Pain raked him as the wound refused to heal. Demonsbane oil. His lips rolled back in a snarl. He leaped, but the demon hunter dodged his attack and swung the sword again, slicing into Grulik's thigh.

Grulik shook his head. Something was different about this one. Tall, muscular, narrow-waisted, slightly wider hips. This demon hunter was a woman.

He kicked out and his claws shredded her leather pants. She slashed his side, cutting him under his rib cage. He grabbed the sword, but it slid through his grip. Grulik ripped her left shoulder and upper back with his claws. She sliced him again, this time severing his hamstring. He knocked her sword across the pavement.

She pulled a dagger out of her shirt. He twisted just enough that the blade missed his heart. He caught her in his arms. She thrust her knife into his throat. If she severed his neck, he would die. He dragged his claws down the side of her neck, and she kicked off him with her feet. She landed on the wharf on one knee. Blood poured from the wounds in her neck and upper body. Strands of dark red hair fell around her shoulders.

Grulik yanked her dagger from his throat and limped toward her. Fire burned in his wounds. He would enjoy taking her soul. "I've never killed a female demon hunter before."

Dark blue eyes glared at him. "And you won't tonight."

"I may be in bad shape now, but a little taste of your soul will fix me right up." He snarled.

"You'll have to catch me first." She staggered to the edge of the dock and dove into the Thames.

He lost track of her in the murky water. The mageborn lords were wrong. There was a demon hunter in London. She was female, which was probably why she kept her identity a secret. Grulik grabbed her sword and dagger and threw them into the river. No point letting somebody get hold of demonsbane-coated weapons.

London had plenty of mageborn souls to choose

from. He'd be completely healed before daybreak.

The demon hunter—no, *huntress*—would not be so lucky. He'd dealt enough death blows to know she wouldn't last more than a few weeks.

There were only two demon-hunting families with female daughters in London. Lady Marleigh was going to be wearing mourning very, very soon.

CHAPTER TWENTY-SEVEN

REGINA SAT IN THE CARRIAGE, her heavy woolen cloak covering her shift and a wool rug wrapped tight around her legs. Still she shivered. Aunt Agatha sat opposite, her mouth dropping at the corners in disapproval.

"What were you doing in the maze with Lord Lindsay?"

"Lord Lindsay escorted me about the gardens, then suggested we tour the maze. He doesn't seem to despise humans or half-bloods anymore. I thought it was a good opportunity for me to carry out our plan."

Aunt Agatha shook her head. "I thought we agreed that a kiss would suffice. Really, Regina, this was too much! Everyone saw you in your undergarments."

"That's not what happened." The memory of the cold blade pressing against her neck made her throat dry. Lord Lindsay had nearly killed her when he thought she was the demon. She still didn't know what had stopped him, but she couldn't tell Aunt Agatha about this. Lindsay had tried to save her when he realized his mistake. "We reached the heart of the maze, and then Lord Falsworth showed up. He was a demon."

"Lord Falsworth."

"Yes." Nobody at the musicale had believed her, especially after Lord Lindsay walked out of the maze holding her tattered dress. They all believed he had attacked her, and that her story of the demon had been an attempt to avoid ruination. "Lord Lindsay fought him after he changed forms. I ran away and the demon chased me. *He* ripped my dress, not the earl."

The look of pity on her aunt's face made Regina cringe. "There are no demons in London. If there were, don't you think someone would have noticed a monster as hideous as the one you described?"

"It could shift forms. Like I said, it looked like Lord Falsworth."

"Lord Falsworth was not at the musicale. My dear, tonight you experienced a trauma no young woman should go through. Most likely the earl used his magic to play a trick on you and drive you into his arms."

Regina stared at her aunt in disbelief. She didn't know whether to laugh at this ridiculous characterization of the earl. "He doesn't need to use tricks. He's powerful, handsome, wealthy, and *an earl.* That's why I chose him."

"Maybe he was just playing a game with you. Who knows?" Aunt Agatha leaned forward and gently patted her knee. "When we get home, I'll have cook make you a posset. It'll set you back to rights. I'm sure things will look differently in the morning."

Regina flung her head back against the velvet cushions, frustration eating away at her. A faint orange gleam from the carriage lights seeped in around the edges of the velvet drapes covering the window. She couldn't tell her aunt about her magic, not now. If Aunt Agatha didn't believe her about the demon, she definitely wouldn't believe her half-blood niece had suddenly developed magic after a lifetime without it. She closed her eyes and slumped against the seat.

As her head bounced on the plush cushion a deeper realization struck her. In the eyes of society, she'd been well and truly compromised. Her future had been ruined tonight by Lord Lindsay. Would he do the honorable thing and propose marriage? If so, her quest for a mentor for Gabe would be over. Thank goodness. She hated attending these mage-born events. Of course, if the earl didn't propose, she wouldn't be attending any more balls anyway since she'd be ruined. And then Gabe wouldn't have a teacher.

"Sleep," Aunt Agatha whispered.

What? No, I don't want to sleep. She struggled to open her eyes, even as the dark heaviness of her aunt's sleep spell claimed her body.

Regina stared at a cloudy night sky. She was bumping along on a horse across the open moors. Something large with leathery arms and sharp claws held her on the saddle. She struggled to move her body but couldn't. A faint purple glow covered her skin and clothing. It reminded her of the dark magic at the maze. Horror filled her. The demon had her. *But how? How did it capture her and how did it get her away from London?*

Power simmered in her blood. She sought to call it forth to fight the spell holding her captive. Her mage energy eluded her grasp. The demon's spell had dampened her ability to harness her magic.

Her thoughts skittered to a halt. Magic? She could feel its power inside her veins, knew how to use it.

I'm dreaming.

She found herself in a field before a soldiers' camp with a huge bonfire burning in the center. Tall evergreens rose behind the canvas tents. A limestone crag loomed in the background, a deep black silhouette against the midnight sky.

A man in a leather jerkin and breeches stood in the torchlight just outside the perimeter of the camp. In this dream world, she knew the man was her husband. Her heart beat faster as she glimpsed a familiar wave of hair and strong high cheekbones.

He spoke and the demon responded. She didn't know what they were saying, but despair filled her at her inability to escape the fiend.

The scene shifted again. She stood before an inky black portal at the foot of the crag. Blood spread rapidly from deep slashes across her chest and abdomen. Her hands cupped the slight mound of her womb. *My baby.*

"Regina," a woman's voice shouted.

Her cheek stung. The pain in her chest and belly

dissipated. She blinked to find herself seated in the stuffy confines of her aunt's carriage.

"Where's the demon? My—" she'd almost said *baby*. But that was impossible. She surreptitiously slid her hands beneath her cloak. No curved mound, just the familiar flat planes of her belly.

A dream, but so vivid. She inhaled slowly, afraid of the pain she knew would come. Nothing.

"You had a nightmare, dear." Aunt Agatha moved to sit next to her and rubbed her right hand between hers. "I shouldn't have cast that sleep spell on you. It sometimes causes bad dreams."

The dream had felt real. More real than the carriage they rode in now. The fragrant aroma of wood smoke, not the oily scent of coal, burned in her nostrils.

"Why?" Regina couldn't help the nudge of betrayal she felt at having a spell cast upon her.

Her aunt rubbed her hands a little faster. "You were overwrought. I thought sleep would help."

Aunt Agatha had accused the earl of using magic to manipulate Regina, and yet she'd done the same. Would she have bespelled her if Regina had had magic? Anger flared, compounded by the sense of helplessness she'd had in her dream. "Please do not do that again."

"I won't. I'm sorry, my dear."

There was no point in lashing out. Aunt Agatha didn't create the nightmare, and Regina knew her aunt had meant well. The carriage rolled to a stop before their townhouse, and they went inside.

After Regina settled in her bedroom, she dismissed her maid. A fire burned in the grate, and cook's posset sat in a teapot on the table. A towel and hot water had been placed on the vanity.

Regina frowned into her bedroom mirror, staring at the thin red line on her throat. It was little more than a scratch, but her blood heated as fury filled her. Lord Lindsay could have killed her. The demon could have killed her. And she'd been powerless to do anything about it.

She had sensed the demon's vile presence at the Sherrington masquerade and in the maze. She had visions. Those dreams she'd had since childhood of being a witch and healer no longer seemed like a product of her innermost longings. Tonight's dream had felt like a real memory. Even the pain.

Were her dreams visions of somebody else's life? Or were these her own memories from a previous life? Did it matter, if she could learn from them?

Regina came from a line of demon hunters. It was in her blood. So was magic. Should she ever encounter that spawn of hell again, she didn't want to be a victim, depending on some mageborn lord to save her. She needed to learn how to wield her power. She couldn't fight the demon, but if she could counteract its spells long enough to escape, that would be enough.

She turned her focus inward. Golden streams of magic burgeoned in her blood. She held her hand out and concentrated. "Fire."

A tiny flame flickered then disappeared.

That was all?

Power pulsed through her body. This time she

tried to channel her mage energy into the image of a flame on her palm. "Fire."

Magic rushed down her arm. A ball of fire burst into life above her palm. Heat warmed her face. She plunged the fiery orb into the bowl. The water bubbled and sizzled, steam rising into the air. The flames disappeared.

Regina slumped in her chair as energy left her in a rush. Breathing hard, she lifted her chin and focused on the thin threads of magic still flowing in her blood. One more test, then she could go to bed. She touched the mark on her throat and closed her eyes. Somehow, in her mind's eye she could see the damage. "Heal."

Magic flowed through her fingertips, warm and soothing, fixing the cut to her skin. When she opened her eyes, the mark was gone, as if it had never existed. Not even a scar marred her throat.

Regina wasn't a magicless half-blood. Not anymore.

She was a witch.

Julian slammed the heavy oak door of his study and headed to the sideboard to pour himself a brandy. He raised the crystal tumbler and downed the fiery liquor in one long swig. His head ached like the very devil. His condition wasn't helped by Langley, who had annoyingly accompanied him home. If his granite-faced cousin wanted to fight about tonight's cock-up, he'd oblige him.

He'd failed again.

Not only did he mistake Lady Regina for the demon, he'd almost killed her. The thought of how close he'd come to shedding innocent blood gave him chills. He would never have been free of that guilt.

And when his nemesis appeared? He'd failed to kill him, failed to protect Lady Regina, and the monster still roamed free. Some demon hunter he was.

To make matters worse, he'd found the young woman's dress lying on the path. Who knew that by walking out of the maze with that tattered piece of cloth he'd completely destroy her reputation?

The entire evening was one giant disaster.

Julian poured another brandy. There wasn't anything else he could do this night, and maybe it would take the edge off his ferocious headache. He turned to Langley and held up an empty tumbler. "Care for a drink?"

"No." Langley planted himself in the center of the Turkish carpet and crossed his arms. His grim stare never wavered as Julian downed the brandy in one gulp, feeling the burn all the way down his gullet. His cousin took a step towards him. "Put it down. We need to talk."

Julian set the crystal tumbler on the polished mahogany sideboard.

"Bastard." Langley balled his fist and threw a punch at Julian's jaw.

Julian deflected the blow with a raised arm. He stumbled back against the sideboard. His stomach roiled, and the room wavered. That bloody demon had nailed him but good earlier, and now his cousin seemed determined to finish the job. "I didn't touch her."

Langley followed up with a jab to his gut. "Doesn't matter. Everyone thinks you did."

Julian's breath whooshed out and he doubled over. Between the alcohol and his muzzy head, it was a struggle to keep upright. He held up a hand. "Stop. I deserved that much for ruining her reputation. However, that's as far as it went. I didn't attack her."

Langley threw another punch. "You're an impostor. You can't marry her."

The horror of that gave Julian a burst of energy. He knocked his cousin's arm aside and slugged him on the chin. "I just lost a wife. I don't want another one."

That comment enraged Langley further. He moved lightning-quick and landed a solid blow to Julian's eye. He stared at him and stepped back. "*Now* we're done."

Julian leaned his elbow on the sideboard for support. He pressed his hand against his eye, which already started to swell. He squinted at Langley. "By His Blood, you have a nasty right hook."

Somehow it seemed a fitting end to a supremely miserable evening.

"I don't know who the bloody hell you are or where you came from, but you've mucked everything up." Langley paced across the wood-paneled study. "You must do the right thing and ask Lady Regina for her hand in marriage."

"I can't. I'm an impostor."

"There's no other way. The real Earl of Lindsay has disappeared, so you must fix the mess *you* created. She's a half-blood." Langley stepped closer and looked like he would like nothing better than to hit him again. "Mageborn society hardly tolerates her presence now."

"There was a demon in the maze. Lady Regina called him Falsworth before he changed into his natural form."

"She announced that to the guests before you walked out of the maze, but nobody believed her. Right now fixing her reputation is more important than finding the demon. She doesn't deserve to have her future destroyed."

"If I propose, what happens when the real earl turns up?" Julian plopped down into the wingback chair by the fireplace.

"The other Julian Rutherford is a beast. He hates humans and half-bloods. If he were forced to marry her, I doubt she'd survive a year without some mysterious accident befalling her."

"And yet you want me to propose to her, knowing that she might marry a monster?"

"I'll write to the marquis. I'm sure he'll find a way to break the engagement that will save her reputation. But in the meantime, we'll do what we can to salvage the situation. You have to visit Lady Regina tomorrow and ask for her hand in marriage."

Julian's head throbbed at the action he must take. He was an impostor, borrowing another man's name and unsavory reputation for the time it took to hunt and kill the demon. And now he had to propose marriage to a young woman whose every mannerism reminded him of his dead wife. Guilt and remorse gutted him each time he looked at her familiar features. Was there a worse torment than to be constantly reminded of how he'd failed the person he'd loved most?

Perhaps Edward Rutherford, the Marquis of Thornwood, could spy a way out of this mess when the time came and his son—the real Earl of Lindsay—surfaced. Julian leaned back in his seat and met Langley's gaze.

"Very well." Let the torture begin.

CHAPTER TWENTY-EIGHT

THE NEXT MORNING, REGINA EXAM-
INED her throat in her bedroom mirror. Even
in the bright daylight, there was no hint of the cut
she'd had. She pulled at the skin, tilting her head so
she could see it from various angles. Not so much
as a faint red line marked the spot where the earl's
knife had sliced her delicate skin. Her reflection
stared back at her, green eyes wide and faintly disbelieving.

She'd done it. She had used magic to heal herself.

But at what cost? She was no longer a magicless
half-blood, but a half-blood witch. The knowledge
settled uncomfortably over her shoulders like the
greatcoat of a stranger when she'd stood shiver-
ing in her underclothes outside the maze. All those
dreams she'd had—of being a witch and healer—
were within her reach, but to achieve them she'd
have to let go of the person she'd always been. Less
like her human mother. More like the mageborn.

The mageborn had always despised her. Their
disdain wouldn't change because she had power,
especially now that her reputation was ruined from

last night's events.

If Lord Lindsay had any shred of honor, he would arrive sometime today to propose to her and salvage her reputation. Then, like many other young debutantes before her, all would be forgiven, though never forgotten. She'd be able to mingle with polite society and attend social events though, and hopefully, Gabriel would have the mentor in magic he needed.

It'd be easier to stay in this room and ignore the world outside, but she had to tell Gabe about last night to prepare him. He needed to know about the demon, and the fact she'd been compromised with no guarantee of an offer of marriage.

She picked up the organza scarf from her dressing table and draped it over her shoulders, then went downstairs to the morning room. No one was there. Her aunt must have already had her customary light breakfast. Regina placed coddled eggs and toast on her plate.

Her brother blew into the room, still dressed in his riding clothes. He flung himself into the seat opposite Regina. A servant quickly set the table before him.

"You're back early," Regina commented. Gabe normally ate a hearty breakfast before anyone else was up, then spent the rest of the morning riding.

"It started to storm." He reached for a roll and slathered strawberry jam on it. "How was the musicale? I heard cook had to make a posset so you could sleep."

Word definitely traveled fast. "It was—" how

could she best put this?—"terrifying. Cook made the posset so I could have a dreamless sleep."

He shoved another bite into his mouth, chewing slowly. He seemed to be thinking about what to say. "Was there another dead body?"

"No, but almost."

Gabe jolted straight up. "Are you saying a demon was there at the musicale?"

"Yes." She summarized what happened, leaving out the part about Lord Lindsay trying to kill her. No point in getting Gabe upset with the mage who might become his brother-in-law and mentor.

"Could you sense the demon's presence? Father always said he could sense them. That's how he could track them."

"I think so, now that I recognize the sensation."

"How did it feel?"

"When the demon was close, I suddenly felt uneasy. Like danger was lurking nearby."

"What did he look like?"

"In the beginning, he looked exactly like Lord Falsworth. But every now and then I saw yellow flames in his eyes. Then he shifted into his demon form." She wrapped her hands around her teacup, for warmth and comfort. "He was enormous— around eight feet tall, giant shoulders, a muzzle like a wolf, and glowing yellow eyes. He didn't have skin like us. Instead he had a thick greenish-brown hide. Lord Lindsay fought him, and I made my escape."

"Is the creature dead?"

"No."

Gabe collapsed into his seat. "No wonder cook made you a posset. You'd have had nightmares otherwise."

Telling her brother about the demon was the easy part. "There's more you should know."

"The demon escaped. I figured that out."

"Not just that." She could feel a flush rising up her cheeks. "I was found in a compromising position with Lord Lindsay, and now I'm ruined." She lifted her head, defiant.

"Ruined? How? Did it happen before the demon came?"

"No. It was a mix-up. The demon knocked Lindsay out, then came after me. We were running through the maze, and he was close enough to grab my dress with his claws. My dress tore and I escaped. Aunt Agatha and the other mageborn were looking for me—they'd heard me screaming for help. I ran out of the maze in my undergarments. The demon didn't follow me. Instead, Lord Lindsay walked out. He'd found my dress in the maze, so everyone assumed he was the one who'd torn it off me."

"Didn't you tell them it was the demon?"

"I did, but no one believed me. Not even Aunt Agatha."

"What? Why not?" Gabe sounded as surprised as she'd felt when their aunt had disregarded her comments.

"The earl is a powerful magelord. She thought he'd used his magic to play a trick on me, or maybe to impress me."

"Is Lord Lindsay going to ask for your hand in marriage?"

"I don't know."

He looked away for a moment, staring out the window at the storm raging outside. Lightning flashed. "Maybe it's better if he doesn't."

Thunder pealed, and she jumped. "What?" Regina was shocked. "I'll be ruined—we'll all be ruined—if he doesn't."

"I don't care." His mouth set in a mutinous line. "Isn't he the lord who attacked you last year?"

She had never told him about the Prinsworth ball. "How did you know about that?"

"I heard you and Aunt Agatha talking about him. He hates humans and half-bloods." Gabe glared at her, his expression hard, every inch the young lord. "You can't marry him."

"He said he changed, and I think it's true. He's not the same at all. He's been polite and courteous to me, even though he knows I'm a half-blood." She shook her head as she struggled to match the boorish man from her memory with the mage she'd recently met. "It's almost as if he were a completely different person. I think he truly has reformed and abandoned his prejudices against us."

"So if he asks for your hand, you are going to accept?"

"Yes." Her goal had been to trap a mage into marriage. Just not so spectacularly. Or publicly. Heat flooded her cheeks as she remembered the leering gazes of the lords as she'd stood in her underclothes outside the maze. "I will not repay Aunt Agatha's kindness to our family these many years with disgrace. Nor will I destroy your future."

Gabe was young, but he already took his burgeoning responsibilities seriously. She could see him struggling with the ramifications. "If you don't want to marry him, refuse him."

"I cannot."

A quiet knock sounded and Deeds opened the study door. "My lady, you have a visitor. Lord Lindsay requests your presence. He awaits you in the drawing room."

"Thank you, Deeds." She noted his stern expression. He bowed and exited the room, closing the door behind him.

Her brother pushed himself to his feet. Although only fifteen years of age, he already stood several inches taller than her. His jaw tensed in his narrow face, and she glimpsed the man he would someday become. "I want to meet him."

She looked up into his stormy green eyes. "Of course."

Gabe preceded her and opened the drawing room door. Regina straightened her shoulders and lifted her chin into the picture of pride her mother had drummed into her. They were half-bloods of noble lineage on both sides. She and Gabe had nothing to be ashamed of.

Lord Lindsay stood by the marble fireplace, studying a landscape depicting the Yorkshire moors in summer. She loved the green hills and how the blue skies looked near enough to touch, but the clouds piled on the horizon in the painting made her sad. As if tragedy waited just behind the far hills. The earl turned at their entrance.

Regina's heart thumped when those silver-blue eyes met hers. There was something about the way he looked at her that felt familiar. As if he'd watched her enter a room many times. "Lady Regina." He bowed.

Gabe moved to stand protectively beside her. Though tall, he was gangly and had yet to fill out. He was no match for Lord Lindsay's powerful frame. She still thought of him as a boy, yet once again, she had proof that he was becoming a man.

"Lord Lindsay, may I introduce my brother, Lord Harbrook?"

"Lord Harbrook." He inclined his head.

"Lord Lindsay." Gabriel didn't nod or bow in return. He was clearly wary of the lord. "To what do we owe the honor of your presence? Most mageborn don't visit the homes of half-bloods."

Regina glanced at her brother in shock. Why was he behaving so rudely to their guest? How would the earl react? Would he be angry? She turned back to him, an apology already forming.

But the earl had a half-smile on his lips, seemingly not bothered in the least by her brother's directness. "Last night your sister and I were caught in a scandal. It was unfortunate, but I'm here to make things right. As much as I can, at least. With your permission, I'd like to speak to Lady Regina privately."

Gabriel straightened. Few treated her brother as

an equal, because of his breeding and his youth. He glanced at her, and she gave a slight nod. "You may do so."

"Thank you, Gabe. I'll send for you after we've spoken." Regina knew her brother would want to eavesdrop. That was probably how he'd learned about her encounter with the earl at the Prinsworth ball last year. With her hand in front of her body so Lord Lindsay wouldn't see, she gestured and flicked her hand away from the door.

From the scowl that crossed Gabe's face, he understood her message. He pulled the door closed.

The earl had ventured out into a thunderstorm in order to call on her, and he'd treated her brother as an equal. Both of these reinforced her opinion that the magelord's attitudes towards humans and half-bloods had changed.

Regina smiled at Lindsay, feeling hopeful for the first time since she'd started her search for a mentor for Gabe. "Now that we're alone, what would you like to discuss?"

◆

That smile—the sweet familiar curve of her lips, the dimples in her cheeks—undid him. Julian's gaze ate her up, from the honey-gold hair coiled in a loose bun, to her wide green eyes, the straight line of her nose, the feminine curves skimmed by her floor-length white dress. His heart pounded as every fiber of his being told him—*this is Evelyn.*

"My lord?" Even her voice resonated with his memory, the tones warm with a slight husky note.

He jerked his gaze away and strode to the window. It was rude, but he had to put some distance between them before he did something unpardonable—like wrapping her in his arms and never letting her go. Carriages rolled slowly by in the heavy rain, and a few unfortunate servants rushed along the pavement, their black umbrellas faint protection from the storm.

She's not your wife. Evelyn is dead.

Lightning flashed followed by a thunderous boom. The turbulence outdoors matched his emotions. Julian reminded himself he was here on a mission. He turned back to confront her and his past failures. "I beg your pardon. I wanted to see if the storm had eased yet. I wouldn't want our conversation interrupted by more visitors."

"You needn't worry. We never have visitors. The mageborn don't visit half-bloods." Her voice held a slight note of bitterness, and why not? The prejudices of the mageborn left much to be desired. She sat on the blue velvet settee by the marble fireplace. "Would you care to join me?"

Julian crossed the drawing room. He couldn't bring himself to sit next to her, not with the yearning still burning in his heart, and took the gold damask chair opposite. The pain that she wasn't his lost love was almost enough to turn him coward and shirk his responsibility, but he couldn't let Lady Regina or her family suffer the repercussions of the previous night's events.

The proposal rose to his lips, but he couldn't utter the words, not while his mind confused her with Evelyn. He searched for something else to discuss. "At the Sherrington masquerade, we never got a chance to finish our conversation."

The light gold color of her skin turned a deep rose as she blushed. "I shouldn't have run off like that, but I was wearing Lady Felicity's costume and you had mistaken me for her. Regardless, I didn't think I could help you."

"What I wanted to ask—was whether or not you had any relatives who could track the demon?" Julian couldn't—*wouldn't*—fail Evelyn and their unborn child again as he had at the maze. But in order to rescue their souls, first he had to find the monster.

"No. Perhaps my brother, but he is too young and has no training."

He didn't want to put a woman at risk, but Lady Regina had shown she was capable of handling herself when faced with the demon. "What about you?"

Her eyes widened at his suggestion, and she drew back slightly.

"You sensed the demon at the Allensworth estate last night. You even outran the creature, which indicates you inherited your family's demon hunting gifts. Could you track it?"

"I don't know." She chewed her bottom lip, and an expression of fear crossed her face. "Why? Is it because the demon killed your wife? I never even heard you were married."

"My wife died a long time ago." He didn't mention Evelyn had been carrying their first child when she was murdered. Discussing her death was difficult enough.

"Did you love her?"

In contrast to the heavy gloom outside, the cream-and-blue room with its classical moldings and comfortable seating cast Lady Regina in a warm, almost golden light, flickering from the flames in the hearth. Once again his mind and body refused to separate her from Evelyn. "Yes." He'd loved her enough to chase a demon through time to save her.

"Did the demon take her soul?"

This same question plagued him, worried him if he failed. "I don't know. But I can't risk doing nothing. Her soul would be trapped for eternity otherwise."

She twisted her fingers in her lap. "I sensed the demon's presence in the maze. But to be honest, I don't know if I can track it."

"Demon hunting is in your blood. With practice, you'll be able to trace its steps." By His Blood, he hoped that was true. "I'll help you learn."

"How?"

"My best friend was a demon hunter." How he wished Harbrook was here to help him. They'd have found the monster by now, and Evelyn and his unborn child's souls would be at peace. "I can teach you what I remember."

She stared down as if reading the future in her palms. Finally, she looked up. "My brother wants to be a demon hunter, but he's too young. I worry that he'll go after this demon himself. I'll help you."

"Thank you. Now that that's resolved, we both know why I am here." Lady Regina's consent to help him track the demon lifted a heavy burden from his back. It also helped him separate her from his wife. Evelyn could never have tracked a demon. It wasn't part of her heritage.

"Because my reputation is ruined?" Now that they were no longer discussing the demon, her chin rose in the air, and her eyes flashed fire, challenging him.

"Yes. It's the only way to restore your name and respectability. To allow us both to remain in society." He spoke the words matter-of-factly, without emotion. As a betrothed couple, they would retain their entry to the balls and to the demon's favorite hunting grounds.

Her gaze searched his face. "There are no other options, are there?"

"None." Although he wished it were otherwise. "Will you do me the honor of becoming my wife?" He said the words as if this was real, as if he weren't an impostor usurping another man's name. But this was nothing more than a societal transaction, a necessity for both of them.

She raised her chin and met his gaze with her own steady green eyes. "I have one condition."

A condition—surely not sharing a marital bed? For a moment, his mind pictured her curving into him in the dark, her body filling the spaces in his, as familiar and right as a sunrise. He swallowed the longing that rose in his throat. The body he imagined was Evelyn's, not Lady Regina's. And yet…a part of him knew the truth was a muddled mix of the two. Betrayal stabbed him, and he dragged himself back to the matter at hand. "Which is?"

"You met my brother. I want you to train him in the magical arts."

The fire crackled in the corner, chasing the morning chill away. The rest of the house was silent, save for the drum of the rain against the window-panes. "Absolutely not. I have a demon to catch. I don't have time to train a young man in magic."

Or involve himself any further with her and her family. Entanglements caused pain, and that was the one thing he'd had more than enough of.

Her spine went rigid, and her green eyes flashed fire. "Then I won't marry you. Nor will I help you find the demon."

"Without you, I can't track the demon. Would you rather people die?" He leaned forward, closing the space between them. "This betrothal is bigger than both of us, Lady Regina. This is life or death."

"So is my brother's need to learn magic."

"Ask someone else."

"We have. Everyone has refused, including his uncles, all because Gabriel is a half-blood. There's no one left to ask."

The amber eyes of his half-blood nephew flashed in Julian's mind. He would have trained Alex in magic, had he shown talent. He rubbed the bridge of his nose as a headache formed behind his eyes. He needed Lady Regina's help to track the demon, and the betrothal to allow them to continue to move in society. "Very well. I will agree to train your brother."

Her shoulders dropped and she sighed in relief. "Thank you. I accept."

Julian's temples throbbed. He hoped they found the fiend soon. The sooner this charade ended, the better.

CHAPTER TWENTY-NINE

———◆———

GABRIEL PACED AROUND THE STUDY, wishing he could go for an early morning ride. He pulled the curtain aside, but the rainstorm showed no sign of easing. He collapsed into a chair before the fireplace. Even the flames in the grate looked sullen. It was a perfectly miserable day. Just like yesterday, when he found out that Gina had been ruined and forced to accept Lord Lindsay's marriage proposal.

He jumped up from the chair, unable to sit still. He paced the room again, tracing the patterns in the Persian carpet. He'd overheard Regina speaking with Aunt Agatha about an incident last year, where the earl had kissed her against her will and spit at her. The man hated half-bloods and humans. How could she be sure the brute wouldn't hurt her? That he had truly changed?

Gabe didn't care if their family was ruined. Mageborn society didn't like them anyway. Gina should have refused the earl. He blinked away the moisture in his eyes. She was too important to him to risk losing.

A soft knock sounded on the study door. "The Earl of Lindsay is here to see you, milord." Deeds opened the door, and the man who'd been occupying Gabe's thoughts entered the room.

Lord Lindsay didn't look like most mageborn lords, who spent their time indoors in the city. Instead he looked like an outdoorsman—broad shouldered, muscular, tanned skin. Gabe wasn't as tall as him. Not yet. But in a few years he would be, if he got his father's height.

Gabe glared at the magelord who had ruined his sister.

One of the earl's eyebrows went up. "Lord Harbrook."

"Lindsay." He crossed his arms. "Why are you here?" Gina would chastise him for his rudeness, but she and his aunt were still sleeping.

"Your sister didn't tell you? I'm here to train you."

The breath stuck in Gabe's throat. He swallowed hard. "You're going to teach me magic?" Then he shook his head. It had to be a joke. The earl hated half-bloods.

Lindsay walked around the study. He assessed the massive oak desk, the wingback chairs, the settee, and the end tables. "This room will do, if we move the furniture out of the way. What do you think?"

"You're serious." He couldn't believe it. His own uncles wouldn't train him.

"Very much so." Lindsay picked up one of the leather chairs by the fireplace and placed it against the wall. "Now come help me, so we can get started."

Gabe scrambled to grab the other chair. He snuck glances at the earl whenever the man wasn't looking. "Why are you going to teach me?"

Lindsay picked up the black lacquered coffee table. "Because your sister asked me to."

"That's it? Because she asked?" Nobody else had ever agreed when asked. After he finished moving his item, he waited by the settee, the last piece of furniture left. It would take both of them to pick it up.

The earl grinned as he crossed towards him, and suddenly looked less formidable. "Nothing slips by you, does it? You're right. There was a little more to it than that, but that's between your sister and me." He took the opposite end of the settee. "Lift."

Gabe didn't know what kind of deal his sister had made with the magelord. She hadn't mentioned it, and he was certain Lindsay wasn't going to tell more than he had. He decided to switch topics. "Is it true you fought a demon the other night?"

"Yes."

"Why didn't you kill it?"

"You don't mince words, do you?" He looked up from placing the settee against the wall. "I tried, lad, but the creature got the better of me. I should have had more knives on me."

"What did you have?"

"One dagger, one knife. Both coated with demonsbane oil. You do know what that is, don't you?"

"No." Gabe had never heard of it.

Lindsay frowned. "Your father was a demon hunter and you don't know what demonsbane oil is?"

"He died when I was little. But he didn't talk about demon hunting much. He hated it."

"How do you feel about it?"

Gabe didn't even have to think about it. "I want to fight demons."

"Then that's what we'll train you to do. Your first lesson will be about demonsbane oil." Lord Lindsay moved into the center of the room. He gestured and an image of a dark, glossy-leaved plant appeared. Long reddish-brown spikes topped with light purple flowers rose from the mass. "This is demonsbane. It's a low-growing shade plant. You'll often find it under trees." He then explained the properties of the plant and how to use it.

"How do you know so much about demonsbane?"

"My best friend was a demon hunter. We trained together, and when we were old enough, we hunted them together as well."

Gabe reluctantly adjusted his image of the earl. He'd never met anyone besides his father who had hunted demons, and Lord Lindsay didn't even come from a demon hunting lineage.

"Now, let's see what you can do. I've heard you are very talented."

Gabe held out his hand. He knit his brows and concentrated. A flame appeared in his palm. Sweat broke out on his forehead as he tried to hold it, then it winked out. He looked up, pleased. That was the longest he'd ever held a flame.

Lord Lindsay had a slight frown. "You're holding back."

"No, I'm not. I tried my hardest." Anger heated his chest. How would the earl know how hard Gabe was trying? Didn't he see how long he'd held the flame?

"I know you tried, but you're not harnessing your energy properly. Here, let me show you." The earl held out his hand. White mist surrounded him, then slowly dissipated. He didn't look the least bit tired.

"Magic flows in your blood, but you have to call it forth. When you do, the streams thicken and grow."

He scowled. Just because he was a half-blood didn't mean he was completely ignorant. "I know that."

"Good. What do you do next? How did you make that flame?"

Gabe glared at him, then paced around the study. It was always easier for him to think when he was moving. "I pictured it in my mind, and then it appeared."

"I want you to try again, but this time, after the mage energy swells, picture it flowing down your arm into your hand, becoming fire when it reaches your palm." Lord Lindsay backed away from the center of the room. "Do you understand?"

"Yes, I do." It'd be impossible not to, the way the earl had explained it. Gabe moved in front of the fireplace. He'd show the magelord what he could do. His power rose in a flood. He imagined it rising and rushing down his arm into his hand—

An enormous fireball appeared in the center of the room.

Gabe jumped back. The acrid stink of burnt hair floated around him. He smoothed his finger over his brow bone. Soft hairs met his touch near the nose, then disappeared by his temples. His eyes widened in wonder. He'd singed half his eyebrows off. The earl was right. He'd been doing it wrong.

Lord Lindsay waved his hand and a mist enclosed the fireball. The flames shrank and disappeared. Steam filled the study.

Gabe stumbled to a chair by the wall. He was exhausted. The power that flowed out of him had taken every last bit of magic and energy he'd had.

Lord Lindsay opened the study door and told Deeds to have tea prepared immediately. He came over and squeezed Gabe's shoulder. "How do you feel, lad?"

"Empty and tired." He never knew he had to channel his power. No one had told him. He looked up at the earl with new respect.

"Food and drink will fix that. You did well. After tea, we'll work on controlling the flow of your magic. Unless you want to singe the rest of your hair off?"

Even though he hardly had the energy, Gabe grinned. He was learning magic from a mage who had hunted demons.

Maybe Regina made the right choice after all. And if not, he'd protect her. He'd learn everything he could, as fast as he could. Nobody would hurt his sister. Not magelords. Not demons. Gabriel had a heritage to embrace.

CHAPTER THIRTY

REGINA POPPED HER HEAD INTO the morning room, but didn't see Gabe. He often disappeared to the stables when upset. After Lord Lindsay had left yesterday, Gabe had spent the day with the horses. Aunt Agatha, on the other hand, had left the house dressed in her best "armor," as she'd called her outfit, to spread the news that rather than being ruined, her niece was now betrothed to a wealthy and titled magelord.

She'd fulfilled her quest and found a mage to train her brother in magic. What she hadn't expected was the earl's counteroffer—that she help him find the demon. Her hand paused on the doorknob as her heart raced. She could still see the yellow-eyed monster leaning over Lord Lindsay's prone form in the garden maze. Could she track it? If she couldn't, would the earl ask Gabriel to take her place? She couldn't let that happen. A demon was loose in London. She and Lindsay had to find it before it killed more people…or her brother decided to hunt it himself.

Sweat beaded on her palms and she wiped them

nervously against her dress. *Think about something else, something happy.* She was betrothed. Surely that counted as a benefit, even though it wasn't a love match?

The magic in her blood cracked open. She tried to stem the flood but couldn't. *Why now?* Power drenched her vision and the world went dark.

She stood in a small forest clearing, fir needles cushioning the ground below her feet. Her own dear Julian knelt on the ground before her, hands stretched out in supplication. "Lord knows I do not deserve such an honor, but I cannot bear to walk this life without you by my side. Dear heart, will you marry me?"

Love for this man who had suffered so much suffused her. He was the bravest man she had ever known, but even more, he loved her with all his heart. It didn't matter that he was only a second son. Marriage to him would not be a sacrifice. She placed her hands in his calloused ones as she knelt before him. "Yes. With all my heart, yes."

His eyes glowed a deep blue as his head lowered. Her lips parted and her eyes closed as she awaited the sweet heaven of his lips on hers...

"Lady Regina, is anything amiss?"

Her eyes snapped open, and she fell back a step, embarrassed. Their butler stood before her, his wrinkled face creased with concern. Heat flooded her cheeks as she pushed the vision of that almost kiss out of her mind. "I'm perfectly fine, Deeds, thank you. I was merely wondering where my brother is. Have you seen him?"

"Lord Lindsay is teaching Master Gabriel magic

in the study," Deeds said proudly.

"He is?" She hadn't expected him to start the training so soon. She hadn't told Gabe the earl agreed to train him, just in case the magelord didn't show.

"They've been in there since nine o'clock this morning."

Regina should have known the earl would keep his promise. He was determined to find the demon. She cracked open the study door and peered inside. All the furniture had been moved to the edges of the room. Her brother and the earl sat at the table by the window, where a very large tea had been prepared. Gabe's plate was piled high with food. Things must have gone well, or her brother wouldn't be devouring everything in sight.

"Good morning. May I join you?"

"Of course." Lord Lindsay pulled out a chair for her.

"Deeds said you were training my brother this morning. How did it go?"

Gabe's face broke out in a wide grin. "You should have seen it, Gina! I created an enormous fireball! Look—" He pointed at his dark-blond eyebrows, which were missing half their lengths— "I nearly burnt them off!"

"And that's a good thing?" She fought the urge to touch her own brows to make sure they were still there.

"Yes! I wasn't doing it properly before, which was why I could only make that tiny flame. Then Lord Lindsay showed me how to harness my power and next thing I knew my eyebrows were almost gone. It was smashing!"

"What else did you learn?"

"After that demonstration I thought it wise to work on controlling his power," Lindsay interjected. "But first we stopped for tea. Magic uses a lot of the body's energy."

"He's right. I could hardly move. After I ate, I felt better. And then when I had energy again I made balls of ice."

"So if I want a cool refreshing drink, all I have to do is come to you?" Regina asked.

"Yes," Gabe said happily, biting into a crumpet.

A warm glow spread in her chest. It didn't matter that she'd been ruined, seen in her underclothes by the mageborn elite, or chased by a demon. She'd found a mentor for her brother, and Gabe's excitement made each of those excruciating moments pale in comparison. She smiled at Lord Lindsay. "Thank you for coming today."

"It was my pleasure. The lad is a quick learner." Sunlight broke through the clouds, glinting on the silver table service. Lindsay glanced outside, where patches of blue rapidly filled the sky. "It looks like the rain has finally passed. Would you like to go for a carriage ride, Lady Regina?"

She met his gaze across the table. The earl had fulfilled his part of the bargain by showing up this morning to train Gabriel. Now it was time to uphold her end. "I'd love to," she lied.

"Then it's settled." Lindsay gestured to the footman and arranged to have his curricle brought to the front. "We'll go after tea."

Regina slid a sidelong glance at Gabe. A demon was on the loose, and monster hunting was in his blood. If she and Lindsay didn't find the demon, what would her brother do? Would he try to find it on his own? "Gabe, what are your plans for this afternoon?"

"I've been waiting to go riding for days. I'm going out as soon as I finish." He shoved a lemon cheesecake into his mouth. After he swallowed, he stood up and held out his hand to Lord Lindsay. "Thank you for training me this morning."

The earl rose and shook his hand. "It was my pleasure. I'll see you tomorrow?"

"Yes." The smile on Gabe's face warmed Regina's soul. If she ever had doubts, all she had to do was remember this moment. The expression on her brother's face made everything she'd done worthwhile.

When the curricle arrived, Regina climbed into the two-wheeled vehicle with Lord Lindsay's help. After he had taken his seat and picked up the reins, she asked, "Where are we going?"

"To the Allensworth estate. Since that's the last place we saw the demon, it'll be easiest to find its trail from there." The earl flicked the reins, and the horses leapt forward on the cobblestone street.

Regina gripped the side of the curricle. They were sitting so close to each other that his shoulder brushed hers and the white fabric of her dress slid over his thigh. Her breath caught in her throat at the intimacy, and her skin flushed as she remembered her earlier vision. The man had looked exactly like Lord Lindsay, except he'd been wearing a linen tunic and hose. Was it a true seeing, or had her magic somehow conjured up a romantic fantasy? She glanced up at him to see if he was affected by their closeness too, but the hard planes of his face remained unreadable. Annoyed at herself for being a ninny, she yanked her skirt back and slid away from him on the seat. "How do I track it?"

He turned to her, a slight frown on his face. "Your father never told you?"

The look in his eyes, as though Lord Harbrook had failed in his duty, stung. "Why would he? I didn't have magic, and Gabe was too young."

Lord Lindsay studied her intently for a few moments. She had a feeling he saw the hurt she'd always kept hidden from her aunt and brother. "To track the demon you need to picture it in its natural form. Then use your magic to search for it."

A breath whooshed out that she hadn't realized she was holding, and her shoulders slumped with relief. He wasn't going to pursue the topic of her father. She tightened her grip on the side of the curricle and then closed her eyes. She called up an image of the monster—its huge form blotting out the stars in the night sky, the sharp claws, and the feral yellow eyes that struck fear deep in her soul. "I see it."

"Now concentrate on your desire to find it."

Reluctance filled her, but a bargain was a bargain. Gold bubbles burst inside her veins. She directed her power at the picture in her mind. *Find the demon.*

She turned her head in different directions, searching for that sense of wrongness she'd felt in its presence. A vague disquiet filled her. The sensation reminded her of the time a neighbor's townhouse had been broken into but no one had had any idea until weeks afterward. She opened her eyes. "I think it has been in this area, but the impression is so faint I'm not sure."

"We'll try again once we reach the Allensworth grounds. The scent should still be strong enough for you to pick up."

Chills ran down her spine as she remembered fleeing the demon. She'd always been fast, but that night she had practically flown through the maze. Her demon hunting lineage had saved her life. "What happens if we find it?"

"I'll kill it." His voice was cold and determined.

"How? It almost killed you, and I barely escaped."

"Langley will join us at the estate. He'll help me."

"What if it defeats you both?"

"You're a gloomy one, aren't you? It won't." He maneuvered around several wagons as they reached the outskirts of the city. "But if it does, take the curricle. You do know how to drive?"

The years spent on her family's country estate had taught her many skills. "Yes."

"Good."

When she'd encountered him at the Prinsworth ball last year, he'd been a drunken brute. This London season, she'd barely seen him take a drop of liquor or lose control. He had definitely changed, and his confidence moved her to trust him. "How do you know so much about demon hunting?"

"My best friend was a demon hunter. We trained together and started hunting demons when we were your brother's age."

"I'm surprised you didn't ask Gabriel instead of me. He's more powerful than I am."

"Is he? How do you know?"

She opened her mouth to respond but swallowed her retort. She had to remember she was a witch now, not a magicless half-blood. What could she do if she had training and time? "I suppose I don't. I just assumed, because he has always been the one with power."

"Your brother has a lot to learn. I'm sure he could track the demon, but I don't trust him not to leap into a fight should we encounter it. You, at least, have the wisdom to run."

"Thanks, I think."

He grinned at her. "It was meant as a compliment."

"Of course, it was." Sarcasm dripped from her voice, but it only made his smile widen.

Although the road leading out of London was packed with carriages and wagons, it wasn't long before they reached the Allensworth residence. Hard to believe only a couple of nights ago she had fled the demon on these grounds. She shivered at the memory of its claws scraping her back. Sweat beaded on her brow.

One moment. That was all she would allow herself to acknowledge her fear. She took a deep breath and lifted her chin. Her family tree consisted of demon hunters going back centuries. No minion from hell was going to best her. She had a bargain to fulfill and a demon to find. If Lord Lindsay killed it, so much the better. Gabriel would be safe.

A large man on horseback waited in the shade beneath a large oak tree next to the road. Lord Lindsay slowed the curricle. "There's Lord Langley. We should be close enough for you to pick up the demon's path."

"I'll try again." A prickling sensation raced up her spine. She scanned the grounds, and a sense of wrongness washed over her. A strong tug pulled her gaze toward the maze. When she looked down the road past the estate, the pull eased, but when she looked east it strengthened. "I have its trail. It went that way."

She pointed back towards London.

Julian wanted to shout his triumph. She'd done it. Lady Regina had picked up the demon's trail.

I've got you now.

He waved at Langley to join them, then turned the curricle around in the shaded country lane. He had no doubts that between the two of them they could destroy the monster. He'd free Evelyn and his unborn child's souls from the demon's captivity, as well as all the others the fiend had taken. Jubilation pounded through his blood, and he had to rein himself in as tightly as he did the horses.

Lord Langley removed his hat when he reached them and executed a surprisingly elegant bow from atop his steed. "Good day, Lady Regina. Congratulations on your betrothal."

"Thank you, milord."

"The demon headed for London. As we'd hoped, Lady Regina is able to track it," Julian interjected. They were wasting time.

His cousin leaned on the pommel of his saddle as he examined her. "You're certain?"

"Yes. But it took a different path." Her brows furrowed in concentration as she gazed over the extended parkland of the Allensworth estate. "It seems to have traveled closer to the river."

Julian stared at the roadway they'd just traveled. She hadn't mentioned feeling the demon's presence along the way. Could she track it now that she had its scent? "That makes sense. There are trees along the river that could give it cover. If we travel back on this road, can you follow its trail?"

She wrinkled her nose. "You make me sound like a hound, but yes. At least for now."

"We'll do that then. Let us know if the trail weakens, then we'll move closer to its path."

"I will."

Langley guided his horse so that he rode alongside Lady Regina. Julian clenched his teeth against the flash of possessiveness that made him want to force Langley to ride behind them. He had to remind himself that their betrothal was a sham. Langley had every right to court her if he wanted. It was probably better that way. Julian couldn't marry the young woman, and no matter how much she reminded him of his wife, she wasn't Evelyn.

"Lady Regina, I find it interesting that you can track the demon, even without any magic. I'd had no idea the demon hunting lineage was so strong." Langley could have been discussing the weather with that mild tone.

Regina stiffened beside Julian. The wet clopping of the horses' hooves filled the silence. Would she tell Langley the truth?

"I'd rather you kept this to yourself, but I do have magic," she said.

"Then the rumors have greatly exaggerated your lack of ability."

Julian felt a twinge of anger. What was Langley getting at?

Some of the stiffness left her shoulders, and she sighed. "It's true I've never had magic. It's new."

"I see," Langley said. "When did you learn you had magic?"

She bowed her head over her hands as if confessing a sin. Who had made her ashamed of her lack of magic? And why was she keeping it a secret, instead of shouting her discovery from the rooftops?

"I'd always felt that I had magic and knew how to use it. But whenever I tried, nothing happened. Then a few weeks ago I had a vision. I was with my brother when it happened, but I didn't tell him." She raised her head and looked at Langley, then at Julian. "You two are the only ones I've told."

A vision. Evelyn had had visions too. Julian

forced words past the tightness in his throat. "What did you see?"

"A young red-headed lord riding on a horse, but his eyes were strange. They had yellow flames flickering in them, just like the demon's."

Julian met Langley's gaze over her head. The young man had to be Lord Higginbotham. The timing of her vision coincided with the fiend's arrival in this time period. Were the two incidents connected? Regina's honey-gold hair and soft curves reminded him so much of Evelyn. What if he was wrong and the demon hadn't taken Evelyn's soul? Could Regina be Evelyn reincarnated?

Hope flared for a second, and then he squashed it. Even if she were Evelyn reincarnated, it didn't change anything. There was no way to prove she was Evelyn, so he had to kill the demon regardless. But most importantly, Regina clearly didn't know who he was. If she had no memories of her past life, she wasn't his Evelyn. She was only Regina.

Julian squeezed the reins in his grip. Now who was the gloomy one? He turned his gaze back to the muddy road, away from the woman who reminded him of a time that was lost to him.

A few minutes later, Langley spoke again. He was like a dog worrying at a bone, Julian thought sourly. "Why haven't you told anyone about your magic?"

Odd that she hadn't. Gabriel and her aunt would be happy for her.

She looked straight ahead, not meeting either of their eyes, then turned back to them. "What if the magic goes away as quickly as it came? I don't want to get their hopes up, until I know for sure it won't disappear."

"Is that possible?" Langley asked Julian.

Julian shook his head. "I don't think so, but it doesn't make sense that she didn't have magic before and suddenly does now. Did something happen?"

"No, nothing. Just that vision one afternoon." She answered absently as she stared towards the river, her attention obviously focused on tracking the demon.

"Hmm." Langley said. "It sounds to me like you've always had magic, but that it's been blocked. I'll look into it. Maybe that's happened before."

"You won't tell anyone that it's me?"

He bowed from his chestnut steed. "You may trust me, milady. I'm the soul of discretion."

Lady Regina's lips curved into a tremulous smile at Langley's words. "Thank you."

Jealousy ate at Julian's heart. "You could attend my lessons with Gabe. You could tell him you're simply there to observe, and practice later on your own."

The smile she gave him was so radiant, Julian felt a momentary pang that he had no intention of marrying her. "Thank you. I might do that."

"Lessons? What lessons?" Langley asked.

"Lord Lindsay is instructing my younger brother in magic."

"He is? Funny you forgot to mention that, cousin." Langley's gaze narrowed as he looked at Julian, then Lady Regina. It was clear Langley didn't appreciate Julian's omission.

"You disapprove?" Lady Regina's voice was sharp. She looked like a hen ready to fight for her chick.

"Not at all," Langley soothed. "I'm merely surprised he's taking on new obligations, considering his other responsibilities."

"I didn't have a chance to tell you, but I knew you'd approve." Lies. All lies. He'd known Langley wouldn't approve—not because Gabriel was a half-blood, but because Julian wasn't the real earl. He was an impostor, and he was going to break this betrothal as soon as they killed the demon. Building ties with Lady Regina and her younger brother was only going to make that situation worse. He'd explain his bargain with Lady Regina later.

"Lord Lindsay agreed to train my brother in exchange for my help tracking the demon. That was the price I demanded."

Or not, since she'd done it for him.

Langley examined them both. Julian shrugged. It was a small price to pay, and truth be told, he enjoyed teaching her brother. "I offer you my congratulations once again, milady." Langley tipped his hat. "Apparently you are a shrewd negotiator."

She laughed, and the moment was smoothed over.

When they reached London, Lady Regina directed them towards the wharves. She led them to a dock bustling with activity, as heavy-set workers and loose-limbed sailors loaded and off-loaded cargo. "It was here. I know that much." She glanced up and down the river Thames. "I can't tell where it went though. The scent is muddied and faint now."

Julian had a memory of standing on a riverbank with Harbrook, who stared in frustration at the swollen river flowing past them. "It must have boarded a boat or entered the water."

"You're telling me I can't track it across water? Or on it?"

"Water constantly shifts, so the trail gets washed away or overlaid by other scents." Julian and Harbrook had tracked a demon for several days, only to lose its trail at a riverbank. It had taken a week to pick up the trail again.

"So now what, cuz?" asked Langley.

"We find the place it came ashore."

the river several times and traveled by boat to this estate. He was as safe as he could be for the moment.

His skin writhed and his fangs retracted into his gums. He had to get the new souls under control. If all went well, he'd only lose a week.

Then he'd kill the witch.

CHAPTER THIRTY-TWO

"LADY REGINA," A PRETTY YOUNG debutante in her second season looked up at her, "is it true the Earl of Lindsay asked for your hand in marriage?"

Regina looked across the ballroom at Lord Lindsay, who stood talking with his cousin. He turned for a moment and their eyes met. She felt a flush creep up her cheeks. She turned back to Miss Hardy, who raised a hand to her mouth and tittered when she saw the earl's gaze on their group.

"Actually—"

"I heard Lord Carlisle threatened to challenge him to a duel if he didn't propose," another young lady interrupted.

"A duel? Was Lord Carlisle in love with Lady Regina too?" gasped another young miss. Her question triggered a spate of chatter and laughter as they explained that Lord Carlisle was Regina's uncle.

Regina stared at the eager faces of the young women surrounding her. Less than a month ago, these women had turned their backs to her, laughing while Lady Coraline ridiculed her human blood. But now that she was betrothed to Lord Lindsay, they chatted with her as if she were a long-lost friend. She felt odd. As if she had stepped into Lady Felicity's life. Was this what it was like to be accepted?

Her mother's voice popped into her head with another of her sayings. *They feed on gossip. Never do anything to catch their attention.*

Too late.

Lady Coraline approached with her closest friend, Lady Agnes. Lady Coraline shot daggers at Regina, though her small lips were pursed in a tight smile.

"I hardly think the Earl of Lindsay would be here tonight if he were going to a duel tomorrow." She smirked as she glided up to their group.

"Lady Coraline." Regina pasted on a smile as fake as the one that graced Lady Coraline's face.

"Lady Regina, pray tell, are the rumors true?"

"Rumors?"

"Yes." Her smile grew larger and so sweet Regina's teeth ached seeing it. "They say a half-blood enticed the Earl of Lindsay into a garden maze. And that when she left, she was missing her dress."

Her mouth pursed in triumph as the young ladies gasped at the juicy on-dit.

Regina fought to calm her racing pulse. Of course, it wasn't a secret. The wonder would have been had they not heard the news. That was why she and Lord Lindsay had attended tonight's ball— to announce their betrothal and end the gossip about her ruination. She took a deep breath. "You do know what they say about rumors?"

They shook their heads.

"They're only as good as their messenger." She met Lady Coraline's narrowed gaze with an icy stare of her own. "But the truth is the Earl of Lindsay did ask for my hand in marriage, and I said yes. Now, if you'll excuse me, I promised the next dance to my betrothed." She turned on her heel, head held high.

Lord Lindsay crossed the ballroom towards her, an expression of concern on his face. "Is everything all right?"

She grimaced. "Yes. But I think I'd rather be chased by the demon in the maze than face the false friendliness of that group."

He scowled at the gaggle of young women who were tittering behind their fans, and the ladies fell quiet and backed away. He grinned down at her. "Given the choice, I'd choose the demon as well."

"Hmm. You did rather leave me to their tender mercies. I never took you for a coward."

"One of the hallmarks of a good soldier is to know when to retreat." Dancers formed sets for the quadrille. He extended his arm. "Lady Regina, may I have this dance?"

"It would be my pleasure, my lord."

They took their places in the middle of the dance floor. Lord Lindsay executed an elegant bow. She curtsied, her eyes downcast. As she rose up, she saw his gaze upon her. The corners of his lips turned downward, and his features were drawn in an expression of pain. Her heart fluttered in her chest at the intense sadness she saw.

"Have I done something wrong, milord?" Why did he look so troubled whenever he gazed at her?

"No. It's just—you reminded me of someone from my past."

His wife? Or someone else?

The orchestra played the first bars of a lively tune, and the chance for talk was over. They joined hands with Lady Quimby, Lord Holmes, Baron Knightley, and Lady Tarbrooke, the others in their dance set. All of them smiled pleasantly at her as they engaged in the dance, and Regina marveled at the change her betrothal had made to her status. Of course, Lady Quimby had always been kind to her, but she doubted she would have been as well received had she not been engaged to the powerful Earl of Lindsay.

Her mind wandered back to the events of that afternoon. The demon had left a trail, and she'd actually been able to follow it to the wharves of London. They had searched along the docks for a while, but she hadn't found any trace of the creature. Aunt Agatha had insisted on their attending tonight's ball as a betrothed couple. Lindsay hoped that the demon would show as well, but so far, Regina hadn't had any hint of its presence.

The dance separated her from the earl, and they moved into different sets. Baron Knightley engulfed her hands with his beefy fists, his grip firm. The innocuous face of the portly middle-aged gentleman reminded her of Lord Falsworth, and her power surged as darkness flooded her sight.

"Drink."

A tall, hawk-nosed man stood in front of her. She knew him, although she didn't know how. She reached out to take the flask he held out to her.

"No! Don't drink it!" Regina shouted in her vision.

"Thank you," she said as she took the flask. She swallowed the mead. Warmth and a delicious languor spread through her body. Her vision wavered as the man before her changed. His face elongated into a snout and rough hide replaced his human skin. The demon! She tried to move, but her limbs didn't respond. Her heart raced as she realized she'd been drugged. Eyes of flickering yellow flame scrutinized her as she lost consciousness.

"Lady Regina!"

The ballroom came into focus as the darkness drained from Regina's view. Baron Knightley frowned with concern, and she heard him call her name again. She whispered, "I'm sorry, but I must sit down. Please excuse me."

She stumbled off the dance floor, her heart still racing with fear. The demon had been in her vision of the past. Why? How were they connected?

◆

Julian excused himself and followed Lady Regina through the crowd. She weaved on her feet, then slipped through a heavy oak door to the right of the ballroom. What happened? Why had she fled in the middle of the dance?

He went through the door and entered a wide

hallway. Candelabra flickered on tables, but he didn't see Lady Regina. She hadn't been so far ahead of him that she could have reached the far exit. He strode to the first room on his right. A fire burned low in the grate, and dark oak wainscoting and rich blue velvet curtains gave the library a cozy feel. Lady Regina sat on the damask couch stretched before the fireplace, her fingers lightly picking at the arm cover as she stared into the fire. The crackle of burning logs filled the air.

Julian closed the door so they wouldn't be disturbed. "Lady Regina."

She looked up at him, and her face was pale. "Yes?"

"You left the ballroom rather quickly. Was the baron rude to you? Shall I call him out?"

"What?" She straightened up and gave a startled laugh. "No, nothing of the sort. I had a vision of the demon, and I needed to sit down."

Tension instantly filled his muscles. "Is he here?"

She shook her head. "No. My vision seemed to be from the past. I saw him handing a flask to a woman. The liquid was drugged. After she drank, he changed into his true form."

Julian's throat tightened. Was her vision of Evelyn? Was that how Kikson had subdued her? "What did the woman look like?"

Her gaze flicked down and she smoothed her skirt. "I didn't get a good look at her. My vision focused on the demon and his transformation. Then it ended."

"Why would you have a vision of his past?" It

seemed odd that she wouldn't see what the monster was doing now. He dropped down onto the couch beside her.

"I don't know. Maybe because I was thinking about Lord Falsworth and his transformation, and so my sight showed me another transformation of his?"

"Perhaps." Who knew why the sight chose what it did? Although Evelyn had been able to control some of her visions, she'd had others that she'd also had difficulty explaining. "Have you had any hint of where the demon is now?"

"None." She sighed and leaned back against the seat cushion. "To be honest, I'm surprised. I expected him to be here, since he's been at the other mageborn balls."

"We'll ride out tomorrow. Maybe you can pick up his trail."

Her eyes clouded as she looked up at him. "Do you think we should tell the Mage High Council about him? The mageborn need to be warned."

"Do you think they will believe you?" The Chancellor had dismissed her when she'd said Lord Pratchett's soul was missing, and the mageborn had scoffed when she'd said there was a demon in the maze. Because she was a half-blood, nobody could see past their prejudices to the truths she spoke.

She closed her eyes briefly, and when she spoke again her voice was resigned. "No. Probably not."

He hated the look of defeat that tugged her lips downward. He took her hand in his, lightly stroking the back with his thumb. "With your help, we'll

find the demon. He won't stalk London much longer."

Doubt filled her eyes. "I lost his trail at the
wharves. What if he left London?"

Julian acknowledged the thought, but refused
to worry about it until they needed to address it.
"We'll cross that bridge when we come to it."

The logs cracked and sparks flared. "My father
could track demons across country. I suppose I
could too, once I learned how."

He smiled at her determination. "Of course
you can. But hopefully it won't come to that." He
released her and stood up. "We should return to
the ballroom before we're missed."

"I suppose you're right. Although now that
we're betrothed the scandal wouldn't be quite as
great." Her head tilted back as she looked up at
him, exposing the beautiful line of her throat. His
hand trembled slightly as he extended it to her. She
moved hers until it hovered above his, almost—but
not quite—touching. Tension strung through him.
Even though there was no contact, he could feel
the powerful attraction vibrating between their
palms.

She laid her hand on his. He drew her up, but
didn't step away to give her more room. Mere
inches separated them, and the smell of lilacs
wrapped itself around his senses. Her green eyes
were wide, the pupils dilated. The firelight flickered, casting a warm glow over her skin. As his gaze
searched her features, the pain he'd carried in his
heart for weeks eased.

Regina.

He lowered his head and claimed her mouth. His lips moved gently over hers, coaxing her to open beneath his caress. She kissed him back, tentatively at first, then more passionately as their kiss deepened. Her arms slid around his back, and the weight of her body against his felt right in a way nothing else in this time had. As if he'd finally come home.

The door to the library creaked open, and they sprang apart. Regina smiled at Julian, her eyes shining.

A maidservant bobbed her head and eased her way into the room. "Pardon me, milord and milady. I came to stoke the fire."

"Please do," Julian said. He walked around the couch and headed for the door. "We were just leaving."

Regina slipped behind him, and her eyes glowed with a new softness as she looked at him. He smiled and pulled her hand into the crook of his arm. And then it hit him.

He had no right to kiss her. He was an impostor.

CHAPTER THIRTY-THREE

FRUSTRATION GNAWED AT JULIAN AS yet again they failed to find any trace of the demon. The three of them—he and Regina in the curricle, Langley accompanying them on horseback—had ridden up and down the Thames for the past week in search of the demon's trail. Today they'd gone as far they could into the countryside and still return before dusk. Since they were near Langley's country house, they stopped to regroup before heading back to London.

They sat in Langley's study, a secluded room with dark oak wainscoting. Although it was midday, the heavy green curtains were drawn closed, and a fire burned low in the slate fireplace. Instead of opening the curtains, a maid came in and lit some lamps. The crackle of burning logs filled the silence.

Regina leaned on the arm of a green and gold striped couch, her chin propped on her palm. She stared into the flames of the fireplace, as Julian and Langley dropped into wingback chairs.

After the maid exited the room and closed the door, Langley said, "My staff knows I like my privacy, so they keep the curtains closed."

Regina nodded and seemed to accept his statement at face value, but the experienced soldier in Julian wondered if there was more to it than that. On their hunts for the demon, Langley had shown himself familiar with the seedier parts of London. Did his cousin have enemies who he worried would spy on him when he was home? What did Langley do when he wasn't chaperoning Julian?

Julian knew his cousin well enough to know he wouldn't get any answers, only evasions. So instead he addressed the issue at hand. "Searching London and its environs has failed to turn up any sign of the demon. We have to try something else."

"What do you suggest?" Langley asked.

"Lady Regina is a seer. Maybe she could scry for the demon's whereabouts."

"What?" She jerked up straight. "I don't know how to do that."

"Scrying uses water to summon visions. Since you already have this gift, you should be able to scry as well."

"I've never actually summoned the visions. They come on their own. However, I'll try. Anything would be better than another day riding around London."

Langley went to the door and asked for a shallow basin of water to be brought. Julian saw the footman hand him a note. Langley frowned as he read. "I have to leave."

"What's going on?" Julian asked.

"Lady Marleigh has requested my presence. She

says Lady Felicity is ill." Langley folded the note and tucked it inside his jacket. "You two stay here and see if you can determine the location of the demon. I'll tell my staff you are not to be disturbed."

Scrying required quiet, so it made sense for them to be left alone. But as Julian gazed at the way the warm firelight turned Regina's hair to gold, he wished Langley had phrased his words differently. Memories of the kiss he and Regina had shared flooded his mind. "If she succeeds in finding the demon's location, I'll send a message to your town-house."

"And please convey our best wishes to Lady Marleigh. We hope Felicity will soon be well," Regina said.

"I'll pass along your regards and await your word. Good luck, milady." Langley left the room as a footman entered with a large silver bowl and a pitcher of water.

"Place them on the reading table," Julian said. He grabbed a couple of candles and placed them on either side of the basin. "Please have a seat."

She took her place at the table, and he pushed in her chair. The footman lit the candles, then closed the door. Julian and Regina were alone. The scent of lilacs that followed her everywhere lingered in the air, and he fought the urge to touch the smooth skin of her shoulder.

"What should I do next?" she asked.

He dragged his thoughts back to the scrying. "Pour the water into the basin until you have a shallow pool. Place your hands on either side of the bowl and look into the water. Then call forth your magic and ask it to show you the demon."

"That sounds simple enough." She followed his instructions. "Can I talk?"

"It's better to wait until you're done. You need to focus on calling up a vision, and talking could break your concentration."

Her hands gripped the sides of the basin. "What do you have to show me?" she whispered.

Julian settled into the wingback chair, where he could watch her. Would she be able to see the demon? What else might her scrying show her? Evelyn had been skilled at calling up visions, but even she couldn't always control what her magic showed her…if it chose to show anything at all.

His brows furrowed. The demon had gone underground. Did it know Regina could track it? Or had it disappeared for another reason? Hopefully she'd be able to spy the demon's location, and they could get back to the hunt. And afterward? There was no going back to his time. Perhaps he should start thinking about a future here.

Regina continued to stare into the water. Her green eyes darkened in the flickering candlelight. Julian slowly eased forward to be sure. Her irises had turned completely black. A vision, then.

She sighed and released the silver bowl. When she looked up, her eyes had returned to their normal color.

"What did you see?"

"First I saw an elegantly-appointed bedroom, and then the demon appeared. He looked strange.

His features kept shifting—sometimes human, sometimes monster—but they never settled long enough for me to get a good look at any of them."

"Could you tell where he's staying?"

"Not really. I know he's on an estate by a river, because I could see the water in the distance when he looked out the window. But I have no idea which estate, nor which river. However, I think it might be near or inside London."

"Why?"

"I had another vision, this time of the future. I saw my Aunt Agatha and Lord Langley in our box at the opera house. I didn't see the demon, but I had a strong sense of his presence."

"You're sure this is of the future?"

She nodded and leaned back in her chair. "Yes. Langley has never attended the opera with us. My aunt and I have tickets to the show three days from now. I'm guessing that is when the demon will show up. I don't suppose you would care to join us?"

He bowed over her hand. "It would be my pleasure to attend the opera with you and your aunt."

"The honor is all mine, milord." Her green eyes were soft and vulnerable.

The moment in the library burned in his chest, and even though he knew he shouldn't, he couldn't resist the connection they shared. He knelt beside her chair. "I have no right to you."

She leaned forward and cupped his jaw in her slender fingers. "You're my betrothed. You have every right." And then she kissed him.

When her lips met his, the ache in his heart disappeared. Impostor or not, he gave into his craving for her.

Regina.

———————

Regina stroked Julian's jaw, the light stubble making her fingertips tingle. They hadn't kissed since the ball, and she'd been yearning for a moment alone with him. His lips were full and smooth beneath hers, his mouth caressing. He let her take the lead, and her heart pounded so hard it thundered in her ears. His kiss was like the brandy she'd snuck a taste of once. Hot and fiery, it burned a trail down her throat and warmed her in secret places.

She licked his lower lip and gently closed her teeth on it. He growled in response and his arms wrapped around her, pulling her deep into his embrace. His tongue delved into her mouth and she gasped at the sweet pleasure.

When she'd embarked on her plan to find a mentor for Gabriel, she'd never dared hope that the magelord she found would be someone she could be happy with. Yet Lord Lindsay was all of that and more. He treated her as an equal, even though she was a half-blood, and when he touched her, her body flamed so hot she thought her magic would burst free and set them both on fire.

He picked her up and carried her to the sofa. He stretched alongside her, and his mouth trailed down her neck, lingering on a sensitive spot she didn't know she had. She drew in a shaky breath.

"Julian," she begged.

He gave her a wicked smile. "So, a few kisses and suddenly I'm Julian, not Lindsay?"

"You beast." She laughed and slid her fingers into the thick waves of his hair. "Maybe you should kiss me more, or I might go back to calling you Lindsay."

He obliged, and his hand cupped her waist, then slowly caressed her ribcage. Her breasts ached for his touch. As if he'd read her mind, he dipped his head until she could feel the warmth of his breath just above the neckline of her dress. She arched her back, pushing her breasts upward, imagining his calloused hands stroking her tender flesh.

He lifted his head to stare deep into her eyes. His cheeks were flushed dark with desire. "Do you want me to stop?" His voice was husky.

Her mouth went dry and she licked her lips. She shook her head. "No."

He bent his head. Liquid fire surrounded her as he took her nipple in his mouth through her layered clothing. Her breath caught in her throat as an ache built down low. She needed more. She craved his touch, needed to feel his skin against hers. She reached up and slowly unlaced the bodice of her dress. He lifted up on one arm, his heated gaze following every movement. She pulled her stays down. Warmth flooded her cheeks as she exposed the smooth swell of her breasts.

"Touch me." She grabbed his wrist and pulled him towards her.

His hands gently cupped her breasts, shaping them so he could better pull her nipple into his mouth. Regina moaned and swallowed hard. The rough feel of his calloused palms as he alternately caressed and laved her nipples made her arch deeper into his hold.

He raised his body and slid higher up against her. He captured her mouth once more. His arousal pressed against her through their many layers of clothes. She widened her legs to allow him greater access, her dress pulling tight across her thighs. He rocked forward and she moaned at the intimate contact. She wanted more. *Needed more.*

She raised her hips to meet his long thrusts, and he moaned against her neck. Her breaths quickened as he stroked the most sensitive part of her with his plunging length. It didn't matter that they were still fully clothed. The sensation was exquisite. Her fingers tangled in his hair. His mouth slid to the side of her neck, where his tongue licked the sensitive skin. She rocked harder against him, aching for release from the pressure building inside her. His mouth closed on the side of her neck and lightly nipped. Her fingers dug into his back as wave after wave of liquid heat pummeled her.

He groaned and laid his head alongside hers. She could feel the coiled tension in his back. He brushed a kiss on her shoulder, and a knot eased inside her heart at the sweet gesture. She lay boneless beneath him, her body so relaxed and content it took effort to raise her hand to softly caress his hair.

He rose up on his elbow and lowered his head. His lips landed gently and she closed her eyes, savoring the rich warmth and taste of his mouth. A light touch skimmed her nipple, and her body jerked with pleasure. Then she felt his lean fingers pulling the fabric of her stays back over her breasts.

He sat by her feet and leaned forward, his broad hands dangling between his knees. She could see his arousal jutting against his breeches and wondered what it would feel like to touch him there.

He caught her glance and gave a shaky laugh. "Don't look at me like that."

She smiled at the slightly hoarse tones, knowing that she was the cause.

"We can't linger here much longer, or betrothed or not, we'll cause a scandal that will put our last one to shame."

"Didn't Langley say his servants were the soul of discretion?" She teased.

"Don't tempt me." He groaned.

She blushed, but quickly laced her stays and adjusted her dress, until she was satisfied her clothing had been put to rights and no one would guess what she'd done. She reached up to check her hair and caught him watching her.

"You're the most beautiful woman I've ever known." The words seemed to drag out of him, unbidden. The air reverberated between them. The crackle of the fireplace roared loud in her ears as their gazes locked.

She almost asked him if she was more beautiful than his wife, but shoved that niggling jealousy away. His wife was dead, and Regina was his betrothed.

"Thank you," she said, and meant it.

CHAPTER THIRTY-FOUR

JULIAN SLOWLY CLIMBED THE STEPS to the Harbrook townhouse, his emotions in turmoil. Images of Regina lying on the damask sofa, her creamy skin exposed to his hungry gaze, burned in his mind. Even though he had no right to kiss her, he hadn't been able to resist. He couldn't help thinking of her as his betrothed. After all, he—not the real Earl of Lindsay—had asked for her hand in marriage.

However, his life in this time period was built on a lie. He hid behind a name and title that were not his own, nor did he possess any funds of his own. Even if he wanted to, he had nothing to offer her.

He knocked at the large front door. The butler, Deeds, was familiar with the routine. As always, he led Julian to the study, where Gabriel paced before the massive oak desk.

"Lord Lindsay!"

Julian smiled at his young protégé. Gabriel was an apt pupil and he enjoyed training the young lad. The boy's raw talent reminded him of Harbrook's as a youth. It seemed Harbrook's line had run true down the centuries.

"Good morning, Gabe. Did you practice yesterday's lesson?"

"I did. Watch."

Gabriel moved to the center of the room. The air turned dense with power, like before the strike of a lightning storm. The boy's magic dropped from his fingers in long misty blue threads to coil on the brown and red Turkish carpet.

"Very good. Now thicken the strands. Once it's solid, form a loop and toss it around me—without using your hands. Let's see how well you can control your magic."

The youth's rawboned body tensed with effort. The semi-transparent length swayed in the air, a cobra dancing from its coiled base. When the rope reached Julian's shoulder, it weaved and thinned like rising smoke.

"Concentrate. Gather more magic to maintain it if you have to. Don't let it disappear."

Gabriel's outstretched arm shook, but the mist solidified. He formed a circle from the misty cord and raised his gaze. The lengths wavered but remained solid. Pride warmed Julian's chest. His student had learned to split his attention. The loop flipped over Julian's head.

"Tighten it and trap me." Thin cord wrapped around Julian's rib cage. "I'm going to try to escape. Stand firm and don't release your magic."

Julian inhaled sharply and rolled his shoulders to try to dislodge his binding. At first the rope slackened, but Gabriel regained control and drew it taut.

Julian grabbed the cord with both hands and yanked. Gabriel stumbled across the carpet. "What can you do to make me let go?"

Gabriel's narrow jaw worked. "I don't want to hurt you."

"Don't worry about me, lad. I'll manage."

The mystic cord flared red, searing Julian's hands, and he released it. "My lord!" The rope thinned and dissolved. Gabriel rushed over. "Your hands. Were they burnt?"

Julian turned them over. His palms and fingers were reddened and had a couple of scorch marks, but nothing more. Thick calluses had protected him from the worst of the heat. "They're fine. You did well." He clapped the young man on his back. When Gabriel continued staring at his hands. Julian arched a brow in question. "Do you doubt me?"

"No." He raised his own hands and turned them over. The fingertips and palms were pale and smooth. "I've never seen a gentleman with so many calluses on his hands. How did you develop them?"

Julian stared at his roughened palms. *Years of fighting.* "Hard work. Lots of it."

Gabriel's entire body quivered in the aftermath of expending his magic. His face was wan.

"Let's take a break."

Gabriel collapsed into a tufted leather chair in front of the desk.

Julian opened the study door. "Deeds."

The butler came swiftly and executed a slight bow. "Already taken care of, my lord. The tea will be here shortly."

The entire household had become accustomed to the new routine. Julian arrived every morning at nine, he and Gabriel worked magic for an hour, had tea, then continued until noon. "Thank you."

He returned to the room and took the winged chair across from Gabriel. "You've made progress since we began."

"Only because you've been willing to train me."

A soft knock sounded on the door, and a maid wheeled the tea service in on a cart. Julian selected an assortment of sandwiches, while Gabriel grabbed every lemon cake he could find and piled them high on his plate. He reclined back against the seat, legs extended in front of him. He munched happily on the sweet dessert.

"If you don't mind me asking, how did your father die?"

Gabriel's happy expression faded as he swallowed the rest of his cake. "He died from a demon's wounds. But he killed it first. When I'm old enough, I'm going to be a demon hunter, too."

"You're not scared?"

The young man's jaw firmed, and he looked as stubborn and determined as his sister. "No. Demon hunting is my heritage and duty. Now that you're here, I'll finally have the training I need."

"I'll do my best. Who trained your father?"

"My grandfather. But he's gone."

"There must be someone else."

The boy shrugged. "I don't know of anyone."

Julian couldn't understand that. Gabriel was one

of the most talented mages he'd ever seen. He could perform magic feats at the tender age of sixteen that men twice his age had difficulty with. "You're very talented. Are there so many demon hunters that they can afford to let one go untrained?"

Gabriel slouched further in his seat. "I don't know of any demon hunters now that my father is gone." The young mage bursting with power disappeared, replaced by a lost and vulnerable-looking boy. "But even if there were, nobody would train me because I'm half-human."

Julian didn't have the special abilities that demon hunters had—the lightning speed, enhanced reflexes and power—but he'd hunted demons with Harbrook. He could teach Gabriel everything he needed to know. "Eat up. We have work to do."

Gabe's face lit up. He smiled and shoved a crumpet into his mouth.

———◆———

Regina awoke in the soft cushions of her mattress, her nightdress twisted around her legs. The mid-morning sunlight streamed in between the bed curtains, falling across her stomach in long rectangles. She rolled over, throwing an arm across a pillow and pulling it close.

She'd slept poorly the whole night long. Sometimes she'd dreamt of the demon's shifting features as it had appeared in her scrying. Other times a hawk-nosed man handed her a cup of mead. When she sipped from it, he transformed into a monster with yellow-flamed pupils. She shuddered and pushed her face into the pillow.

She pictured Lord Lindsay instead, and the disturbing images of the demon evaporated like smoke in a strong wind. Last night she'd lain in bed, replaying the things they'd done in Langley's study. Julian was the first man she'd wanted to kiss. The first man to ever touch her. She should feel ashamed of her wantonness, but she didn't. He was her betrothed.

She rolled onto her back and closed her eyes. Her breathing deepened as she remembered the rough caress of his calloused hands. She pictured him seated on the couch, the evidence of his arousal plain to see. Her palms dampened with desire. She wished she'd had the courage to touch him last night.

The door to her bedroom squeaked open. Her heart dropped a beat and she froze, feeling like a child caught doing something wrong. Embarrassment flooded her at the familiar tread of her maid on the carpet.

Soft pops and cracks filled the air as the maid added a log to the fireplace and stirred the coals until the fire caught. Footsteps approached the bed and she slid deeper under the thick blanket. When her maid pulled the bed curtains back, Regina's breathing had calmed to nearly normal rhythms.

"Good morning, milady."

"Good morning, Bess. Is my aunt awake yet?" Her cheeks still flushed. Could the maid see it and perhaps guess the cause? Her face burned hotter. She turned so that her hair cascaded forward, masking her face.

Bess walked to the window and pulled the curtains back. "No, miss, she's not. But your brother is. He's in the study with the Earl of Lindsay."

"Lord Lindsay?" she answered so quickly that Bess looked taken aback.

"He's been here every day this week."

"Yes, I knew that." She shook her head. "We got home so late yesterday evening that for some reason I didn't think he'd come for Gabriel's lesson."

"Well, he did, milady. The young lord was mighty pleased to see him."

A different kind of warmth filled her. Even after their long day, he still kept his promise to instruct her brother.

Regina dressed, then went downstairs, where Deeds stood polishing the silver. "Deeds, where is my brother?"

"He's in the study with the Earl of Lindsay, but I wouldn't recommend going in there."

She paused with her hand on the doorknob. "Why not?"

"They're working magic. Things don't always go as they should. It isn't safe."

She understood what he didn't say. It wasn't safe for someone without magic to protect them. She did have power now, but it was still her secret. "I shall keep that in mind. Thank you for the warning."

She cracked the door to glance inside. Caution being the better part of valor and whatnot.

Gabriel's laughter filled her ears. There was a

large thump, and then Lord Lindsay said, "Excellent!"

She opened the door wider and found Julian sitting on the floor. A thin blue rope wrapped around his legs dissolved as she watched. Her brother sat on the edge of their father's desk behind the earl.

"Gabe, did you make that rope?"

"I did." He shot her a wide grin. He jumped off the desk and leaned over to give Lord Lindsay a hand up.

Lord Lindsay was twice Gabe's size, but he didn't hesitate to take her brother's hand.

"Can you show me what you did? What was that thump I heard?"

Gabe snatched a cucumber-watercress sandwich off a tray and took a bite. He looked at Lord Lindsay, who leaned against the desk with his arms crossed. "Go ahead," the earl said.

She didn't trust that mischievous glint in Lindsay's eyes, but she wanted to see her brother utilize his magic. She'd missed most of their lessons, because she hadn't wanted to be a distraction. But today—she was honest enough to admit that she wanted to see Julian.

Gabe rushed to the center of the rug before the desk. "Stand right here."

She joined him on the carpet. "I'm here. Now what?"

"Don't move." He frowned in concentration and raised his hand before him, palm down. Blue specks of magic streamed from his fingers and coiled in the air.

He shifted his stance as if bracing against an unseen force. Air hissed from between his clenched teeth. His hand was steady though, as the blue mist solidified into a lengthy rope.

He whipped his hand in the air and the rope flew above her head. The coils quickly bound her from her chest to her ankles.

Then her brother jerked his hand and her feet went flying out from under her. "Gabe!" she shouted as she fell.

Lord Lindsay caught her before she could hit the floor.

Gabe waved his hand and the rope, which had felt so real a second ago, dissolved into a blue mist. He doubled over laughing.

Lord Lindsay helped Regina straighten up. His hands lingered for a moment, and her mind flashed to the last time she'd been in his arms.

"Is this how you ended up on the floor?" She asked, raising her brows.

"Yes."

"I suppose I should be grateful you were here to catch me," she said.

Julian grinned, looking more relaxed than she'd ever seen him.

"Next time, I think I'll skip observing your lesson, Gabe."

Her brother laughed harder. He was learning magic and working pranks with it. She couldn't remember the last time she'd seen him so happy.

She smiled at Julian and Gabe as tears welled in her eyes. The hunt for the demon wasn't over, but today was a wonderful day.

CHAPTER THIRTY-FIVE

LADY FELICITY WAS DEATHLY ILL. Instead of recovering as Langley had hoped, her health had worsened. Regina stared out the carriage window at the sodden London streets, her mood as bleak as the weather. Rain poured down, turning the buildings and people into a dreary blur. Aunt Agatha sat opposite, her delicate features pinched with worry. They were on their way to Lady Marleigh's townhouse. A footman had delivered a message that afternoon. Aunt Agatha immediately sent for a carriage upon reading it.

"What did Lady Marleigh say in her note?"

"Merely that Felicity had been involved in a boating accident and fallen into the Thames. And to please come, since her dear daughter was lying at death's door." Aunt Agatha's lips trembled, and she dabbed at her eyes with a handkerchief. "Lady Marleigh has been my bosom friend since childhood. I hope we arrive in time."

"I'm sure we will." Regina squeezed her aunt's hand, trying to offer some comfort despite her own fears. She didn't know Felicity well, but the young woman had always been kind whenever they'd met.

When they reached the Marleigh residence, Aunt Agatha rushed inside. The butler asked them to wait in the front parlour. Despite the delicate green and cream decor and the fire burning in the grate, the room had a mournful air. It was the awful quiet. That same hush had permeated the house when Regina's father had been on his deathbed.

Lady Marleigh entered the parlour. She wore a white morning dress and a delicate cap covered her faded red hair. Dark circles shadowed her eyes.

"Oh, Elaine." Aunt Agatha threw her arms around her friend in a tight hug. "How is she?"

Lady Marleigh clung to her friend. When she raised her head and pulled back, tears filled her brown eyes. "Not well. Thank you both for coming."

"Did you send for a physician?" her aunt asked.

"Yes, but there's nothing that can be done. I'll take you upstairs. Perhaps she'll be awake and you can speak with her."

Regina followed her aunt and Lady Marleigh up the stairs. The healer had said the same thing about her father. *"There's nothing I can do for him now. He should have sent for me sooner."*

The drapes in the bedroom were partly drawn back, but the rainy weather added to the gloom indoors instead of relieving it. A small lamp sat on a table next to the bed. A chair had been pulled up beside it.

Felicity lay asleep. Her skin had a greyish cast,

and her breathing was rapid and labored. Large bandages wrapped her neck and shoulders. Knowledge rose within Regina. Felicity would not last the night.

Lady Marleigh sagged against Aunt Agatha. "You see?" she whispered. "I sit there and hold her hand. I want her to know she's not alone."

Regina looked at Felicity's mother and her aunt. "I can sit with her for a while. If she wakes, I'll come for you."

"Thank you, dear," Aunt Agatha said. She turned her friend towards the door. "Come, Elaine, we can talk while Regina keeps Felicity company. A hot tea will do you wonders."

Lady Marleigh looked back as Regina settled into the chair next to the bed. "You'll send for me if there's any change?"

"I will," Regina promised. She scooted closer and wrapped her hands around Felicity's cold one.

Felicity's red hair splayed across the embroidered linen pillowcase, her finely chiseled features so still and pale that she looked as if she'd already gone to meet her maker. Regina held her breath as other images assaulted her—her father's silent form stretched on his ornately carved bed, his eyes staring blankly into a future that no longer included his children. Tears welled, both for Felicity, and for Regina's own lost years as she'd taken over the responsibility of raising her younger brother.

Five years ago, she had sat next to her father's bedside. Bandages wrapped his torso where the demon's claws had torn through his chest and abdomen. The effects of the demon's blood poisoning could have been reversed, but her father hadn't sent for a healer until too late.

Bitterness and anger churned in her breast as it always did when she remembered those dark days after her mother's passing. Her father had withdrawn from her and Gabe, shutting himself in his study. Regina had taken over running the household by then. She saw how little he ate. Her father wasted away before her eyes.

Phillip Westcott despised his demon-hunting heritage, but a terrible eagerness had stamped his features the day of his final battle. Regina knew then he was lost to them.

Her father could have lived. Instead he'd deserted her and Gabe.

A moan broke the stillness.

Felicity's fingers had paled from Regina's tight hold. She released her vise-like grip, cursing the buried resentments that caused it, and the blood rushed back into Felicity's hand. "I'm sorry," she murmured. "I didn't mean to hurt you."

The witch's head moved restlessly on her pillow. Regina grabbed a small cloth and dipped it in the basin filled with water. After she wiped the sweat from the young woman's brow, she held her hand again, gently this time.

Felicity was going to die, just like her father had. And there was nothing she could do to prevent it. Regina rested her head on the bed as tears slipped down her cheeks.

She stumbled from one body to another on the battle-

field, checking for signs of life. A young mage had a large sword wound to his abdomen. There wasn't time to take him to the medical tent. He'd die before her men reached them.

Placing her hands on his arm, she gathered her magic. She closed her eyes and sent a small thread into his body, searching for the damage. His wound was grievous, but she thought he could be saved. She poured her magic into his body. Working from the inside out, she repaired the torn bits, burned out the diseased sections, coaxed his body into healing itself, using her magic to feed it. When she was certain he wouldn't die, she released him.

Blue eyes opened and fixed on her face.

Regina opened her eyes to find herself still in Felicity's bedroom. What happened?

Her magic still laid dormant in her veins. Unlike her normal visions, there was no moment of pure black, no exhaustion from the surge of power. She chewed hard on her lip and stared at the petals of a pink cabbage rose on the coverlet. This had felt like a memory. She could see it as clearly as this morning's breakfast of buttered rolls, preserves, and hot chocolate.

Why did she have visions of another life? Who was she?

Regina's entire identity had been rooted in her lack of magic and her human mother. This blossoming of her power unsettled her. Those dreams of hers—the ones her grandmother had said were a product of her hopes—came to vivid life in her waking hours now. She wasn't a magicless halfblood anymore, but she wasn't ready to claim the mantle of witch yet either.

A soft hitch of breath brought her attention back to the matter at hand. Felicity's slender fingers lay limp and cold in Regina's warm grasp. Purple mottled the pallid skin. Long seconds passed before the floral coverlet rose again over the young lady's chest.

Up until a few weeks ago, Regina had had no magic to speak of. Not a speck. Not a bubble. She was a half-blood, not a healer. What made her think she could heal Felicity when all the other doctors had failed?

An angry red stain pooled on Felicity's bandages. Magic thrummed hot along Regina's veins, banishing the cold fear she'd felt since entering this room. She hadn't called up her power, and yet it built, as if in preparation.

She gently removed the sodden cotton wrappings. Gaping wounds slashed across Felicity's neck and shoulder, and a putrid purple-black slime oozed alongside rivulets of pus. Lady Marleigh said Felicity had been in a boating accident, but Regina recognized the injuries. She had seen them before, and the memory ran through her with a shudder. Her father, lying in bed, his eyes wide and sightless, his body cold and still, his wounds identical to Felicity's.

The clear marks of a demon attack—not a boat, or an oar, or a tree. She cleaned the lacerations and replaced the wrappings with clean ones. Why had Lady Marleigh lied?

It didn't matter. Knowledge boomed in Regina's

head, drowning out all the questions. *Clear the poison around the heart.*

Regina obeyed, pouring her magic into Felicity through their clasped hands and using every golden drop to counteract the demon's poison. When the witch's faltering heartbeat gained strength, she spread her healing to the other organs. Sweat ran into Regina's eyes, and she blinked it away. She couldn't stop. She dove deeper into her own blood, grabbing more and more of her mage energy as she repaired the jagged wounds.

Exhaustion drained Regina's limbs. Grabbing the last dregs of her magic, she repaired Felicity's skin, until all signs of her injuries were gone.

Regina collapsed against the bed, her hand still holding Felicity's. Her body felt as if it had been hollowed out.

Felicity's head no longer tossed on the pillow, and she breathed deeply in sleep. Her skin had returned to a healthy color. All the violet splotches covering her limbs had disappeared.

She's going to live. I healed her. Regina rested her head on their clasped hands, too tired to think about the ramifications.

A hand shook Regina's shoulder. Her eyelids felt weighted with lead.

"Regina," Aunt Agatha whispered. "It's time to go."

Regina sat up slowly and popped the crick in her neck. How long had she been in that position? "Felicity?"

Her aunt glanced at the head of the bed, where

Lady Marleigh, with a soft smile, gently pushed the hair out of her daughter's face. "She appears to be much better."

Felicity was deep in sleep, her chest rising and falling with each breath. Her skin still had a healthy color, and the lines of pain had disappeared.

It hadn't been a dream.

Gratitude—and a slight sense of disbelief—filled Regina at her success. Neither Aunt Agatha nor Lady Marleigh looked at her any differently. They probably thought Felicity had turned the corner on her own.

Regina smiled at her aunt and Lady Marleigh. Felicity would get well, and Regina's secret was still safe. She smoothed the blankets, squeezed Felicity's hand in farewell, then followed her aunt out of the room.

Lady Marleigh softly closed the door.

CHAPTER THIRTY-SIX

———◆———

THE NEXT EVENING, REGINA AND Aunt Agatha attended the opera with Julian and his cousin Langley. The rain had stopped earlier in the day, and the air was warm and humid. Regina prayed they caught the demon tonight. The longer the monster roamed London, the more likely it was that Gabe would step into their father's shoes and try to find the demon himself.

"I've heard so much about tonight's opera. I'm so glad we'll finally be able to see it," Aunt Agatha said. "Thank you, Lord Lindsay, for joining us tonight. I do hope you'll enjoy it."

"In your company, Lady Carlisle, I could do no less." Lord Lindsay inclined his head and smiled. His black hair was pushed back off his face. He looked so handsome in his evening finery, his black coat tailored to perfection, that Regina felt a pang they weren't here for pleasure.

"Tut tut." Her aunt smacked him with her closed fan and laughed. "Such a flatterer."

Lindsay and her aunt ascended the stairs, while Langley escorted Regina. She had told him about her vision, so he knew they thought the demon would appear at the opera sometime this night. "Lord Langley, would you keep an eye on my aunt?"

"Of course. Have you sensed the demon yet?"

"Not even a whiff." Regina had been unable to track him, despite their best efforts to locate him. Her vision was the only lead they had.

"I'm sure you'll find him."

"Assuming he shows up. That's the question, isn't it? Lindsay says visions of the future may or may not come true." She wrinkled her nose in disgust. "That isn't very useful."

"It helps you to be prepared though. Forewarned is forearmed."

"I suppose." Regina would have preferred more definitive answers though. She loved the opera, but she wouldn't be able to enjoy this one, not with the demon's potential appearance lurking in the background.

She and Langley followed Julian and her aunt to a box framed with heavy red velvet curtains. Aunt Agatha settled herself on a padded chair at the rear. She waved her hand towards the front. "Have a seat, my dear. Lindsay, you too."

"Wouldn't you rather sit up here?" Regina asked.

Her aunt pulled out a fan and flipped it open. "I prefer it back here. No one can really see me, while I—" she leaned forward and whispered conspiratorially—"can observe them. Besides, sometimes the music makes me cry, and I'd rather not give anyone reason to comment."

"I'll keep your aunt company," Lord Langley commented, as he took the chair beside her.

Her aunt's machinations worked in their favor, since Regina had an unobstructed view of the crowd. She called up her magic and searched for the demon. Nothing.

The mageborn lords and ladies in the adjacent boxes stared at her and Lord Lindsay, and just as rudely refused to greet them. A few weeks ago that would have bothered Regina, but a demon on the loose had a way of clarifying one's priorities.

She leaned over to whisper in Lindsay's ear. "No sign of him yet."

His gaze deftly searched the opera house. "If he doesn't show up during the performance, we'll search during intermission."

"What if he doesn't come?"

"Let's worry about that later, hmm?"

The lights dimmed and the curtains behind them were pulled closed. The rich tones of the string orchestra filled the theater, but Regina's eyes were on the crowd more than the stage. If she were an evil being from hell, where would she go?

With any luck, the opera.

When the lights rose for intermission, Aunt Agatha tapped Regina on the back. "I'm going to go visit with the Countess Allensworth for a bit."

"I'll join you." Langley rose and offered Lady Carlisle his arm.

"Any luck?" Julian asked Regina after her aunt and Langley had left the box.

"Nothing."

"Let's walk around before the next act begins. You should be able to detect his presence if we cross his path."

"I like that idea better than sitting here waiting." She took his arm, and they exited the box. Instead of heading towards the foyer, they strolled the length of the hallway. She leaned closer to him and inhaled the clean scents of pine and woodsmoke. How did he always manage to smell of the outdoors here in the crowded city of London?

"Lady Regina!" Her shoulders tightened at the false cheer that came from behind her. She gritted her teeth and plastered a fake smile on her face.

"Lady Coraline." If Regina didn't see her again until hell froze over, it would still be too soon.

A malicious glint sparked in the petite blonde's pale blue eyes, as she and Lord Brambly approached. Like Lady Coraline, he'd made many barbed comments disparaging Regina's human lineage. He'd been part of Lord Lindsay's crowd when the earl belonged to the Mageborn Purity League. This mage was Lindsay's friend. How would he react to their betrothal?

"Lord Brambly." She channeled her mother's haughty disdain. *Don't be a lamb, child. Show them your teeth. In a smile, of course.*

"Lady Coraline, Lord Brambly." Lindsay's voice was so cold shivers ran down Regina's spine.

"Lindsay, I couldn't believe it when I heard you were betrothed to one of *them*." Brambly flicked a sneering sidelong glance at Regina.

"One of *them?*"

"Half-blood. I knew you found her attractive, but there were other ways of having her. You needn't have stooped so low as marriage."

Lindsay removed Regina's hand from his sleeve. He stepped forward until he loomed over Brambly, who tilted his head back to meet Lindsay's gaze. "Apologize."

Lady Coraline watched the proceedings with a smug expression.

"I won't apologize to that filth. What were you thinking, attending the opera with a half-blood? You weren't thinking. At least, not with your head." Brambly leered at Regina.

She wrapped her shawl closer about her shoulders, covering her bosom.

There was a flurry of movement. Lindsay pinned Brambly against the wall of the hallway, his forearm crushing the shorter man's throat. Lord Brambly gurgled, his fingers clawing at Lindsay's arm.

"Apologize."

Lord Brambly shook his head.

Lindsay lifted him higher. "You might want to rethink that," he said calmly as Brambly's face purpled.

Regina felt a familiar tingle of magic. Lord Brambly was attempting to gather his power. Lady Coraline merely looked on, an expression of boredom and disgust on her face.

The air turned oppressive and heavy with magic. A gold light exploded with a muffled boom over Lord Brambly's head. He quit fighting. Lindsay released his hold on his throat, and Lord Brambly slid slowly down the wall.

"Do not insult Lady Regina again or venture within my presence," Lord Lindsay growled. "Or next time you will not fare as well."

"You're a disgrace," Lady Coraline said to Lord Brambly, who sat dazedly on the floor. "You needn't bother returning to our box after intermission." She cast a venomous look at Regina and Lord Lindsay and stormed off.

Regina looked down at Lord Brambly. "What did you do to him?"

"I cast a stun spell on him. He'll be blinded for a while and his ears will ring."

"Did he hear your warning?"

His grin was positively wicked. "Probably not, but I'm sure he got the message."

They headed back to their box. A sharp tug and a ripping sound made Regina look down. The lace edging the bottom of her dress had separated from the hem.

"My lord, would you excuse me? I need to fix my gown."

"I'll accompany you."

She shook her head. "You can't come into the retiring room with me."

"I wasn't planning on it." He placed a gentle finger under her chin and her lips parted. "I merely wanted to ensure that no one else bothers you tonight."

He wanted to protect her. Warmth flooded her being. "In that case, I would be delighted to have your company."

Julian led the way, using his broad shoulders to forge a path through the glittering crowd. A bell sounded indicating that intermission was over. Groups of people headed back to their seats, and the hallway in front of the retiring room emptied.

"This shouldn't take long," she said.

"I should check the room first."

"I'll look." She opened the heavy oak door and glanced inside. "It's empty. Don't worry. I haven't had any hint of the demon yet."

"I'll wait for you here then."

Regina sat on a small velvet chair, glad that she had the room to herself. She wasn't in the mood for company after the encounter with Lady Coraline and Lord Brambly. She placed her reticule in her lap and dug through it, looking for the small felt sewing kit she kept inside. When she found the kit, she pinned the lace to the hem.

A door opened behind her. She looked up, a feeling of unease overtaking her. A maidservant in a black dress and white apron and mobcap entered the room. "Can I assist you, miss?"

Pressure built within her head. Regina's heart raced as a sense of danger washed over her. She looked into the young woman's brown eyes. Yellow flames flickered in the pupils. She rose abruptly, dropping her sewing kit onto the floor. "No, thank you. I just finished."

"You dropped this, milady." The maid held out the little felt book.

Regina hesitated. Did the demon know she could sense his presence? If she didn't take the kit, would he realize she knew he was the maid? But what if he tried to grab her when she reached for it?

Nerves jangling with tension, she stretched out her hand and took the proffered object. "Thank you."

"My pleasure, miss." The maid curtsied. She pushed the footstool nearer to the chair, then fluffed the gold tasseled pillow, placing it neatly against the back of the seat.

Regina dropped the kit into her reticule. It looked like the demon didn't realize she knew who he was. The maidservant continued to straighten the room. Regina's back tensed as she strode for the door. She had to get to Julian. She had almost reached it when a blow knocked her to the oak floor.

"Not so fast, milady." Sharp claws dug into her side and flipped her onto her back.

"Jul—" Purple mist poured into her mouth and nose, choking off her scream. She looked into the jagged snout of the demon, unable to breathe as his monstrous form pinned her against the ground.

Her heart beat fiercely, protesting the lack of air.

His fetid breath steamed against her cheek, and she flinched. "I've waited long enough. Tonight your curse ends."

Curse? What was he talking about?

Purple motes of demon magic flowed into her and covered her body. He opened his jaws and she felt a pull from deep within her being. Pain knifed her from head to toe, as the demon's magic fought to tear her soul from her body. Tears slipped from the corners of her eyes. She was losing the struggle. Her soul loosened its moorings, and she suddenly felt weightless.

Dark limestone cliffs flashed in her mind, along with the demon's hot yellow glare as he rattled her body beneath a wintry night sky. She couldn't let the beast steal her soul. She'd die.

I can't die. Not again.

<hr>

Julian paced the hallway. The opera had recommenced five minutes ago. A woman's voice trilled in a thrilling crescendo then dropped off as the music descended into a menacing and deep build. How long did it take for a woman to fix a hem?

He approached the door to the ladies' retiring room and raised his hand to knock. A soft thud sounded from inside. "Regina!"

The door was locked. He gathered his magic and flung his fingers outward. The heavy oak splintered into pieces. The scene in the room was Julian's worst nightmare brought to life.

Regina lay immobile on the floor, engulfed in a purple mist. Her eyes were wide with terror. The demon leaned over her, his jaw and sharp teeth open above her mouth. He snarled at Julian.

Julian blasted the demon with his magic. It hit the fiend's torso and knocked him flying off Regina. The violet motes writhed around her. Her eyelids fluttered. Rage thundered through him. He had to break the demon's hold on her.

A fiery rope burst into the air and hit the demon. It encircled the monster like a snake winding itself around its prey. Julian twisted his hands and blue flames licked out to fill the gaps between the magic coils. The acrid odor of burning hide permeated the room.

"You think your mage magic can hold me?" Baleful yellow eyes glared at him over the top of the magical cocoon. "I've taken thousands of mageborn souls, and their power feeds me. Even now my skin heals."

Julian tightened the flaming spirals, which had reached the creature's throat. The demon flailed against his bonds, throwing himself around the room. The padded chairs and coffee table fractured under the creature's weight. Julian directed a glance at Regina. The malevolent mist still covered her. Her eyes had closed. His heart raced. He had to save her, but he couldn't get close enough to the demon yet to kill him.

Suddenly the dusky mist withdrew from Lady Regina and attacked the blazing column of blue fire surrounding the demon. The recoil knocked Julian back against the doorframe. Purple motes intermingled with the flaming coils as the two magics battled for control.

With a rasping gasp and feeble moan, Lady Regina rolled to her side and crawled towards Julian.

Sweat dripped into his eyes. His hair plastered to his forehead. His magic was starting to wane. His attack on Lord Brambly seemed a supreme act of folly now. He'd squandered his power on a fool, despite knowing the demon might appear. "Get out of here," Julian commanded Regina.

Violet magic flecks rapidly overcame the flames holding the fiend hostage.

"Regina, you need to go. Now!"

She rose shakily to her feet and stumbled past him into the hallway. Julian gathered all his magic into his hand. His skin glowed deep gold from the power roiling beneath the surface. The mass of energy swelled and burst across the room.

The demon flew backward, crushing the vanity table and knocking the standing mirror to the floor. Julian reached inside his coat and pulled out the long, cross-hilt dagger Harbrook had given him before he strode into the portal.

He leaped onto the monster and stabbed the blade deep into his throat. Thick claws hooked into Julian's back and flung him across the room. The dagger's steel blade jutted from the beast's neck. Purple-black blood gushed from the wound. The demon howled as he pulled out the shank, then dropped to his haunches, staunching the wound with a massive clawed hand. The yellow flames in his eyes flared red with hate.

"Let's finish this, shall we?" Julian reached down and pulled another dagger from his boot. He blocked the doorway. If the fiend wanted to leave, he would have to go through him.

The demon circled the room. "We'll finish this, but not tonight." He leaped, crashing through the closed window into the alley behind the theater.

Julian dashed across the room. He looked down, but the demon had already disappeared into the tendrils of fog undulating in the dark depths below.

"By His Blood!" Julian crashed past the broken door into the hallway, searching for Regina. Small tables topped by brass candelabras filled the ornately decorated hall to the left. He charged right, stumbling into a table placed next to the door. "Blast!" He grabbed the candlestick before it hit the Turkish carpet and froze.

Regina huddled against the dark oak wainscoting next to one of the side tables. Her green silk dress, smeared with dirt, puddled on the beige and blue carpeting. She looked fragile, as if the wrong word would cause her to shatter. He reached out a hand to the wall to steady himself, willing his rage to calm.

"Regina." He lightly touched her shoulder, and she lifted her wet face. Her pupils were dilated and slightly unfocused, as if she were still staring at the horror from earlier. He gently gathered her into his arms and pulled her against his pounding heart. "You're safe now. The demon is gone."

Her arms slid around his waist, and her face burrowed into his chest. He cradled her close as she cried and tried not to think of her lying on the floor as the demon attempted to steal her soul. He pressed a kiss against her hair. He'd almost been too late.

"You're safe now. I promise." He wasn't sure if he was saying it for her benefit or his own.

Her sobs quieted, then she wiped at her eyes.

"We should go back. Aunt Agatha will be wondering what happened to us."

"Do you feel like watching the rest of the opera?" She looked drawn and shaky.

"No," she admitted.

"I'll have my carriage brought round, and we'll send a manservant to fetch your aunt and Lord Langley."

"That would be wonderful."

"Come with me first." He headed for the ladies' retiring room.

"Why are you going back there?" She stopped at the doorway, as if she couldn't bring herself to enter.

"I need to get something." The retiring room was a disaster. Furniture had been tossed and broken in the fight. He spotted his dagger on the floor, among shards of mirrored glass. Purple-black blood congealed on the blade.

He wiped the blade clean, then burned the handkerchief. Ashes drifted down to the hardwood floor.

"What will we tell the staff? They'll never believe there was a demon here."

"We'll tell them you walked in on a couple of thieves. You screamed and I chased after them. It's close enough to the truth."

She inhaled deeply and nodded.

They walked into the foyer. Julian called the theater manager over and explained what happened. The man came back quite shaken.

"Sir, the place has been ransacked!" he exclaimed.

"Have the bills for the repairs sent to my man of business. I will ensure everything is paid in full."

The manager stared at him in shock, and his color lessened. "Very good, my lord. Thank you."

"Please have my carriage brought to the front. Lady Regina is overwrought from the experience and would like to go home."

"Yes, my lord, of course." The manager beckoned to a footman.

"We also need someone to notify her aunt, Lady Carlisle, and my cousin, Lord Langley. They'll be sitting in her box."

"I'll take care of it now, my lord." He bowed and walked away.

Regina took a seat on a padded sofa in the foyer, while Julian paced, waiting for their carriage to be brought around. She interlaced her fingers on her lap. "I don't think the demon's attack was a coincidence."

"What do you mean?"

"Before he tried to take my soul, he said he'd been waiting long enough. That tonight my curse ends."

"But you never cursed it."

"No. I've barely learned how to use regular magic. Even if I knew how, I wouldn't use dark magic." She clasped her arms around herself.

"You're saying you've been the demon's target all along?" Regina resembled Evelyn, but did she also have his wife's soul? Was the fiend trying to finish the job he'd been summoned to do? But if so, why go after Regina? Why not come after him?

"Yes." Her voice broke. "Those people who died. Their blood is on my hands."

"What?"

"Lord Pratchett was with me before he died, but I was the demon's target. He died because of me. All of them—Lord Falsworth, the maid, the others—their deaths are my fault." When she looked up, her eyes were wet with tears.

He knelt in front of her and took her hands in his. "Their deaths are not your fault. The demon killed them, not you. The blood is on his head, not yours."

She shook her head. "I—I don't know."

"It's not your fault, Regina." He held her uncertain gaze. "Say it."

"It's not my fault," she whispered.

"No, it's not. But if you are the demon's target, I'm surprised he never attacked you at your townhouse."

"He can't."

"What do you mean?"

"Our house has a blood ward on it. No demon can cross that barrier."

"Then we need to get you home." Julian wanted to go after that devil's spawn, but Regina had barely survived the demon's attack. He couldn't ask her to track it now. "Once you're safe, Langley and I will return. The demon was injured. With any luck, he left a trail."

"Do you want me to help you track him?" Of course she would offer. That was his brave girl.

"No. I want you to rest." He squeezed her hands.

"We'll find him, and you won't need to worry anymore."

CHAPTER THIRTY-SEVEN

GRULIK DARTED DOWN THE ALLEY and into one of the mews. His clawed hand clutched the wound in his neck.

So close. He'd almost had her.

Lord Lindsay kept getting in the way. No wonder his summoner had wanted to get rid of Lindsay and his line.

The slice in his neck continued to burn. He pulled the claw away. It was dripping with blood. He needed souls. Immediately. It was the only way to heal from the demonsbane oil that had coated the blade.

Voices sounded from down the street. He slunk to the edge of the brick building at the end of the mews, keeping himself hidden in the shadows. Two gentlemen stumbled down the foggy lane. His sensitive nose detected the smell of spirits. Perfect. Only mageborn frequented the gambling establishment they'd just exited from. He'd get what he needed from them.

A little later, he strode down the street, straightening his clothes, neck healed. After disposing of the bodies, he'd shapeshifted into the form of the younger gentleman, whose clothing had been expensively tailored, indicating greater wealth.

Ahhh, now I am Lord Sinestra. Pleased to meet you, my lord. He laughed to himself.

He was tired of Lord Lindsay rushing in to save the day. It was time for a new plan.

He found Lord Sinestra's carriage and climbed in. "Take me home."

CHAPTER THIRTY-EIGHT

REGINA ENTERED THE HALL OF her townhouse, feeling drained from the demon's attack at the opera house. Julian held her close to him, his arm draped comfortingly around her back. Aunt Agatha moved to confer with Deeds about having cook make up one of her special possets. Lord Langley waited near the front door.

Julian took her hands in his. The concern in his eyes melted the cold lump in her chest, and she fought the urge to ask him to stay with her. He had to find the demon before the trail went cold. "Is there anything I can do for you before we leave?"

"No, I'm fine. I just need to rest." She also needed time to think. What curse was the demon talking about that had sent him after her?

Julian raised her hands to his lips and kissed them. "I'll call on you tomorrow. But if you need me sooner, send a message and I'll come right away."

Her throat tightened, and her gaze moved from him to Langley. "Be careful," she told them both.

"We will."

Aunt Agatha returned. She held her hand out

and Lord Lindsay took it. "Thank you, my lord, for attending the opera with us tonight." She cast an anxious glance at Regina. "I'm sorry it ended like this. I've never heard of such a thing happening before. To be accosted by brigands, in the theater! I will watch over her and make sure she gets some rest."

"The pleasure was mine. Please contact me if you need anything. In the meantime, I'll do my best to make sure the culprit is found."

"Thank you. We appreciate your help tonight," her aunt said.

"Good night, Lady Regina. Try to get some sleep if you can," Langley said.

"I will."

The two men bowed, then left. Regina hoped they found the demon. She'd sleep better once that threat was gone.

"My dear, you look terrible," Aunt Agatha burst out. She came up to Regina and put an arm around her waist to guide her towards the stairs. "The first thing we're going to do is get you upstairs. A bath will be brought up, and cook is making you a posset. We'll get you set to rights and then you can put this whole distressing evening behind you."

Regina nodded. She wove on her feet. They reached the top of the stairs, and she breathed a sigh of relief. "Thank you."

"You're welcome, dear." Her aunt's eyes were worried. "I've never seen you so shaken. What happened in that room?"

Regina's step faltered on the smooth wood floor.

Would her aunt believe her if she mentioned the demon? She'd have to think on it. "I was attacked, but Lord Lindsay rescued me."

Her aunt's face paled. "Were you harmed?"

"No. He arrived in time."

Her aunt followed her into her room. A fire had already been lit and burned brightly in the grate. Regina dropped into the broad-cushioned chintz chair before the fireplace and curled her feet beneath her. Instead of cheery flames, she watched a bonfire burning high against a night sky in the middle of a camp, while soldiers with swords stood guard.

A soft knock sounded and a tub was carried into the room by a couple of footmen. Her maid brought in a tray with a steaming pot and a cup.

"Cook sent this up for you, milady." She curtsied.

"Thank you, Bess." Regina took a sip and choked, feeling the warm burn of alcohol in her throat. "What did cook put in this?"

"Brandy, milady. She said it would do you good."

"She's right," Aunt Agatha chimed in. "Drink it slowly."

Regina cradled the warm cup in her hands. She sipped it slowly, and gradually the ice melted from her limbs. Footmen brought in buckets of hot water, followed by cold. Steam rose from the tub. The servants left the room when the bath was ready.

"I have to admit I wasn't pleased when Lord Lindsay compromised you, but his behavior has been above reproach since then. Thank goodness he was nearby and able to reach you in time tonight."

"Yes. I was very fortunate." She took a deep breath as she remembered her struggle for air.

"What happened in there?"

Regina gazed down into her cup. "I'd rather not discuss it." She finished the cup and placed it on the table. "All I want to do is take a hot bath, drink another cup of cook's posset, and go to bed. I don't want to think about tonight's events anymore. I want to forget about it."

"Very well. We'll talk more in the morning." She bent down and kissed Regina's cheek. "Try to have a good night, dear. Don't hesitate to call if you need me."

Bess placed her nightdress on the bed and a couple of towels over the back of the chair next to the tub. She placed a tray with the soap, shampoo, bath oils, and a cloth on the chair seat.

"Thank you, Bess. I'll do the rest myself."

Bess hesitated. "Are you sure, milady?"

"Yes. Let everyone know there's no need to wait up. The tub can be removed in the morning."

"Very well. Have a good night, milady."

"You, too, Bess."

After the door closed, Regina stripped off her clothes. She stepped into the water, which at first felt almost too hot for comfort. But as she sank deeper into the tub, her skin quickly adjusted. She leaned her head back and closed her eyes. Her mind drifted.

The air inside the canvas tent was quite chilly despite

the fire burning in the pit in the center. The water in the bathtub steamed. Julian approached her.

"Happy anniversary."

"How did you find a tub?" It was a small, hip size copper tub, but the closest item to luxury she'd seen since joining the camp. She loved it.

"I traded for it the last time I went to town."

"What did you have to give for it?"

"The family's well was running dry. I used my magic to find a spot for a new well and dug it out."

She remembered that he'd been gone for a few days last month. She smiled. "I don't know how you kept this secret from all the women in the camp."

"I never brought it to the camp. I hid it."

She laughed.

"I have another gift for you." He pulled a velvet pouch from one of his saddlebags. "I know you missed having these."

He placed the item in her hands. She could feel a couple of long handles through the luxurious fabric. Her heart pounded with hope. She pulled out a silver backed mirror and brush. Tears filled her eyes. She'd left these at her parents' home when she'd gone to join Julian on the battlefield. Her fingers lovingly traced the name engraved on the back of the mirror—Evelyn Duarte.

She flipped the mirror over to see how much she had changed over the past year.

Her cheeks had hollowed. Her eyes looked a lighter green in contrast to her sun-kissed skin, but her face had a pallor the healer in her didn't like. Her honey-colored hair was streaked with light blond strands from long days spent under the sun.

"Thank you. I have a special gift for you too, but it won't arrive for a while."

Even though the war had been difficult, she'd never regretted her decision to join him on the battlefield. They were together. That was more than enough.

"What is it?"

"Your present should arrive in about seven months." She grabbed his hands and slid them to her belly. His eyes softened with wonder.

He gently lifted her chin, turning her face up to his. "Your present is best."

His lips came down softly on hers and her heart ached with love for this man and the child they would have. Evelyn raised her arms and slipped them around his neck…

Regina's eyes flew open. No tent, no loving eyes of a man who looked like Lord Lindsay. Only blue floral wallpaper and a white marble fireplace. The water in the bath had cooled and she shivered.

Evelyn.

That name—she swallowed hard—sounded so familiar, as if she'd heard it many times before.

"Evelyn." She tried the name out on her tongue. The word settled over her like a heavy winter cloak. If Regina weighed two stone less and spent more time outdoors, she and Evelyn could have been twins. Who was Evelyn? Why was Regina experiencing visions of Evelyn's life? And why did Evelyn's husband—coincidentally also named Julian—look like Lord Lindsay?

Regina sank further into the tub. She was too tired to make sense of this. The only thing she understood was that Evelyn and her husband shared a connection that went far beyond the physical.

She closed her eyes against the yearning that swamped her. Would Lord Lindsay ever love her with that same abiding passion?

Julian rapidly descended the stairs of the townhome, Langley trailing behind. The temperature had dropped significantly and the mist had thickened, dense enough to obscure the lines of the tall carriage waiting in the street. He jumped inside and rapped on the roof.

"Take me back to the opera house, as quickly as possible."

Langley climbed into the carriage. "Why are we going back?"

"To find the demon. You can come along or get out and find your own way home."

Langley settled into the cushions. "Of course I'll come. That was clever to say that Lady Regina was attacked by a thief."

Julian's legs jerked with the need for action. The carriage tumbled over the cobblestones as the driver raced across the London streets. They each grabbed the leather straps to keep from being thrown around.

"It was easier to say she was accosted by a thief than explain she was attacked by a fiend from hell."

"True. It would have been difficult to explain there's a demon on the loose in London that no one knows about. It might have caused quite a stir."

"Joke if you must, but Lady Regina almost died tonight." The vision of her still body on the floor filled his mind. He'd almost been too late.

"I'm sorry to hear that. But you saved her, and she's safe at home now with her aunt."

For the moment. They had to find the demon. Julian never wanted to come so close to losing her again. "The beast is injured. I managed to stab its neck before it escaped."

"If it left a trail, we'll find it."

"Demon blood is purple-black. I'm hoping we'll find traces of it in the alley."

The carriage stopped down the street from the opera house. Carriages were still lined up in front of the building, as the opera had not ended yet. They'd have time to look for the demon's trail.

Julian headed for the right side of the opera house, where the monster had jumped through the window. "Stand guard," he told Langley.

He gathered his magic and cast a light spell. A ball of golden light hovered above his hand and he used it to explore. Shards of glass showered the ground. Giant claw prints in the dirt—too big to belong to any animal in London—showed the demon's landing. The prints led deep into the murky alley.

Julian raised his hand and the ball of light hovered in the air about four feet off the ground. Because of the heavy fog, he couldn't see more than five feet around them. Other than the whuffling sounds of the horses hooked up to the carriages and the occasional shouts of the ostlers, the night was quiet.

"Let's go." The thick night air carried sounds

clearly, so Julian kept his voice as low as possible.

They followed the tracks through the back streets of London. Langley moved quickly but silently alongside Julian. Neither spoke. Where did Langley learn to move with such stealth? Julian suspected his cousin would be deadly in a fight. Luckily the magelord was on his side. At least as long as they hunted the demon.

The tracks ended at a cobblestone thoroughfare where gaming halls spread up and down the street. Julian released his ball of light. A carriage stopped at an establishment two doors down. A couple of gentlemen stepped out.

"Lord Henry and Fitzhugh," Langley commented quietly. "White's is popular with the mageborn. Do you think the demon went there?"

"The demon is injured, so he won't be able to shift into a human form. Let's see if we can find more tracks. I'll take the right."

"On it." Langley headed left.

Julian passed the gambling houses but found no sign of the soul sucker. After a couple of blocks he crossed the street and met up with Langley.

"I think I found something," his cousin said.

Large claw marks scored the dirt in the midst of a jumble of prints. Julian knelt to take a closer look. There had been two men—one a good deal heavier than his companion, judging by the depths of the impressions—as well as the beast. It looked like a scuffle had ensued in the alley.

"If the demon took their souls, we'll find the bodies nearby." Julian had enough experience to know there wasn't much hope of the men surviving.

They investigated the alley. The boot prints disappeared, replaced by parallel drag marks.

"You were right. That demon is a monster to be reckoned with. Judging by the markings in the mud, it dragged both bodies at the same time," Langley said.

They crossed the cobblestoned lane to a steep road that curved down to the Thames. The tracks and drag marks ended at the edge of the riverbank.

Rank fish, dank mud, and slow-moving water permeated the damp air. Thick fog hung over the Thames.

Julian stared into the murky river. The drag marks ended a foot from the edge. Only the creature's massive claw prints could be seen. He cast his magelight over the water, but it was impossible to see anything below the surface.

"Poor bastards," Langley said. "Depending upon how the demon discarded the bodies, it might take a while for them to turn up."

"They'll be avenged. We'll find him and free their souls." Julian vowed as he stared at the slow-moving depths below.

They searched the riverbank for more clues. The claw marks disappeared, but a set of human footprints appeared, followed by boot prints. The demon had shifted form once again. The tracks headed towards a cobblestone lane that led away from the Thames.

When the trail turned cold, Julian turned to

Langley. "Let's see if we can find someone who saw something."

"Sounds like a good plan."

"We'll start with the gaming establishments. With any luck, we'll find out the identities of our victims."

"Do you want to split up?" Langley asked.

"No. This demon is too dangerous. Our hunt will be slower, but if we encounter him, we'll at least have a chance."

Julian braced himself for a long night. At least Regina was safe.

CHAPTER THIRTY-NINE

MORNING SUNLIGHT STREAMED THROUGH THE curtains into Regina's bedroom. The events of the night before tangled in her mind. The demon's attack on her at the opera, followed by her vision of the woman named Evelyn. Even now, all she had to do was close her eyes and her cozy bedroom dissolved, replaced by the walls of a canvas tent and a burnished copper tub with steam rising from its midst.

Even though she craved rest, there was no point in going back to sleep. A white porcelain bowl decorated with blue flowers waited on her dressing table, along with a matching pitcher of water. She'd scried for the demon at Lord Langley's house. Could she use her magic to find some answers?

She poured the water into the bowl and set a couple of candles to either side, then seated herself at her dressing table. Her reflection in the mirror flickered, reminding her of Evelyn's gaunt features. Who was Evelyn? Regina wanted to know, but she had a more important question she needed answered. What was the curse the demon spoke of? Why was the monster after her?

She gathered her magic and looked into the bowl. The blue flowers at the bottom disappeared as the clear water clouded. "Show me the curse the demon spoke of."

Limestone cliffs rose black against an early dawn sky. She stood in an open meadow, and a fiery pain knifed her chest and abdomen. The demon held her up. Then she noticed it. A separate heartbeat deep inside her womb. Tears poured from her eyes as she felt the heartbeats stutter.

Dear God, no, not again. Paralysis and anguish filled her. It was so much worse this time. Because this time, she could feel her daughter's soul, its power and beauty burning bright within her.

The demon snarled its spell, and a dark purple mist coalesced in the air. She—they—were running out of time. The demon was using her blood to open its gate to its hell, and then her daughter's soul and her own would be stolen. Enslaved for all eternity.

The flame of her daughter's soul winked out. Evelyn moaned. She stared at the craggy snout of the foul monster. He continued to mutter his spell, not even noticing her. He'd already dismissed her. A desire for revenge filled her like nothing she had ever felt before. Her blood gleamed red against her pale skin, and the demon's purple blood leaked slowly from the wound on his arm. Her mage magic was dwindling, but she could use the power of blood magic.

One of the darkest magics, blood magic was forbidden. She'd never used dark magic, but knew its usage carried a price. As she stared at the flaming yellow eyes of the demon, she didn't care. She would have her revenge for her child's death. If not in this life, the next.

She dipped her fingers into her chest, groaning at the effort and pain. Then her hand fell onto the fiend's open wound. Power surged from their comingled blood, even as her strength faded. The icy hands of death crept along her limbs. Death had its own power.

With shallow breaths, she struggled to grasp the motes of death magic, weaving it with the power of their mingled blood. And then she felt it, the surge of gold in her own blood, as her mageborn power responded to the blood magic she harnessed to her will.

"By my blood and thine, our lives intertwined." Even though her voice was a whisper, power resonated in the words. "I curse you, demon, to be trapped in this world and barred from your own, until the day my heart is reborn."

"What are you doing?" He shook her like a ragdoll, and only the power of the magics suffusing her body kept her alive.

She looked up at him and let all the hatred she felt pour from her gaze. "One day we will meet again. And when that happens, you will die, not I." Magic pulsed through her body, surrounding her and the demon in a blood red nimbus, shot with black, purple and white.

Her spirit separated from body. Relief flooded her that the demon failed to get her soul. It would take centuries, but one day, she and the foul creature would meet again. And the next time, she would have her revenge.

Dark magic carried a price. As her consciousness faded, she wondered what the cost would be.

Whatever it was, it would be worth it.

Regina gripped the table so hard her knuckles ached. Her mind rebelled against the knowledge that made all the missing pieces fit together.

I am Evelyn.

Magic flowed hot beneath her skin. She looked at her reflection in the mirror, watching as the last dregs of black drained from her eyes. She understood why she'd only been able to use her magic after the demon's arrival in her time period. Why she'd had no memories of the curse or her past life. Dark magic had a sense of humor. Curse a demon, but don't have any defenses or memory of it until almost too late. That was the price she'd paid.

If she hadn't tried to scry for the curse, would she ever have remembered who she was? Somehow, she didn't think so. Scrying for the curse seemed to have been the key to unlocking her past.

Memories of her past life flooded her. Evelyn's childhood, her sister Lisette, Harbrook, and most of all, Julian, the love of her life. Regina knew why the demon was after her now. She'd cursed him when she was Evelyn, trapping the monster in their world. A cold icy knot formed in her chest as she remembered the loss of her daughter. Evelyn's healing magic could sense her child's life, but Regina's demon hunter lineage enabled her to see her daughter's soul. That had been Regina's magic, not Evelyn's. Somehow, when she'd relived that moment, her own magic had infused the memory.

Anguish and the hard desire for revenge flooded her. Heat thrummed beneath her skin as her power flared. Evelyn had been a healer, but Regina was something more. The blood of demon hunters churned within her blood.

"I will find you, and you will die. I swear it." The vow rushed out of her along with her magic. She collapsed against the back of her seat. Unless, she amended, Julian and Lord Langley had already found the demon and killed him.

Like Evelyn, Regina was a healer. Thanks to her heritage, she also had the potential to be a demon hunter. Her unusual height, her abnormally quick reflexes, her powerful magic, her ability to track demons—all of that came from her father's side of the family. Maybe fate had a sense of humor too. Because Evelyn had not come from a demon hunter lineage, but Regina—who had a demon to hunt—did. Fate had given Regina all the tools she needed to have her revenge.

She changed into her morning dress and went downstairs. The demon had made several attempts on her life. She needed to warn Gabe and Aunt Agatha. Could she tell them she was the reincarnation of a witch from the past and about the curse? In all the fantastic tales and stories of the mage-born, she'd never heard of anything similar. Maybe it would be best to simply say that the demon thought she'd cast a curse on it. Her family didn't need to know that she'd been the one to cast the curse centuries ago to understand the danger they were all in.

Regina entered the breakfast room, surprised to see Gabe was still there. Normally he'd be ensconced in the study for his daily lesson with

Lord Lindsay.

Gabriel sat at the table, hunched over his food. He looked despondent.

"Where's Lord Lindsay?" She slid some kippers from the buffet onto her plate, as well as a couple of pieces of toast.

"He sent a note early this morning. He said he lost something at the theater last night, and he was still trying to find it."

Her hand froze in midair with the tongs and kippers. Did that mean he'd found the demon's trail? Or did it mean he was still searching for it? "I'm sorry he isn't coming."

Gabe shrugged. "His note said he'd come this afternoon if he could."

"I hope he does. You seem to have made a lot of progress."

He looked up. "It's a whole new world. I never realized magic could be used to do so much. We were going to work with the elements today. He was going to teach me how to manipulate air. Not even Father mentioned it was possible to control the elements!"

"Hopefully you'll still get your lesson."

"How was the opera last night?" He ate more vigorously now.

"Terrifying." Regina slid into the chair across from him and leaned forward. "You remember that demon I encountered at the maze?"

"Yes." His youthful face turned serious.

"He attacked me last night. I was alone in the retiring room fixing my hem when a maid walked in. She was the demon."

"Could you tell the maid was the demon?"

"Yes. When she entered the room, I had this sense of danger. I could see yellow flames flickering in the maid's brown eyes, and I knew then she was the demon."

"How did you get away?"

"I didn't." She struggled to push away the horrific memory of the demon pulling on her soul and her powerlessness. "He trapped me with his magic and tried to steal my soul. Lord Lindsay arrived in time to save me."

Gabriel's jaw hardened. Despite his youthful cheeks and lean boy's face, he reminded her of their father. "We have to find him and kill him."

"Lord Lindsay is already hunting for the demon with his cousin Lord Langley. They went back last night to try to find its trail. But if they don't find it, Lord Lindsay and I will continue searching for it."

"You've been trying to find the demon? How? You don't have any magic."

His worry filled her with guilt. Her desire to keep her ability secret seemed so selfish. What kind of person was she? She'd been lying to everyone in her family. "I do have magic."

"What?" He looked at her in disbelief, as if he couldn't understand what she was saying.

"I discovered I have power that day Aunt Agatha went to ask her brother to train you. Remember how you asked me to try your lesson? I had a vision that day. I saw a red-headed lord riding on a horse. I didn't realize it at the time, but he was the demon. I thought I'd imagined the flames in the young man's eyes."

The hurt in her brother's eyes was like a knife twisting in her chest. "Why didn't you tell me?"

Her fingers smoothed the linen tablecloth while she searched for the right words. "I was afraid it would go away as quickly as it came. I wanted to be sure I had magic and could use it before I told anyone."

"Does Aunt Agatha know?"

"No. I plan on telling her today."

"Have you used your magic?"

"Yes. I can call up visions and do some healing. And I can track the demon."

"You can track the demon? Like father?"

"Yes. The more I've encountered him, the easier it has gotten to sense him. I can tell when he's close now, and I can track him. That's what I've been doing during my afternoon rides with Lord Lindsay. He's hunting the demon and wanted my help."

"Why didn't he ask me? I could have helped him."

"You're too young. Demons are powerful, more than I'd ever imagined. He'd kill you."

"I have magic and Lord Lindsay has been teaching me to use it. I need to learn how to hunt demons anyway. I might as well start now."

"No."

"But he's letting you help him, and you don't have any training." His gaze turned mutinous.

"I'm helping him because he knows I'll run." She dipped a toast point into the yolk of a soft-boiled egg. "If he asked you to help him, he's sure you would stay and fight."

"Of course I would!"

"That's why he asked *me*. It's too dangerous, Gabe. You'll have plenty of time to hunt demons when you're older and trained."

"That's not fair."

"Perhaps not, but that's the way it is." Regina reached across the table and grabbed his hand. "I will do everything I can to protect you. You are the one who will take over our family's legacy, not me. And in order to do that, you need to stay safe and learn. Eventually you'll be the one hunting demons, and I'll be the one waiting for you to come back."

"Do you think the demon will come here looking for you?" He sounded excited and worried at the same time.

"I don't know, but we're safe here. Demons can't pass the blood ward on our property. But if you go out, you need to be careful. If something doesn't seem right, or you have a strange feeling of being watched or of wrongness, that could be the demon. If you ever sense it, get away, as fast as you can. *Promise me*."

He hesitated. "I promise."

"Thank you. I couldn't bear for it to take your soul."

There was the soft scuff of a boot on the carpet. She jumped. Deeds entered the room with a slight bow.

"I beg your pardon, miss," he said in his gravelly

voice. "This just arrived for Master Gabriel."

Gabe reached out and took the envelope. Made of elegant linen paper, the envelope bore the crest of the Earl of Lindsay. He opened it and his eyes widened. "Lord Lindsay wants me to meet him at Kensington Park! We're going to have our lesson there."

Her shoulders sagged in relief. Lord Lindsay was alive. She smiled at her brother's flushed cheeks and excitement. "He must have killed the demon if he wants to have your lesson at the park. What time does he want you to arrive?"

"As soon as I can." He jumped to his feet and tossed his napkin on his seat. He leaned over and brushed a kiss on her cheek. "I can't wait to ask him how he killed the demon."

"Tell Lindsay to come here when you're done," she called after him. She had to see Julian for herself and make sure he was all right. "You're not the only one who wants to hear the story."

He poked his head back into the room and grinned. "I will. 'Bye."

CHAPTER FORTY

GABRIEL RODE INTO KENSINGTON PARK, accompanied by his groom. Since it was early morning, the grounds were mostly empty. He breathed in the crisp morning air and felt his chest lighten after the morning's revelations. Regina had power. It hurt that she hadn't trusted him enough to tell him sooner, but he understood. If he'd never had magic and one day it suddenly appeared, he would have kept it secret too until he was sure it wouldn't disappear.

His older sister had been looking out for him for as long as he could remember. If she'd had magic and training, he knew she would have trained him herself. Instead, she'd convinced Lord Lindsay to train him. She'd helped the earl search for the demon—Gabe still had trouble wrapping his mind around the fact his sister had been able to track a demon—and Lord Lindsay had killed it. And now Gabe was on his way for his first outdoor training session.

Gabe had never been sure he'd be able to fulfill his family's duty and become a demon hunter.

How could he, when no one would train him in magic? Aunt Agatha had done her best, but she couldn't teach him how to track demons, or use his magic to fight, or even how to become a demon hunter. Then Lord Lindsay had entered their lives.

It didn't matter to Gabe that Lindsay had once hated humans and half-bloods. The magelord had changed. He must have, or he would never have agreed to train Gabe. Gabe was young, but he wasn't a fool. He'd noticed the way the earl's gaze followed his sister, how her smile would cause the magelord's shoulders to relax. The earl cared about his sister. He'd saved her from the demon, although Gabe was sure he would have done that for anyone.

Lindsay's note said to meet him by the pond near the west entrance. As a more secluded section of the park, it would be perfect for working magic.

Gabe's imagination filled with all kinds of scenarios for today. Would he learn how to levitate objects in the air? Could *he* levitate in the air? A huge grin split his face. That would be *amazing.*

Or maybe he'd learn how to control liquids. He could spin the water in the pond round and round into a spout as tall as Buckingham Palace. He laughed. Lindsay was usually more prosaic in his lessons. He'd probably teach him how to speed a boat over the surface.

But first, he'd ask Lord Lindsay about the demon. Maybe the earl would show him how he fought it. Gabe's heart raced. Was it possible he'd learn how to fight today?

He dismounted and had the groom lead the

horses to the other side of the pond. That way the horses wouldn't be spooked by his lesson.

Hoof beats sounded behind him. Lindsay rode down the grassy hill, followed by his groom. "I brought something for you. Catch!"

An object flew through the air towards Gabe, twice the distance a man could throw without the aid of magic.

Gabe caught the item. It was wrapped tightly in heavy paper. He sniffed and caught the rose scent of Turkish delights. He unwrapped it. Turkish delights were a rare treat.

"Go ahead, eat one. If we're going to work magic today, you'll need your energy."

"Thanks!" Gabe popped one of the chewy treats into his mouth. *Delicious.* He'd eaten two more by the time Lindsay reached him. He dismounted and his groom left to join Gabe's on the other side of the pond.

As Lindsay came closer, Gabe's stomach turned over. He swallowed hard to keep the sweets from coming back up. Had he eaten them too fast? Gina was constantly nagging him to slow down when eating. She always said he'd make himself sick. He grimaced. He didn't want her to be right. She'd never let him forget it.

His head spun and he weaved on his feet. Sweat burst out on his forehead.

"I think I'm going to be sick," he murmured to Lindsay, who came up beside him.

"Here, let me help you." Lindsay placed an arm across his back.

Gabe's skin crawled and a blur of faces popped into his mind. What was happening? He looked into Lindsay's eyes. For a second, he thought he saw a flicker of yellow flames in the black pupils. He froze. This wasn't Lord Lindsay. It was the demon.

Gabe tried to gather his magic, but he couldn't focus. The dizziness grew. His legs collapsed beneath him and all he could think was—

Lord Lindsay was dead.

CHAPTER FORTY-ONE

JULIAN POUNDED UP THE STEPS of the Harbrook townhouse. By His Blood, he was tired. He and Langley had spent the entire night trying to find someone who'd seen either the missing men or the demon. They'd finally found a footman who'd seen two mages leaving White's around the same time the beast had fled the opera house.

They'd gone to the young men's terrace houses. One had returned home then left shortly afterward. The other never returned at all. Julian couldn't be sure these were the lords the demon had taken.

It'd been near five in the morning when Julian dropped Langley off at his home. He penned a note for Regina's brother to let him know he'd be there later today. He'd needed some rest and food before going to perform magic with the young lord.

Deeds looked at Julian in surprise, and then leaned around him to look down the stairs towards his carriage.

"Where's Master Gabriel?"

"Isn't he home?"

Deeds frowned and his forehead creased with

worry. "Come in. I need to get Lady Regina."

Julian followed him to the drawing room. Deeds opened the door. "Please have a seat. I'll let Lady Regina know you are here."

A few minutes later Regina rushed into the room.

"Where's Gabe? Deeds said he isn't with you." The words tumbled out of her mouth.

A bad feeling hit Julian in the gut. "I thought Gabe was here at home. I told him I'd be by later today for his lesson."

"He received another letter from you after that one. Asking him to meet you at Kensington Park. Please tell me you sent it." Her glance pleaded with him.

Julian absorbed the import of her words. "I only sent the one. We need to get to the park. Do you know where he was told to meet me?"

She pulled the letter out of her dress pocket and handed it to him.

The handwriting was different from his, which wasn't surprising. However, the stamp on the wax seal was identical to the one he used. If his suspicions were correct, then the Marquis of Thornwood's son was another one of the demon's victims. They needed to get to Kensington Park as soon as possible.

"My carriage is still outside. Let's go." He strode for the door.

"Deeds," Regina said as she left the townhouse, "please tell my aunt we went to find Gabriel."

"I will, miss."

"Kensington Park. Hurry!" Julian called to his driver. The carriage lurched forward. The horses' hooves clopped loudly on the cobblestones. A whip cracked and the horses picked up speed. Lady Regina tumbled across the seat, and he reached out to pull her close against him.

She clasped his hand and looked up at him. "Did you find the demon last night?"

"No."

"Do you think the demon sent that note?"

"We know the demon is after you. My guess is that he is using Gabe to draw you to him."

"It's my fault. The demon has killed everyone near me. And now he has my brother."

"We don't know that for sure. Gabe has the power of your bloodline. With any luck he realized it was the demon and got away."

She bit her lip and her eyes were uncertain. "The demon is after me. If anything happens to Gabe, I'm responsible."

Regina blamed herself, but it wasn't her fault. Events that happened centuries ago had led to this moment. If blame fell anywhere, it belonged on Julian's shoulders. "You're not to blame."

If the demon had impersonated him in order to get close to Gabriel, that meant the Julian Rutherford of this time period was dead. There was no way the demon could shapeshift into Julian's likeness unless he'd taken the soul of the marquis's son.

To bring up this possibility, Julian would have to tell Regina he was an impostor. She would be hurt. He'd lied to her and been intimate with her, all the while knowing that he couldn't marry her.

She stared out the carriage windows and his breath dried in his throat. It didn't matter that she raised feelings in him that he couldn't deny. He had to tell her the truth, even if it destroyed everything between them.

You're not to blame.

Regina mulled over the earl's words. He was wrong. It was her curse that had brought the demon here and put her brother's life in jeopardy. The only consolation she had was that she didn't think the demon would kill Gabe. At least, not until he had her in his grasp. She had a feeling the foul creature knew she would give her life to save her brother.

As much as she wanted revenge for the past, she wasn't Evelyn anymore. She lived in this time with her brother. Gabe was all that mattered.

The question she faced now was—should she tell Julian she knew why the demon was after her? It sounded so ridiculous, this story of reincarnation and blood magic and a dying witch's curse. But the very fact the demon was hunting her confirmed it. Demons recognized souls, which meant the monster knew she was Evelyn.

No matter how unbelievable her story sounded, she needed to tell Julian. He was her partner in hunting the demon, and he'd saved her life more than once. And, she admitted to herself, she loved this magelord who didn't care about her human blood and willingly trained her brother when everyone else refused to. She turned away from the window and met his gaze.

"Lady Regina." His expression was so serious, her heart clenched in her chest. Was this about Gabe? Did he think her little brother was dead?

"Yes, milord?"

"There's something I must tell you." He angled to face her on the seat, but he didn't release her hand.

"What is it?"

His jaw worked, as if he struggled to get the words out. "I'm not the Earl of Lindsay."

"I beg your pardon?" The blood rushed into her head as she stared at him, uncomprehending. He couldn't be the demon. He'd gotten past the wards in her townhome. "What do you mean you're not the Earl of Lindsay?"

"I've been impersonating him. I think the real earl is dead, killed by the demon."

"You're saying you are not the son of the Marquis of Thornwood?"

"That's correct."

She yanked her hand out of his grasp and slid away from him. No wonder he seemed so different from the drunken lout at the Prinsworth ball last year. He wasn't the same man. Her stomach roiled as she stared into his indigo eyes. He was a liar. She'd fallen in love with a person who didn't exist. "Who proposed to me?" she snapped.

"I did."

Lord Lindsay had betrayed her, just like her

father. Just because she was half-human, it didn't mean she didn't have a heart or soul. What was wrong with the mageborn, that they thought half-bloods did not matter? "Why would you do this? Is it because I'm a half-blood?"

"No! It had nothing to do with you being a half-blood. I needed your help to find the demon. I only proposed because your reputation would have been ruined otherwise. I never meant any harm."

"You meant no harm? What will happen to my reputation once word gets out that Lord Lindsay is dead? That I've been taken in by an impostor?"

"Nobody will know about my impersonation. As soon as we find the demon I'll disappear, and then people can learn the earl is dead. Your reputation will be safe."

"I don't care about my reputation." Her voice echoed loud and angry within the carriage. "I let you into my heart and home. I begged you to train my brother in magic. I let you touch me in ways that no man other than my future husband should. And you tell me that all will be well as soon as you disappear?"

"I'm sorry."

Magic bubbled up in her blood as her rage built. "My brother looked up to you. All he ever wanted was to follow in his father's footsteps and become a demon hunter. Until you came along, he had no hope of receiving the training he needed. And now you are going to leave? Was this your plan all along? To find the demon and then disappear? How could you?"

"I had planned on asking Lord Langley to continue training your brother."

"Even if he says yes, Langley has never hunted demons. He doesn't have the experience you do. And what about me? The real Lord Lindsay hated humans and half-bloods. Were you going to leave me to my fate if the demon hadn't killed him?"

"I would have had you break the betrothal."

"*Of course* you would have. What is your real name? As your *betrothed*—" she infused the word with enormous sarcasm—"don't you think I have the right to know?"

He hesitated. "You can call me Julian Rutherford."

She shook her head in disgust. She'd thought she'd known him—that he was an honorable man. How could she have been so wrong? "You can't even tell me your name?"

"It's complicated."

"Only because you are a liar."

He winced and she felt a perverse joy that her dart had landed.

"If you aren't the marquis's son, are you the by-blow of a relation of his? Because the resemblance is uncanny."

"I'm not the bastard of anyone."

"If you're not a by-blow, then who are you?"

"I'm not at liberty to say."

"Of course you aren't." She glared at him. "I hate you," she bit the words out. "You betrayed us all. My brother worships you. If he survives, there won't be anyone to train him to become a demon hunter. He'll be defenseless. And you and I both know that Gabriel will never turn his back on his heritage. Training or no training, he will fight. Do you really think Langley can give Gabe the knowledge he needs?"

"Regina, I'm sorry. I hadn't planned for things to happen this way." He looked devastated, but she hardened her heart. "Maybe there's a way I could continue his training."

If the real earl hadn't died, they could have continued this ruse. But once people knew the earl was dead, this Julian Rutherford would not be able to show his face in London anymore. "I believe you, but it doesn't change anything. You can't marry me, and you can't continue to train Gabriel. There is no future for us now."

A few moments later the carriage slowed down as they entered Kensington Park. Lord Lindsay—she refused to call him Julian or Rutherford since both of those names implied an intimacy she no longer acknowledged—called directions to the driver. The coach rolled to a stop. Julian descended the coach and turned to assist her.

She glared at his outstretched hand, but took it. No point risking a tumble. She'd probably fall right into his arms. As soon as her feet touched the ground she stepped away.

The early morning sun sparkled on the dewy green grass, and the pond gleamed a deep dark blue. The steady hum of bugs and bird songs filled the air. Regina could tell where the demon had been, could sense that thread of uncanniness disturbing the tranquil meadow. "The demon was here, but he's gone now."

Lindsay picked up a paper wrapper that lay on the grass with a few sweets. "Turkish delights."

She sucked in a breath. "Those were Gabe's favorites. How did he know?"

"It could have been a lucky guess. Turkish delights are very popular." He placed the wrapper in his pocket. "But we don't know for certain that the demon has your brother."

Two servants and their horses waited on the other side of the pond. She held her hand up over her eyes to shield them from the bright sun. "Gabe's groom is over there."

"I see my groom as well. I'll have them come here." He waved at the men, who mounted up and headed back.

Regina knelt where Lindsay had found the paper wrapper and reached for the sweets. The image of a brown-eyed man with a beaked nose holding out a flask flashed before her. *Kikson.* She pulled her hand back, leaving the candy untouched. "I think the demon used these to drug Gabriel."

"That would make sense. If your brother ate these, he could have been incapacitated before he realized it was the demon."

The grooms arrived at the clearing. The older one said, "Lord Lindsay, why is a carriage here? Where's the young lord?"

"We're not sure," he answered. "Could you recount the events of this morning, from the time you arrived?"

Lindsay's groom looked at them oddly, but nod-ded his head. "Certainly, my lord. You and I came here to meet with Lord Harbrook. Buck and I took the horses to the other side of the pond so they wouldn't be spooked by all the magical goings-on. It looked like young Harbrook needed a moment to sit down, because we saw you help him sit. Then there was a burst of magic. I don't quite know what happened next. One moment you and Harbrook were here. The next thing we knew you were here with a carriage and Lady Regina."

Gabriel's groom nodded his head in agreement.

"Thank you. You both may return home now. We'll take the carriage back."

"As you wish, milord." They rode off.

Regina stared after the men. She didn't want to look at Lord Lindsay, or see the pity on his face. There was no question now. The real earl was dead, and the demon had her brother.

"We'll find them, Regina."

"I know we will." She didn't think the demon would kill Gabriel, not when her brother was his only bargaining chip. That didn't mean the evil fiend wouldn't hurt or torture him though.

She looked up at Lindsay. Fear for her brother and Lindsay's betrayal created an ache in her heart that nearly brought her to her knees. The earl—fake earl—had been her support. He'd been the one person she'd thought she could tell about the curse. But she couldn't tell him her secret, not anymore. His betrayal hurt too much. But if any-one would kill the demon for her, he would. He'd stolen another man's identity and even proposed marriage to her in order to hunt this creature down. He'd do anything to kill this demon.

Of course he would. The demon had killed his wife. The tightness in her chest grew. Had anything they shared been real?

"Can you follow his trail?"

Forget about Lindsay and his past. She had to find Gabriel. Regina called up her magic. The demon's scent was fresh and easy to trace. "Yes, I can."

They returned to the carriage, and she called out the directions. The trail wound out of Kensington Park and through the streets of London until they came to the Great North Road.

"We should return to your house and let your aunt know what is going on."

She raised her chin. "No. We must follow it now. We can't be more than an hour or two behind them."

"They're traveling on horseback. Wherever they're going, they'll make much better time than we will in a carriage. It doesn't matter if we wait a little longer. We won't be able to catch them regardless."

She looked down at her dress and thought for a moment. "We could ride too."

"Are you sure? Traveling by horseback is very tiring."

"We'll make better time. I have to get to Gabe. Why don't you drop me at my townhouse then fetch your horse and bags. When you come back, I'll be ready."

"I'll see if Langley can join us."

"Very well." She scrutinized him. "Does your cousin know you aren't the real earl?"

"Yes. So does the marquis."

Did everyone except her and Gabe know the truth? "I see."

"They only agreed because they wanted to help me catch the demon. I resembled the real earl too much to use a different identity. I knew the monster had gone to London in the form of a lord. I never meant for you to get hurt by this, Regina."

"When you made yourself a part of our lives, knowing it was only temporary, you made hurting me inevitable. I can handle my own pain, but Gabriel won't have anyone to train him to become a demon hunter anymore. That's the part I can't bear. Assuming the demon doesn't hurt him."

"We'll get him back, and then we'll figure out what we can do about his training. I won't leave Gabriel on his own."

He sounded sincere, but she wasn't sure she believed him. Once he'd killed the demon, he wouldn't need her or her brother anymore. Would he really stay to help a pair of half-bloods? Yesterday she would have answered yes, unreservedly. Today—she wasn't sure she knew him anymore.

The carriage halted in front of her townhouse. "I will be ready within the hour."

"I'll see you soon." He leaned back against his seat and the footman shut the carriage door.

CHAPTER FORTY-TWO

JULIAN WALKED INTO LANGLEY'S STUDY, where his cousin sat behind an oak desk flipping through a sheaf of documents. "The demon kidnapped Lady Regina's brother."

"That's a bloody rotten turn of events. How did it get past the blood ward?"

"It didn't. It sent a letter to Lord Harbrook asking him to meet me at Kensington Park for this morning's lesson. The note was marked with my seal."

Langley's fingers stilled on his papers and his gaze flicked up.

"The grooms were still there when I arrived with Lady Regina. There seemed to be a gap in their memories, but they remembered me meeting Lord Harbrook."

"So unless *you're* the demon, the real earl is dead."

"Yes, poor bastard." Although from all accounts the Marquis of Thornwood's son had been an unsavory character, losing his soul to a demon was a fate nobody deserved. "Considering the circumstances, I had no choice but to tell Lady Regina the truth."

"That you're a man from the past?" Langley's eyebrows rose.

"Hardly. I told her I was an impostor. It didn't go over well." That was an understatement. Every word she'd thrown had left him bloody and writhing in his guilt. He'd betrayed her trust. The familiar ache of loss rose in his chest. After he'd killed the demon, he'd somehow assumed she and her brother would remain a part of his life. Now any hope of a future with them was gone, and he had to find Gabriel before the demon tortured or killed him.

Langley leaned back in his seat and steepled his fingers. "Did I ever tell you I did some investigating?"

"Of what?"

"I dug into the Marquis of Thornwood's family tree."

Where was this leading? Had Langley found someone Julian could be descended from that would account for his resemblance to the earl? Was this a background that could be used to allow him to stay in London? "What did you find?"

"Nothing. No uncles, nephews, cousins, aunts, sisters, or bastard children. The marquis and his son are the last of the family line."

The news rocked Julian. After all the generations between him and the marquis, they were the only two left? "No one else?"

"Your family seems to have been cursed with reckless bravery over the centuries. If there was a war anywhere in this hemisphere, your family got involved. If there wasn't a war, your family started one. It's a wonder anyone was left at all to continue the line."

"What are you saying?"

Langley dropped the mocking tone and leaned forward. "There's no one for generations that you could be descended from other than the marquis, and he says it's impossible that he has a by-blow. Of course, the resemblance could just be coincidence, and yet, you did have the original signet ring of the Earl of Lindsay."

"Are you saying you believe I'm from the past?" Julian was incredulous.

Langley leaned back. "I'm saying that when you've ruled out the possible, sometimes the only thing left is the impossible. So yes." The side of his mouth lifted in a smile. "I suppose I am."

Julian blew out a breath and raked a hand through his hair at Langley's surprise support. "I'm honored. Thank you." It meant a lot to him to have the backing of a man he respected.

"So what are your plans now?"

"Lady Regina tracked the demon to the Great North Road. We're going after it. I want you to join us."

Langley's expression sobered. "I can't."

"You've been helping me search for the demon for weeks. Why can't you come?"

"It's complicated. I can't leave London right now."

"Change your plans."

"Believe me, I would if I could. But it's impossible."

"What's more important than catching a demon and rescuing a young boy?"

"I can't say."

"You mean you won't tell me."

"I can't. I'm sorry." And to his credit, Langley actually did seem sincere.

"How long do you have to stay in London?"

"Days, possibly weeks."

"So you won't be able to join us later."

"No, but I have every confidence in you."

If Langley couldn't go, so be it. He'd kill the demon on his own. But just in case things didn't go as planned—

"I have a favor to ask you." As much as Julian wanted to keep training Gabriel, he didn't know if that would be possible. "Would you continue Lord Harbrook's training in magic? Once word gets out about the real earl's death, I'll have to disappear."

Langley stood up. "Of course."

"He wants to be a demon hunter. Any training you can give him in fighting would be appreciated. I'd like him to have a long career in defeating the monsters."

"You have my word."

Julian reached across the desk and held out his hand. He didn't know what business his cousin was involved in, but he knew it must be serious for Langley to stay behind. "If all goes well, I'll tell the marquis the news about his son in person. If not, I'm afraid you'll have to find a way to hunt the demon on your own. You've been a good ally. I'm glad you were there to watch my back."

"Godspeed, Julian."

Regina rushed into the townhouse. She didn't have time to waste stewing about Lord Lindsay's lies to her or what his real name was.

Deeds met her in the hallway. "Thank goodness you're here, milady. Your aunt wants to see you."

"Where is she?"

"She's upstairs in her sitting room."

"Does she know Gabriel is missing?"

"We told her you and Lord Lindsay had gone to Kensington Park to look for him." His long face sagged. "You didn't find him?"

"No, but we know what happened to him. He was—" She couldn't say her brother was captured by the demon. Even if Deeds believed her, he'd worry terribly. Their stern butler had a soft spot for her brother. She decided to go with a slightly less frightening option. One that didn't involve the stealing of his soul. "He was kidnapped, but we found his trail. Don't worry, we'll rescue him."

"You and Lord Lindsay?" Deeds frowned, looking even more anxious than before.

"Yes. Please have Gabe's horse brought around front. I want it saddled with his saddle, not a side saddle. And I need saddlebags for travel brought to my room."

"Are you sure you don't want to take a carriage?"

"I'm going after my brother, and I need to be

able to move quickly. Lord Lindsay should be here within the hour. Please let me know when he arrives."

"Very well." He bowed, and scuffled away as fast as his arthritic legs let him.

Regina gathered her skirts and ran up the stairs to her aunt's room. She knocked politely then entered the room. "You wanted to see me?"

Aunt Agatha sat on a settee in front of her fireplace. She dropped the embroidery hoop she was holding to her lap. "Have you been keeping secrets?"

Regina's heart pounded. Did her aunt know about Lindsay's lies? How did she find out? "What do you mean?"

"I just came back from Lady Marleigh's."

She released a breath. So much had happened that she'd completely forgotten about the Marleighs. "How is Lady Felicity doing? Is she all right?"

Her aunt's head tilted to the side and her eyebrows arched high. "She's still very weak—after all, the poor girl hadn't eaten in weeks—but her wounds seem to have miraculously healed. Without leaving any scars, if you can believe it."

"That's wonderful!" Her magic had worked. If the demon hurt Gabriel, she could heal him too. "Maybe all she'd needed was rest."

"Honestly, Regina, I know I'm older than you, but I'm not senile." Her aunt shook her head reprovingly. "Soon after we left, Felicity sat up and started talking. She ate her first meal in days. When they removed the dressings from her injuries, the wounds were gone. Do you want to explain what you did while I spoke with her mother?"

The time for truth had come. "I healed her."

Aunt Agatha didn't say anything, just looked at her and waited.

The words Regina had kept bottled up for weeks poured out. "I discovered I had magic that day you went to ask Lord Burlington to train Gabriel. Mostly I've had visions, but I've also been able to heal minor cuts. When we visited Felicity, she reminded me of father on his last day. Somehow I could see her injuries, and I fixed them."

"If I hadn't seen Felicity for myself I wouldn't have believed it. But she remembers. She knew you held her hand, and then she said her body suddenly felt like fire was burning it from the inside out. After the fire passed, she felt fine." She sighed. "When were you going to tell me?"

"Today." Remorse flooded her that she hadn't told her aunt sooner. "I didn't tell you because I feared it might disappear as quickly as it came."

"Power doesn't work like that. Once you have it, it's yours to keep."

Regina laughed. Warm affection filled her toward the aunt who had fulfilled the role of mother and father after her parents had passed. "I should have come to you right away then."

"No, my dear, you needed time to adjust. It's a big change to think you are magicless then one day discover you are a seeress and healer at once."

"Thanks for understanding. I have so much to tell you." Regina told her aunt everything that had happened in the past few weeks, leaving nothing out.

"So Lord Lindsay is an impostor?"

"Yes."

"That explains why I find the earl so likable now. I positively detested him before."

"You did?"

"Oh yes. But he seemed reformed and I could tell he was besotted with you, so I thought he would be a good match."

"But he lied to me."

"Yes, he did, and I would expect you to make him grovel before you forgive him. In the meantime, he's going to help you rescue Gabriel, and he wants to find a way to continue your brother's training. That's not the sign of a man who doesn't care."

"But I don't know who he is." How could they have a future when the world thought he was the Earl of Lindsay, who was now dead?

"He's a magelord who wants to kill a monster and rescue your brother, and he's not ashamed to ask for your help. You already know quite a bit about him. See what happens after you find the demon. Things might work themselves out."

Regina hugged her aunt. "Thank you."

Her aunt squeezed her tight and sniffled. Then she patted Regina's back and said, "Now then, we need to get busy. Don't you have some packing to do?"

Regina went straight to her brother's room. She wasn't going to hunt the demon riding sidesaddle and wearing a dress.

She wasn't quite as tall as Gabe, but close enough for his clothes to fit. She'd taken one of her sturdiest scarves and wrapped it tightly around her bosom to flatten her chest. Then she'd pulled on her brother's shirt, trouser, waistcoat, and jacket. She pinned her hair up, and then hid it with Gabriel's hat, pulling the rim low over her forehead. She looked at herself from all angles. Dressed like this she could pass for a young man, if people didn't look too closely.

She finished packing, adding a dress just in case, then went downstairs. "Deeds, please show Lord Lindsay to the morning room when he arrives."

His eyes opened wide when he saw her, then his expression blanked, ever the consummate butler. "Yes, milady."

Regina paced in front of the window, glancing out at the bustling street for any sign of the earl. It had been nearly an hour. Where was Lindsay?

The door opened and she turned.

Lord Lindsay entered the room and walked towards her. His gaze traveled over her body, a hot, sensual look that made Regina's skin burn. Although she knew her figure was hidden by the jacket and waistcoat, she blushed. When he drew close, his eyes had an intensity that made her catch her breath. He'd looked at her that same way before kissing her at Langley's estate.

They stared at each other silently for a few moments. Would he beg her forgiveness? Take her in his arms?

Instead he said, "It's a good disguise."

"Thank you." She forced the words past her suddenly dry throat. "I'm lucky Gabriel isn't so much larger than me that I couldn't wear his clothes."

"Very lucky," he agreed, as his eyes continued to devour her.

"Aunt Agatha will be back soon," she said, desperate to ease the heated tension. What was she doing? She was still mad at him for lying to her. Could she really forgive him that easily?

He straightened and took a step back, and the chasm between them was more than physical. "That reminds me. Here." He handed her a sheathed dagger. "It's coated with demonsbane oil. You should have something to defend yourself with."

Memories flooded her mind as she stared at the weapon. The pain of Evelyn's lost baby and death merged with Gabriel's disappearance, and a desire for revenge flared hot in Regina's soul.

"I never once imagined that I would be the one following in my father's footsteps. It was always going to be Gabriel." She wrapped her fingers around the cold metal hilt. The action weighed heavily on her, as if by taking the dagger she was choosing a different future. "But here I am, holding a blade, and there's nothing more that I want than to use it."

"What do you mean?"

Her voice was fierce when she spoke. "My father dreaded going after demons. Hated it. But I'm so *angry*. That fiend kidnapped my brother. There's nothing I want more than to hunt him down and make him pay."

"We will, I promise. Are you ready?"

"Yes."

Aunt Agatha rushed into the room, carrying two wrapped packets. "Good, you're both still here. Take these." She held the items out.

The scent of pickles, bread, and beef wafted up. "Sandwiches?"

"Yes. I thought you might get hungry on the journey."

Regina hugged her. "You are the best. I didn't think to pack any food."

"I brought provisions too, but nothing that smells as good as this. Thank you." Julian placed the parcel in his jacket pocket.

"Lord Lindsay, must you and Regina go after the demon? Shouldn't the Mage High Council be notified? Surely they have someone they could send."

Regina shook her head. "We don't have time to wait for the council members to convene, make a decision, and find someone to track it. Since father's death, I haven't heard of any other demon hunters, have you?"

"Well, no. But who knows what resources the council has? Going after the demon is dangerous. You might get killed."

"Lord Lindsay fought the creature and saved my life. I'm certain he'll be able to save Gabriel if we can find them in time."

"I'll do my best to keep your niece and nephew safe," Julian promised.

"We need to go." Regina squeezed her aunt's hand. "I'll send word as soon as I know anything."

"Be careful, my dear," Aunt Agatha said, wrapping her in a hug. She pulled back with a half-laugh. "It's like hugging Gabriel. You even smell like him."

"I *am* wearing his clothes." Regina swallowed the lump in her throat. She hoped this wasn't the last time she'd see her aunt. She kissed her cheek. "I love you. Thank you for taking care of me and Gabe all these years."

"Tut tut," her aunt admonished, her voice thick with tears. "Don't talk like that. I'll see you both soon. Take care of them, Lord Lindsay."

Julian stepped forward and took her aunt's hand. "I will. You have my word."

CHAPTER FORTY-THREE

REGINA PULLED HER HORSE TO the side of the Great North Road. At her family's country estate, she'd ridden often with Gabriel, who loved racing across the hills with her. Fear clenched her heart as she worried she'd never get another chance to ride with him again. She had to find him.

Her brown gelding snorted and stamped the ground. She could feel its teeth chomping on the bit through the reins. She loved the feel of the powerful animal beneath her, and the security of knowing that compared to riding sidesaddle, sitting astride put her much more in tune with the powerful creature.

She leaned forward and patted her mount's neck. "We'll get going soon, I promise," she murmured soothingly.

First, she had to pick up the demon's trace again.

She called up the memory of the huge monster crushing her to the floor, his magic clogging her throat and nostrils, his rank breath hot on her skin as he tried to take her soul. Then she concentrated on her need to find him.

There—a pull forward on the Great North Road. She turned to Julian, who rode a large grey stallion. "I've got his trail again."

"Good. Do you have any idea where he might be going?"

"Not yet. He won't do anything to hide his tracks though. He wants me to come after them."

"We'll find them." His voice was strong and determined.

"I know. But what condition will Gabriel be in? Will he torture him?"

"I doubt it. We don't know how far they're going, but it'd be hard to travel with an injured man. My guess is the demon will keep your brother drugged and unconscious. They're probably in a conveyance of some kind—most likely a private carriage. We'll catch them."

She'd felt ice cold since learning of Gabriel's disappearance, but his words consoled her. He was right. They'd rescue Gabe. If the demon hurt her brother—well, she'd healed Felicity. She could heal him too. After the fiend was dead.

She and Lindsay rode off at a steady, ground-eating pace that would not tire the horses. The dirt road was dry and packed down. There were many carriages and wagons at first, but the further they got from London, the emptier the route became.

Regina focused her will on finding the demon. That steady pull never diminished. After a while she didn't even need to focus. She could feel the sharp tug, like a splinter lodged beneath her skin.

The terrain gradually changed from the flat environs outside of London, to tree-lined fields surrounded by dry stone walls, to thick forests. Her back and bottom ached from riding. She'd kept her hat brim pulled low. Not once had anyone remarked on her gender. Instead, people tipped their hats, saying "Gentlemen." Julian had responded each time. Regina merely nodded.

The sun sank below the horizon. The road through the forest was full of shadows. In less than thirty minutes, the path would be completely black.

"We need to stop for the night," Lord Lindsay said.

She agreed. She was exhausted, and already, the road was difficult to see. The last thing they needed was for one of their horses to get injured. Plus, there were highwaymen to watch for. Lord Lindsay might be powerful enough to ward them off with his magic, but she didn't want to risk it.

"There's an inn not far ahead, The Wandering Magician. Langley and I stayed there on our way to London. It's clean enough and the food is decent."

A sudden worry struck her at the name. "I'm a half-blood. If they somehow found out, would they allow me to stay?"

She'd heard stories of places that required a small feat of magic as the price of entry.

His expression turned fierce. "They will."

Warm light fell through the inn's windows onto the cobblestone courtyard. Regina slid her leg over the saddle, feeling the ache of being in the same position for hours. Julian stepped towards her, but she gave a slight shake of her head. If he helped her, he would give away her disguise. She finished dismounting. Two grooms stepped up to take the reins.

Julian unleashed the straps on the backs of the horses and removed the saddlebags. Once he had them, the grooms led the horses away to the stable. He easily slung one pair of saddlebags over his shoulder. The other pair he held out to her.

That's right. She'd have to carry her own saddlebags. Julian raised them high enough that she easily slid them onto her shoulder. The weight settled against her back and chest. She was thankful for her brother's gloves. They hid her slender fingers and fine-boned hands. "Thanks."

He led the way into the inn. A hearty fire crackled in an enormous, sooty stone fireplace at the back of the room. A bar stood to the side of the entrance, and a large handwritten sign on the wall stated: Magic Required.

What trick could she do? She didn't think "I can track demons" would suffice. She gripped the saddlebags more firmly, her fingernails digging into the hard leather.

A large burly man stepped towards them from behind the bar, a towel in his hand wiping out a glass.

"We need a room for the night, and a hot meal," Lindsay said.

The barman gestured at the sign with his head. "That won't be no problem, if you can meet the requirements."

"What do you need?"

The man shrugged. "Anything that proves you're mageborn."

Julian snapped his fingers and a bright orange ball of light flashed into being right before the man's face. The man blinked and leaned back. A second later the orb was gone.

"We'll take that spot over there," Julian said, indicating a table against the far wall that was slightly in shadow.

"Not yet. It's his turn."

Regina cleared her throat as deeply as she could and croaked, "I have visions."

The man sighed and shook his head, as if he'd heard this excuse many times. "That's not good enough."

She saw Julian tense. "I can try to call up a vision for you. What do you want?"

The man's eyes flicked towards a blonde woman in her early thirties wearing an apron over her gown and a ruffled bonnet over her hair. She was serving plates of food and drink to the customers at their tables. "That's my wife. I want you to tell me what you see."

Regina noticed sadness and longing in the barman's eyes when he looked at his wife. "Have her come here. I need to touch her."

The barkeep scowled.

"Just her hand, nothing else."

"Gertie! I need you here."

His wife turned and flashed him a beautiful, if tired, smile. She finished depositing the dishes from her tray on the table then tucked the tray against her side as she made her way to them. "Yes?"

He waved his towel and glass at Regina. "This young man says his magic is visions. I asked him if he could see anything about you, and he said he needed to touch your hand."

Gertie looked up into her face. Her eyebrows rose slightly above merry brown eyes. She slid a sidelong glance at her husband. "This *young man?*"

Regina silently begged the woman not to tell. She could feel the tension radiating from Julian beside her.

"Yes." Her husband flapped the washcloth in Regina's direction.

Gertie shrugged. "Very well." She held out a hand that was rough and reddened from hard work.

As tired as she was, Regina called up her magic. It took a moment to find the gold bubbles in her blood. Heat blossomed beneath her skin. "I'm ready."

Julian reached forward and pulled the saddlebags from her shoulder. She took her gloves off and laid them on the counter. She touched her fingertips to Gertie's palm. A spark jumped from the contact. The barmaid gasped and Regina gripped her hand tightly, her thumb pressing firmly into the woman's flesh. She raised her head to look into Gertie's eyes. Magic surged down her arm into Gertie's body and back. Gertie's mouth fell open.

A moment later she released Gertie's hand and her own dropped by her side. Her breaths came quick and fast. She felt drained.

Gertie rubbed her hand and her eyes were a little frightened.

The barkeep looked between them. "What happened?"

Gertie shook her head. She looked unsure.

Regina stared straight ahead at the image she saw as clear as day before her. "Your wife will be blessed with a healthy baby boy by Christmas. Congratulations." Her voice came out soft and deep.

Gertie gasped. "How did you know? I told no one, not even Bart." She cast a pleading look towards her husband. "I wanted to wait a little longer. We've been disappointed so many times."

The big man's eyes filled with tears. "It's true then?"

Regina's shoulders fell. She felt weary. "I saw Gertie cradling a little baby boy in her arms before the fireplace, you leaning over them both. The fire burned low, and holly decorated the mantle. That's all."

The man swung his wife around and bussed her on the lips. "You wonderful woman. We're going to be parents!" He reached forward and shook Regina's hand in his large grip. "Gertie, please lead them to the table at the back wall. Your first drink is on the house."

Gertie's eyes were full of tears, but her smile was bright. "Welcome. We are honored to have you stay."

They followed the barmaid to a battered oak table in the far corner. Gertie left them and said she'd be back shortly with their drinks and some food.

"How do you feel?" Lindsay asked.

"Good. Glad to be sitting down." She slumped against her chair back. It felt wonderful to have something to lean against.

"I thought you would be upset about the test."

"I'm so tired right now that it's hard to care about anything," she said with a half-laugh. "I'd sleep in a barn and be happy about it."

"That was a nice vision you had. They'll have a happy Christmas."

"It was lovely." She smiled softly to herself. "I could feel the presence of another soul inside her, burning so bright. Even without the vision, I knew she was carrying a baby boy."

"I thought demon hunters could sense souls. Is this so unusual?"

"I suppose not, but it's a new ability for me. I hadn't realized I could sense souls through a mere touch."

His dark gaze was inscrutable in the flickering candlelight from the wall sconce above. "Can you feel my soul?" He reached his hand across the table.

What would she find? Would she learn anything new about him? She looked up at him. "You're not afraid I'll learn your secrets?"

"No."

"Very well."

Breathing deep, she gathered her magic and then touched the back of his hand. Power surged between them, hot and almost violent. Images flashed through her head—Evelyn, laughing and kissing Julian, dashing through the meadow as he gave chase—then Lindsay, the dark moodiness in his blue eyes when Regina had first met him, and the sweet intensity with which he'd kissed her at Langley's estate. Through it all the weight of ages pressed down on her, burdened even further by a sense of despair, rage, and love.

Grief etched the hard planes of his face. She jerked her fingers back.

"What did you sense?" His voice was hoarse.

"Your soul feels *old*." Was it possible he was Evelyn's Julian reincarnated? That they were both being given a second chance at love and a life together?

"Old?"

There was so much to explain to even begin this discussion. Evelyn's dying curse, Regina's blocked memories and magic. Would she even survive to have a future?

She was exhausted, physically and mentally, and her worries about Gabe tore at her constantly. It was cowardly, but she couldn't muster the trust to open herself up so fully. "I know it makes no sense."

◆───

Julian hadn't become the leader of the Mageborn rebellion just because he was Eric's brother. He'd also been a good reader of people. Regina was being evasive. "Old in what way? How did Gertie's soul feel?"

Her gaze darted up to his. Why was she surprised he wanted to know?

"Hers felt current. The baby's soul felt new. Yours

had the weight of years attached. What do you think that means? Do you believe in reincarnation?"

He remembered his thoughts a few weeks ago, when he had wondered if she was Evelyn reincarnated. Almost everything about Regina reminded him of Evelyn, but while his wife had grown up knowing she was loved and been unafraid to go after the things she wanted, Regina had grown up without loving parents and been despised for her half-blood status. How Regina had survived her upbringing to develop into such a warm, generous woman was a mystery.

Could she be Evelyn? Despite their different upbringings, they were surprisingly similar in character. But if Regina didn't remember him or her past life, what difference did it make if she was his reincarnated wife? "Maybe. Who knows what is possible?"

"Do you think that could be why your soul feels old?"

He almost choked on his ale. "You think I've been reincarnated?"

She drew circles on the scarred and worn tabletop. "I don't know. I'm just looking for explanations for why your soul feels the way it does."

This was his chance to tell her the truth. Was traveling forward through time harder to believe in than reincarnation? By His Blood, yes. Even stories of the darkest magics never talked about time travel. Immortality, yes. Crossing boundaries between worlds, yes. Disappearing into faerie worlds where time passed differently, yes. But actual travel through time? No.

She already thought he was a liar. If he told her he had traveled through time, she would think he was making fun of her. "I suppose that could be it. What about life experiences? If a person had lived through many hardships, could that make their soul feel older?"

"I don't know. I suppose it could."

"Anything is possible, isn't it?"

She shrugged and looked away.

He didn't think she realized it, but Regina was one of the strongest women he'd ever known. She'd risked everything to track the demon. If she had any reputation left, dressing in men's clothing would shred it. Yet she'd done it without hesitation, all to save her brother. His eyes drank in her golden skin, delicate nose, and stubborn chin, all tucked under a yeoman's floppy hat. She'd never been lovelier to him than in that moment.

Gertie arrived with their food. She placed bread trenchers filled with heaping amounts of a mouth-watering beef stew on the table. "Please let me know if you need anything else. I'll return shortly with more ale."

"Thank you," Regina answered with a weary smile. "The food smells delicious."

Julian caught the loving exchanges between Gertie and Bart as she walked away from their table. He was glad for them, but his heart ached to have a family of his own. He looked across the table at Regina. Sometime during these weeks of hunting down the demon and training Gabriel in magic, Julian had found a new life. Even Langley, his cousin only in name, felt like family. When had he accepted that Evelyn was gone?

If he found a place in this world, could he still marry Regina? Would she accept him?

After eating and drinking, Regina's color returned, a sure sign that her mage energy had been replenished. Her hands cradled the large mug of ale placed before her on the table. She'd drunk nearly the entire thing. Her eyes were bright, her cheeks flushed, but her expression was sad.

"Are you thinking about Gabriel?"

Her fingers tightened on the pewter tankard. "Yes."

What he knew she left unsaid was—would her brother still be alive? "You don't need to worry. They'll have to stop too. Although the demon can travel by night, your brother and any horses they have won't be able to. He's safe for now."

"I hope you're right."

"I am." He stood up and left money on the table. "Let's go. We've got an early start tomorrow."

She nodded and pushed her chair back.

He bent down and picked up his saddlebag, then slung it over his shoulder. He grabbed hers with his free hand. He headed for Bart, who still manned the bar.

"We're ready for our room."

Bart looked at Lady Regina, who stood weaving slightly on her feet. "Is he alright?"

Julian forced a grin. "A little too much to drink.

The lad isn't used to it. He'll be right by morning."

Bart laughed. "That's how we all learned." He gestured to a nearby maid. "Take them to the blue room upstairs. We serve breakfast early, if you're interested."

"Thank you. I appreciate it."

The maid was already ascending the stairs. Julian let Regina pass before him. The blue room was a corner room at the back of the inn. The furthest from the tap room, and therefore the quietest. It was also larger than the room he'd had the first time he stayed there, and better appointed. Bart was showing his appreciation for Lady Regina's vision.

Julian gave the maid a few coins. She curtsied and quietly exited.

The room was comfortably furnished. A fire already burned in the small grate, keeping the damp at bay. The bed was a full size with room enough for two. An armoire stood along the side wall. Two extra blankets were folded inside. He grabbed them and a pillow.

"You can have the bed. I'll take the floor." He dropped the items on the rug before the fireplace.

"Very well."

She moved gracefully around the room, her lithe form comfortable in the men's clothing she sported. Her long legs were clearly delineated by the breeches, and he swallowed the yearning that rose in his throat at the sight. The jacket hid her waist and bosom, but his memory was sharp. He had no problems filling in the hidden details.

She sat down before the dressing table and removed a pin from her hair. One long, dark honey lock fell to her shoulder. He lit a candle and set it on the table so she'd have more light. Their eyes met in the mirror. His heart pounded. All he could hear was the sound of his blood coursing through his veins.

CHAPTER FORTY-FOUR

T HE CANDLE JULIAN SET ON the dressing table enclosed the two of them in its golden aura. Regina met Julian's gaze in the mirror, watching the play of shadows across his cheek.

"Don't you have to get ready for bed?" Her voice came out husky, without the snap she had intended. She inwardly groaned. Instead of a call back to reality, her words sounded like an invitation.

"Yes." He lifted a lock of her hair off her neck. His fingers skimmed over her skin and she shivered.

In the candlelight he looked dark and dangerous…and hungry. What would happen if she gave in? Would it be worth it, even knowing that after they found the demon he would disappear from her life? She was so tempted, but if she got with child—just thinking about explaining that to Gabe made her shudder.

She fought the intimacy of the moment and hardened her tone. "*Now*, Julian. I can't get ready with you here."

"Very well." His gaze lingered on her face, then he released her and strode to the area before the fireplace where he would bed down for the night.

Regina blew out her breath. Her fingers trembled as she removed the rest of the pins from her hair. Between her worries for Gabe and her desire for Julian, how was she going to get any sleep?

She watched Julian in the mirror as he undressed. He removed his jacket and neatly placed it over the back of a small wooden chair at the table. Then he loosened his cravat and unbuttoned his waistcoat. When he pulled his shirt out from his trousers, she jolted to her feet.

"I'm going to change." She grabbed the candle and dashed behind the carved wooden screen in the corner.

Regina removed her clothes and draped them over the chair. She slipped her chemise over her head. Muffled thumps sounded as Julian moved about the room. The rustle of his clothing put her on edge. Did he leave any clothing on? Would he be lying in her bed when she came out?

An image of him—no, *Evelyn's* Julian—standing next to a lake in the late afternoon sun, naked above the waist and shaking water out of his hair, popped into her head. What would *her* Julian look like? Would he be as broad and muscled as Evelyn's husband had been?

She fervently hoped he'd taken his shirt off.

Damn Evelyn and her memories.

They weren't married, and yet tonight felt strangely like a wedding night. She'd never spent a night alone with a man before. She felt vulnerable, exposed. Maybe she shouldn't have changed into her nightdress. The fact that she had done so without a thought told her that despite his lies, she trusted him. She picked up the candlestick and moved from behind the screen.

Julian knelt before the fireplace and placed a fresh log onto the flames. His linen shirt stretched taut across his back, and she squelched her disappointment that he was fully clothed. He stoked the fire. His thick black hair rippled in the flickering light, sometimes flashing a deep burgundy. She longed to run her fingers through the rumpled waves. He rose and returned the poker to its stand.

When he saw her, he froze. Their gazes locked.

"I've put my life and my brother's in your hands. Can you at least tell me your real name?" She had to know. How could they possibly have a future without the most basic of trusts between them?

"It's Julian."

She closed her eyes, swallowing her bitterness. When she opened them, she had to force the words past the regret blocking her throat. "Even now, you won't tell me the truth? Fine. I'll call you by another man's name. What does it matter anyway? As soon as we kill the demon you'll be gone."

He approached warily, as if she were a wounded animal.

Or maybe he thought she'd hit him over the head with the candlestick if he said the wrong thing. Which wasn't such a bad idea.

"My name truly is Julian Rutherford. I have no

title, no land, no funds, no home. If not for the Marquis of Thornwood's generosity, I wouldn't have any resources at all. This journey—every last bit of it—is paid for with his money."

"Why is he doing that for you? Are you a relation?"

"It's complicated." He raked a hand through his hair and paced a couple of steps before turning back. "You should go to bed."

"That's it? End of discussion? Run along and go to bed?" Knowing his name didn't change things at all. They still didn't have a future together.

"Regina."

"Yes?"

"I'm sorry I lied to you. I have nothing to offer you or anyone. But if I could, I would marry you."

Her chest burned with anger. "You can. I'm an heiress. My dowry is more than enough for us to live off of."

His jaw clenched and he glared at her. "Absolutely not."

The fire in her chest flared higher, burning away her fear. She was done hiding her emotions or accepting that she wasn't good enough. "Do you love me?"

Dear God, the expression on his face would melt glaciers and flood the earth. "Yes." He approached her and gently lifted her chin. "But I can't marry you like this. You deserve better."

Despite her best intentions, tears welled. "I *deserve* a man who loves me."

"And one who will take care of you. A man with

a name to leave you and his line. Not a nobody who must beg for every penny he spends."

She knocked his hand away. "You love me, but you won't marry me." She glared at his stubborn stupidity. "I guess rescuing my brother will have to be enough. Good night."

She climbed into the bed and blew the candle out. Julian settled down on the hard floor with nothing more than a thin rug and blanket. For a second Regina felt pity, but she squashed the emotion. The alternative was inviting him to sleep next to her, and she couldn't do that. It was all too easy to imagine his body curled around hers, those muscled arms wrapped around her midriff, those firm lips kissing her neck…

Why did he have to tell her he loved her, and in the same breath say he couldn't marry her? Men and their ridiculous honor.

"Good night, Regina. Sleep well." His husky baritone frayed her nerves. Even his voice attracted her.

She punched her pillow and rolled over so she wouldn't be able to see him. Firelight cast shadows on the wallpaper, and she watched the roses pop with color then disappear. The sounds of Julian tossing before the fire in what she assumed were attempts to get comfortable made her feel guilty. Eventually the long day caught up to her. She yawned and fell asleep.

The jarring gait of a horse brought her back to consciousness. Her head bobbed in time with the horse's steps. She opened her eyes and saw the black head and mane of a giant steed before her. Enormous hide-encased arms enclosed her.

Not again. How many times must she relive this memory? She struggled to wake up, but the vision sucked her deeper.

Kikson had drugged her—how long ago? She tried to move her head away from the demon's chest, but couldn't. Her hands lay limply in her lap. She attempted to curl her fingers. No response. Her mind was awake though. The potion had started to wear off.

She could feel her magic inside her, a dormant thread lying in her body. Could she control it? She reached out. It slipped through her will like water between spread fingers. What herb had the devious fiend given her? She'd never heard of one that could weaken both the body and the will. Bitterness churned inside her. She couldn't fight back. Not yet. But the drug was wearing off. Please God she'd get her power back soon.

The night sky was black before her, streaked with fast-moving clouds. The few stars she could see glinted coldly, giving her body a bone-deep chill that had nothing to do with the bite of the moor wind. Because now she knew where they were. She could see the limestone field before them, the backdrop of the forest with the stark limestone cliffs behind, and the bonfire and torches of a camp across the limestone field the demon was riding recklessly across. And one man, larger than the others, who strode into the torchlight.

Julian.

***

Julian bolted upright at Regina's soft cry. She

whimpered in her sleep and her fingers gripped the covers above her belly. In the dim light from the fire it looked like a sheen of tears coated her cheeks. She moaned and twisted in the bed, as if trying to escape.

"Regina," he called softly.

The flickering flames cast moving shadows over her features. It was hard to discern if her expressions were truly changing so quickly or if it was simply a trick of the light.

"Regina," he repeated, louder this time.

"Julian." Her voice was hoarse but full of relief and something else he didn't recognize—gratitude? "You're here."

"Of course I am." He sat on the edge of the bed. Did she really think he'd leave her to face the demon alone? "Did you have a nightmare?"

"No, I had a vision." She pushed herself up into a seated position.

"Of Gabriel?"

Tears rose in her eyes when he mentioned her brother. "No, the demon. From the past."

The Sight showed information that was relevant to the seer. How was an incident from the past significant? "What did you see?"

"I saw the demon kill a woman."

He only knew of one woman the monster had killed in the past. *Evelyn.* "What happened?"

"He used the woman's blood to open a portal back to its world. As she was dying, she cursed him."

"Did the demon get her soul?"

"No. She died before the fiend could take it."

There it was. The missing piece. He bowed his head as relief washed over him. Evelyn and his baby's souls were safe. He still had to rescue Gabriel and free the souls the demon had stolen, but at least one of his worries if he failed was gone. He stared at Regina. Did she realize this was why the demon was after her? That she was Evelyn reincarnated? "At the opera house, the demon said tonight your curse ends. Do you think your vision showed you the curse he was talking about?"

"Yes."

"Demons recognize souls," he said carefully. He wanted to gently lead her to the realization if she hadn't already.

"Julian, I'm not an idiot. I know what this means. Somehow, I was that woman. I've been reincarnated." She shook her head. "Or she's been reincarnated. That's why the demon is after me."

"Do you have her memories?" Did she remember her life as Evelyn? Did she remember him?

She looked away. He stared at her profile as he waited.

Finally, she turned back to him. "I have visions of her life sometimes. Bits and pieces. But I'm not her. I'm me."

"I know." He took her hand in his and caressed the back with his thumb. Knowing she was Evelyn reincarnated didn't change his feelings for Regina. He'd long ago accepted that despite Regina's resemblance to his dead wife, she was her own person. A woman he respected and admired. Evelyn was part of a world that had been gone for centuries. "You're worried about Gabriel, but if you are the one the demon wants, we can be sure he'll keep your brother alive—at least until he has you."

"And then what?"

"I'll kill the demon."

"I don't want to worry about the future anymore." Her green eyes met his, and she squeezed his hand. "Stay with me."

"Do you know what you are asking?"

"Yes. I don't know what will happen when we find the demon. Who knows if we will survive? But you love me...and I love you." She touched his face with a gentle caress. "Right now I only want to be close to you. We may not get another chance."

"You love me?" Julian swallowed the emotion that clogged his throat. He'd suspected, but hadn't dared hope to hear her say it. The husky warmth of her words filled the empty space inside that he'd carried since Evelyn's demise.

"I do." Her expression was tender. "Now stop talking."

She kissed him. He tried to pull away but she tightened her arms around his back, pressing him against her soft curves. When the tip of her tongue slid against his, the desire he'd been fighting all night took over. *As long as she was sure...* He plundered her open mouth, while her hands wandered up his back, stroking the length of each rigid muscle.

She slipped her hands beneath his shirt and he

sucked in a breath at the feel of her cool fingers against his heated skin. The fireplace gave off little warmth, but Julian was burning with need. He wanted to worship every inch of her body until she forgot about the demon, the past, and her fears.

"Would you remove your shirt?" Her cheeks flamed in the dim firelight. "I want to see you."

"Are you certain you want to do this?" He craved to know her fully, but he didn't want her to have any regrets.

Her tongue moistened her lips. "Yes."

He pulled his shirt over his head and tossed it to the floor, watching her expression as she absorbed every move. Her gaze openly admired him, and he'd never felt prouder of the scars he'd earned. He slowly pulled back the thin quilt and sheet covering her. The sheer linen chemise revealed every glorious curve.

Her breathing quickened. Nerves? Anticipation? He spread his fingers wide on her stomach.

"Julian," she begged.

He leaned down and kissed her. Traces of ale still lingered, but she tasted as sweet and fiery as his favorite whiskey.

He slipped his mouth from hers and brushed a thumb over the soft skin at the nape of her neck, then drew her nightgown down, exposing her creamy skin. She blushed but didn't cover herself. He'd never seen anyone so lovely. His hand cupped a breast and the rosy nipple peaked beneath his touch. He sucked it into his mouth and she arched against him. The sweet taste of her made him shiver as he slid his tongue along the pebbled bud. She gently pulled his hair, making him ache for her.

He moved his hand to the deep indentation of her waist and slowly caressed the smooth curve of her hip. She moaned and slid a hand behind his neck. Her fingers threaded into his hair.

He grasped the edge of her nightgown and her body stilled.

"Do you want me to stop?" *Don't say yes.*

"No." Her green eyes burned bright with desire. "I need you."

He touched the center of her womanhood and traced a long finger along the cleft. She was so hot and wet he burned to taste her. She gripped his forearm and he paused. Then he swirled his tongue over her nipple and a flood of liquid heat coated his finger. Her grip loosened and he rubbed his thumb over the button of her sex. Her body jerked.

He rose up and took her mouth. His tongue stabbed deep at the same time his finger plunged into her. She gasped and her mouth opened wide, taking his tongue deeper. He inserted another digit far into her center and her hips rose. She was so responsive that his body thrummed with almost unbearable need.

His thumb caressed the nub at her entrance while he continued to stroke deep inside her. Her legs fell open to allow him greater access. She moaned and clenched his shoulders. He pulled out his fingers and sucked them clean as she watched.

"You taste so sweet." He slid down her body.

"What are you doing?" Her voice was ragged.

"I need to taste you." He raised her nightgown higher until she was exposed to his gaze. So beautiful. She tried to close her legs, but he gently grasped her knees and spread them apart until he could fit his shoulders between them.

He nuzzled the inside of her thigh as she gasped. She grabbed his hair. He inhaled the sweet musky fragrance of her body. He loved everything about her. The way her skin glowed warm in the firelight, the way she writhed beneath him. Tonight would be her first time. He'd do his best to make it memorable for her.

He cradled his hands beneath her hips, raising her up to his mouth. His tongue stroked along her entrance. She was already wet and ready for him. He suckled the nub above and she bucked beneath him. His tongue delved into her, licking and tasting the places his fingers had been just moments before. *Delicious.*

She gripped his scalp as she ground her hips against his mouth. His tongue sank in deep, licking her tight passage, savoring the sweet honey her body offered. Whether she realized it or not, they were destined to be together. Regina belonged to him.

CHAPTER FORTY-FIVE

R EGINA GASPED AND ARCHED BENEATH Julian's hot and hungry tongue. Moisture pooled within her core and she gripped his head. His tongue dove deep inside her and she shuddered. She shouldn't be so wanton, but she couldn't help herself.

Who was she? Regina? Evelyn? She didn't know anymore. So what if he wasn't the Marquis of Thornwood's son? She was with the man she loved and that was all that mattered.

His tongue flicked back and forth and his fingers slid deep. She convulsed with pleasure, as wave after wave of ecstasy rolled through her. When the ripples subsided, he kissed the inside of her thigh and moved away from her. He moved to the edge of the bed and removed his breeches. Her eyes widened when she saw his sex. It stood out from his body, large, long, and stiff. She swallowed hard. He caught her watching him and his member jerked.

"Did I ever tell you there's more?"

"No." She was nervous, but ready to explore.

He gave her a wicked smile. "There's still more."

"Show me." She spread her legs beneath his gaze and held her arms out to him. A sense of familiarity rippled through her.

His blue eyes darkened with desire as he crushed her to the bed. Their tongues tangled in a fevered kiss. The tip of his sex probed at her opening. Warmth flooded her and he slid inside. She nuzzled his throat, reveling in the coiled strength of his muscles.

"Give me more," she gasped and wrapped her legs around his back.

He plunged forward slightly then slid in slow. His thick rod spread her wide, wider still, until she didn't think she could take any more. His tongue trailed down her throat, and his calloused palm glided over her breast as he squeezed her nipple. Pleasure pooled within her. He drove his hips deep, impaling her.

She caught her breath at the pain, her heart pounding at the unexpected jolt. Julian held still within her. The pain faded and she relaxed. He drew out slowly then slid back to the hilt. She writhed beneath him as a delicious pressure built inside her. His mouth claimed hers. His urgent kiss matched the rhythm of his thrusts.

She gripped his back, her hips bucking up to take him deeper and deeper within her. Their bodies melded, as if they'd done this many times before. He pulled his mouth from hers and sucked the sensitive spot where her neck and shoulder met.

Regina flew apart. Her fingernails scored his back as she gasped with pleasure. Her body convulsed, squeezing him to the point that he shouted as he released his seed. The steady pulsing of his shaft inside her caused her to peak again. She cried out, her head thrown back as she held him tight.

She lay in bed, her breaths calming down, her body sore but sated.

He raised his head to kiss her shoulder. "How I love you, Evelyn."

Regina froze, all contentment gone. How did he know that name? The weight of his muscular body, so welcome only minutes before, oppressed her. "Get off me."

He rolled off her, his expression bewildered. He raked a hand through his hair. "What's wrong?"

"You called me Evelyn." She shoved against his chest. The warmth and comfort she'd felt in his arms had disappeared, leaving her with the desire to flee. "Who is she?"

Realization flashed in his eyes. "I'm sorry. It was an accident."

"Who's Evelyn?"

He raised up on an elbow. His sigh was heavy. "Evelyn was my wife. She died. I must have said her name out of habit."

Evelyn. The woman from Regina's previous lifetime. The woman who'd been married to a man who'd looked exactly like Julian. Her head throbbed and she rubbed her temples. It wasn't possible. His soul was old. She'd thought he'd been reincarnated…except he spoke of Evelyn as if she'd recently died, not as someone he'd known in a previous life.

The words seemed to wring themselves from deep within her soul. "*When?* When did she die?"

He seemed taken aback. "A little over two months ago."

Two months ago. That was when she'd had her first vision of the demon. She thought about his equivocations when she'd asked what his real name was. Time travel was impossible, wasn't it? "What year was that?"

"That's an odd question."

"I had visions of you and your wife." She left out the fact that in her visions, *she* had been Evelyn. "The time period was not recent."

"How do you know that?"

"In my visions, Evelyn was a healer in the Mageborn War, and her husband—who shares your name and looks—led the rebels. You say your name is Julian Rutherford, but that you are not the son of the Marquis of Thornwood. Which makes me think—as unlikely as it seems—that you somehow traveled through time. Did you? Are you the Julian of my visions?"

"Yes." He sighed and fell back onto the bed. The sheet slipped down to his waist.

Regina strove to ignore the pain that filled her at the sight of his muscular chest. She'd caressed him as though she'd had the right to, had opened herself up and loved him. She gathered the sheet around her and scooted to the edge of the bed, wishing she could escape this moment and disappear. Julian had been the one person who didn't care she was a half-blood, but she still wasn't good enough. She was just a substitute for his dead wife.

"How did you travel through time? Nobody can do that."

He frowned up at the ceiling, his hands locked behind his head. "The demon we're chasing is the same one that killed my wife. He used her blood to open a portal. When he jumped through, I followed. I thought we were going to his world, but I found myself here. I lost his trail and went to the Lindsay estate where I met the marquis. He believed my tale and agreed to help me."

"As did Lord Langley?"

"Yes, but not because he believed me. He just wanted the demon stopped." He reached up and gently pulled her hand away from the lock of hair she'd been twisting. "I'm sorry I called you Evelyn. When we came together, it felt so natural and familiar, and the words just came out. But I love *you*."

Doubt tore at her. He knew she was Evelyn reincarnated—and he'd called her Evelyn after they'd made love. Did he truly know the difference between them? Or was Regina just a replacement for the woman he'd lost?

She loved him, but she was greedy. As a halfblood, she had spent her life in mageborn society accepting the few crumbs that had been tossed her way. In this, she found she could not compromise. She could not accept less. She'd been second best her entire life. She refused to be second best in love.

She grabbed the extra pillow and laid it between

them. "You can share my bed. You need your rest."

His eyebrows rose in inquiry and she steeled herself against the heat in his glance.

"If you want to sleep here, that is all you will do. Sleep." She lay down and faced away from him.

She couldn't bear his touch. Not when he was thinking of another woman.

Even if that woman was her.

CHAPTER FORTY-SIX

THEY'D BEEN RIDING SILENTLY ALL morning. Julian had slept in fits and starts, aware of Regina's warmth a few inches away. The slight perfume of lilacs on her skin had tempted him to move nearer, to touch her, to haul her to him in the dark and prove to her that she wasn't a substitute, but the woman he loved. Even now he couldn't believe he'd called her Evelyn. He'd bloody blown it with that slip of the tongue, and she had rewarded him with a stony visage ever since.

When they'd left The Wandering Magician, the heavy rain had been a suitable accompaniment to their moods, but the showers finally stopped. Julian stretched in the saddle to loosen his back and shoulders. His stallion continued its steady plodding along the muddy road, the hooves making a slight sucking sound.

Regina's shoulders curved forward with weariness, but she still sat straight in the saddle, her gaze focused on the road ahead. Her quiet strength and determination were unlike any other. She thought all he saw when he looked at her was Evelyn, but he saw so much more. Her expression whenever she gazed at him was so sad, he ached to make the pain go away. He didn't see her as a substitute for his dead wife. But how was he going to convince her of that if she wouldn't speak to him?

He grimaced. Her stony silence hung as heavy as this morning's storm clouds. By His Blood, Evelyn could hold a grudge. He'd hoped Regina would be more forgiving. He nudged his horse forward to catch up to hers. One way or another, she was going to talk to him. They had to settle this before they caught up to the demon, or they might not get another chance.

He spied a lush green pasture on the other side of a bridge. "The horses need to rest. Let's stop over there."

She nodded. The rhythmic clack of horseshoes on stone filled the air as their mounts clopped onto the bridge.

They rode down to the grassy meadow next to the creek. The loud buzz of insects thickened the air. Regina stopped a few feet behind him. She already had one leg slung over her horse's back by the time he reached her. He placed his hands on her waist and helped her down.

"Thank you." She avoided looking at him as her boots landed on the ground. She patted her gelding's flank and murmured, "Good job. I bet you could use a little rest."

Julian led the animals to the creek to drink. Afterward the horses grazed on the rich meadow grass.

Regina wandered over to the stone bridge. The parapet walls were about thigh-high. She sat down and took a thick slice of bread and a cheese wedge from her pocket.

He joined her, choosing the opposite side of the bridge.

She drew a small knife from her pack and sliced off a piece of cheese. The crown of her wide-brimmed hat hid the heavy wealth of her glorious hair, but a few silky gold strands escaped to curl around her delicate cheekbones. Her skin had deepened to a darker gold. When she looked up, she avoided looking at him. Instead, she looked towards the horses, which were chomping happily on the deep grass by the stream. "The pull is growing stronger. I think we're getting closer."

"Regina, we need to talk about last night."

Her shoulders stiffened, but her gaze didn't waver from the field.

"I'm sorry I called you Evelyn." When they'd been together in bed that night, her openness, the easy way she'd touched him—as though she'd known every contour of his body and what affected him the most—had reminded him of his wife. It had felt so familiar that he'd slipped and called her Evelyn. But he'd never forgotten it was Regina he kissed, Regina who he held in his arms. "I made love to *you*. I wasn't thinking of her at all. I don't know why I said her name, except perhaps from habit."

The knife stilled in her hands.

"We both know you were Evelyn once. When

I'm with you, everything feels right. I haven't been reincarnated. I'm still Julian Rutherford, the brother of the lord who started the Mageborn War, but I don't feel like the same man anymore." His heart thudded with the need to convince her. "Back then, I was an earl's second son and the leader of a rebellion. Now, I'm nobody. I'm posing as the son of the Marquis of Thornwood, but I have no name, no title, no home. As much as you resemble Evelyn, you're not the same woman. That period of my life—*our* lives—is gone. When I look at you, I don't see Evelyn. I see *you*—a woman who will do anything to save her brother. I love *you. Regina.*"

Her chest heaved on a sob, and tears slid down her cheek, glinting in the weak light. He crossed over to her and pulled her into his arms. The knife she was holding clattered against the stones at their feet. She wrapped her arms around him and held him tight as she wept.

He drew her close, grateful to have her in his arms again. Love for her swelled, so intense he couldn't speak. He blinked away the moisture that welled in his own eyes. Whether she had forgiven him or not, she was here with him. That was all that mattered.

She leaned back and wiped her eyes. "I don't know why I cried so much."

A lump filled his throat. "I didn't mean to hurt you. It truly was an accident."

"I know. It's just hard knowing how much you loved her. I can't believe you love me too."

"Why wouldn't I?" He lifted her chin. Her green eyes were wide and damp with uncertainty. How could she not know how much she mattered to him? She was the love of his life. His past and his future. "You're the only woman I've ever met who can outrun a demon."

She half-laughed and a smile tugged at her lips, even as a couple more tears fell. "That's it? You're impressed with my demon-hunting lineage?"

"And your bravery." He kissed her tenderly. "Your willingness to sacrifice everything for your family. There aren't many people who would do that."

"Evelyn would."

"Yes, but she wasn't tested the same way. She had the support of a loving family. Even after the war started, her parents did as much as they could to help her. You didn't have that. Your Aunt Agatha is a wonderful lady, but you've had the burden of raising Gabriel, made harder by the fact that both of you are half-bloods."

When she met his gaze again, her green eyes were luminous. "Very well. I forgive you." And then she smiled at him, for the first time that day.

He laughed and hugged her tight. "I love you." And then he kissed her, and they didn't speak for a while after that.

They ate their lunches, sitting side by side on the bridge, shoulders touching. The gentle burble of the stream added a peaceful backdrop to their break. Soon, they'd have to get back on the trail.

"How are we going to kill the demon?"

Julian pulled out the dagger he kept sheathed on his belt and held it out for her inspection. "This is what I plan on using."

Regina's eyebrows soared when she looked back up at him. "That's it?"

He opened his jacket and showed her his pistols. "I also have these." Whoever had invented pistols had been a genius. After his encounter with the demon at the opera house, Langley had trained him in their use. He'd said it never hurt to be proficient in modern weapons, especially since Julian couldn't to go around London with a sword sheathed at his belt.

She shook her head. "The pistols won't work. Bullets have no effect on demons."

"Are you certain?"

"My father tried bullets. They failed. In the time it takes for a bullet to pass all the way through, he said the demon could heal itself of the wound. He said daggers or swords made of iron worked best."

"So be it." Julian reached inside his pants pocket and pulled out a small jar wrapped tightly in several layers of worn leather. "This is demonsbane oil. I was given this by your ancestor, Lord Harbrook. It slows the creature's regeneration. Do you have any weapons?"

She reached inside her pocket and drew out a dagger. The sheath had been cleverly hidden within the lining of her coat.

"Hand it to me."

She passed it to him, handle first. He pulled out a linen cloth that he used for cleaning his dagger.

After dipping it in the oil, he slid it along the steely length, making sure he coated every inch of the blade. "Do you have any other weapons?"

She reached down and pulled a couple of smaller daggers from her boots. "These are my backups. My father always took them when he went on demon hunts."

She was full of surprises.

"Do you know how to use them?"

"I think so." She gripped the daggers, one in each hand. She eyed a tree stump approximately fifteen feet away from where he sat on the bridge. She threw first one, then the other dagger. They stuck into the side of the wood, no more than an inch apart.

He grinned, impressed. Evelyn had known how to throw knives as well. Maybe Regina retained more knowledge than she realized. Not that he'd mention that to her. He wasn't about to stumble into that briar patch again.

She retrieved the daggers, wiped the blades on her pants and handed them to him.

He proceeded to oil these blades as well. "Who taught you to handle knives? Was it your father?"

"No. No one taught me. I remembered." Her expression was troubled as she gazed at her hands.

He decided to change the subject. "I know about your father, but what happened to your mother?"

"She died in a carriage accident a couple of years before my father. I've often wondered if my father had taken more risks than he should have as a result."

Julian thought of his own life. When Evelyn died, he'd cared nothing for his own. He had chased the demon through a portal leading to a place unknown, all in the hopes of saving the souls of his wife and unborn child. Would he have taken the same risks if he had a son and daughter waiting for him at home?

No. Deep in his heart he knew if he had family of his own depending on him, he would have chosen to stay.

"I'm sure he did the best he could."

"Yes, I think he did," she said slowly. "I wish things had been different, but you're right."

His heart ached for her. She'd borne a heavy burden, it seemed, for most of her life. "If you're ready, we should get back on the road."

"I'm ready." Regina's head lifted, and her honey voice was strong and determined. "Let's go."

***

The sun had barely cleared the horizon when Regina rode out of the innyard with Julian beside her. The niggling sensation had been growing steadily stronger each day. Now the pull was a constant drag on her, making her want to dig her heels into her horse's sides and gallop the rest of the way to ease the summons. The thick wooded forests had given way to the bare open moors of the dales. Today the sky was clear, the cool moist air refreshing in the early morning.

Julian had shared her bed each night. Their lovemaking had been sweet and hot, both of them determined to make the most of their time together. Her left hand slipped surreptitiously to her belly. A tiny little glow flickered beneath her hand. She'd first noticed it this morning when she woke up. The more time passed, the stronger that little flame grew. Soon, she would have to make up her mind whether or not to tell Julian. Once again, she had the sense that things had come full circle.

As they traversed the countryside and got closer to the dales, the memories from her life as Evelyn took over. A cultured field divided by long drystone walls was overlaid by a vision of a battlefield. She'd walked among the fallen, looking for the wounded she could yet save. A winding river recalled the time she and Julian had slipped away to picnic on its banks. The ruins of a castle sprawled in forgotten splendor in an overgrown meadow reminded her of the first time Evelyn and Julian had met, at his brother's mage-day celebration. She'd had a premonition that night that they would always be together, their fates intertwined.

A squirrel scampered down the drystone wall that lined the path, charging across the dirt road before their horses. Regina pulled tight on the reins to keep her mount in check, but beside her Julian's stallion tossed its head, raising its front legs up high in protest. Julian's voice rumbled softly to the beast, soothing it.

Her gaze absorbed the man she'd loved in two different lifetimes. Her premonition the night they'd met had been right. She and Julian been inseparable, growing in friendship and love as they'd matured. Even death hadn't kept them apart.

Although Regina hadn't had a vision, she sensed today would conclude the events set in motion centuries before. That time, she had lost. Her hand shifted to the comforting weight of her cross-hilt dagger.

She refused to lose again.

CHAPTER FORTY-SEVEN

JULIAN'S BACK TENSED AS MEMORIES of camps and past battles rose in his mind. Numerous sheep grazed the lush meadow grass, baaing their complaints at the horses. He recognized the rock-strewn field where he'd battled Lord Harbrook. A dense forest cloaked the back of the valley, where limestone cliffs towered ominously.

As Regina directed her mount towards the base of the cliffs, the hair on the back of his neck rose. The scene was all too familiar. The demon was leading them straight to the escape route Evelyn had followed the night she died.

When Regina reached the foothills, she dismounted. "The demon went this way." She pointed up the slope to a tumble of rocks next to a large tree and small shrubs.

Julian tied their horses to a giant yew tree. His guts knotted as she drew near to the rock fall. He knew what lay hidden there, the false promise of safety. He scrambled after her up the slope. Her slender fingers grabbed a few pebbles and raised them to her nose, almost as though she were sniffing the demon's trail. A few steps further up she brushed aside the low-growing branches of a woody shrub, exposing a hole at the base of the cliff wall that was barely wide enough to fit a grown man.

"He went through there." She bent down to look inside.

Julian reached forward and grabbed her shoulder. "We can't go in that way. The hole is too narrow. The demon could kill us before we even poked our heads through the other side."

"What do you suggest we do? This is where the trail leads."

"There's another way inside. Evelyn was supposed to wait in the caverns with my personal guard until it was safe to return. We made sure there was another exit in case she needed it."

Her eyes squeezed shut as if in pain. "I remember. Kikson was the demon. He drugged me."

"You said, '*Me*. He drugged *me*.'" Did she realize she spoke as if she and Evelyn were the same person?

The wind whistled around the rocks, and loose strands of her hair lifted in the breeze as her dark green gaze met his. "I know. I have her memories too. The closer we've gotten to these cliffs, the stronger my past has become. I'm still me, but I also feel like her. And right now I want my revenge."

His throat thickened. "I failed you. I should have listened when you asked me to let you stay at the campsite."

Her fierce gaze met his. "You didn't know. None of us did. You thought you were sending me to safety."

"I don't want to lose you again." He stepped up to her and she moved into his arms. He laid his cheek against her hair. So many lives were at stake. Somehow he had to defeat the demon without Regina or Gabe getting hurt. His pulse jumped at the challenge ahead of him. He had to save her. He couldn't handle life without her again.

She placed her hand on his chest. "I don't want to lose you either, but we have to save my brother. Gabe comes first. Promise me."

Every instinct rebelled at her request. She was asking him to protect her brother instead of her. He cared about Gabriel, but Regina was the love of his life. Without her his future was meaningless. He suddenly sympathized with her father's lack of interest in living after her mother had died. Maybe Julian was more like the man than he'd realized. "I promise."

The words hung heavy on his heart, but it was the right thing to do, no matter how selfish he wanted to be.

Her breath whooshed out in a sigh. "Thank you."

"Speaking of Gabe, maybe we can find some clues about how he's doing." He examined the sandy soil around the small entrance to the caverns. It took a couple of minutes, but he found what he was looking for. "There are two sets of prints leading up the slope. It looks like your brother was at least well enough to walk."

Her shoulders fell with relief. "That's good news."

"We'd better get going. It'll take some time to

get to the other entrance."

They retrieved the horses and descended to the base of the rocky crag. Julian led them along the ridge until the land dipped once more, revealing another valley. Sheep grazed the verdant fields lying alongside the broad river that crossed the dale. The thick forests of his time had disappeared. Had it not been for the position of the limestone scar, Julian would have doubted his memory.

He rode parallel to the river until the trail climbed once more and stopped when they reached a large fall of tumbled granite slabs. In his era a large ash grove had hidden the rock overhang that led to the cave network beneath these hills. Now a rockslide had filled the old entrance, and only a few ash trees remained.

Bloody everlasting hell. They'd gone from a tunnel where the demon could have lopped off their heads to a blasted stone mountain.

"Was that the entrance?"

He ground his teeth. "Yes. We'll have to find a way to reach it. It's still the better option." He searched for gaps between the granite stones and found a narrow one on the north side of the rock fall where a large slab had toppled onto another. He crouched down. Cool damp air brushed his cheek. The entrance still existed.

He walked back to Regina, who waited on her horse. "Can you sense the demon here?"

She closed her eyes and squeezed her lips together. "I can still sense its presence, but it's not nearby. I don't have any awareness of it having been here."

"Good. We'll go in this way." He helped her dismount.

She tended to the horses, while he went back to the gap. The top slab was too heavy to move. He gathered his magic and sliced into the bottom hunk approximately a foot from the edge. Blasting the lump would be easier, but the noise that would create could alert the demon. Sound traveled inside caves.

A thin orange-red line glowed where his magic etched itself onto the rock's surface. Julian carved deeper into the stone, his muscles aching from the strain of maintaining a constant flow of power. When he judged he'd gone more than halfway, he stopped.

He bent over and rested his hands on his thighs, breathing deeply to catch his breath.

Regina came over to him and held out a flask. "Here, this will help."

He gulped the warm ale and handed it back. While he'd been slicing into the stone, Regina had removed the saddlebags and hobbled their horses so they could graze in the valley. A small stream passed near the trees. Their mounts would have plenty of water to satisfy their thirst while he and Regina were gone.

Julian strode over to the saddlebags. After a minute of searching, he found the chisel and hammer he'd packed.

She eyed the tools. "You brought a chisel and hammer? You knew we would have to cut into rock?"

He grinned. "I brought other tools as well. A length of rope, flint and tinder, and an axe. I thought we might end up back here, so I came prepared. I even brought charcoal in case we need to mark our path inside the caverns."

"I see you haven't lost your ability to plan ahead."

She followed him back up the slope. He harnessed his magic once again. He inhaled deeply and cut into the slab. Julian could feel the resistance of the hard granite. A hand touched his shoulder. Power flowed into his body and surged into the stone. The pressure disappeared and he stumbled forward a step. He raised a shaky hand and thrust his hair back from his face.

Regina gulped from the ale flask then handed it to him. He drank deeply then wiped his mouth with the back of his hand. She handed him an apple.

"Thanks. That stone was stubborn."

"Eat this too. You need to rebuild your strength." She pulled a sandwich out of her pocket.

He took the food she offered and headed for a large rock away from the jumble of stones. "You should also eat. You fed me a lot of energy."

He took a giant bite of apple and chewed quickly. He was ravenous.

She sat next to him and pulled out a sandwich for herself. "What happens when we find the demon?"

He swallowed quickly. "We get Gabriel, and then we kill the monster."

"How?"

He chewed slowly, the smoky taste of the ham

sharp on his tongue. "The best option is to behead him. He can't regenerate without a head on his neck."

"There's no other way?"

"If his injuries are severe enough, he'll die. But that means using demonsbane oil-coated blades to slow the healing. Stabbing him in the throat would probably work if we can sever the artery. Unless you know of a better way. How did your father kill the fiends?"

"He did something similar. He tried to ambush the demons when he could. The element of surprise gave him an edge, he said."

"I don't think we'll have the element of surprise on our side. The creature knows we're coming and will be waiting. The only thing in our favor is that he'll expect us to come in the other entrance." He frowned. "If he was Kikson, he'll know of this entrance as well. It was to be the escape route should the enemy find the forest entrance."

She patted her waist where she kept the dagger close. "I'll be ready."

Her eyes reflected her determination, and Julian knew she wouldn't let the demon catch her unawares again. "I know you will."

He inserted his chisel into the slender cut in the slab and levered the two pieces further apart. The stone budged less than an inch, but it was enough. He slid his magic into the narrow gap, and an orange web spread over the surface of the separated piece. Once the netting glowed on every side, he tapped it lightly with the hammer. A bright gold shimmer spread from the strands, and the rock trembled and disintegrated.

A pile of rocks and sand now filled the space.

Regina handed over the remainder of the ale and knelt to scoop the rocks out of the opening. "I don't suppose you packed a shovel in that saddle-bag of yours."

He laughed. "No. My apologies, milady."

"No apologies necessary, but I will expect full recompense later." She smiled at him mischievously.

He returned her smile, but his thoughts turned to what would happen once they entered the caverns. Could he kill the demon before anyone got hurt?

His light mood fled.

CHAPTER FORTY-EIGHT

REGINA FINISHED SCOOPING OUT THE small broken rocks between the slabs. Julian had made a couple of rough brooms out of branches from the nearby ash trees, and the tools had been much more effective than their bare hands. They'd cleared most of the opening, then Julian left to grab the saddlebags.

She crawled into the tunnel. Sunlight filtered through the granite slabs, filling the space with dim light. Something scurried above her, and she froze. A soft swish followed, and a thin trail of sand drifted down. She was jumpy, knowing the demon was inside the caverns. They were so close now. She prayed Gabriel was alive and unhurt.

"Regina," Julian called softly.

"I'm in here." The entrance to the black cavern opened before her, and she finally had room to stand.

"I have the supplies." He pushed the saddlebags through the opening. She bent down and pulled them clear. He crawled forward, his shoulders rubbing against the rough stone on both sides.

"I can tell the demon is inside the caverns, but he doesn't appear to be near this entrance."

"That's good to hear."

"How are we going to kill him?"

"I'll blast the demon with my magic. With any luck, it'll stun him long enough for me to kill him." He rose to his feet and pulled a torch out of the pack.

"And if that doesn't work?"

"I'll fight him, while you and your brother make your escape."

"What if Gabriel can't walk?"

He looked at her with exasperation. "We'll improvise."

"You have to save him. Gabe first, then me. You promised."

His jaw clenched. "I'll keep my promise."

She chewed her bottom lip. Should she tell him? The demon would realize as soon as he saw her. She couldn't let Julian be surprised. "There's something you should know."

Even in the dim light, his blue eyes were striking against the burnished bronze of his skin. He sighed. "What is it?"

Her pulse jumped. How would he react to her news? She placed her hand on her belly where her daughter's soul burned bright. "I'm with child… again."

His throat worked several times before he got the words out. "You're pregnant."

"A daughter." A lump rose in her own throat. "The one we would have had. When I relived Evelyn's memories, I saw our child's soul. I recognized her. We've all been given a second chance."

Julian fell back against the wall and placed his head in his hands. "You made me promise to save Gabe, even though I might lose you both?"

"I won't let him kill me again."

"You might not have a choice!" His voice burned with anger.

"You'll be there. I know you'll save us. And if you can't—I'll kill the demon or die trying." Her heart ached with the welter of emotions inside her.

His eyes were damp when he raised his face. "I can't lose you again. I need you."

She rushed into his arms and looked up into the beloved features of the man she'd loved in two life-times. "I love you so much. But I don't know what else to do. I vowed to keep Gabriel safe. I have to protect him."

He rested his forehead against hers. His voice was gruff when he spoke. "Don't die. Don't make me go through that again."

"I'll do my best." She kissed him, then squeezed his arm before stepping back.

Julian sighed and moved away from the wall. "You have rotten timing."

"I would have told you sooner, but I didn't know until this morning." She looked at him, hoping he could tell how sorry she was.

"We'd better get going. The demon and your brother are waiting." He straightened, and suddenly he was the magelord who'd led the rebel army to victory centuries ago.

He lit the torch and stepped forward into the darkness. A deep sense of foreboding filled Regina as she followed him. Black deeper than anything she'd ever experienced surrounded them beyond the wavering torchlight. Julian followed the wall to their left. It gleamed, as did the smooth rock below their feet. She lightly dragged her fingers across the surface, expecting her fingers to come away wet, but the wall was dry.

She didn't know how long they walked through the caverns. The soft scuff of their leather shoes on stone was accompanied by the constant trickle of water, unseen but nearby. The air was damp and cool. She shivered, glad for the warmth of her wool jacket and multiple layers of men's clothing.

Julian stepped onto a slender ledge alongside a deep pool. The rock wall curved low, and Regina ducked to keep her head from scraping the top. Her lower back ached from hunching over, and she tread carefully, afraid of slipping and falling into the hidden depths beside her. The orange-red torchlight reflected off the inky surface. She pressed back against the wall, panting. She remembered Kikson waiting for her beyond another ledge, his beaked nose like a bird of prey in the flickering light. She'd been so afraid of sinking into the stagnant water, but he'd been the true threat.

"Just a little further and it will open back up," Julian murmured. He seemed to sense her unease.

She breathed deeply and forced herself to let go of the wall. Julian moved forward again. Regina focused on placing her feet carefully on the slick stone, ignoring the ripples that lapped against the edge.

The rock that arched overhead ended, and they entered into a vast cavernous space.

"You see where that wall ends?" Julian pointed the torch. "A tunnel shoots off to the left there. It leads straight to the campsite. Can you tell if the demon is there?"

She felt a powerful forward draw. "Yes. I can sense his presence very strongly now."

"Before we reach the edge of that wall, I'll put out the torch. I'll hold your hand and guide you. If you sense the monster approaching, squeeze my hand twice."

"I will."

He strode forward and she followed quietly. When they neared the edge of the cavern wall, he snuffed the torch. His hand touched her arm and slid down until he clasped her hand. A faint whisper of sound and he tugged her forward. She followed him, her left shoulder as close to the wall as she dared, the soft bumps a comfort in the dark.

A couple of torches glowed in the distance. As they got closer, a rock platform came into view. Gabriel lay stretched out on the ground. Julian stopped and she halted beside him. Had the demon killed him? When she saw him stir and move a leg, she had to bite back a moan of relief. He was alive.

The demon stepped out of the shadows in his natural form. He looked straight towards them, as if he could sense their presence. Perhaps he could. The glow of his yellow eyes reached out to her, even from this distance. "I've been waiting for you to join me. I have to admit, I expected you to arrive a day earlier."

"Unfortunately, the weather refused to cooperate." Julian strode forward.

Regina could feel the tingle of magic as he gathered it. They had to stun the demon, but she had no experience using her magic to fight, not even as Evelyn. Julian would have to do it.

"What did you do to Lord Harbrook?" he asked.

"Nothing he won't recover from. Simply a little mead and food, doctored with an herb from my realm." His eyes fixed on Regina. "You're not the only one with experience with herbs, my dear."

Julian's shoulders tightened and an orange fireball shot from his fingers.

The demon negligently flicked his hand. The glowing orb dissolved in a series of sparks. Then he hurled a spell at Julian.

Julian deflected it into the pool, making the water glow with an eerie lavender light. He fired another bolt, which the demon diverted to the wall, causing rocks to explode and slide to the platform.

The fight was too near to Gabriel. She had to make them stop. "Give us my brother," she demanded.

The demon stopped mid-throw. He lowered his arm and a purple mist slid across the platform and crawled up her brother's prone figure. "Tell Lord Lindsay to stop his attack."

"Julian, please." The monster was too powerful. They'd have to find another way to defeat him.

Frustration twisted Julian's features, but he acquiesced and dropped his hand.

The demon gripped Gabe's hair and tilted her brother's head back, exposing his neck. The tips of his claws dug into the soft flesh. Gabe's eyes fluttered and his forehead creased in pain.

"Don't hurt him!" she shouted.

"You can have your brother, dead or alive. The choice is yours."

What a ridiculous question. "Alive. What do you want in return?"

"You."

Even though she'd prepared for this moment, hearing it brought back all of Evelyn's memories of being at the demon's mercy. Her blood roared in her ears as her pulse thrummed in her veins. She had vowed to protect her brother, and she would—even if she had to sacrifice her own life. "You must allow Lord Lindsay to take my brother to safety. Then you may have me."

"Agreed."

"No." Julian glared at the demon. "Take me in Lord Harbrook's place and let them leave. This is between you and me."

"I'm afraid you are mistaken. This is not your concern." The fiend's hot yellow glare turned to her. "If Lord Lindsay refuses to leave, your brother dies."

"Julian, remember your promise. You must save Gabriel."

"I can't lose you. Don't do this."

The demon couldn't be defeated with magic.

His power was unlimited compared to theirs. Regina studied the beast who had destroyed her life, and cold determination wrapped itself around her heart. It was time to improvise.

"I have no choice." She stepped away from the wall. "You must agree to let Lord Lindsay and Gabriel leave."

"The bargain is struck." The demon released her brother's hair and stepped back. "If you attempt anything, Lord Lindsay, the lady dies."

Julian climbed the platform, while the monster backed away from his reach. He squared off with the demon, tension riding the taut lines of his body.

Regina's pulse raced. *Don't do anything. He'll kill us all.*

He knelt and gathered Gabe's limp body in his arms. Of course he'd keep his promise. She shouldn't have worried.

"How is he?"

"He seems to be in a deep sleep." Julian came towards her, his arms easily bearing her brother's weight.

She smoothed Gabe's hair away from his face and kissed his cheek. He moaned. "You're safe now. Lord Lindsay will take care of you."

She turned to Julian. She couldn't tell him her plan, not with the demon so close. She could only hope he'd trust her and return as fast as he could. "Take him where the demon's magic can't reach and he can escape."

The brute raised a clawed hand and pointed it at her. "Milady, if you want your brother to live, you had best come now. My patience only lasts so long."

"Don't go to him before I'm back." The anguish in Julian's expression nearly undid her resolve. "Regina, promise me."

Hot tears slid down her cheeks and she roughly swiped at them. "I'm sorry. Take my brother to safety. Please."

"Regina."

"Save him like you promised." She couldn't look at him anymore or she'd try to leave with them. She knew the demon well enough to know he'd kill them all in retaliation. She turned and walked briskly towards the platform.

"Regina!"

She ignored his shout. Her steps didn't falter, not even when Julian's footfalls faded from the chamber, leaving her alone with the foul creature. Her father often said surprise was the best weapon against demons. Her powers were no match for the fiend's dark magic. She would have to outmaneuver him instead.

She stopped next to the platform and felt a disturbing sense of déjà vu. Once again she could see Kikson before her. "I'm glad you don't have a flask of mead for me this time. Not that I would drink it."

His leathery snout opened slightly in what appeared to be a grin. "I see you remember who you are. That makes things easier."

"I'm the one you want. Why did you kidnap my brother?"

"Lord Lindsay kept interfering. I thought it would be easier to get you this way."

"All this because of a curse?"

He looked at her and snarled. "Your curse trapped me in the human world. I can't return home. I want to go back."

"Then I'll break the curse and you'll be free to go."

The hulking beast snarled and hissed in laughter. "That's my plan."

"How do we break the curse?"

The flames in the creature's eyes flickered faster and gleamed a brighter yellow. "There is only way I can think of—I eat your soul."

"Or you could simply kill me. You don't *have* to take my soul." She noticed he neglected to mention the other alternative. *She* killed *him*. That would end the curse as well.

He hissed with laughter. "I missed our conversations, Lady Evelyn. Or should that be Lady Regina?"

"What if I don't choose to die?" The tiny glow in her belly reminded her that there was more than one soul at stake.

"I'm afraid that's not an option."

Of course it wasn't.

Regina listened intently. No further noises echoed through the caverns. All she heard was the trickle of water that had been a constant accompaniment in this underground world. Did the silence mean Julian had escaped the caves with Gabe?

She took a breath. It was up to her now. "Demons

like to bargain."

"That is the nature of the beast."

"I'll willingly give you my soul, but you must promise not to go after my brother or Julian."

"That doesn't sound like much of a bargain."

"You must also agree not to take the other soul inside me." His eyes bored in on her womb, and she crossed her hands protectively over her belly.

"You want me to give up three souls for the price of one?" He paced across the platform, his snout turning from side to side, before he fixed a glare on her. "What do I get in return?"

"I won't fight you." She mentally crossed her fingers and begged forgiveness for her lie. "You get my soul. The curse will be broken, and you will be able to return to your home world."

"You make a compelling argument, although it still doesn't sound like a good deal for me. However, I have always liked you. I agree." He tilted his monstrous head, and the flames in his eyes flared slightly. "You do realize the child will die once I take your soul?"

"Yes." But at least her baby's soul would not perish. Perhaps her daughter would have a chance to be reborn once again.

She wanted to bargain for Julian's safety, but she had nothing left to offer. He was strong and powerful. She had to believe he'd be able to kill the demon and keep Gabriel safe.

"Very well. Come here," the fiend commanded.

She scrambled onto the platform, thankful once more for the men's clothing she wore. His blazing gaze searched her face and body. *Show nothing.*

"You are quite famous throughout mageborn society," the demon said in a surprisingly cordial tone of voice. "Your father, the most powerful demon hunter of his era, a mighty half-blood son no one will train, and the poor half-blood daughter who inherited nothing from her father but his height."

She winced at his characterization. "Must you flaunt my family's flaws to my face? That isn't very polite."

He hissed and snarled again. "I only mentioned it to point out how little society knows. Thanks to your demon-hunting lineage, you are even more powerful than you were as Evelyn. Your soul will give me enormous strength."

No, it wouldn't.

She'd kill herself before she let the fiend take her and her daughter's souls. She could stop their hearts no matter what he did with his magic. "You promise not to take my daughter's soul?"

"I may be a demon, but I keep my word." He stroked the back of a claw along her cheekbone. Every instinct screamed at her to flee, but she didn't move. This was her only chance to end their battle. "I'll enjoy having your soul to keep me company through the ages. I was always quite fond of you."

He grasped her shoulders. His jaw opened wide and a purple mist poured into her nose and mouth, suffocating her. Her heart thumped in protest. Tension gripped her muscles as she forced herself to remain still. She had to convince him that she accepted their deal…that she wouldn't fight. If she didn't, he would use his power to bind her.

Her skin itched from her scalp to the soles of her feet.

Relax, she commanded herself. *Wait for your chance.*

A burning sensation ripped through her. Her soul was separating from her body. There was no time left.

Regina burst upward, her arms rising up and out, knocking the demon's claws off her shoulders. Her skin tore but she didn't care. She dove forward, using her momentum to carry her into the demon, pulling the dagger from her coat. When her body collided against his chest, she grabbed his shoulders and hooked her feet around his knees. The demon fell backwards to the stone cave floor and his snout jerked up. She drove her dagger into the soft portion of his exposed neck as they fell.

Dark blood spurted and hit her face, scalding her skin. Ignoring the agony and gagging on the smell of her burning flesh, she dragged the dagger downwards. The force of their landing loosened her grip. The demon's claws ripped into her back muscles and she arched in pain. She released the demon's shoulder and grabbed the dagger with both hands. She couldn't pull it out, so she rocked it back and forth in his neck. More blood spurted, blinding her. Her hands smoked under the inky ichor. The mist faded and she breathed through her nose, determined to inflict as much damage as possible before her strength failed.

CHAPTER FORTY-NINE

JULIAN LAID GABRIEL ON THE floor near the exit where their saddlebags still sat. He took off his coat and placed it over the sleeping youth. Enough daylight remained that Gabe would be able to see his escape route when he woke up. Julian had fulfilled his promise.

He turned and dashed back into the cavern. He had to get to Regina.

Julian raced to the campsite where he'd left her, his heart pounding from his mad sprint through the cave system. A nightmare unfolded before him.

Regina straddled the demon, her black-coated hands gripping a dagger. His claws were sunk deep into her back. She stared blindly in front of her, her face covered with the demon's poisonous blood. She rocked the knife in his throat in long arcs forward and back, but the fiend was still alive. He struggled to drag her off, but she clung to the dagger, all her weight leaning onto the slender blade.

Julian leaped onto the platform and threw himself at the combatants. He slashed his dagger across the demon's throat. Blood spurted in a giant ebony fountain. He dragged Regina off the demon and away from the spray.

The beast's body spasmed. Purple mist flowed out of it and sank into the pale rock floor, staining it black.

Regina's face was badly swollen. Angry red streaks spread across her inflamed skin. Patches on her neck and forehead had already blackened and oozed pus. He'd never seen the blood poison work so fast.

Did she realize how badly she was injured? Fear made his limbs shake. *Don't die. I can't lose you.*

If he could clean the poison off, maybe they could gain enough time to get her to a healer. Julian ripped off his shirtsleeve. He gently wiped the blood from her eyes. Her eyelids were puffy and red.

"Can you see?" he asked.

Her eyes opened and she nodded. Tears rolled down her cheeks as she grimaced with pain.

A humming filled the air, the reverberations making the hair on his arms stand on end. He froze and looked at the demon's body.

The monster's leather hide glowed with a brilliant light. Misty white forms poured from its mouth. Julian could clearly see their features and clothing. Dock workers, a maid, lords he didn't recognize, Falsworth, Pratchett—and then a chill raced down his spine as he saw his twin, the real Earl of Lindsay. Kikson appeared, followed by soldiers Julian had thought died on the battlefield…the stream continued. The beings floated up towards the ceiling then disappeared.

No wonder the demon had been so powerful. He'd taken many, many souls.

Julian looked down at Regina. Her gaze fixed on the demon and the glowing forms that continued to flow out into the darkness.

Pride and love welled hot in his heart. "Their souls are finally free. You saved them."

Her glance flicked up at him, and her lips trembled.

"Don't try to talk."

She blinked in acknowledgment.

Her injuries were severe. The muscles in her back had been torn, and the front of her body swelled in reaction to the demon's toxic blood. He needed to wash the poison off her skin. "I need to move you closer to the water. I'll be as gentle as I can, but it will hurt."

She blinked again.

He scooped her up tenderly. She moaned. Julian carried her to the edge of the platform and stepped down carefully. He laid her down on the ledge. A groan passed her lips. He took off his waistcoat and shirt and ripped the material into long lengths.

Dipping the improvised bandages into the water, Julian washed the venom from her skin. Even if he could remove all the poison, the wounds in her back were grievous. Blood pooled beneath her body. Iron bands tightened around his chest, choking off his air. He wasn't a healer. He couldn't save her.

Unsteady footsteps plodded on the stone behind

him. He turned and saw Gabriel stumbling towards them. The young mage carried a lit torch in one hand, Julian's jacket in the other.

"What happened?"

"Your sister killed the demon."

Gabriel's eyes widened. Regina's face was swollen now beyond recognition and marred by oozing black patches and red streaks. The bands had spread down her throat to her chest. The poison was progressing, the same as it had in Julian's hand.

She moaned and opened her eyes when she heard her brother's voice.

"Gina!" He collapsed beside her.

"Don't move her. Her back is injured."

Gabe glanced down. He stilled and Julian knew he'd seen the blood on the stone. "You'll recover. We'll find a healer and you'll be fine. You'll see."

Tears slid from her eyes and she opened her hand. Gabe grasped it.

Julian grabbed his jacket from the ground to cover her. A small jar banged against his thigh. *Demonsbane.* He opened the jar and dipped his fingers into the oil and gently spread it over her face. "Demonsbane countered the demon's poison when I was injured. It might give us more time."

She blinked, her eyes slightly unfocused.

Julian finished spreading the oil on all the places the fiend's blood had touched her. If nothing else, the demonsbane would relieve some of the pain.

Before she died.

Regina's back burned as if she'd been sliced open by a thousand swords. Her face and chest felt blistered and hot, like she'd been stung by a nest of hornets and then set on fire. She drifted in and out of consciousness. Wet warmth pooled beneath her. Water? Why was she lying in—

Blood. Her blood.

Memories rushed back. She'd stabbed the demon and his poisonous ichor had drenched her face and hands, searing her skin. Even the inside of her mouth and throat hurt, where the dark droplets had gotten past her lips.

Torches lit the area around her with an orange-yellow glow. She was still in the cavern. Gabe's face wavered into her blurry vision. His bottom lip trembled. He looked terrified. His grip on her hand was steady, though, and comforting.

Julian knelt on her other side. He held the jar of demonsbane oil that they had used to coat their weapons. Firm fingers lightly spread the oil across her throat and chest. Each pass was agony. She lost consciousness.

Cold stone pressed against the lacerations in her back. The pain prodded her awake. Her breaths were shallow and rapid. A strange falling sensation deflated her chest.

I'm dying.

Julian's tortured expression made her long to touch him and soothe the pain from his brow. She loved him so much. Had loved him in two separate lifetimes. More than anything, she wanted to live to raise a family with him.

Her limbs turned heavy. Death's numbing touch seeped the warmth from her bones, and the flame of her daughter's soul dimmed.

She struggled to speak. "Julian."

"Hush, save your strength." He raised his gaze from the dusky purple haze spreading across her arms and met her eyes.

She was a healer, but her magic had drained away with her lifeblood. Only a dribble of power remained. It wasn't enough. She swallowed, even though the action hurt. A memory popped into her head of Evelyn's vision after she'd cursed the demon. She'd seen herself in the future with Julian and their children. They'd been happy. There had to be a way to make that dream a reality. She couldn't heal herself, but maybe…

"Heal," she whispered. Tears rose in her eyes. She lifted her fingers. "Help me."

A look of understanding crossed Julian's face. He grabbed her hand. Deep furrows creased his forehead, and then a rush of power flooded her body.

Julian's magic was strong, but her body was weak. She gathered her will and wove a cocoon of protection around her womb to ensure she wouldn't accidentally draw on her daughter's magic. The demon's poison hadn't reached her child, but if Regina didn't heal herself quickly, they'd both die.

She directed the magic into her wounds, staunching the flow of blood, knitting her torn sinews back together. Deep pangs pierced her as she reset her bones. It hurt to breathe. Every gasp rasped her raw throat. There was worse damage, but she healed her lungs, throat, and mouth. Her next breath was a painfree sigh. Worth it.

Julian continued to feed her energy, but the deluge had dwindled to a trickle. He bent over their clasped hands, his shoulders trembling with effort. Regina repaired the rest of her internal organs, then the shredded skin of her back. As new layers filled in the gaps, the cool stone underneath her no longer stabbed.

Despite her massive efforts, her nerves were still on fire. The demon's blood continued to poison her, devouring her swollen and festering skin. She looked into the faces of the two people she loved more than life itself. To survive, she needed to counteract the toxin.

"I can't heal the rest of my injuries." Her puffy lips hurt, but she could speak above a whisper now. "I don't have enough magic."

"You are not going to die," Julian said. The fluttering torchlight glinted wetly on his cheek. "Gabriel."

Her brother looked up from where he sat cross-legged on her other side. "Yes, milord?"

"How would you like another lesson?"

"Now?"

"Your sister needs more magic. I've given her all I can. You must help."

Her brother nodded. "Tell me what to do."

"Take her hand."

Gabe wrapped her hand in his and she winced. The demon's blood had burned her hands when she'd stabbed the monster in the throat.

"Gather your magic and feed it to her through your linked hands."

A tiny surge of power jolted her palm, then ebbed. Her brother frowned down at their linked hands, and her skin tingled. Then, like a dam bursting, a welter of magic surged up her arm and into her body. She sucked in a breath. Her brother's magic overwhelmed with her with its strength.

She turned her attention to her skin. Working her way down from her scalp, she eliminated the poison and rebuilt her blistered and pus-ridden flesh. Bit by bit the fierce burning eased. The swelling in her face subsided, and her vision improved. Finally, she dammed the flow of Gabe's magic. Her limbs trembled, but all the pain had fled. Her new skin tingled. She looked at her fingers, pale now, instead of light gold from the sun.

Julian reached forward and gently caressed her cheek. She turned her face into his palm and smiled at her two favorite men in the world.

"Thanks for helping me, Gabe."

Her brother grinned. "Thanks for not oozing anymore, sis."

She laughed and stood up with their assistance. The little glow inside her womb was bright and content.

This time, they were *all* going to be fine.

CHAPTER FIFTY

ALTHOUGH REGINA HAD HEALED ALL of her injuries, she was too weak to walk very far. Julian carried her from the caverns, while Gabe led the way with the torch. When they reached the tumble of rocks blocking the entrance, night had already fallen.

It would probably be safer to make camp inside the cave, but Julian wanted to make a fire. Regina needed to get clean and change her clothes. She also needed to warm up. Plus, they could all use the comfort.

Gabe slid through the gap in the rocks, followed by Regina. Julian passed the saddlebags to them. He crawled through the tunnel, feeling strangely reborn. Somehow, he'd left his past in the darkness of the cavern. When he reached the end, Regina waited for him, a smile lighting up her features. He wasn't a mageborn leader anymore, a rebel, or a son who could never please his father. He was simply a man in love, with a bright new future wrapped in honey-gold hair, laughing green eyes, and the tantalizing scent of lilacs.

The horses were still grazing nearby. He could see their outlines under the bright moon. Soft snorts and whuffles floated to them on the gentle breeze. The fact that the horses were still there was a good sign that they were alone.

"Let's make camp over here." He pointed to a level spot near the stream that was sheltered on one side by trees, and backed by the cliffs on the other. "Gabe, we need wood for a fire."

Gabe headed for the edge of the woods, where dead branches littered the forest floor.

Julian gathered some rocks and quickly lined a pit for the fire. Regina sat on a stone nearby as he worked.

"Julian," she called softly.

He looked at her and contentment rushed through him. Her clothes were filthy and blood-soaked, but she looked more beautiful than ever. "I saw a small pool of water where you can bathe. You can clean up while Gabe and I finish making camp."

She tilted her head to the side and her eyes crinkled mischievously. She looked like she wanted to say something, but Gabe arrived and dropped an armful of firewood next to the pit. She abruptly shut her mouth. "Very well."

Julian knelt and showed Gabriel how to lay the wood to ensure a steady burn. "I'm going to show your sister a pond where she can wash. Can you start the fire?"

Gabe looked around. "I don't see anything to start it with."

Julian smiled and clapped him on the shoulder. "Use your magic. But go easy, we don't want to burn the forest down."

Gabe grinned back. Julian felt a tingle and then a small flame burst into being at the base of the logs, in the fine wood and tinder they'd laid at the bottom. Gabe carefully stoked the fire.

Regina finished going through her saddlebags. She pulled out another set of men's clothing and a small bag. "Where's the pool?"

"This way." He headed upstream. The pond was near the base of the cliffs. When they arrived, he pointed to a large rock about twenty feet away. "I'll be over there if you need me."

He heard her hiss as she entered the cold water. He fought the urge to look at her as she bathed in the moonlight.

"You could join me." Her voice floated on the wind.

He resisted only a moment before turning. The water covered her breasts and her hair floated on the water. The bright moonlight reflected off her skin and hair, making her a mysterious blend of light and shadows.

"No, I can't. Your brother is waiting for us."

She sighed. "You're right. I'm almost finished. Just give me a minute to get out and dressed."

He looked away, because if he didn't, he'd join her. Soft splashing filled the air. A few minutes later, footsteps approached behind him. Regina was fully covered once more. Her wet hair hung loose down her back. She held the clothing she'd been wearing inside the caverns. "We should burn these."

He stood up. "Lay them on this rock."

She did.

"Stand back." He gathered his magic, and his fury and frustration at being unable to protect her from the demon burst forth. The clothing flashed bright orange-blue and burned to ashes within seconds.

"That was quick."

"Just releasing some frustration."

She stepped closer and placed both hands on his cheeks. "Maybe I can help." Soft full lips touched his as she kissed him.

With a groan he wrapped his arms around her and hauled her close. Her full breasts pushed into his chest, spiking his desire higher. He ran his mouth along her jaw, bestowing kisses all the way up to her sensitive earlobe, where he gently nibbled.

She moaned in response and wound her fingers in his hair.

He laid his cheek against her silky hair, inhaling the scent of lilacs. "I thought I'd lost you. I couldn't get back to the campsite fast enough."

"It wasn't your fault, and you and Gabe did save me in the end."

"I love you." He swallowed the lump that rose in his throat. "It will take a while, but I believe I can make a living as a tutor, instructing half-bloods such as your brother. If you can wait for me to establish myself, I would like you to marry me. It wouldn't be the lifestyle you are accustomed to—"

"Of course I will marry you. I've been waiting centuries for you to ask. For real, this time. Not because I was ruined." Her arms tangled around his neck. "I love you too."

He gathered her to him and kissed her deeply, fervently. Grateful beyond words that he'd found her again. That they'd been given a second chance at a life together.

They left the limestone cliffs early the next morning, after breakfasting on fish they'd caught from the stream and cooked over the fire. The ride passed quickly. Gabe told them how the demon had tricked him, but said other than being drugged, the monster hadn't harmed him. Regina recounted her tracking of the demon and their journey. Julian answered questions about demon hunting and listened as Regina and Gabe discussed the events of the past few weeks.

The Lindsay estate rose in all its glory before them. The long elm-lined drive provided welcome shade as they passed beneath the branches. Regina sat before him on his stallion, while Gabriel rode her mount.

"This is your estate?" Gabe asked, his eyes wide in wonder.

"Yes," Julian responded. It was the truth, in some manner.

Julian dreaded the exchange he was going to have to have with the Marquis of Thornwood about his son. They rode from beneath the trees to the top of the drive, where it curved in front of the manor.

A stableboy hurried over. "Milord."

"Is the marquis in residence?" Julian asked.

"Yes, milord. May I take your horses?"

"Please. I'd also like the saddlebags sent to our rooms."

"Of course, milord." The stableboy bowed, then took the reins of the horses and led them to the stable. Julian led the way up the stairs to the main entrance.

He had barely set foot on the top step when the heavy oak doors were opened by a footman. The butler awaited them inside the foyer.

"My lord, to what do we owe the pleasure of your company?" His gaze took in their dirty and rumpled clothes, but he didn't comment.

"I have come to see—" Julian paused as the words, *the marquis*, first came to mind—"my father. Is he available?"

The butler pursed his lips. "I will check."

"I'd also like rooms to be made up for Lady Regina and her brother. Please arrange for baths to be sent, as well as some food. We've had a long day's travel and my guests are weary."

"Yes, my lord." It was evident he thought little of their attire.

Julian had to sympathize. At the moment, although all the damage from her encounter with the demon had disappeared, Regina did look rather disreputable dressed in her brother's clothing…and wildly attractive. He grinned at her and she blushed.

What was the butler's name again? "Thank you, Thomas."

The butler straightened at his words. "It's my pleasure." He had the footman who'd opened the door fetch a maid. When she arrived, he gave her directions. "Please take the master's guests to the blue and green suites, then have the footmen fetch a bath for them."

The maid curtsied. Her eyes were curious as she eyed Regina. "This way, please."

Julian looked at Regina and her brother. "I have things to discuss with my father. Feel free to join us for dinner, or you may rest in your rooms and have dinner brought to you."

"Thank you," Regina said. Her eyes were sympathetic. She placed a hand on his arm. She knew how much he dreaded his task. He'd always hated telling families about the loss of their loved ones on the battlefield.

The butler returned. "The marquis will see you now."

Julian followed the manservant to the library.

A fire burned low in the hearth. The marquis sat in a winged leather chair before the marble fireplace, a glass of brandy in his hand. "I take it this isn't a social visit."

Julian crossed the room and took the seat across from him. "My lord, I came to update you on the occurrences since we last met."

Thornwood looked up. His face was expressionless, and Julian had a feeling the older gentleman would not be surprised by his news.

"I know what happened to your son."

The marquis waited. His knuckles turned white

on the glass, but he said nothing.

Julian regretted the pain he would cause this man whose generosity had helped him so much. "I'm sorry, but the demon got your son."

Thornwood's eyes closed in pain and his grip tightened on his glass. His throat worked. "How?"

"I don't know. But the demon impersonated him in order to kidnap Lady Regina Westcott's younger brother, Lord Harbrook. I know it isn't much consolation, but we succeeded in killing the demon. All the souls were released upon the monster's death. I saw the earl. Your son's soul is free."

The marquis downed the rest of his brandy. Julian quietly took his glass and refilled it.

"You compromised Lady Regina Westcott and asked for her hand in marriage. What do you plan to do next?"

"She knows that I am not your son, but we still plan to marry. I have been training her younger brother in the use of magic. I believe I could support a family as a tutor. There aren't many people willing to train half-bloods in magic."

"You would be ostracized by mageborn society." Julian shrugged.

"How do you plan on explaining the similarities in looks between you and—"

Julian made his voice as gentle as possible. "With your permission, I'd prefer to claim a distant relationship, or perhaps one born on the wrong side of the blanket. I would change my name as well."

The marquis's fingers drummed on the arm of his chair. "Why don't you return to the past?"

"I cannot."

"You came here."

"That was not my doing. I thought the demon had opened a portal through time, but I was wrong. My wife cursed the demon upon her death. She used blood and death magic to send it to a time where she could have her revenge."

"I don't understand."

Julian raked a hand through his hair. "It's complicated. Lady Regina is the reincarnation of the wife I lost. The demon was stalking her in London. I foiled several of its attempts to kill her, which is why it resorted to posing as your son—or me—to kidnap her brother and force her to a place of its choosing. All this time, the demon was hunting her. The curse she'd cast when she died had trapped the monster in our world. It sought to break her curse so it could return to its own demon hell."

"Lady Regina was your wife?"

"In the past. Not only does she remember our life together, but she is identical in appearance to my wife. The first time I saw her, I mistook her for the demon and nearly killed her."

Thornwood laughed softly at that. "If she'd been your wife in a previous life, it explains why she is willing to sacrifice a life of comfort to marry you."

"I'm sure it will be difficult in the beginning. She says she has a large dowry we could use to set up a home. But I'd rather earn my way and provide for her on my own if possible."

The sharp tap-tap-tap of the marquis's fingers on the armrest grated on his ears.

After a few moments, the marquis looked up. "With my son's death, I'm the last of our line."

"You're still young enough to father more children. You could remarry."

"No, I have no interest in that." He gazed at the family portrait of him, his wife and son that hung above the fireplace. "Our titles would revert back to the crown." He turned shrewd eyes upon Julian. "I find I cannot tolerate the thought of our titles reverting back to King George."

Sudden hope burned fierce in Julian's chest.

CHAPTER FIFTY-ONE

REGINA WANDERED PAST TALL BRICK columns into the Lindsay estate gardens. Shrub roses mixed with an assortment of perennials burst from the flower beds, and the quiet hum of bees filled the air. After the dark underground world of the caverns, the sunlight on her skin felt like a caress. She strolled down the grassy paths, enjoying the sweet aroma of roses.

After Julian had gone to speak with the marquis, Regina had gone upstairs to freshen up and change clothes. She'd luxuriated in the warm water—a big improvement over her frigid outdoor bath the night before, but lacking a certain something without Julian to tease. No sign of her ordeal remained. No scars, no burns, no redness. Although she hadn't planned it, she'd removed every trace of her battle with the demon, the same as she had when she'd healed Felicity.

A profusion of white roses climbed the brick wall at the back of the enclosed garden. She cradled a full bloom in her hand and pulled it towards her to inhale the scent. Would it be spicy or sweet?

"I thought I'd find you here." Julian's voice came from behind her.

She started slightly and turned with a smile. "Not hard to guess. These gardens are beautiful."

He'd bathed and was clean-shaven once more. She wondered how Julian's talk with the marquis had gone, but his expression gave her no clue. "Where's Gabe?" he asked.

"Checking out the estate's mounts. I'm sure he's already made friends with the head groom." After riding all day, one would think her brother would be tired of horses, but the stable was his favorite place to be.

"I'm glad he's settled in. The events of the past few days don't seem to have affected him too badly."

A far-off look and certain seriousness sometimes crossed her brother's face, but then he'd shake it off and the old Gabe would be back. Whatever he thought about in those moments, he hadn't shared with her. "No, he's handling it well overall."

"Let's walk. I haven't seen much of the gardens yet."

He held his hand out. Regina took it without thought, the movement as familiar and natural as breathing. "Did you tell the marquis about his son? How did he handle the news?"

"He didn't seem surprised. I think he'd suspected something had happened to the earl when Langley couldn't find him."

Pity rose in her breast for the marquis. He'd been estranged from his son and had never had a chance to see his only child again. She could only imagine how devastated he must be.

"The marquis gave me something for you." Julian stopped to face her in front of an arbor covered with pink roses, and she remembered another garden, and their wedding day, back when she'd been Evelyn.

"He did?"

Julian reached into his pocket and pulled out a stunning gold ring set with a round sapphire surrounded by diamonds. "This is a betrothal ring. It's a family heirloom."

She gasped and looked up into his blue-grey eyes. "He's giving this to me? Why?"

"Since the earl died, the marquis is the last of his line. Upon his death, the title will revert back to the crown."

Regina's heart pounded. Julian's face was almost stern—what was he trying to say? "I don't understand."

"It means—" He lifted her hand and slipped the betrothal ring onto her finger—"that you'll be marrying the Earl of Lindsay after all."

"I beg your pardon?"

He laughed and bussed her on the lips. "You'll be marrying me. No one knows I'm an impostor except you and Langley, and the marquis wants to keep it that way. He thinks the title should remain in the family, rather than revert to the crown."

She felt lightheaded as joy bubbled through her, the smile on her face so wide her cheeks hurt. Julian—so worried he had nothing to offer her—

had found a place in this world and a new family to replace the one he'd left behind.

Events had come full circle, and she and Julian were back at the point they'd been when the Mageborn War had ended. They had planned on returning to his estate and raising a family. It wasn't the same era or the same life, but they could still live out their dream.

Regina wrapped her arms around the magelord who'd risked everything to save her soul. Heart bursting with love, she kissed him and welcomed a new future.

EPILOGUE

REGINA RECLINED ON THE PICNIC blanket on the grounds of the Lindsay estate, laughing as she watched five-year-old Grace chasing after her little brother, who had just turned three. Julian shepherded both children, his laughter booming as he picked up first one, then the other in his arms. The children squealed with laughter as her husband nuzzled them. He carried them over to their nanny. It was time for their nap.

She gazed over the gardens to the forest beyond. It was the perfect summer day. Warm and mild, with blue skies and clouds like fluffy sheep. Julian joined her on the blanket, and she laid her head on his shoulder. He laid a gentle hand on the rounded mound of her belly. The baby obediently kicked. He smiled with wonder. "This one has a strong kick. Will it be a boy or a girl?"

"I'm not telling," she said and smiled. Of course she knew. He always asked, but whenever she was about to tell him, he'd change his mind and say he'd rather be surprised. "What is your father doing?"

The marquis had accepted Julian into the family.

It had taken a while for him to get over the loss of his son, but eventually the two men had formed a strong bond. Julian had much more in common with the lord than his own son had. Regina loved the dear marquis, who'd become a surrogate father to her as well. Plus, Thornwood did love children. "The more the better," he'd said to her with a gruff smile.

"He's showing your aunt and uncle his latest hybrid rose. He's named it Gracie's Rose, since it's her favorite color combination—pink and cream."

"And Gabe?"

"He's with Langley and their brood, showing off his latest magic tricks."

She laughed. Gabe had come fully into his power, and knew how to use it, thanks to Julian. Their loved ones had traveled to the dales not only to celebrate Edward Thomas's third birthday, but the impending arrival of another family member.

A hard contraction gripped her and she gasped.

Julian took one look at her expression, then picked her up and started carrying her towards the house.

"Julian, I can walk," she insisted, even though she delighted in his strength. She was not a delicate woman, even less when with child.

"I know." He smiled at her.

Another contraction seized her and she held her breath until it passed. She settled her arm around Julian's neck and placed the other hand on her belly.

Contentment filled her.

Once, centuries ago, she'd had a vision of her husband carrying her across a green field towards a stately manor house, where their children and family awaited. That was the vision she'd clung to when all hope had seemed lost.

It had taken a long time to realize the vision, but the wait was worth it.

She leaned her head against her husband's brawny chest and smiled.

Welcome to the world, little Alex.

Acknowledgments

I'd like to thank Chicago-North RWA®. When all I had was the dream of writing a book, you gave me the confidence that I could be an author.

Thank you to Windy City, Hearts through History, Celtic Hearts, FF&P, and the Beau Monde for being excellent resources and wonderfully supportive people.

The Aphrodite Writers—Cici Edward, Katrina Bauer, Sonali Dev, Denise DiLeo, Clara Kensie, Hanna Martine, Savannah Reynard, Robin Skylar, and CJ Warrant—for their support and the best writing retreats ever!

Thanks to Yasmine Phoenix, Barbara Weitz, and Sonali Dev, for their feedback on *Demon's Bane*. Especial thanks go to my critique partners—Cici Edward, CJ Warrant, and RQ Bell—for their willingness to repeatedly read and discuss my book.

CJ Warrant, for calling me every day and pushing me to finish. Your dedication to your work inspired me to keep going.

Savannah Reynard, for your support and thoughtfulness, and amazing ability to juggle many things at once.

Cici Edward, for being there through thick and thin. Thank you for your constant support and encouragement. Whenever I was discouraged, you helped me get back on my feet, and celebrating with you made the wins sweeter.

Nancy M. Bell, for editing an early version of my manuscript, thanks to a critique I won through Brenda Novak's Annual Online Auction for Diabetes Research.

Mary Kole, my editor, whose insightful feedback made this a better book.

Shirley Jump, whose classes helped me to deepen the impact of my scenes.

Mary Beth Moran, for making me realize writing could be a second career instead of just a hobby.

Beth Laffin, for listening to me talk endlessly about my book and writing, and still being interested in reading it.

Kim Killion and Jennifer Jakes of The Killion Group, for their amazing website design, book covers, promotional materials, and formatting services.

And most importantly to my family. Thank you for your love, your support, and your faith. I couldn't have done it without you. You are my world.

AUTHOR BIO

INDIA POWERS WRITES PARANORMAL HISTORICAL ROMANCES set in England. Her novel *Demon's Bane* finaled in Romance Writers of America's 2013 Golden Heart Contest and won West Houston RWA's 2013 Emily Contest. She lives in the Midwest with her husband and son and enjoys home improvement projects, sewing, and watching sci-fi/fantasy shows and movies.

To learn more about India and her books, visit her website at: *www.indiapowers.com* or follow her on Facebook: *www.facebook.com/IndiaPowersAuthor.*

www.ingramcontent.com/pod-product-compliance
Lightning Source LLC
Chambersburg PA
CBHW060725190726
48285CB00001B/80